Once Upon a Time
There W

D0766079

Once Upon a Time There Was a Traveller

Asham Award-Winning Stories

virago

VIRAGO

First published in Great Britain in 2013 by Virago Press
Reprinted 2013

Introduction copyright © Lennie Goodings 2013

The moral right of the authors has been asserted

A CIP catalogue record for this book
is available from the British Library.

ISBN 978-1-84408-684-9

Typeset in Melior by M Rules
Printed and bound in Great Britain by
Clays Ltd, St Ives plc

Papers used by Virago are from well-managed forests
and other responsible sources.

MIX
Paper from
responsible sources
FSC
www.fsc.org   FSC® C104740

Virago Press
An imprint of
Little, Brown Book Group
100 Victoria Embankment
London EC4Y 0DY

An Hachette UK Company
www.hachette.co.uk

www.virago.co.uk

Contents

Contents

Introduction

We know the adages about travel, the most famous surely being Ralph Waldo Emerson's 'Life is a journey, not a destination' and Leo Tolstoy's theory about fiction, marvellously, economically expressed as: 'All great literature is one of two stories; a man goes on a journey or a stranger comes to town'. So it seemed we'd be on to a good thing if we combined stories and travel as the theme for Virago's second book with Asham, and Carole Buchan from the Asham Literary Endowment Trust – to whom this book and authors owe much thanks – agreed. Happily, joining me as judges were two women who represent some of the finest of travel writing and of literature: Sara Wheeler and Helen Dunmore.

We were given a longlist of forty stories and off we three went on one of the best kinds of journeying: armchair travelling. Unsurprisingly for a book about travel, many of the stories are on the move: on planes; on

trains; on the road; and even on the school run. There
are mischievous outings; missions to save a life (possibly); memories of childhood journeys and a story about
discovering that staying home is sometimes best. We
read and emailed, shortlisted and made notes.

When at last we met to make our list of twelve writers and to choose our winners, we did not have an easy
time of it as there are many stories of a very fine quality.
Says Helen Dunmore, 'Like travel itself, these stories are
full of the unexpected. I love the polish and boldness of
the writing, and congratulate the authors.'

But we did eventually come to an agreement and
chose a spare and brilliant story set in South Africa, *The
Journey to the Brothers' Farm* by Pippa Gough, as our
First Prize winner. We judged the stories without any
knowledge of even the authors' names, but now that I
can read Pippa Gough's biography I see that she spent
most of her childhood in Africa. She writes evocatively
of the land and the haze of the heat, the dust and the
grass roofs warming in the early morning sun. As she
leads us slowly, reluctantly, down the road to the brothers' farm, we are torn between desperately wanting and
never wanting to know what's at the end of the track ...
There we find a place where brutality and justice are
sometimes too close to separate. Brilliantly handled and
powerfully, simply told.

Our Second Prize winner is by Dolores Pinto. Her
story, *Where Life Takes You,* is about a young woman

who has somehow ended up in Whitby, a small seaside town, where she doesn't belong, where she feels different, where she knows everyone is looking at her. She wants to travel back to London 'to walk unnoticed between tall buildings'. How can this place be where she will stay? It is a beautiful, deceptively slight story about longing, loss, love, and finding out what home is.

The Elephant in the Suitcase by Deepa Anappara is a fantasy – or it is reality? – about a forest guard working for ten years in a place full of shrieking birds, wild dogs, sambars and a very pooky nocturnal elephant who makes him see it is high time to leave! Playful and truthful, it is wonderfully unexpected and winner of our Third Prize.

And we decided to award an Honourable Mention to *Pay Day* by Dawn Nicholson, a heart-breaking story about a teenager who sacrifices everything to send his young brother off on an adventure, to save his life. Powerful and touching.

Sara Wheeler expresses all our pleasure with the final selection: 'I so enjoyed reading these richly diverse stories. They took me to many new places, real and imaginary, and constantly confounded my expectations. Bravo les filles.'

The tradition with Asham is to invite a few established writers to publish alongside the debut ones. Here is Susie Boyt's glorious story set in an old people's home with a pair who've come 'an awfully long way from the

Dudley Hippodrome'; Helen Dunmore's startling and disturbing glimpse of youth as it passes through an airport on its way to fight in Afghanistan; and an extract from Angela Carter's beguiling 1967 novel, *The Magic Toyshop*, about a young girl's journey away from innocence. Ultimately, I suppose, that – a journey from innocence – is perhaps what all journeys are about. But no one does it the same way and this is a great book of talent with laughter, ruefulness, sadness, wisdom, absurdity, curiosity, melancholy all packed up and ready to go.

Lennie Goodings
Publisher, Virago

Once Upon a Time
There Was a Traveller

Departure Time

Tessa Green

Patras station is tall and yellow with pale marble floors, more solid than the bus station and less crowded; it looks like a grown-up building that could save you. The woman in front of Samantha buys a First-Class ticket and it seems so cheap that she copies her.

The seats in First Class are wide and green with three across the carriage not four. Samantha has never travelled First Class before. She looks down at her bitten finger-nails and makes fists to hide them. The ticket says 14A but when she sits in it the seat slides and swivels so she moves. The guard comes in and fixes 14A with a kick of a lever, looking at her snottily. You can turn it to face forwards or backwards, that's why it slithered. The old woman with a stick and gold leather shoes across the aisle – the one who'd been in front in the queue – is

3

watching her. Samantha is too embarrassed to move back to her real seat. And anyway she's set herself up in the new one, barricaded by plastic bags. But now she's anxious at every station and ready to leap up and vacate. In her mind she practises the smile and 'my mistake' gesture. She tries a little grin but her lip wobbles and it feels like a sneer. She's regretting First Class now but if she moves down the train everyone will stare.

Out of the carriage window she sees orange trees like lollipops dotted with fruit. After five years she still can't believe they're real. A line of small children dressed for winter (although it seems warm to Samantha) stand holding hands by the track. When the smallest boy on the end lifts his arm in a wave, she lets her head sink to the table then fumbles a small blue cardigan out from one of her bags.

Each station takes her further away which is good and bad. She screws up her eyes and concentrates on the good: Mam and Dad; her sisters; feeling normal; nights on the town with the lasses; home. She rubs out nights on the town and adds an NVQ in hairdressing (if she's not too old now).

The bad side is a hard grey lump sitting in her stomach. She sings 'All Things Bright And Beautiful' over and over in her head to block it out then lifts the little cardigan to her face; breathing in. How long will his smell last? Will she suck it all out? A sudden panic makes her insides lurch and she hugs the carrier bag. It's the first time today she's really felt anything. Since she got up this morning and put on her church clothes she's been doing everything from a distance: catching the bus; getting to the station; changing her clothes in the toilet. She can't allow herself to think too much. She holds on to the idea that when she gets home, Mam and Dad will sort it all out. They'll get Alexander later. But she keeps it in a corner of her mind, skirting round it because she knows it's fragile and empty like the blown egg on the nature table that she held too hard and then lied about. She hasn't told them she's coming. And part of her is just embarrassed about running home ('tail between her legs' she hears in her Nana's voice) after all that showing off of her tan; starting sentences with, 'Well in Greece, we ...'; and ordering in Greek in the restaurant in the Bigg Market. But that's too shameful to admit. And too small – a tiny spot on the bigness of it all.

The biggest thing she's ever done before was in a whoosh of romance and wanting to be different from her sisters. She had nothing to lose then but a job on the check-out at Morrison's. It didn't even seem like a decision. This one she's gnawed at for ages: hanging it out with the washing; chopping it up with the vegetables; turning it over and over. She's been heavy with it for months. She pictures her mother's face as she walks through the door. A warm thought, spongy with relief, but then she can't stop the next one sneaking in as her mam's voice asks, 'But where's the bairn?' She hates it when thoughts jump out of nowhere or creep in behind others. She wants to blank them out but they keep coming back like felt-tip pen under emulsion paint. She pictures a NEXT CUSTOMER, PLEASE sign between one clump of thoughts and another. If only. The checkout doesn't seem so hard now. She thinks of those men whose wives have left them, getting seedier every week with their ready meals and cans of Carlsberg. She always chatted to them. Nikos won't go like that. He has his mother and sister and aunts and cousins. Sometimes the same man would come in all smartened up, buying wine and foreign cheese, and you could tell he'd found someone new. She thinks of another woman putting on Alexander's little shoes. He hates anyone doing it, even her, and the blank-faced woman won't know about the boat game. She jumps up; she's got to go back. But the old woman is moving down the carriage like a crab, stick in one hand, the other papery and yellow, fluttering and landing on each seat in turn. And Samantha sinks back down. As the woman's hand settles on the top of 14A, the chair twists round and the woman twirls and crumples, a bundle of sticks, too many arms and legs; her Gucci sunglasses now wonky on the thin pale face. Her paper-bag brown hair splays out so you can see her pale blue scalp underneath. At first all Samantha thinks is 'I fucking told you so!' to the guard, but then the woman crashes down, her head catching on the corner of the drinks tray. As she lands in Samantha's lap a thin stream of blood runs down her forehead, disappears under the glasses and trickles out like a tear. Samantha cradles the woman, reaching into her bag for a tissue. Quickly she wipes the wound, all the time whispering words in Greek, hugging the fragile body. A whiff of rabbit hutches pokes through the smell of perfume and talc and hair-spray. When Samantha has helped her back to her seat, the old lady, in a hard, high voice refuses any more help and forbids her from telling anyone.

Samantha flinches at the dressed-in-black voice and knows she can't go back. Not to the house where Nikos's mother sits in the corner like a big spider watching her and making noises that mean she's doing something wrong though she never knows what. Sometimes she rips Alexander out of her arms, making him cry. Samantha cries later. She lies awake waiting for Nikos. If she complains he takes his mother's side now, so she keeps quiet, swallowing the sobs as he turns his back. And it's not just at home. The tentacles slither into every corner of the town. She can't walk down the street without someone shouting, 'Where are you off to?' or 'What are you up to?' The whole town is his cousin. At first she thought it was lovely.

When Nikos lost first one and then another job they had moved to the mainland to live with his mother. It was very different to when she had first visited. Then she was pregnant and everyone had made a big fuss of her. She had been trailed round to all the relatives who said how tall she was (the best thing for a girl to be in Greece), how pretty she was (like Lady Di) and how good her Greek was. She'd liked the attention then. And after Alexander was born it was like being a celebrity. But it didn't last and the new house with an en-suite bathroom that Nikos had promised stopped being mentioned.

A few months ago she'd started going to the English church in Patras. She always dressed in smart clothes and got the bus. His mother accepted it because it was religion. Nikos or Yiannis would pick her up afterwards. The first time she had poked her head in and it smelt familiar, although in England she only went to church for weddings. The vicar had said, 'It's not an uncommon phenomenon, Samantha, there's an enormous cultural gulf,' and 'My door is always open'. She had lied about the time, and before the service just walked round the city or sat in cafés. Of course she was watched, but strangers' eyes have no befores and afters. They thought she was a blonde tourist. Eyes in the town were on long stalks stretching back to her husband's mother. 'Husband' felt like a fib.

The train is moving so slowly and so close to the street that she can see the pink insides of people's mouths as they stand chatting. Four teenage girls in identical black trousers stand in a group, all of them on their mobiles talking to someone else.

Samantha was seventeen and on holiday when she met Nikos. At work they said things like, 'On the phone again, Shirley Valentine?' After two months of drizzle and relegation to shelf-stacking for being late back from her breaks, she moved to the island to live with him.

She'd only been there three weeks when she and Nikos were down in the old port. You couldn't tell where the sea ended and the sky started. And the door she leant against was the exact same colour. Marriage wasn't on her mind at all but he begged her. He danced round her in his blue Tommy Hilfiger shirt with a huge bunch of jasmine saying, 'Samantha, love of my life, you *have* to marry me to save me from the sheep.' He meant the Greek girls his mother had got lined up, and she felt superior and sophisticated and thought 'Why not?' Nikos is very, very good looking, everybody said so. He's in a different league to the lads back home though he wears the same clothes and likes the same films. And when they visited his family on the mainland, it was her and him together. He made jokes about his parents' old-fashioned ways in English in front of them that make her giggle and blush and punch his arm when they got outside. That first year was like one long holiday. Samantha wonders now if she's spoiled holidays for-ever.

The Gulf of Corinth is on the left. She'd looked on the map on the dentist's wall. Deep in the canal a tug boat like a tiny shoe inches through. Corinth is where she and Nikos and the family would always stop on the way to Athens; a whole crowd piling out of the bus or car downstairs to the loo. People she knew but didn't know. Sometimes they would have a souvlaki standing in the car park. As she thinks about it, she can smell the pork and *rigani* and diesel from the lorries. She always stuck out, and strangers talking to them gave her little sideways glances as they flicked their cigarettes.

The train is running right along the cliff edge and there's only blue sea to the right. She thinks of Alexander's nose pressed against the train window. Breath marks and spit. The road above juts out on stilts. She's been along it loads of times. No one in the family ever goes by train. That's why she's chosen it although it takes longer. She'll get off in Piraeus after Athens and catch the airport bus from there. She unzips her shoulder bag and feels her passport.

When Alexander was tiny and they had gone to England for Christmas, Nikos had put the baby on his passport. He's got his own now. The photo makes him look like a little boxer. All the family documents are locked in the big trunk upstairs in Nikos's mother's room. One day when Samantha was alone she'd crept up and with the bent prong of a fork had picked the lock. She thanked God she'd gone out with Philip Gudgeon when she was fourteen although her dad had banned him. The trunk smelled of the house in the village where they always go at Easter. She'd taken out the

boy's passport, running her fingers over the gold letter-
ing, kissing his photo although he was only downstairs,
then slid it back under the embroidered tablecloths in
exactly the same place that she'd marked with a piece of
red wool. Hers was there as well inside a leather cover
someone had given her for Christmas.

After that it was like a drug and if there was no one
around she'd go up and get the two passports out. Then
one day the boy's wasn't there. She'd nearly thrown up
as she pulled out all the old linen looking for it. She'd
sat on the bed with her head on her arms knowing that
now she could never leave.

But as she put the stuff back, not caring how, she'd
taken her own passport out of its case, put the empty
cover back in the trunk and slipped it down the front of
her jeans. It pressed on the top of her pubes and grew
warm as she made the meal and did the washing up and
put the child to bed. Later when the men had gone out
and the old woman was in bed too, she'd wrapped it in
tissues and put it in the box of panty liners with the
packets of the pill that Marie sent her.

Marie's the eldest and Samantha's the baby. She
knows she was spoilt. She knows now they'd all been
playing along when she said she was going to be a
model (just catalogues not catwalk), cutting out the
photos for her scrapbook and helping with her daily
beauty regime. But she is pretty. Nikos used to say she
was the most beautiful girl in the world.

11

Recently she'd started to pray it would be Yiannis who picked her up from church not Nikos. He's older and still not married. He was the only one who was kind to her. He did little things to help her that no one else knew about, explained things she didn't understand, whereas Nikos went out all the time: eating at tavernas when she'd spent ages cooking; gambling on the football; coming home in the early hours.

The landscape has stopped being like a postcard now. It's scrubby and dry, and full of corrugated iron shacks and factories. They pass a field packed with row after row of dusty cars. She thinks of her father with his big cracked hands that smell of soap and oil; the creases that stay black no matter how hard he scrubs. And as she's explaining it all to him, he strokes her hair and calls her princess. But Marie's there too and Samantha tries saying, 'It's not an uncommon phenomenon, there's an enormous cultural gulf.' But the words don't work. Her sister, who has had five failed IVFs, looks back at her with the eyes of the world.

They're so close to the flats that she can see the OshKosh B'gosh label on a pair of dungarees hanging out to dry. When a voice announces that the next station is Athens, Samantha shifts in her seat looking to see which side the platform is. A group of people appears and the man at the end walks just like Yiannis. With a shock she realises it *is* him, looking into the carriages, his head going from side to side like a goalkeeper. As he turns towards the other end of the train, she dives beneath the wide double seats and jams her whole body under, face down on the dirty lino. But one foot is sticking out into the aisle and there's nothing she can do to move it. She's wearing the big fluorescent trainers she bought in London that Yiannis always laughs at. She's so tense that she wants to jump out and run to him but she's stuck anyway. She's thinking maybe he won't look in First Class when she hears his voice from the end of the carriage, 'I'm looking for an English girl – she's tall with blonde hair ... '

She's just about to crawl out when the old woman's voice cuts through, clear now like a teacher's, 'Well, she's certainly not in here. I've been quite alone since Corinth.' Samantha can see the walking stick stretched out between the seats, blocking the aisle.

There is a slow silence before she feels the engine through the floor on her bare stomach where her shirt has risen up and then a little shudder as the train pulls forwards towards Piraeus.

Leaving Her

Diana Swennes Smith

Mornings this clearing smells of damp mint and wild onion. I imagine it might have been the kitchen garden of some pioneer family that had put down roots for a while, or maybe it was the optimistic beginnings of a patch started by some transient miner following an off-shoot of the mighty Fraser River during gold-rush days long past and forgotten. Either way, the party moved on.

I collect our scant toiletries from the old Malibu's glove box and follow Mary down the faint path we've made to the creek. The dozen-odd campsites are overgrown with weeds and even the money collectors have crossed this place off their to-do lists. Three weeks and no one's bothered us, but Mary still looks up and down the shallow water tumbling over rocks polished to egg smoothness and tries to cover both breasts as she wriggles out of her top. I like her when she's not so cocky. Satisfied that we're alone, she steps out of her shorts and pads barefoot across the flat shale, laughing with that rusty sound of the day's first utterance. I shed last night's work dress and join Mary at the creek's edge, trying to figure out how to leave her.

We kneel where the water's fast and roiling, and scrub our teeth, kneecaps grinding on the rocky shelf. White foam drips from my mouth. We rinse and spit and lay our tooth-brushes on the flat to dry, then step into the glacial run-off. Mary's hands fly up as she shrieks with the shocking thrill of cold. Birds startle from the trees at her voice.

The creek swoops south in a great rush as if it knows a better place. We'd planned to be away by now, off to the next town, leap-frogging easy jobs all the way to California. That's what we decided laying on our backs in the muddy fields of home – Hudson Bay, moose capital of Canada – watching the stars come out, killing a twenty-sixer of rye between us. Every fall when geese flew over I felt stupid for being too drunk and broke to get up and move with them, away from that misery town with its pellet factory and pig farms. Dumber than a goose: that's low. Mary threw our empty rye bottles at them.

We wade downstream to calmer water where all time slows and pools beyond the half-submerged branches of a fallen maple, me with my black dress crumpled to my chest, Mary with the soap bar before her in her hollowed palm like a supplicant making peace with her gods. She looks Egyptian with her hand that way: her face sun-coppered; chocolate hair cropped to her chin; that proud-humped nose. She was thirteen when she moved with her dad to our street in the north part of that too-far-north town, and we walked to school together the first day. Cheekbones like Cleopatra and she chose me: smaller, blonder, paler, weaker.

The creek deepens and my belly draws away from its scald; my breath comes in jerks. But Mary, she dips the soap and rubs it over her raw-boned arms as if pain was a pleasure. I pinch my dress by its straps, unfurl it like a dark pennant and lay it down in the current. Water fills it like a blousy wind. Mary dips the soap in the water and rubs it over her bluing wrists.

Currents in this creek pull so strong that when you let something slip there's no recovering it. When we washed our clothes yesterday, my last pair of underwear got away like a slippery fish from my fingers' dull hooks.

'This guy at the bar last night, he knew I was going commando.'

Mary throws back her head and laughs in disbelief, teeth strong and even as bowling pins. 'Your wicked ways,' she says. 'They'll get you in trouble.' Brown eyes slick in the dimpled shade.

I look at her quick, wondering if she knows the trouble I'm in. But she turns and bends close to the water, peering as if she can see the bottom, though our coming has churned up sediment and the water is cloudy.

'Think there's any gold in this creek?' I ask.

'I don't know. Hard to say.'

Her hair is plastered to her cheek like painted tiger stripes. She smooths it back and soaps her neck and shoulders with infinite care, scoops water to rinse. I reach for the soap; she grins and smacks the surface, sending a chill spray across my flinching torso. She knows I hate that. Now I'm the one studying the patterns in the water as I soap and rinse. Mary spreads her arms, closes her eyes and falls into a back float, lifting her flat feet. I place the soap on her navel and her lids flutter but she won't open them. The creek holds her buoyant and aloft. I force my numb legs up-stream and climb on to the sun-baked shale to wait.

Back pressed to the unyielding rock, my dress bunched beside me, I close my eyes and listen to the robins in the willows and the rumouring grasses twitch. After a while my muscles stop quivering. I feel super-charged – like I could juggle a grizzly. Like I should get up and do something. A beer would go down smooth. The sun has warmed the grass: the smell is dry now, oaty and domestic.

There's a splash on the rocks as she leaves the water. I feel her shadow move across my feet and up my legs, cool droplets on my stomach. I open my eyes, and she's standing above me, her head in the sky. Water runs down the hollow between her ribs and over her prickled flesh. Her pubic hair drips like tree moss in rain.

'You're making me cold!' I screw my eyes tight and when I open them again, she's stepped off and gathered her clothes in her arms. I follow her up the path to the campsite cradling my wet dress.

Pinch-browed, she checks around, afraid someone's been snooping, worried about things that don't matter. The tent has plastic bags sticking out everywhere to plug the leaks. We borrowed that rag from Mary's dad. Tent of a thousand holes. Our sleeping bags are patched with duct tape. The battered camp stove is almost out of fuel. One burner works. Other than the old Malibu, which we would have heard backfiring if anyone started it, there's only a dime-store Styrofoam cooler, Mary's jumbo-sized ketchup, and half a loaf of Wonder bread. I'd say to anyone who wanted any of these things: *Take it. No – thank YOU!*

What Mary doesn't worry about is what we'd do if we ever hit California. The way she sees it in her crazy head, we'll camp on sun-kissed beaches and trade in beer and rye for Chi-Chi's and pina coladas. That's the shiny goal. And I'm supposed to get a permanent job at some quaint seaside margarita stand while she guards our stuff.

I hang my dress on the clothes twine, unpeg our towels and toss one to Mary. She rubs it over the hair on her head and see-saws it behind her back. Then she pulls on clean underwear and her red shorts, and I watch her disappear down the long path into a jungle of wild rhubarb and raspberry bushes that have grown out of all proportion in the fertile oasis of the outhouse. The raspberries are black and withered now. That first morning after our arrival I picked the last of the ripe ones for our breakfast cereal.

Her cigarettes are on the stump where she left them. I light one and take a drag, drop the flaming match in an empty beer bottle on the stump. A stream of smoke curls out the neck. Then I remember and throw the cigarette in the cold fire pit, pour a little water on it from the dish-pan. Expectant women shouldn't smoke. When I was twelve, I stole cigarettes from my mother, sneaking to the kitchen after she was asleep, pulling one or two from the open pack on the table, trying to hold them between my fingers and tap them on the ash-tray like she did.

The best place to leave Mary would be Harrison Hot Springs, before we cross the border. Lots of tourists there. I'll take her to a nice bar, buy her drinks. Not too many because she's liable to throw punches. When she's had a few, though, she makes friends easily – starts insane conversations with the crowd at the next table about the time she ate an entire jar of hot banana peppers on a dare, or how she can do a handspring and kick out a light bulb on a ceiling. I've seen her do that one. Hell, she's amazing.

She comes up from the creek now, shaking water from her hands, and sits at the picnic table to flick ants off the camp stove. That's one thing she does to feel useful. Her long brown finger catapults them over the yellow grass towards a line of dusty poplars that screen the campsite from the road. They probably crawl back within two minutes.

'Full-time job right there,' I tell her. Her concentration intensifies.

I watch for a bit, her legs pushing out of her shorts, levered at the knees, her tanned ankles folded primly under the bench. Birds sing of urgent business in the willows and shadows are bunched small and close to their solid forms. It must be about noon.

'Any live ones left in the cooler?' One beer won't hurt, I don't think.

'Nothing but dead soldiers.' Her toes poke at a Labatt bottle under the table. 'We need more ice too. Eggs are going to rot.' We tried keeping eggs in the creek but raccoons got them.

'We should eat those eggs,' says Mary. She lifts the lid off the cooler.

'I can't stomach eggs right now.'

'Your appetite's gone for shit.' She puts the lid back on.

Her thighs push out from her shorts even more as she stretches her legs under the table. Then she pulls them back and folds her ankles again, pushes her pink toe-nails into the dirt as she coils her finger. I shuffle into my flip-flops and over to the Malibu.

I take the roll of money out of the glove box and glance up. She catches my look, asks the question that's been stuck on her tongue all morning: 'Tips any good last night?' Her finger's poised over the stove, gathering tension.

'No better 'n usual.'

She lets go and the ant arcs forwards, a black speck above the grass. I imagine flailing legs, a sickening rush of wind.

I open the trunk, push clothes and shoes out of the way. 'Twenty dollars for the California jar.' I hold up the jar so she can see me stuff money in it.

'Cheap town for a Friday night,' says Mary.

'No worse 'n last town.' I shove the jar under the clothes.

Mary's concentrating on the ants. I flip back the carpet and tuck a twenty inside the other bills in the plastic baggie. Maybe one more week, if tips stay good. I fold the carpet in place and pat it down, spread out the clothes and slam the trunk, and walk over to Mary.

'Here's for groceries.' I hand her two tens.

She draws up stiff like she always does. 'You know I'd take a turn if I was any—'

'You don't have to say—'

'I'm just saying—'

'I know.'

22

Mary did have a job for about two days outside of Calgary, helping in the laundry at a private girls' school. I remember on her first day I went to pick her up and was waiting by the window in the common room. Girls' voices and laughter floated up from the yard below. I could see them with their books spread on the grass – sharing answers, I guess. It was around the time I started thinking about leaving Mary. Hudson Bay wasn't the problem. It was her – it was us. Who we were together, aimless and lost. I was sitting there in that chair staring dumbly at a patch of chequered light falling through the wire mesh of the window across the tiled floor. Just then, with the laughter stirring such a longing in my chest and the impossibility of our situation making me feel heavy and worn down, Mary wandered idly through the square of light with a basket of clothes balanced on one hip. She was wearing leather sandals and sparks of dust danced in the wake of her shuffle. The bones of her feet moved like strings, a kind of music as she walked. I don't know exactly why she got fired from that place. Some mix-up in Mary's head about rules, what you could and couldn't take from the pantry, and how much and how often.

I find my watch under the driver's seat where I keep it, but it's still dead and I don't know how to fix it. I could turn on the car ignition to check the time but that would drain the battery. Shadows are creeping out from under the trees and by my unskilled reckoning it's one o'clock. I pick up the comb and make futile jabs at my hair.

'You going to work?' she asks.

'Yeah.'

'Don't forget the rye.' She lifts a beer bottle from the table and examines the contents.

'Mary, that's from last night.' This is why I have to leave her.

She rubs the back of her head and regards me without concern. 'You're a mess,' she says. 'Come here.'

Mary takes the comb from my hand and runs it through my hair, catching a tangle. I wince, but she teases out the knot with a gentleness that makes my eyes well. In one week I'll tuck a bus ticket in her purse and walk out some side door while she waits for me to come back from the lady's room. I crave a cigarette and remember my mother at the kitchen table smoking quietly, picking at the chipped Arborite with her nicotine-browned nail all through my growing-up years as she waited for my father to come home from the Naughty Spruce. His truck dug such a groove into the parking lot that the wheels turned of their own accord after a while, instead of staying the straight course home. Finally he didn't come home at all. He left that parking lot one night dead drunk and drove straight into a logging truck.

'All done,' says Mary, and pushes me away.

As I'm skinning into my wet dress she edges over,

biting her lip, hands deep in her pockets. 'Hey, you know ... ?' She pushes through the dirt with her toe, burrowing towards me. I nod and give her a tight smile.

Afternoon shadows lay long across the gravel as I steer the Malibu towards Chilliwack. It must be later than I thought. I hardly know how long we've been on this broken journey. It was May when we started, a week after Mom's funeral. Now it's Indian summer. The leaves will be falling in Hudson Bay, the farmers will be cutting their muddy fields and spreading shit before winter. Geese will be flying over the town, honking past the pellet factory. At change of shift, men and women will glance up briefly to mark their passing, then down to the scratched metal of lunch kits and the dullness of their boots.

The Cloud's jumping, and evening accelerates in a blur of full glasses and empty ones as I manoeuvre between chairs and elbows and hands and fingers, swaggering and staggering bodies, sweaty paper coasters piled with wet change. It's stripper night and tips are fantastic. Outside, shadows purple. I need a smoke so bad I'm ready to light my finger and suck that, but I settle for a draught on the house. Bottoms up for a job well done. The bartender slips me a bottle under the table for Mary, and I remember ice.

On the drive home I figure out money. How much for the California jar, how much for my get-away. I think of Patrick back in Rocky Mountain House, try to recall his

features. Wavy hair, longish, dirty blond. He had a
habit of tucking it behind his ears when he bent over
the drink orders. A space between his front teeth.
Whiskers. A blue enamel fleur-de-lis that hung from his
neck on a silk cord. Blue eyes? Yes. That was a nice
town.

The fire's low at the campsite. She must be asleep. I
kick off my shoes, pour ice in the cooler.

In the tent, I can't make out her face, but her grey
form curls foetal around the darker lump of her sleeping
bag. Her knees are drawn up close to her abdomen.

'Can't sleep?'

'I couldn't find my pills.' She moans in the dark.

'Oh.'

This is so like her. My hands frisk clothes and blankets, magazines and dirty socks and damp paper cups
and I come away empty-handed. I feel along the edges
where plastic bags are stuffed in failing seams along the
canvas floor. I pull bags out from their holes and rifle
their insides and throw them down. I pluck bags from
the walls and bags from the ceiling, squinting my eyes
at myriad shafts of moonlight. I can see her more clearly
now: her mouth twists meanly and her hair splays damp
across her face, black as crow feathers. She's kicked off
her shorts and her underwear gleams white in the
weird, streaming light.

'How could you lose them? You know what happens!'
The words sound harsh against her stifled cry.

I throw wood on the fire and find the smoke-black pot on a stump half-full of tomato soup from a day not this one, and fling the soup in the grass. Under a lopsided moon the creek runs molten. I dip the pot; the water burns my skin. I carry water to the fire and set it on the grate, shove clothes around the Malibu until the hot-water bottle reveals itself and when the water boils, I fill the bottle and wrap it in my sweater and take it in to her. But she doesn't want it.

I remember a nameless store in a nameless town, the shapeless woman with frizzled hair, her green apron smeared with fine powder like dust on a chalkboard. She sold dried cures. Mary and I saw nothing we knew or wanted and were about to leave when the woman said: 'Raspberry leaves are good for the female complaint.' Mary pulled me by my jacket strings on to the bright sidewalk where we laughed like drunks down the street past the fiddle player on the corner, Mary throwing our last coins at his old shoes.

Moonlight glistens off a meaningless calligraphy penned in slime by the bellies of monstrous, horned slugs that criss-cross the outhouse path. I beat back wild rhubarb, its giant frills like prehistoric lizards. The child curls salamandrine in my womb, dreams of blue eyes and curly hair, opposable thumbs, frontal lobes, a name. Patrick or Patricia. I rummage among the raspberry in utter inadequacy, fingers pricked and clumsy, slow as sloth and Mary waiting.

The leaves steep until they smell like swamp. I drain the brew into a mug and blow on it and carry it to her with both hands. 'Can you drink this?' But she's rocking her knees and she says she wants ice.

'Come by the fire then. I have to see to do it.'

She brings her sleeping bag and lies by the fire, shivering in her underwear. I pull the waistband low and put the ice on her belly. The tea sits by, turning cold with the night, the settling dew. Ice skates under my fingers, gliding in figure eights, crossing where I think her womb might lie, circling her ovaries on either side.

'Keep doing that,' she says.

I push the ice over her skin and watch it melt and fill her navel and roll down her waist, spreading like a dark map across her sleeping bag. Firelight gilds her torso. She closes her eyes and seems to be concentrating, then she opens them and looks right at me, and I can't look back because there's a plastic bag of money in the trunk that's going to save me.

She lifts one hand as if to touch my face and all I can say is, 'Hush now, baby,' as I move the ice on her belly. She draws her knees up hard, then pushes them down and takes a sharp breath. I smooth the ice to numb her, and wonder about all those words my mother didn't say.

I remember one day Mary and I had gone up the creek to the warm, shallow pools and stripped out of our bathing suits, not quite believing that the world wasn't ours alone, and we were playing there, splashing each other and laughing at everything and nothing, watching the sun catch and hold the water's light, water filling our hands with a light that overflowed, when I saw a man and a boy fishing, making their way downstream in our direction. They were watching us with calm amazement, and I shouted a warning to Mary. We crashed shrieking through the water to crouch behind the boulders where we'd left our suits, and we wrestled them over our thighs, Mary and I, laughing, always laughing, spandex pinching our skin. But the quietness of the boy's gaze and the man's careful movements with his rod stilled me for a moment and it was like we all held our breath, a single unified breath, and the muddy waters of the creek opened before us. Look, it was saying. Look, what is here. And for that one moment I could almost see.

She's breathing deep and regular now, her body slack. She closes her eyes as if she might sleep. Then she rolls gingerly on to her side and pushes herself up. Her dark hair falls over her face and she smooths it back the way she likes it. 'Anything to eat?'

I fumble for the can opener, a can. She disappears down to the creek and comes back, flicking pearls from her fingers.

When our soup's ready we huddle over it, spoons dipping, and talk of California beaches and grass-skirted margarita stands. Moonlight spills over the tent; plastic bags take on a glow like pale hands punching through. The sky's a deep blue bowl filled with stars. The fire tosses orange sparks into it – they fall back cold to the touch, cold as coming snow. Mary opens the fresh bottle and pours.

School Run

Kate Marsh

I meet my future husband when I'm five years old. He's my brother's best friend and we give him a lift to school every day. I develop a crush on him while he's teaching me to read by spelling out the shop names on the awnings we pass each morning. He sings in the school choir and has perfect pitch; he can recite from memory every line of the Goon Show's *Dreaded Batter Pudding Hurler*, doing all the voices. Whenever we bump into his parents my mother insists, in the same tone with which she praises the artwork I bring home from school, how much she enjoys his early morning performances. Yes, sometimes it would be nice to listen to the *Today* programme on the car radio, but it's a pleasure to be reminded of these favourites from her own childhood. How unusual that a schoolboy in this day and age would appreciate them. But then Magnus is a very unusual boy.

As I enter my teens I realise that my friends seem to fall in love for reasons I haven't considered. Can he drive? they ask. Is he cute? Does he have any cute friends? My answers to these questions don't sound right. He rides a bicycle. He has trouble pronouncing his Rs which I find endearing in someone older and cleverer than me; he's friends with my brother who I don't think you would call cute. At sixteen none of my friends are impressed with the skill of Magnus's card tricks or his promise never to saw a woman in half; their expressions tell me that they do not consider leather elbow patches to be a sign of sophistication, or even of scholarship. They ask if I have ever tried going out with normal boys: the kind of boys we meet at parties, who gel their hair and save up for motorbikes.

He goes away to university and sends me letters every week or so, always set out as neatly as a lab report. Sometimes with diagrams, and often a bibliography. I feel there is something supremely trustworthy about a man who has never given an unattributed reference. But I struggle to glean particles of news from our correspondence to pass on to my family and friends. 'Do you ever think about matter?' he writes, in the washable blue ink I have persuaded him to use after an accident with blue-black over the car upholstery. 'How matter can never be created or destroyed, but only altered? I would think that would be comforting to religious people. I don't know why they seem to think science is cold.'

'He's enjoying his philosophy classes,' I tell my mother. 'He's thinking about joining the choir.'

My friends, as they prepare for another Saturday night, say: 'Do you really think it's a good idea to try to keep the relationship going while he's away? What if he's met someone new and doesn't know how to tell you? What if you meet someone?' They ask, 'Doesn't he ever invite you up there to parties and stuff? Maybe we could all go one weekend. Have you met his friends? Are they cute?'

He writes to me, 'A group of us is going to Bletchley to see the Enigma machine. Do you want to come? It's got 10^{114} possible combinations.'

After I leave university and get my first job, he goes on to study for his postgraduate degree. My friends say to me, 'What happens when he finishes this degree – is that the highest you can get? Will he stop then?'

He says to me, 'I was going to buy you an engagement ring but I wasn't sure whether we should buy it together or if I should choose one and surprise you. There appear to be two schools of thought.'

I tell him that my mother has put aside my grandmother's ring for me and he inspects my face for clues as to how I feel about that.

'I underestimated the variables,' he says sadly. 'I should have done more research.'

My mother seems to feel responsible for my marrying a man who wears corduroy year-round and who thinks that Scotch eggs are canapés.

'Who was that other boy who used to sing in the choir too?' she asks. 'The one who got that very high-powered job in the City. I remember how excited you were when he joined the school run and his father's chauffeur drove you in a Rolls-Royce.'

'Nicky Mott. He takes cocaine and picks up women in nightclubs. The son-in-law you've always dreamed of.'

Her face falls. 'Oh no, really? He had such a lovely singing voice. Or that boy who won the art prize and went to study in Italy. You always liked him.'

'George Stefanidis.'

'That's right, George. Do you remember how he could never get up in the morning? Half the time we'd have to leave without him. I suppose he must have taken the bus.'

I ask her, 'Are you wondering if I would be engaged to George Stefanidis if we had only driven him to school more often?'

We decide to wait until he has finished his thesis and I ask my friends if they would like to be bridesmaids. The reception will be small and simple – which they understand to mean that they should bring dates as they will be unlikely to meet attractive men there. They ask me with genuine concern if Magnus is going to ride to church on his bicycle and arrive with one leg of his suit trousers tucked into his sock. They worry that I will have to carry a plastic bouquet to avoid triggering his pollen allergies.

At the birth of each of my sons my mother comes to stay to help out for a while. She bites her tongue when Magnus takes a calculator to the lavatory with him in the morning instead of the newspaper like a normal person. She averts her eyes from the double-helix-shaped mobiles hanging over the baby's cot. She makes tea in the kitchen for my girlfriends, sharing their disappointment at having to find presents for boys. Chunky wooden puzzles, clock-work trains and pull-along toys are not as much fun as pink accessories, fairy wings and miniature baking sets.

'You hated all that stuff when I was growing up,' I remind her. 'If anyone gave me a Barbie you would accuse them of gender-role stereotyping.'

'I know,' she agrees with a sigh. 'You couldn't just be a recreational feminist in those days. You had to go the whole hog. I'm sorry now that I didn't wear a bra more often. I'm sorry I missed out on all those bonding mother-and-daughter activities. I'd hoped to relive them through your children.'

She tries to make up for it by buying toddler-sized football strips, which make Magnus anxious. He has trouble with the responses at football matches, as poor attendees do at church. He is never sure when to sit down and when to stand up. He checks with me that I am not expecting him to take them, in baby sling and pushchair, to Stamford Bridge while their Chelsea all-in-ones still fit.

'Don't worry,' I tell him. 'She'll just keep buying them new ones when they grow out of them. You'll have plenty of time.'

Around the time the boys start secondary school I notice a change. Not in us, but in the world around us. Recently I have begun to see young men from my husband's department, and on the train and on television, wearing sneakers with their suits with varying degrees of nonchalance. Magnus has, for fifteen years, worn Dunlop Green Flash with his corduroy and tweed, winter and summer. I often have to cut the laces out, like a surgeon snipping stitches, because he is fond of tying complex knots and then can't untie them. In a post-breakfast panic, he has been known to lace them with garden twine, the twist-ties from freezer bags or birthday ribbon from my gift-wrappings drawer. Our older son tries to interest him in Velcro fastenings, opening and closing the straps on his own trainers. Look, how easy.

Wherever I look, the contact lenses that my contemporaries thought as necessary for adulthood as a driving licence are being replaced with black, square-framed spectacles. At friends' parties and at drinks with neighbours, the opinions of Richard Dawkins and

Stephen Jay Gould are being passed around with the crostini and the wasabi peanuts. Debates about the Large Hadron Collider break out at summer barbecues and copies of *A Brief History of Time* and *The God Delusion* have begun to appear in the bags of jumble I collect for the PTA.

Astronomers and physicists are no longer paunchy stand-bys, late-night TV fodder for insomniacs and Open University students. My husband occasionally appears on television-panel shows these days, when unthreatening displays of erudition are called for and Stephen Fry is unavailable. He answers the questions with the same unforced patience with which he once taught me that the letters on the butcher's window spelled Purveyor of Fine Meats, and the same serious attention to detail with which he has answered the boys' questions over the years about the weather on Mars and the relative merits of different dinosaurs.

When my friends ring up I can hear the embarrassment in their voices as they flip through my family news and wait for me to pause so that they can get to the true reason for their call: a child's essay on electromagnetism; a glitch in the latest Microsoft upgrade; a charity quiz night in need of a host. When I look over at Magnus he'll be snoozing in his chair. He has always been able to sleep bolt upright, silently; a gift which has carried him through various religious and sporting events, and every single movie I have taken him to see. He relies on his glasses to hide his closed eyelids, not knowing that the softening of his mouth, the gentle rise and fall of his lamb's-wool chest, give him away to anyone who really knows him. I wave the boys aside when they go to wake him and tell my friend on the phone that it's been good to catch up with her and that I'll be sure to give him the message.

A Sense of Perspective

Penelope Macdonald

It's a game we play, testing each other. One has to arrange the journey – that's usually George, he likes doing business on the phone. Sometimes he mentions to the coach company that we're blind – sometimes he thinks it will be more amusing to keep them in the dark about this detail. After all we are experienced travellers. There's not much we haven't faced before.

We've been friends a long time, since school. We were there seven years. You get a lower sentence for GBH, George always says – and you don't get sent there when you're eleven. Still, that's how it was then, and that's where we met. Not much we don't know about each other by now.

George likes his little jokes; he likes to land us in it sometimes, to see how we manage, and we always do manage somehow. As for me – I've always been up for it. It's an adventure, living on the wrong planet, trying to understand the natives; I might even marry one of them one day. Then there's Pete – he's special. He was born one of them, joined us a little late – some obscure disease of the retina the GP failed to spot. But it gives him a different perspective: well, it gives him the memory of perspective. It makes a difference to our outings when Pete comes along.

So there we were in the coach on our way to Coventry. George had been enjoying some mothering from the woman behind us. It's one of his cast of characters – The Inadequate. He began as soon as we got on.

'I got no lunch. I forgot my sandwiches.' That happens often enough – but it was the voice he used, the little hurt voice, so I knew what to do. I ignored him. Sat across the aisle with Pete and we waited to see who he'd catch.

She was a nice woman, Irene. She introduced herself right away from the seat behind him. She was an older woman, her voice oozing concern. One of those who thought we shouldn't be allowed out alone, so I had no worries about him taking her for a ride. Best way to educate them – to take advantage.

George played her a treat, got some crisps from her when the coach stopped, and when she heard we were going to the cathedral she offered to show us the way. Normally we pick up a taxi from the bus station: we've tried different things, but that's the simplest. The problem is people are so bad at giving directions. I know exactly how far I walk in five minutes, I can count how many roads we cross, know my left from my right even; but I can't see that school the guy points to, where we should turn, or aim for the spire 'you can't miss it really'. Well really, I can.

Anyway we arrived in Coventry, and Irene offered to walk us there. She said she'd take us past the ruins, which was nice of her, but showed how far she missed the point. She had George by the arm – she'd obviously decided we weren't quite as blind as him and could manage with each other – which was fine by me. Pete was trying to trip me with his stick, which is his level of amusement most days. So I whacked him on the leg with mine and after that he stopped.

Cathedrals were Pete's idea. He said they'd give us something to aim for, a sense of purpose. Not a religious purpose, but a list of places we were going, and he reckoned if we could understand them, get the point of it all, then we'd be that much better at understanding the natives. So far it all seemed pretty pointless to me, but he was right – having a list, places we were going to – it helped. None of us had what might be called a job, or not one worth having. At school if you had an idea, something you wanted to be, the answer was always the same: nothing was possible. Anyway, I couldn't get on with Braille and my exams didn't go so well – so all they could offer were work placements with firms who had to have you to fulfil some percentage they were set. Pete worked in his aunt's shop but he could usually get days off. George – he was still planning on going back to college, finishing his degree. I didn't reckon he'd ever go back though, not after five years.

Anyway Coventry was the one Pete had picked this time: a modern cathedral, he told us, standing beside the ruins of the old, where the German bombs had fallen.

Irene made a lot of noise as she walked – a sort of bustle, like she'd got plastic bags hanging under her skirt, and her footsteps sounded decisive. Our sticks swept and tapped and our shoes scuffed the edges of the paving slabs. The traffic was a few streets away. There were voices all around; every few steps someone said 'sorry' as they moved out of our way.

'Nearly there now,' said Irene. 'There are the ruins – we could walk through that way?'

'No, straight to the cathedral, please, Irene,' George told her.

There were fewer people now and I was getting excited. It was nothing really, but we were nearly there and it had been easy this time. There was a flight of steps – too narrow, and they seemed to slope away to the left. Not designed with us in mind. Then we were in the entrance, and Irene, a bit breathless now, said she had to go.

'We can manage from here all right, thanks,' Pete told

her. George was pretending to sulk, and hardly even said good-bye. He was expecting her to stick around for a while, but I liked it better that way. Just us and the cathedral.

We went in, pushing the heavy glass door open. Pete led the way. The smell got me first – outside it was just that general city smell of dust and cars and damp; but inside the air seemed cared for: cleaned, waxed, scented with lemons and floor cleaner. Then the sound was different, the world shut out as the door swung slowly closed behind us. Our sticks echoed, the sound going way up above my head. The other voices seemed small, swallowed up by the distance. I tried to imagine it – if we joined hands and spread ourselves wide would we reach the walls? And above our heads too – how many Georges, standing on my shoulders, to reach the roof?

And that's Pete's idea – to have us understand the scale. The first time, he got us a model of the place, St Alban's Abbey that was. One of their guides saw what Pete was doing, trying to have us understand the shape of the building by feeling the model, so he came over and tried to help. It was quite interesting, about the blocks of stone and the years it took, and he had us feel some of the carving on the pillars and on the pews. I couldn't understand how the walls stayed up – how this huge roof he kept telling us about didn't just push the walls over. So he took me outside, this guide, and introduced me face to face to my first buttress. I could feel the angle of it, and it made sense now I knew there were all these props round the place. Like people leaning against each other. Like fingers spread when you're doing press ups.

He was okay that guy but most can't leave us alone, not once they realise we're all blind. No native to take our hands, unless George has beguiled someone. They take us to the designated area for a bit of touching stone. Trying to 'see' with your fingers – it's all bumps and lumps. Does it really look like a flower? It's not how a flower feels to me: a vegetable softness, spoiling and falling apart in my hands.

Why shouldn't the blind lead the blind? Who else can understand? Trying to speak to us in colours and distances. Thirty miles is time to me – the bus, the speed of my feet: my father's car taking me back there, back to George and Pete, back to being one of us.

But I'm forgetting Coventry. We're still there, by the door, our shoes sliding on the marble floor; my stick bumping over the edges, where the pieces join. George wanted to sit down. He was still in a mood. There were rows of seats in front of us. Not solid wooden pews but a line of chairs, and when George tried to move one to feel its seat as he sat, he knocked it over. He didn't know what he'd done – just legs there where there should be a seat, and he was getting cross, swearing at it. Pete tried to help him, but I was laughing already. I know George. He was getting physical with it now, trying to twist the chair back to what it should be, and I could hear him shoving it and swearing, pushing, and Pete saying – 'No, like this' – and then a great glorious crash as he sent the whole line of chairs falling forwards, and I could hear where the ceiling was now – how high it was, how high the sound of those chairs fell back at me.

They were sympathetic, of course, understanding George's frustration; how he could not see that the chairs were joined. We were assigned a guide, to help us 'make the most of the cathedral'. To keep us out of trouble.

George never lets us stay free for long. He calls attention to us. Maybe I'll have to start going on my own. Maybe just me and Pete. Or someone like that girl they got to show us round, someone like Annette.

She shook our hands one by one. She seemed younger than us and at home there. She told us her father worked in the cathedral, a clergyman. Not the bishop, I guessed. 'No,' she said, 'not him!' She laughed, as if I was deliberately being funny, as if I too knew the bishop – and I felt I did, a little.

She took us to the main attractions. George was subdued, and I had taken over as interpreter, lead alien. I could hear him and Pete muttering as they followed. It's what he wanted – a fuss made, but it was me she liked.

She had flat shoes on and a skirt, and something, I thought, swinging round her neck, moving against the material of her shirt. I followed the flap of her feet across the stone floor. I did as she told me and ran my hand around the stone of the font. Rough surface, obligatory bumps, and smoothed inside where the water went. Damp, rough, smooth. That's stone for you.

We stood in front of Sutherland's 'Great Tapestry of the Christ'. Her voice told me it's not so great. We walked by the stained glass windows – and I could feel how narrow the slits were in the stone. She told me there were colours on my face. I could feel the sunlight coming through the glass. She said we were all standing in the colour; it fell in stripes on the floor by our feet. She didn't try to explain it to us – but I knew anyway. I know light emanates like heat; I know how it passes through and takes that colour with it. I have been told of refraction and waves.

I followed her down the steps into colder places. George and Pete were talking somewhere behind me, but she was telling me about the pictures we passed – about the fish in the glass – 'here,' she told me – 'here.' Her fingers traced the shape with mine. The glass was flat and smooth. I told her I could feel the shape of the fish under my hand. She laughed at me – the sound of her like cream in my mouth. I wanted to touch her face, feel how her mouth moved when she laughed.

We went on down the stairs, my hand on her arm. The others followed knowing nothing of the fish. I wanted to walk on away from them, but she was responsible for all of us. 'Hi' she said to them as they caught us up, so I said 'Hi' too, so they would know it was us waiting there. I knew Pete and George were waiting for me to do something stupid, to say something rude to her. That's usually the game I play. They would be waiting all day.

We went along the corridor, and she slowed and then coughed. We all stopped. She should just have said. We didn't know what we were waiting for. Someone came out.

He said: 'You looking for the Gents?' and I realised what had happened. 'Thanks,' I said, and took George's arm. Pete followed us in.

It's a distinctive smell, however clean. There was no one in there except us, but it's always a bit awkward getting the geography right. I usually opt for a cubicle; give myself a space I can manage. I told the others to wait for me, and thought about what I should say to them.

I knew it was mad – that we were too far from home. However much I thought I liked Annette there was no way I would see her again. But you know what they say – carpe diem.

I was washing my hands. Pete said 'watch it', but I had already heard George at the next basin. I jumped back before the spout of water hit me.

'Bugger off, George!'

He was laughing, and I knew he'd be wet himself. Another of his great jokes. You get a splash of water down your front and it's like – well, you know how it looks.

'Tell him to lay off, Pete. I want to talk to you.'

We calmed George down – I had his head, and Pete had his legs. We got him quiet.

'I want you both to lose yourselves when we get out of here. Whatever she suggests, say you're bored with it – go out to those ruins or something.'

'We could say we want to touch some more stone,' said Pete, helpfully.

'Why?' said George. I let go.

'He likes her.' said Pete. 'He likes Annette.'

'The girl outside?'

'She's waiting. Come on, guys, do me a favour.'

'There's really no point—' Pete said.

'I know.'

'Okay,' said George, 'that can be your challenge for today. Get a date with Annette. And Pete's can be to sort out supper.'

Pete said, 'What's yours then?'

'I'll get us home.'

We went back out and turned towards the stairs. Annette was in the hallway waiting for us. She said we could visit the crypt next, and I nudged Pete. He said he wanted to go outside, and George said he'd go with Pete.

'Do you all want to go now?' she said. I thought she sounded disappointed. I told her I wanted to see the crypt. 'Okay, good.'

She wanted us to make an arrangement to meet up –
there was a café.

We agreed to meet in an hour. They went off, back up
the stairs.

'Will they be okay?'

'They'll be fine. We usually do this on our own.'

'I'm sorry.'

'No, it's really nice of you to take me round. I'm sure
I usually miss the most important things.'

I have to say she was pretty useless at first. She kept
making the usual mistakes then apologising. I don't
think she had ever really thought about what it was like
being blind. Mind you, I've not got much of an idea
what it's like to be sighted. I have no idea, for example,
what you mean by a horizon. It's a concept too far for
me. I think I get the sky – thunder puts a kind of roof on
the world. Like those chairs falling.

I should have guessed the crypt was modern like the
rest of the building. There was some sort of audio pres-
entation about the cathedral. I didn't fancy it – though
that's what I would have done with George and Pete.
She took me back upstairs a different way.

After a bit it didn't matter where we were. I asked her
what it was like being the daughter of a clergyman and
she asked about my family. I said I was a bit tired, could
we sit somewhere? She took me to a side seat, our backs
against a window, our knees touching. We chatted. I
remember thinking how different she was to the other

girls I knew. I thought how odd it must be to be brought up with all this religion around you. It must make you seem older than you really are, more serious. She said she thought we were brave. I said it was just life and you had to get on with it. She asked, 'Why cathedrals?' and I said they had a special feeling about them. It seemed rude to say that it was just a list of cities, somewhere to go.

It was like talking beside water, the way other voices carried across the space, the echoes around us. It was quite distracting. I had to focus on her quiet voice, the way she shaped her vowels. The plum stone she balanced on her tongue as she talked. Her hair was long – it brushed against my face when she stood up. I caught a strand in my mouth. I nearly asked her then – can we meet again? I was sure she would tell me she had a boyfriend and that I lived too far away. But everyone comes to London sometimes, don't they? And Barnet is almost London. I could have taken the bus in, met her in Covent Garden. I know bits of the city quite well.

She told me the time was up – that we should meet the others. I was running out of time. The café was back in the crypt.

'Can we go past the fish?'

'Okay.'

'Show me where it is again.'

'Right here.'

Annette – can we meet sometime? But the words wouldn't come.

She could see George and Pete at a table in the café and one of the staff bringing their drinks. Maybe word had got around and they had heard what George could accomplish with a tray. Maybe they always carried the tray for their customers. We joined them – they offered us a drink, some cake. She went to get another cup.

'Any luck, mate?' Pete asked.

'I haven't asked her yet.'

'Blown it,' said George, slurping his tea.

'Not yet,' I said, though I knew I had.

We should have heard her coming, but there was someone collecting cups from the table next to us, rattling them and pushing a noisy trolley.

I said 'I've just got to find a way to say it. Like – "Wanna fuck, sweetheart?"'

The others laughed. I laughed too. Then I heard her feet moving away. I knew those shoes by now. George was still laughing. The trolley moved on to the next table. I stirred my tea and waited to see if she would come back.

I asked how they had got on. Pete had enjoyed the ruins. Much more his idea of what a cathedral should be.

'Until it started pissing down and we realised there was no roof,' said George.

'I knew there wasn't a roof,' said Pete, and George

laughed at him. We were back to being us, larking about. I felt at home.

When Annette came back we had finished our tea. 'Sorry I abandoned you, I met a friend.' I thought she'd been crying. I wanted to tell her it was just a joke, but I didn't want to admit I knew she had heard me.

'That's okay. We can manage on our own,' George told her.

'Right. I better go back to the desk then – in case anyone else needs a guide.' She was talking to them, not to me, but they didn't seem to notice.

'Our time's up is it?' he said, nudging me.

Pete said, 'It would help if you could show us back upstairs.'

'Okay. All set then?'

'What about your tea?' I asked then.

'No, that's fine. I don't usually stop at this time.' She was spurning me. We walked back along the corridor; she was asking Pete what they had seen. He was nice to her, but she was embarrassed. He fell back beside George so I was with her again.

I said, 'Don't worry about it. It's easy to say the wrong thing. He won't mind.'

We came to the stairs. I wasn't using my stick – it seemed too obvious somehow with her beside me. I could manage without if I was careful – but I was a bit distracted right then and I tripped on the first step. She offered her arm. I put my hand through and slipped it down to hers. She let me hold her hand. I said it then as we were going up past our fish. I said it quietly so only Pete and George could hear.

'Can we meet up sometime?'

'I'm sorry. I don't think it's a good idea.'

'Just for a drink I mean, a chat?'

'No, I'm sorry.'

'I knew it. You have a boyfriend.'

'No, that's not it. I don't really go in for boyfriends. I'm going to be a—'

I didn't let her finish. I couldn't bear the thought of all the jokes George would make, of the endless stream of humour it would provoke, that I wanted to date a nun. I stumbled again as she said it, pulling her against me as I fell, her body against mine. Feeling her fingers reaching for balance as we fell, reaching me.

'I'm sorry. I'm so clumsy,' I said, as hands came from every direction, pulling us upright.

I could have hurt myself. It was a risk on that unfamiliar stair. It was worth it, just to stop her talking.

I've thought about it since, and tried to finish the sentence another way. I'm going to be abroad, I'm going to be a bit busy. But I know, really, my instinct was right. That crucifix she was wearing hit me in the face as we fell.

I got it wrong. I thought she was flirting, when all the time it was just her Christian duty. No doubt she loves all God's creatures, especially the blind ones. I could

Penelope Macdonald

hear the pity in her voice; she was just another Irene
really. That's why we tend to stick together I guess; you
know where you are with your friends. But she's why I
remember Coventry – my stupid attempt to reach out, to
presume – and how I got away with it. At least they've
never mentioned her again.

We made it back okay – of course we did. We're sea-
soned travellers by now. It was just another adventure –
quite an easy run. Pete thinks we should try an
overnight trip next time. He quite fancies flying to
Edinburgh, when we've saved up a bit. George, kilts,
Scottish accents. It could be an entertaining trip.

54

Birds Without Wings

Angela Readman

Last summer it was Eva and me against everything evil
in the world. Swimsuits, kale, something that buzzed in
our room. Yet I couldn't stop thinking about Diana
Pinter – some girl at school who went to Paris with her
mother. I lay on a bunk scratching mosquito bites and
pictured them outside the Eiffel Tower eating salad in
the rain. I flicked through the magazines Mom posted,
girls with eyes lost as gazelles. Their hair was molasses,
toffee-apple shiny, the colour of Twinkies. My stomach
growled. It would be dinner soon, something steamed.
A postcard and cash fell out of *Vogue*, my mother's
handwriting like spun silk. *Hope you're having a good
time. Be good! We'll go shopping when you get home.* I
knew what 'be good' meant. I shoved the twenty in my
sock and dangled to high-five Eva on the bottom bunk.

This summer would be different. Mom wanted us to

take a trip. Dad was working and my brother wouldn't come; Ed was oddly self-maintaining. He lived in a fort of science books in his room. At nine he wasn't interested in space camp. If there had been an accountancy camp he'd jump in line. A camp where boys learnt to give bad financial news, and crinkle their brows exactly like their fathers, would suit him just fine.

'What do you think? Just the two of us,' Mom said, 'Won't it be fun?'

I wasn't sure. *Fun* and *Mom* went together as well as she said my shoes matched my blouse. I watched her fiddle with lilies in the vase in the lounge again, fingertips unable to resist giving them tips on which way to turn to be elegant.

No camp! I thought. No hikes, kale or treasure hunts (hikes in disguise – except with fruit and a whittled wooden otter, rabbit, any animal that could be described as a 'critter', at the end).

'Where d'you wanna go?' I said.

'Mexico,' my mother replied.

Not Paris or Venice, which was weird. Her friends usually took their daughters to glistening cities of tiny espresso cups and art galleries to cram in a few more 'sit up straights' before school pushed them out into the world.

'Why Mexico?' I said.

She let the lilies be, looking down like she did when she told Dad the drapes were a steal.

'I don't know. It's different,' she said, 'I read something about the spiritual side.'

I supposed being different was the appeal, and maybe the cost, though she'd never admit it. In the contest of who had the best holiday, I guessed spiritual trumped cultural every time.

'Suppose it might be cool,' I said.

My mother smiled, something up her cashmere sleeve. Mexico? Whatever. It couldn't do any harm. I phoned Eva to break the news.

'Mexico?' she said. 'Well, at least she won't make you go clothes shopping.'

She was wrong.

I followed my mother past counters like ice cubes. The air-con was on overdrive. My shirt stuck, sweat from the street chilled on my arms – shopping was a fever, hot and cold at the same time. My mother strolled, confident her hands were clean enough to stroke every dress on the rail. I pictured Diana Pinter and her mother swapping clothes in Parisian changing rooms, laughing when a cocktail dress suited Diana, and a pleated skirt and blazer looked inexplicably apt on her mom.

'How can I help?'

The assistant's suit was endive pale. She smiled at her commission in the form of a woman with a Chanel purse and hair like a cinnamon bun, coiled at the nape.

'I'm looking for something for my daughter for a trip,' my mother said.

The assistant's smile slipped; she pinned it back into place on her face. I knew the look well. Sales girls and I have a history. She looked at me now, wondering how to squeeze me into something that fit my mother's sense of style.

'She looks like a very mature young lady,' she said.

And off we went, following her towards the back of the store. I was far too 'mature looking' for Junior Miss. I wondered what 'she's a mature-looking young lady' is in Spanish. My shame would translate.

Mom pushed another dress into the changing room. Some things never changed.

'How you getting on? Don't force the zip. You need another size.'

Her voice peered through the curtain. It reminded me of the bus home from camp. For two minutes a year my mother looked hopeful. When the bus pulled in, I'd see her on tiptoes, watching me walk from the back seat. Moving from window to window to the front of the bus, my head and shoulders were all she could see. Anything was possible.

'Lovely to have you back!' she said, looking me up and down.

She paused, like she had to swallow the words her mouth wanted to say.

'Is that you? What happened to you!? You look . . .'

We walked past parents using words we didn't use. Mothers hugged daughters, fathers hugged sons, amazed how little of their arms were needed to fit round.

Outside the changing room, my mother said, 'Twirl.' I twirled. She stood back and frowned.

'Maybe something with a smock waist?' she said.

The sales girl flitted away, dresses like failed parachutes in her arms.

If Mom could free me from camp, I could give her the sky on the plane. We switched seats so she could have the window. It was our first trip alone other than weekends in Cape May – long days of Gramps on the boat, Gran trawling yard sales and Mom looking ashamed. Every night we met in the kitchen, Gran taking an interest in fishing in exchange for Gramps looking at the junk she'd bought, listening to the haggle of getting a dollar off, the drama of beating a neighbouring hand. I thought about their exchanges on the plane. Eating Mom's leftover chicken, I waited to hear: 'Are you sure you aren't full?' It didn't come. If anything she smiled a private smile, maybe the same way I sometimes could when she tilted the lilies in the vase. I took her giving me her cookie as a sign. I wanted to believe we could be friends.

The bus wound down the dizzying road to the hotel. Out of the window were pine trees I hadn't known Mexico had. I didn't know a lot, I could smell the pine, the orange of the Japanese man behind us, and the perfume of the woman in the seat in front nursing a kid old enough to chew jerky. My mother had a million pictures of churches in her purse. She looked at them, determined not to look at the woman. Most of the passengers weren't American.

'San Cristobal,' she'd said. Certain. 'Says here, it's popular with Europeans. I found out about something local we have to see. It's ...'

She changed the subject to the hotel.

We got off the bus and took our passports to the desk to check in.

Mom held on to them with white fingers. 'Do we have to leave our passports?' she said, 'I have American Express.'

The clerk shook his sad head. We handed over our passports – two little faces in bad light.

'We can manage,' she said. 'Men can take things the wrong way,' she whispered, hauling our cases to our room.

The room was peach. Two beds, an iron table on the balcony, and chairs with scrolled backs. My mother wiped the rail in the wardrobe to hang our clothes. Then she laid stuff out on the bed to assemble a survival-kit tote: Spanish phrase book, guide-book, traveller's cheques, handkerchiefs, toilet paper, toilet-seat covers, bottled water from home, pepper spray, Sweet and Lo.

'We have to smile but not be too friendly,' she said, reading about women travelling alone.

I smiled in a not too friendly way.

I kept a journal on vacation though I was never the diary type. I hated the idea of my thoughts all being in one place to be used as evidence against me sometime. Dad gave me a journal before we left. It had a bunch of blue and lilac stamps printed on the cover and a quote in typewriter print: *A traveller without observation is a bird without wings.* Dad customised the pages inside. Under each day he wrote: *Stuff I Liked, Stuff We Did, Stuff We Ate.* He gave it to me with a smirk, an acknowledgement passing from hand to hand.

Under *Stuff I Liked* I wrote: The smell of cinnamon, mountain views, jack hares, markets, little tin things, red, bicycles, breakfast, the tile rose on the table, hot chocolate, raffia baskets, a whole family woven from corn on a craft stall, not knowing the language, being aware of my smile because it had to do all the work.

Under *Stuff We Did* I wrote: Walk, look, photograph old buildings, look in our phrase book, sneeze, touch milagros, be afraid to haggle, smile (in a not too friendly way), say 'No, thank you', say everything slower, tell taxi drivers we're on the way to meet Dad, walk away.

Stuff We Ate had two columns, one for Mom, one for me.

Grapefruit	Mexican breakfast
Coffee and cigarette	Pozol
Egg white omelette	Mole chicken
Orange juice	Pozol
Grilled fish	Fish tacos
Banana & bran	Burrito
Coffee and cigarette	Pozol

Then I got bored with Mom and just did my own. Pozol was like sippable chocolate popcorn. I had it at the hotel, in a café in the old square and from carts. On the street my mother shaved off my milk moustache with her fingertip. I decided to add a new column to my book.

Stuff I Don't Like: My clothes laid out every morning like instructions of how to match Mom's purse. Hills. Cobble-stones & Mom's heels. Mom's fork turning over every bite to spot food poisoning lurking beneath. The dummies in The Museum of Mayan Medicine – a midwife and a spread woman with no mouth. The long walk through unknown streets to get there, one of Mom's hands on the zipper of her purse, her other clutching American water. (It reminded me of Eva and her coke, a can in her hand all day; it stopped her fidgeting, she said. She missed it so bad at camp she poured water into an empty can, trying to trick herself.)

*

Most mornings I took buses with my mother to small villages and lakes surrounding the town.

'Now this is what I had in mind,' Mom said.

People with backpacks squinted off the bus like turtles with ill-fitting shells. Most wore slacks and took sloppy photos. They looked like they were saying, 'I was here, next to this crumbling church. Okay, I looked sloppy – so what?' Outside the church in San Juan Chamula was a market crammed with pottery, woven blankets, paper Frida Kahlos and skeletons in red skirts. I touched strange milagros: tin fish and angels, the Virgin Mary, disembodied hearts, silver hands and feet that looked like they'd snap on the weight of a prayer. I wasn't sure what they meant but I bought a stripey armadillo for Eva (a hard little shell). Mom bee-lined to a stall of hand-embroidered skirts, peasant blouses and lace shawls.

'Stand back,' she said.

I stood under the canopy. Two old women looked on, silently embroidering in wicker chairs behind the stall. My mother draped a shawl over my shoulders and another on hers. Both were white lace, delicate feathers on our arms.

'Do you like it?' she said, combing fringes.

'I like this better,' I said.

I reached for a black one embroidered with white flowers. She stroked the quality and picked up another covered in red roses, a garden on her back. She bought all four shawls, an embroidered and lace one each. It was the first time she had asked what I liked without saying I had no idea what suited me.

Back at the hotel Mom wrote postcards to Dad and Ed. I started one for Eva at camp – I only needed two sentences, but none were right. What I wanted to send was a river of pozol, tamales like rafts. I wondered if Eva had managed to find a junior counsellor saving for college this year. There was always one, looking both ways, sliding down a zip in the boat shed, a duffle bag of Peanut Buttercups, Butterfingers, Tootsie Rolls. Eva and I stared at plastic packets glistening like jewels in the half dark. The counsellor smiled the way shop assistants eyed our mothers in stores. 'This is a customer who knows what she wants. Take your time. Look. Anything else I can get you? No trouble at all.' Every night, Eva and I sat by the lake talking about our moms, eating chocolate with a mark-up to make them blush, laughing till we could burst a gut.

'You're peeling,' my mother said, rubbing lotion on my shoulders before bed. I thought about Eva peeling sunburn off my back at camp. She had held up a mirror like a hairdresser showing a lady she was fit to go dancing. Carefully, I had set about Eva's back, wishing we could just peel off a layer and reveal, underneath our old skin, the sort of daughters our moms could take on a trip.

*

It was Thursday when my mother suggested we wear the white shawls. She got me up early, insisting I wear my best, and least comfortable, dress. I put it on. I still wanted to please her.

'Hannah, get a move on,' she said.

Her fingers twitched as if looking for lilies. She tucked my hair behind my ear. I didn't see what the big deal was. I'd had my fill of ruins, mountains and villages. Tomorrow we were spending the day in San Cristobal doing last-minute shopping before our flight. Suddenly my mother looked as eager as she did the morning of the sale at Bloomingdale's. This village wasn't in the guide-book, she said. No tour buses went from the square; all she had was a slip of paper with instructions on how to get there. Outside the old cinema we rammed ourselves into a *colectivo* – a van packed with backpackers and locals. The driver's music was deafening. The van jerked to a stop outside fields to let people on and off. We got off at a dirt track surrounded by corn.

'This way,' my mother said, looking at her map.

'Where we going?'

'You'll see,' she said.

I think she was smiling. Later I wanted to remember if she was smiling so bad it hurt. I hoped we weren't visiting another old church; pretty as they were, they didn't mean more to me than an hour in the shade. Walking around them my mother looked sort of bored, revived only when she saw tiles or woodwork that would look great in the summer house she was trying to persuade Dad to buy. I followed her uphill now, stopping to sip water and whine about the bugs picnicking on my arms.

'There's nothing here,' I said.

I looked around at cattle sheds, the odd house with a rickety tile roof.

'Here,' she said, 'I think.'

I panted behind her towards a white, stone house with a skinny guy stood aside. He leaned against the wall, watching us approach. My mother took a handkerchief out her purse and wiped the dust from our shoes. The man walked towards us, not smiling, just watching our clean shoes.

'Hello. Is this the right place? We're here to see, we heard ...'

My mother fumbled in her purse, digging for her phrase book buried under breath mints and flyers.

The man nodded and held out his palm, sky up.

'Yes, of course.'

She handed him pesos – I'm not sure how many – and we followed him to the house.

'Here? Thank you.'

My mother zipped her bag closed over her camera, like she did before we went into churches.

'What is this? Some cheese-making place or something?'

'*Sshhh*,' she said.

We stepped into a narrow hallway. My mother's hand rested on my back. Someone, an old woman, was coming out of the door at the end of the dim hall, rubbing her eyes. I squeezed in my stomach to let her pass. She stopped right in front of us, cupping my cheek with the walnut of her hand, she cried, '*Señorita gorda encantadora. Señorita gorda encantadora.*' There were tears in her eyes. I stared at her lips, like a drawstring bag, tightened around contents I couldn't recognize.

'*Bendígale. Bendígale,*' she said.

She rushed past us to cry at the unsmiling man outside. My mother nudged me through the door at the end of the corridor and I lurched into the room. It was bare, a girl lay in an iron bed. In the corner was a woman on a chair. She stood, her hand gesturing us to the bed. She spoke in short bursts.

'Look,' she said, 'my daughter. She not eat since year of too much rain. Crops fail. Only small water touch her tongue for two years. Yet she alive. Is miracle. She a saint, everyone say. '

Her English was bare as the room. She made a cross with her fingers over her shoulders and head. My mother followed, dabbing on a cross like perfume. I don't know why but I did the same. I stared at the girl asleep in the bed, the light from the shutters making gold bars across her pale face. Her eyes were closed, her eyelids dark. I could hear her breathing, I thought. The white sheet, pulled up to the neck, barely moved.

The mother lifted the sheet for us to see stick legs, twig arms poking out of a white nightdress. Through it I could see ribs; frail as a house of matchsticks it looked like a sigh might blow her down.

'We lost cattle. Corn. My daughter dream about angel. She know she did not have to eat,' the woman said.

My mother nodded as if she understood. Something about the woman looked proud. My cheeks burnt hot and red. I stared at the girl, then the mothers. Why? I wanted to yell, Why are we here? What good does it do? How can this happen? Who let it? Who would it save? I looked up at the shutters and had the urge to throw them back, let sun flood the room, drown us all. I wanted to grab my mother's purse and drop mints in the girl's mouth one by one, feed her like a bird. I glared at my mother, opened my mouth and not a word came. I was close to the bed. I couldn't move. My hand touched the back of the hand of the girl, so cool it washed the heat from my own.

'Thank you,' my mother said, 'Bless you.'

The words were alien, spoken like a child repeating something she didn't know the meaning of but wanted to know. The mother of the girl looked at me and patted my mother's hand. The door opened then, a skinny man and a boy with crutches limped into the room. My mother and I stepped into the slim hall, following the jangle of coins in the man's pocket outside.

Trawling downhill, my mother said we were lucky to

see a miracle, a living miracle, in our lives. Even if it wasn't a miracle, they believed it, she babbled, they really believe.

'How many people can say that?' she said, opening her purse to take a picture of a farmer skinning a duck, that little extra bit of local colour rammed in her purse.

I didn't speak. I walked behind her, sun strapped to my back, our shadows swallowing each other if we got too close.

'We have to hurry,' she said, sipping water. She handed me the bottle. I shook my head, refusing the breath mints she offered. I just marched on, downhill towards the *colectivo*, the village, a little gift shop in town where we found a plastic money box of some saint with pink paint smeared on her lips and a slot in her crown.

'Your Gran would love this!' Mom said. She combed tangled fringes on my shawl. 'Is there anything you want?'

I shook my head. No. There was not.

'

Duty-Free

Helen Dunmore

They were the cleanest airport floors I've ever seen. Even so, a man was buffing up sparkles in a corner of the duty-free, beside a display of silver leprechauns. I was not quite the only customer in the half-acre of perfumes, whisky and cosmetics. Two or three of us drifted, desultory, fingering but failing to buy. The goods that shone inside the cabinets seemed to have nothing to do with us. A sound-system played music that broke on our ears as waves break on the shore. The staff were so attentive, so knowledgeably eager to carry out the tasks which could not be completed without the absent passengers. Even as you quaked for their jobs, you couldn't help warming to their unfounded optimism.

Friendly were the security staff, gassing to one

another about a football match. No one mentioned the result. Perhaps they'd all stopped watching at the same moment, to keep up the suspense for yet another working day. Warm and tasty drifted the smells of chilli con carne and mushroom lasagne in the restaurant. I ordered a cup of coffee.

'Will there be anything to eat with that?' sang the young man behind the counter, and I had to fight not to ask for the whole sweep of it, piping hot, just so that his face would light up. But he flourished the coffee on to the counter before me and smiled as if mine were exactly the order he'd been hoping for.

The mica glitter of the floors was getting to me. I'm easily disorientated, and on my way back through duty-free I was busy counting the small airport tasks that I had yet to carry out: buying a bottle of water and the newspaper if they had it, checking my email and the price of Chanel No 5 ... So I organise even my empty hours. There was a recycling bin handy, and there I sorted and threw away the papers from the conference I'd just attended. I held on to the timetable for a moment. It was marked out with notes, and the couple of sessions I'd presented were highlighted in green, the colour of a knot in the stomach. Strange how things could be so important, and then not important at all.

When I looked up the desert had flowered. The duty-free was packed. Scores of soldiers, men and women both, a hundred of them, no, many more than a hundred, milled purposefully around the displays or lined up in front of the tills. They had big boots and pale sandy uniforms. They were large, eager, polite, weary. You could see their health and youth in their springing hair and quick, observant glances. Their skin, however, was poor.

They all wanted to buy something in the short time that they had. Packed into bulky trousers, women soldiers compared lipsticks. Men queued for cologne. Names were murmured like prayers: L'Oréal, Shiseido, Versace, Prada, Paco Rabanne ...

Even though the duty-free hall was now full, it was not far from quiet. The assistants had risen to great heights and were changing dollars into euros in their heads as they advised on a set of headphones while clicking up a fragrance purchase. Politeness flowed over us all, ample as a river.

'This one is seventy-three euros, or would you prefer the larger size?'

We were at home again, in the kingdom of our preferences. Cabinets were opened and disclosed their contents to eager hands. White glossy packages were fetched down from the highest shelves. Leprechauns tinkled against one another. I fell into the swing of it and began to search among the lipsticks for number 719, the one I always wear. A young woman soldier alongside me waved a porfume-tester strip beneath her nostrils.

She had stains of fatigue under her eyes. Maybe this one wasn't right for her, she said. All she could smell was aeroplane.

'You can't go wrong with Chanel No 5. It's a classic,' I said, as I say to my daughter.

The soldier's face lightened. 'I guess it is, but I don't know that it works on me,' she said. She sprayed again, on her wrist this time, and turned it this way and that. She had a Southern voice. Her skin was pitted, not beautiful.

'Where are you all going?' I asked her.

'Afghanistan.'

'I think it works on you,' I said, breathing in the wrist she held out to me. There was her body smell under the perfume. It was dry, powdery and somewhat metallic. She was correct. She smelled of aeroplane.

It was a short stop-over for refuelling. These soldiers must have spent thousands of dollars in their brief time off the plane. After they had made their purchases they sat quietly on banks of plastic seats in the hall outside the duty-free, waiting for the tannoy. The bulk of their uniforms made them sprawl somewhat, legs apart, but not as students sprawl, ostentatiously at leisure, infantry of the gap-year dream that other travellers can only envy. These soldiers rested. The group beside me talked of mobile phones as if there were nothing else in the world.

How vast the airport was, and how bare of purpose. The life in it, for which it had been built, had sunk down to barely a murmur. Cafés, departure gates, transit lounges and scanners were becalmed. A coffee machine hissed to itself. Only everywhere, as far as the eye could see, there were these soldiers.

'Where are you all going?'

'Afghanistan.'

They were not even born in the days when the boldest of my generation took the Magic Bus to Kabul in search of Afghan gold. Here they sat, composed, under orders, touching Irish soil; or at least their boots touched mica particles in the flooring that caught the light as far as the eye could see. They were not unhandsome, some of the men. The girls, too, rested utterly, closing their eyes so that the harsh overhead light exposed the pure cut of the lids and every blackhead on their overworked skins. All the same, they were not unbeautiful.

There was one low-key call for their flight. Immediately they were on the move, down the long hall through an exit which had nothing to do with the civilian airport. There was no gathering of hand-luggage, mustering of children, wheel-chairs, pushchairs. The soldiers were there one minute, filling the lounge, and then they were gone through a flap that had appeared somewhere in the wall of the airport, revealing it to be no more than a transit shed which had served its purpose. On my left the duty-free still glittered. Now there came four or five stragglers who had just succeeded in making their purchases. They loped past me, and for the first time I saw that they were fit and fast for all their heaviness. They quickened almost to a canter, laughing for the first time, then they too disappeared. The tin shed turned back into an airport. The soldiers' big-bellied plane was already receiving them into itself.

An incident, I thought. A notable moment, equal to the sighting of rare passerines. But I was mistaken, because at that time they came in almost daily. A quarter of a million US military personnel, it seems, went through that airport in one year alone.

Backwards and forwards the planes go, settling briefly on this small space of Irish soil, releasing their uniformed passengers. The lifeblood of the duty-free now that the Celtic Tiger is a shamefaced joke and the acres of car-park around the airport stand empty.

They go up slowly, those big-bellied planes. They are far from new, and they labour sometimes under the weight of what they carry. The youth inside them, packed into flesh, packed into uniform and then filling the metal skin of the DC-10. The youth that comes once, and doesn't come again.

'Where are you all going?'

'Afghanistan.'

*

Beautiful place, Shannon, in its arrivals and its departures. A dream of water, an enlacement of low-lying land by shining tributaries. As your plane rises you see it clear, and then the wing tilts and the sky is there instead, reeling away from you, all that greyness thickening to muffle your eyes, your ears, your lips. You will never see earth again. You say good-bye to it without emotion, among the whiteness, as if this is the death you have always expected; but as it happens this time the plane keeps climbing, and you punch through the clouds and out into the blue.

Hwyl

Emily Russell

The summers at Tanodd Carreg were jade and myrtle but the winters were black and white.

Tanodd Carreg was a solid Welsh farmhouse – though no farm remained there, having been eaten up by bigger ones to the north and south. The exterior walls were three feet of impervious grey stone. Great square blocks one atop the other.

The house stood alone and undaunted on a natural ledge. To the back, the hill rose up steeply and disappeared skywards. To the front, forty yards of solid ground dropped away, down to a dark-green valley dotted with plastic cows. So high up was Tanodd Carreg that often the valley was obscured by thin low-lying slips of cloud. Some days the cloud was no more than a grey whisper, other times it was dense and opaque, and then the valley became a giant's mixing bowl filled with the soft peaks of egg whites. In early spring the cloud would gather around the house itself and on those days Tanodd Carreg was a ghost; a phantom in damp swirls of cold, white silk.

The link to the outside world was a long stony track, lined with foxgloves in the summer and nothing in the winter. It curled up the hill, which rose sharply on the right and dropped away to the left, between slopes of soggy, gawking sheep. Three hollow steel gates barred the way along it. Named the 'wailing gates' by the two children who lived in Tanodd Carreg, they sung in the wind – a desolate noise that sank into Nina and Jay's bones as they slept and nourished them like calcium.

Past the wailing gates and at the top of the track ran the mountain road. This was the way out. But they never went up that road. Up was the way things got mad, with the ruins and the hares and the sky. Down, eventually, over cattle grates and through muted woods of Sitka spruce, led to villages – chapels, post offices, schools.

It was on this road the children stood for three mornings running one January, waiting for a school bus that didn't come. It had been snowing since New Year. Nina was six and her brother, Jay, a year younger. By 8.45am, abandoned, frozen and excited, they trudged back down to their world to change out of school uniforms and into matching green snow-suits.

The snow drifts on the east side of Tanodd Carreg had reached the first-floor windows and the lie of the land around had become tacit beneath ten billion sticky flakes. Even the cottage of their only neighbour, Gwen, which usually stood out like a splinter on the scrub-land to the south-west, was barely there any more. But while the earth slept the children played and that week was one of the busiest of their lives. They only went indoors when they could no longer feel their toes, and then their mother, Vivien, would fill them with sweet porridge. Woollen gloves were hung above an old Rayburn in the kitchen until the wool was dry and crispy and smelt of the tangy woodsmoke that permeated everything at Tanodd Carreg.

Nina and Jay's father, Steve, worked six, sometimes seven days a week chopping down tall pines for timber. That week, unable as he was to get further than the second wailing gate, was the longest he had ever spent at home. He exhausted most of the short daylight hours in the barn, fixing holes in the roof, oiling the generator and chop, chop, chopping the logs. By the time the snow thawed there would be enough firewood to last them until the following Christmas.

Vivien spent her time in the kitchen – boiling up scraps, frying up leftovers and trying to make the freezer bigger than it was.

The cooking and the chopping of logs was nothing compared to the plans of Nina and Jay, who went to sleep every night concerned that the morning might bring a melt and leave so much undone.

On the first morning they built snowmen and decorated them with soggy chips of wood and a great aunt's old hats, which they found buried in the back of their mum's wardrobe. When they were done they built snow monsters and then a snow bear before they grew bored and decided to go hunting for real bears. Several times Jay thought he found promising tracks in the snow. Nina wasn't so sure but they followed each of the leads anyway, all the way to disappointment.

The next day their dad took a break from chopping logs to build them some simple sledges from the obscene amount of wood which had filled the barn. They were basic but they went fast and Jay eventually had to be picked up and carried home, while Nina stomped behind in the fading light.

The third morning Nina woke to find flakes the size of party rings sneaking down around Tanodd Carreg. Beating like a heart, she woke Jay. He looked out of the window and then at Nina and laughed. On their way down the narrow staircase she whispered in his ear, 'You know that wishes count for more today?'

'Why?'

'Because of the snow. It's magic, and the stone will be covered in it.'

Their mum was leaning against the kitchen sink drinking tea. She was dressed in jeans and a large grey jumper, her brown hair tied back. The radio was on but she didn't seem to be listening. 'Nina, you shouldn't wake your brother.'

Jay had cornflakes, and Nina had toast and peanut butter.

'I want toast,' Jay said, looking at his sister's.

'You said yesterday that you hated it.'

'It looks different today.'

His mum picked up the bowl of dry cornflakes and poured them back into the box before putting some more bread in the toaster. 'Nina, I don't want you taking Jay up to that rock today. It's too far.'

The outside door opened and their dad walked in, stamped snow off his boots and on to the doormat. 'Morning, you lot.' He moved over to the table, sat down and started on a plate of plain buttered toast.

'I think we'll find the bear today,' Jay said.

Their mother looked at him blankly for a second over her tea and then at their dad, who had already risen from the table, toast still in hand, and was heading back towards the door. She raised her voice slightly, 'Well, actually, Steve, before you go, I think someone should go down to Gwen's today.'

'You mean me?' He was pulling on his boots.

'Well, what if she needs the path cleared?'

'She doesn't leave the house.'

83

'Me and Jay can clear her path!' Nina interrupted. 'We'll take our spades.'

'There you go then,' he said as he opened the door and walked out, leaving some errant flakes of snow dissolving on the doormat.

Later that morning as they left the house Nina saw that the first-floor windows on the east side were now entirely obscured by the drifts. After the calmness of the last two days the wind was becoming strong and all three gates were singing in certainty. Just for a second as they passed through the first gate Nina thought she understood what it was saying to her but then the song changed and her understanding was lost with the wind, like a dream you can't hold on waking.

Gwen was somewhere between middle and old age and lived alone in the little tumbledown dwelling in which she had been born. Had been born, had grown up, had seen her parents die and had never left.

What must have once been a sweet but modest cottage now more closely resembled one of the many abandoned residences up in these hills. It stood on a low, scraggy bit of land that could have been nice if Gwen could have been bothered. Poor Gwen. Everything about her was lopsided. The cottage appeared to lean slightly to the left, and the fence around it to the right. Even Gwen herself always looked wonky; if she put her long greying hair up in a ponytail it flopped to one side. If she put on her best lilac cardigan it was covered in hair and lint and sagged off one shoulder. She had narrow shoulders and wide hips. Whenever Nina saw her she couldn't help but think of a particularly overripe pear she had once found at the bottom of their fruit bowl.

They cut straight down from the track towards the scrub-land to Gwen's, though marsh and scrub-land now looked much the same, and the Tan Woods beyond were just a dark line in the distance contoured with a thick pallid stripe.

The three of them picked their way along what they thought was the garden path – a dangerous path made more hazardous by the mantle of unadulterated snow disguising the many rusting objects and cracks that lay beneath. When they knocked on the door Nina could hear the startled scurrying of little hooves on bare tiles.

'It's tea with the goats then,' Nina heard her mum mutter.

Gwen appeared, wrapped in several matted blankets, hair up in a sideways bun that rested over her left eye.

'*Duw, duw, duw*, what have we here? You've come to check on me? That's nice of you. Me and the girls are fine though. Come in, come in.'

Gwen's Welsh accent rose and fell like the hills and valleys of the country, coming from somewhere far deeper than her throat. When Gwen spoke Nina some-times wondered if her voice came straight up from the stone below the ground, through the tiles, up her stout legs and out of her mouth.

As they entered the dusty space that served as dining and sitting room, the white goat with grey patches, Gloria, trotted over to nibble at their shoes. Their mum did her pretend smile and patted the animal on its head as the children giggled and stroked Gloria back.

'Sit down, sit down.' Gwen motioned to the small round table in the middle of the room. 'You didn't have to come. I've seen worse snow than this.' She gave Gloria an affectionate pat and laughed for no reason, a loud, rolling laugh. 'I'll get you all a drink. You sit there, sit tight ... '

'Actually Gwen, we really can't ... ' Vivien began, but Gwen was already pretending not to hear as she vanished into the kitchen.

The three of them waited in silence. They could hear Gwen chatting to the second goat, Gail. Gloria began nuzzling something which used to be a cushion and then wandered out to the kitchen to see what was happening, leaving them in the dark. The curtains in the room were illusory slips of stained grey lace but light still failed to penetrate through the ancient window panes.

When Gwen returned she was carrying a tray with three small glasses filled with fresh goat's milk and with several short hairs floating on top. She placed them down, one each, around the table.

Hwyl

'The best thing about snow is the thaw – and then the spring. With spring comes *hwyl*.'

'What's that?' Jay asked.

'It means "good-bye",' answered Nina, confidently.

'Lord no, girl! You went sledging yesterday, didn't you?' Gwen continued. 'I saw you. You know how you felt when you was on that sledge and it started to go fast? That's what *hwyl* is.'

'Oh,' Jay said. He looked down at the glass of milk in front of him then caught his mum watching and saw the narrowing of her eyes as if she dared him to try it. He looked away quickly.

As Gwen pottered back out to the kitchen, her slippers flopping off her feet, Vivien reached into her handbag, which she had clutched to her body just below the rim of the table. The children heard the familiar soft rotation of a large cap being unscrewed. Their mum reached across the table for Jay's glass. Nina handed hers over gladly. The flask cap was just being tightened when Gwen reappeared.

Vivien spoke quickly. 'Listen Gwen, I know you probably don't need anything but I've put a casserole on for dinner and there's much too much for us. Shall I drop some round to you later? I hate to waste it.'

'Well, if it's going to be wasted I won't say no. *Duw, duw* – we mustn't waste food!' Gwen laughed and grinned at Nina. Next to her Gloria looked as if she was grinning too with her strange oblong eyes.

On their way out the front door they all turned to say good-bye. Gwen gave Nina a wink. 'Off with you then.' She laughed. But halfway down the path Gwen shouted after them, 'You're doing it wrong, you know!'

They all turned around.

'What?' said Nina.

'You're wishing wrong. I can see the stone from here. I see you two wishing.'

'How is it wrong?'

'Come here, girl, and I'll tell you.'

Before her mum could stop her Nina set back off along the path at a run, hopping over the bumps in the snow.

Gwen bent down and whispered the secret in her ear. She whispered for a long time. Nina didn't say good-bye again but came bouncing back down the path to her mum and brother, a glossy rubber ball that Gwen had launched in their direction.

On their way home they took the marsh route on the lower ground. It was divided in two by what was once a dry-stone wall. Now it was completely overgrown with moss and acted as a causeway across to the woods on the far side. In the spring they went hunting frog-spawn along it. But on this day the wall was no more than a slight bump in an otherwise perfect mantle, which they wanted to corrupt. The sky had closed for a while and hung low and grey above their heads. They walked in silence. Vivien paused halfway along the causeway to empty the flask of milk. It made a sound like someone putting out a fire.

The wall ended abruptly in a steep bank that was overhung by trees. As they went to hop down Jay suddenly dropped to his knees. When he stood up he was holding a skinny little robin carefully in cupped hands. It lay on its side and was quite stiff and crusted with frost so that it sparkled.

Nina made a sound that began as delight and ended in dismay.

'Poor thing, it must have died of the cold.' Vivien went to give it a closer look.

Jay pulled his hands back, 'Can I take him home with us?' he asked, his voice high with emotion.

'What would you do with it, sweetheart? You can't keep a dead bird in the house – it will rot.'

'We could bury him,' Nina said, and saw a look of relief swell over her brother's face.

Jay carried the bird all the way home with his arms outstretched in front of him. It made it hard to climb the bank but he wouldn't let Nina help.

When they got home they immediately set about making funeral arrangements. The snowman was stripped of the great aunt's hat, and Nina stood in front of her mother's mirror and placed it very carefully on her head. Jay named the robin 'Sir' like a knight. On a piece of cardboard Nina wrote in red felt-tip: *Here lies Sir Robin who fought bravely against the cold but lost.* Their mum gave them an old shoebox, which they filled with cotton wool, and Jay set the robin in it with painful slowness.

Using spades designed for sand-castles it took a long time to clear away the snow and dig a hole in a patch of soil in their garden. It had taken them ages to decide on the best place. Eventually they chose an area at the far end that overlooked the valley. Once the coffin was in place they covered it back up. The hard earth made a hollow noise as it was scattered over the box. Then Jay forced the cardboard headstone down on top. The two of them stood for a moment looking down at the grave. Nina, elated by solemnity, tried hard to hide a smile.

Following the ceremony they went back into the house to change out of their smart clothes.

As they left Tanodd Carreg by the front door, the light was not quite waning and the casserole was not quite ready, and their parents were in the kitchen bickering over who would take some down to Gwen later that evening.

Beyond the garden the snow reached their waists in places and it was hard going. They had to take the long way round up the track to the second wailing gate and then double back on themselves across the hill. There was a thick flurry falling again and they stopped often to look up until they were dizzy. Even though the air was quite still the flakes whirled and spun on their way down, moved by some other force. When they reached the top of the hill their legs ached superbly from the effort. Breathless and glowing the two children turned to view their kingdom.

Straight below they could see Tanodd Carreg – the roof completely covered, a thick plume of smoke rising from where the chimney must be. Far to the south the open space of the marsh ended at the dark forest beyond. They could make out Gwen's cottage to the right of it. And Gwen herself. In a red and blue tartan blanket she was the only bit of colour in the entire realm. She lay on the ground next to the goat shed. She was waving. Nina waved back and Jay copied. '*Bore da!*' they shouted.

'She's making a snow angel,' Nina said. 'Let's make one too.'

They made them deep – waving their arms for a long time. When they stood up and shook the snow out of their hoods, Nina remembered Gwen's special word.

'*Hwl!*' she shouted down as loud as she could. '*Hwyl! Hwyl! Hwyylllll!*'

Gwen was a long way away so she just waved back, though Nina was sure she could hear.

It took their eyes a minute to pick the stone out, so deep were the drifts around it, but its shape was clear – a perfect oval, the size of a small van.

'Gwen said it was put here by a wizard,' Nina told Jay.

'Like Merlin?'

'Yes, he put it here to show where the little people live. They're below the ground and they haven't come out for a long time but they can hear our wishes if we do it right.'

The children approached the rock slowly and quietly, their new knowledge weighing them down like pebbles in their pockets. Everyone knew the stone was for wishes. Even the sheep knew it was magic. In summer they would lie for hours on its solar charged surface. But today it was cold.

Nina went first so Jay would know what to do. She marched around the stone three times before pausing significantly at the far end for several seconds to remove her gloves. Then she shut her eyes tight and plunged both hands deep into the snow until her palms met the solid rock. She made her wish and Jay followed.

Steve found Gwen later that evening after eventually agreeing to deliver the casserole. Nobody knew exactly why she'd gone outside – it seemed she may have crawled there. The stroke hadn't killed her, but the cold had.

'If only we'd taken the food round sooner,' Vivien could be heard saying over and over on the phone to various friends and relatives for the next few days.

Nina began shutting herself in her room whenever the phone rang.

It stopped snowing but the cold stayed. When a week

later Nina and Jay passed by the spot at the top of the hill, two shallow dents could be seen in the crust. They looked nothing like angels.

Some weeks later, on her birthday, Nina's parents took her outside and told her to wait by the barn door. It was late spring and the morning mist was so thick that she could barely make it out. The humid air clung to the new green of the ash tree above her and as it became too heavy it fell in a drop on to Nina's left cheek. She watched her parents disappear into the cloud side by side.

A minute later she heard a noise she had been dreading. She closed her eyes and heard her wish become a ticking that became a purr. The dark shapes of her parents began to emerge from the mist, her dad encumbered somehow. Slowly a bright red pierced the grey between them. A deep emerald ribbon was tied to one of the handlebars, becoming the hundredth shade of green that Nina had counted that morning.

It was a boy's bike but her dad had repainted it and fitted a new bell. He rang it proudly. A beautiful, clear note echoed out into the nothing. *Hwyl*, it called to her. *Hwyl, hwyl, hwyyllllllllll.*

The Journey to the Brothers' Farm

Pippa Gough

One day, oh, it must have been when I was about seven, Miss Kotzee read a story about Dulcina, a beautiful young girl with milk-white skin and flaxen hair of the purest silk, who married a prince. 'Dulcina was fine-boned,' Miss Kotzee said to the hushed class, 'and her face was her fortune.'

For many days I puzzled over the mystery of skin, bones, faces and fortunes. I knew about skin – black skin and white skin – but how did all the other things link together? I studied the other children in the playground. Bettina, I noticed, had very pale skin and white-blonde hair but she was an albino and her eyes juddered from side to side behind her thick glasses. Was this strange face her fortune, I wondered?

At home on the farm I looked at the familiar tough-skinned faces of my father, brother and Auntie Das. The person who stared back at me every morning from the mirror on the back of the kitchen door looked the same. My face wasn't as creased as Auntie Das's, whose skin resembled a screw of brown paper from the butcher's shop, but for the first time I noticed the plainness of the Lourens' features: the small chin, brown eyes too close together, the lumpy nose, the coarse hair.

'Do you think a prince would ever want to marry Bettina?' I asked Miss Kotzee one break time. She hesitated and looked around nervously. 'I mean, out of Bettina and me,' I persisted, 'who has the best chance do you reckon? Or out of the whole class?' I took a bite of my sandwich and waited for her reply. Miss Kotzee pondered my question and, as I watched, her face reddened up to the roots of her cropped hair and her thick, wide neck became marbled with weals and blotches.

'I'm not sure marrying a prince is going to be your fortune, Annelie,' she said slowly, and sucked in her breath between orange lips. We both looked out of the window at the other kids in the playground.

'You see,' she continued, 'in the story, from the moment Dulcina was born, it was in her stars to meet a prince. Her prince. That was her destiny, her fate, her path in life.'

Miss Kotzee took another quivery breath and her blunt fingers stroked my cheek.

'So, Annelie, in that way her face was her fortune. Your fortune, meisie, will lie in other things.'

I thought this over. 'So ... she got all that just because she was so mooi?'

Miss Kotzee nodded.

'You mean, she just sat around on her jack?' I could feel sudden tears pricking at my eyes. 'She never had to fetch the cattle from the low field because the waterhole had dried up?'

'Ja,' Miss Kotzee said, shrugging her big shoulders. 'That's about right. And don't say "jack".'

I understood then my face was never going to be my fortune. Nor was Miss Kotzee's or she wouldn't have been our teacher here in Bultdorp. But that was a long time ago. There weren't any fortunes in the way my family looked, or anyone else around our farm. Our fate was to work with our hands, our big-boned, squared-off hands, swinging pick-axes into the dry, red earth, where dust like chilli powder rose up to choke us from between the rows of whispering maize.

This is the sworn statement of Annelie Louw, née Lourens, made on this day 17 February 1977 at Tweekopfontein Police Station.

I own Louw Stores, 37 Main Street, Bultdorp. I have run this on my own since my husband Vernon Louw died three years ago. Every Monday I drive to

Tweekopfontein to stock up on goods for the store from Van Riebeck Wholesalers. Today, Monday 17 February 1977, I left the store at sunrise for the usual Monday run. My journey takes me past the turn-off to Veldplatt, the Krugers' farm ...

I loaded the bakkie with water for the journey and put Vernon's old rifle in the front with me. For many years we had done this journey together. It had been our day out, away from the store. After Vernon had died Croenke's youngest had offered to do the run instead but I found I still liked the break. And now I no longer minded travelling on my own.

I have known the Kruger family all my life. I grew up on Bloumeer Farm. The Kruger farm, Veldplatt, was the nearest farm to us going on up the valley. Hendriks Kruger and I went to the same school in Bultdorp. He was five years older than me. His younger brothers, the twins Jacob and Isaac, never went to school. They had brain damage from birth. They hardly ever left the farm. Hendriks had no wife. He took over the farm when his father died. I have not retained a friendship with Hendriks and before today I had not been to the Veldplatt farm for thirty years. Occasionally I would see Hendriks when he came to town, in the hotel bar ...

The Soweto riots – they talked about it all the time in the hotel bar, especially on Fridays when Hendriks came to town. 'You've got to treat them like animals,' he lectured from his place at the end of the bar. 'Show them who's boss. Crack the bull-whip, my friends.' His loud mouth, big frame and drunken arrogance pushed other drinkers into silent agreement. Like others in Bultdorp, I had learned to steer a wide path around him. And my path was wider than most.

It was one of those days in high summer when the cool of night had failed to curb the heat of the previous day. The dirt road ahead of me swam in a haze, fired already by the early sun. Fine, red dust coated the windows and settled over my arms. I mopped away the beads of sweat gathering under my chin with my hankie and stuffed it back into my bra. The rains couldn't come soon enough. Looking up, the brittle, blue sky gave no hope of salvation. In the town tempers frayed and dogs fought. The hotel bar erupted into brawls more often at this time of year. Water and money were scarce.

The turning to Bloumeer farm came into view on the right. My father's original hand-painted sign still pointed the way. I slowed as I always did and looked down the road as I passed. Swirls of dust blew across the familiar old track that wound its way into the distance across the veld, weaving through the small outcrops of rock that punctured the dry and wizened landscape. I guessed my brother would have put the cattle in the lower field until the rains came.

I still dreamt about the farm. Twenty years didn't dim the memory. These were happy dreams of waking to the rustling and creaking of the grass roof heating up in the early morning sun; of the soft wash of pink light hitting the gauzy walls of my mosquito net; of the gentle cooing of doves and raucous crowing of the cock who scratched around with his hens below my window. At weekends and holidays I would be up and out at dawn. Rumba would be waiting in the stable and I would sing to him as I saddled up. Like ghosts we would move slowly down the track, the baobab trees blackened against the sudden reddening of the sky, thin wisps of wood smoke curling up from the cooking fires in the farm workers' compound. Thabo would be waiting at the edge of the kraal, making clucking and clicking noises to Rumba who would drop his head and whinny back his response.

I have known Thabo Kefentse since I was a child. His father was our Head Herdsman. Thabo went to work for the Krugers when he was about sixteen ...

Thabo. We were inseparable back then, when it didn't matter. Then, quite suddenly, childhood had melted away. 'Mix with your own type now, Annelie,' my father had said one day. 'Play with kids from your school.

Leave the workers now, hey?' So I took to spending time at Veldplatt with Hendriks and his brothers. Thabo hadn't wanted to work for the Krugers but we couldn't afford to take him on. We never really spoke to each other after that. When I did see him around the farm or in town, sitting in the back of Hendriks' bakkie, he would lower his eyes. I became 'madam'. He remained 'Thabo'.

The sun was climbing fast as I approached the Veldplatt farm turn-off. I still had dreams about this farm too; dreams shot through with disjointed memories of storms, of pain and bruises and Hendriks' face looming over mine, blotting out the sky. The welling sense of shame on waking would leave me sweating and choking. Every week I passed the turn-off and every week I gritted my teeth. I would gladly have travelled another hour to avoid it.

The track leading down to the farm was overgrown with thorny scrub and tall, stubborn bush grass. It clogged the storm drains either side. Talk was that the farm had been disintegrating since Oupa Kruger had died seven years ago. Everyone knew the brothers were in trouble, even though no one from the town had been down there for years. We just watched as Hendriks slowly poured away the money on whisky and beer. His brothers, the twins, were never seen. Hendriks mentioned them sometimes with bitterness and a curled lip.

I kept my foot hard on the accelerator as I passed. Then, a sudden quick movement in the culvert caught my eye and instinctively I slowed. An animal, maybe. Leopard had been seen on the farm many years ago. Again the movement – a hand clawing at the stones and grass on the side of the ditch. I slammed on the brakes and the bakkie slithered sideways on the dirt road, snaking to a stop. A red cloud plumed up from the spinning tyres. Taking Vernon's rifle I scrambled out of the cab. A figure crouched at the verge, holding his arm over his head. I stopped and pointed the gun. The wind whipped the stinging dust against my legs and arms.

'What's the problem?' I asked. My voice sounded thin and strange. I felt my heart in my throat. The man raised his head. He tried to speak but his mouth was too dry to allow words and sound to form. Slowly I recognised the face.

'Thabo?'

I stumbled back to the bakkie, threw the gun across the seat and reached for the flask of water. Wrenching the cap from the top, I ran back and held the bottle to his mouth. He gulped and swallowed greedily.

'Waiting,' he said at last. 'Monday. Knew you would come past, madam.'

Thabo took another sip from the bottle. I tipped water on to his face and wiped the dust out of his eyes with my hankie. I looked around. The road was empty. I sensed he didn't want to be seen.

'Come, Thabo,' I said. 'I need to get you off the road. Can you stand?'

Thabo nodded and painfully heaved himself to his feet.

'I'll get you into the bakkie. Then you can tell what's happened.'

With a growing sense of foreboding I helped him into the cab. I climbed back into the driver's seat and took a large mouthful of the remaining water. I swilled it over my teeth and swallowed. My hands trembled against the steering wheel. I wiped my palms down the side of my dress and stared across the ochre veld to the Kruger farm, just visible on the horizon. I reversed quickly and turned the bakkie on to the overgrown and potholed track. A little way off a large, spreading baobab dominated the flat and scrubby bush-land. I recognised the silvered smoothness of the vast, old tree-trunk and the way the blue of the sky was cut out around the huge, spiky branches, tufted with green. I remembered back in Oupa Kruger's time, his cattle had always gathered under its shade, stamping flat the ground and clearing the scrub. I pulled in out of sight of the road and slowly exhaled. The inside of the cab was stifling. I opened the door and let the breeze, cooled by the shade, blow over us. I turned to Thabo. For the first time I realised he was bleeding.

'Thabo, you're hurt.'

'There is a fight, Madam Annelie,' he whispered. 'Up

at the farm last night. Baas Hendriks he was very drunk ...'

Thabo's voice tailed off. He looked terrified, ashen under his brown Tswana skin. He indicated the direction of the farm limply with his right arm. Blood, a lot of it, was dried on to his shirt and smeared across his hands and arms.

'Thabo. Here, show me.'

Thabo shook his head and held his arm stiffly to his side, his left hand moving to hold his shoulder.

'I tried to stop Baas, but he was wild, like an animal. Baas Isaac and Baas Jacob ... they are very hurt.'

'How hurt, Thabo? How bad is it?'

Thabo shook his head.

'It is very bad, Madam Annelie.'

'Did you call the police, Thabo? Did you ring Sergeant Van de Merwe from the farm phone?'

Thabo slid his eyes to look at the ground.

'No, madam.'

'For Christ's sake, Thabo, why not?'

Thabo looked up and let his gaze drop again.

'Because it is too bad, madam. I came to find you.'

Thabo lifted his eyes again. I nodded and took his hand.

'Okay. I'm here now, hey. So, let me look.'

He sighed, then let me gently lift his arm. I could see a long, deep cut obscured by congealed blood that curved away from the top of his shoulder across his chest. As I moved the arm, fresh blood pooled in the wound and spilled on to his chest. It must have taken everything to manage the long walk to the main road.

'Who did this to you, Thabo? Was it Baas Hendriks?'

I already knew the answer. The wound was made by a panga knife –

Hendriks' weapon of choice when squaring up to his farm workers.

'What about the others, Thabo? Your wife and daughter, her children? Are they safe?'

'Yes, madam.' Thabo paused. 'He did not get them. I had to stop him, Madam Annelie.'

Today, as I drove past the turning to the Veldplatt Farm, Thabo Kefentse waved me down. He explained there had been 'bad trouble' at the farm. Hendriks had been drinking all weekend and there had been a fight. He, Thabo, had made his way to the main road to find help. He was wounded and confused. He had lost a lot of blood. He said that he had tried to stop Hendriks and had received his injuries as a result. I believed this to be true. My first thought was to get Thabo back to the farm and ring for help from the phone ...

I felt suddenly exhausted. I didn't want to think about what Thabo was saying. I had struggled all these years to blank Hendriks from my mind.

'I've got to stop the bleeding, Thabo. Come, let me use your shirt.' I pulled him forwards and gently lifted his shirt over his head. It was already tattered and torn, stitched and darned many times. As it came away from his skin I saw the weals and cuts on his back, extending up his neck and across his head. Hendriks had been generous with the bull-whip as well. I tore the shirt into strips and tightly bound up the wound. I gave Thabo more water and settled him back against the seat.

'Okay. Let's get you to the hospital.'

Thabo caught my hand, his grip strong, urgent.

'No, madam. You must go to the farm first.'

I looked at his face, pinched, desperate. He released my hand but his eyes held mine. I nodded, started up the engine and swung the truck around towards the farm.

We ground our way along, dipping and twisting, every jolt causing Thabo to grimace in pain. With every kilometre, memories were flooding my mind. I was back by the reservoir above the farm with the three brothers. I was thirteen years old. Hendriks towered over me. The day was hot and suddenly dark as a storm blew in from the distant hills. We could see it rolling over the veld – a black pillar of cloud joining ground to sky. The air crackled with electricity and lightning forked and flashed on the horizon. Hendriks was in a wild mood. The static lifted his hair from his scalp. I too felt electrified and excited. The twins were whispering and giggling. I knew I should go home before the storm broke but I stayed. I was flattered by the attention I was getting from Hendriks. I remember feeling hot and pleased. I didn't have milk-white skin and hair like gold but Hendriks thought I was pretty. He was telling me so. I smiled up at him. The twins smirked and chattered behind their hands. Hendriks was holding me by my wrists and leering at his brothers. I had giggled, unsure of what was happening, and then I remember the pressure of the hard ground on my back, the sound of my clothes tearing and Hendriks breathing heavily into my neck. The sudden pain between my legs took me by surprise and as I cried out, lightning sparked across the sky, lighting up Hendriks' face and hair. Over his shoulder I caught a glimpse of Jacob crying. Isaac was standing quietly at his side. Then there was shouting and Hendriks was on his feet, pulling me up roughly behind him. Catching me by the elbow he spat into my ear, 'You asked for that, you little tease. Tell anyone and I'll let them know how easy you are.'

The din around us grew louder and I suddenly recognised Thabo's voice. He was screaming. 'Baas Hendriks, come quick. Baas Hendriks, I have just seen the leopard over by the vlei-side waterhole.' Hendriks ran off, bellowing for his brothers to follow him. I sank down on to the grass as the metallic scent of the rain on dusty ground filled the air. That's where Thabo found me. He gently took my hand and helped me up, smoothing down my dress, dusting off the burrs and ground dirt. 'Go home now, *tsala ya me*,' he said.

I never went back to Veldplatt. I would see Hendriks in the town but we never spoke. Some years later in a quiet moment together Auntie Das asked me what had happened at the farm the day of the storm. 'Was it Hendriks?' she said. Shame had stripped me of the words but my silence exposed my secret. It took Vernon to help me lift my head again.

Eventually the old farmhouse came into view and I stopped at the top of the drive. The neat, ordered farm I had known as a young girl had gone. The roof of the low-slung house had collapsed on one side. The front door was propped against the wall, its hinges rusting and useless. The paddock where Oupa Kruger had kept a couple of horses was overgrown, the fences rotting and trampled down. The neat orchard – 'Jacob's patch' they used to call it – over to the right of the house had long since been reclaimed by nature, although the lemon trees still waved above the long grasses that tangled around their slim trunks. Hendriks' old Land Rover stood in the yard. After rolling home from the bar he had probably carried on drinking all weekend. I slid out of the bakkie and reached for the gun. Thabo stayed my hand.

'Madam ... You won't need that.'

I nodded and let the rifle slip back against the seat. I reached over and took his hand.

'Thabo. *Tsala ya me*, my friend. It's all right. I believe you have done nothing wrong.'

I found Isaac almost straight away in the main room of the house. A wide trail of blood showed he had dragged himself in from the back yard and propped himself against the leg of the large, rough-hewn table that dominated the room. He had pulled the thick family bible on to his lap from its place at the end of the table. I don't know how long it would have taken for him to bleed to death from the shotgun wound in his stomach. Outside I followed the sound of the flies and found Jacob in his orchard, lying face down where he had fallen. The blood had dried thick and black across the wound in his back, clotting the long grass around him. I turned and followed the path from the back of the farmhouse along a rocky ridge towards the workers' compound. I squinted into the distance. Nothing stirred. No smoke rose up from the cooking fires. From what Thabo had said I knew I would find Hendriks somewhere between here and the compound entrance. It didn't take long. He was lying below the path in a shallow ravine. His gun lay at his side. The panga and a pool of blood on the path marked the place where Thabo had fought to protect his wife, his daughter, his grand-daughter. I stood looking down at Hendriks' broken form.

*Once I got to the farmhouse, I found all three broth-
ers were dead from gun-shot wounds I believed to
be from Hendriks' shotgun. Isaac was in the house,
Jacob in the orchard. Hendriks was further away
from the farmhouse, lying below the path to the
workers' compound. He had the gun with him. I
returned to the farmhouse and called Sergeant Van
der Merwe from the phone in the kitchen. After
that I went to find Thabo's wife and family. They
were hiding in the compound but uninjured. I then
returned with them to the bakkie and waited ...*

As I slithered down the crumbling bank, Hendriks suddenly moaned and turned his head. I stopped, horrified,
paralysed. I slowly took another step. His leg was shattered, bent backwards at an angle. His face was obscured
by blood. His eyes moved in swollen sockets, unseeing
in the glare. He forced his cracked lips apart, tearing his
tongue from his mouth.

'Dank God,' he moaned. 'Water, help me.'

I knelt next to him, my head shielding the sun from
his face. His eyes found mine. He reached out his hands
and clung to my arm.

'Annelie, dank God. Help me. Annelie, dank, dank
God.' His face twitched and his eyes rolled. 'Bloody
kaffir ... beat me, pushed me. I'll see him bloody
hanged.'

I looked at Hendriks for a long time. Eventually I sat

back on my haunches and glanced around. In the distance I could hear the wind rustling through the grasses on the veld and the cicadas singing loudly in the nearby Boer-bean tree. The sky was a deeper blue than earlier in the day and I found myself wondering again about rain. Hendriks' hands pawed at my arms and clothes and his good leg kicked helplessly at the ground. Finally I reached over and pulled his gun on to his chest. I took his hands from my arms and placed them over the stock, wrapping his fingers round the trigger. I slowly eased the barrel up to under his chin. He muttered and tried to turn his head away. I caught his chin firmly with my fingers, pressing it on to the gun's muzzle. I leaned closer to his ear.

'Listen to me, Hendriks. Your brothers are dead. You shot them. There's nothing left. It's over.'

I pulled back and spat full into his face. His bloodshot eyes stared.

I stood up and clambered back on to the path. I hadn't even reached the compound before I heard the shot.

Pay Day

Dawn Nicholson

I joined the Sea Cadets because they meet on Tuesdays and Tuesday is Mum's big drinking night. When I say that, I don't mean that she goes down the bingo and has a few pints while she and her mates have a laugh and lose all their money. It's not like she stays home the rest of the week, baking cakes and washing our school uniforms. When I say 'Tuesday is Mum's big drinking night', the important word in that sentence is 'big'. Mum drinks every night. She drinks every day; all the time, in fact. Look in the cupboard under our sink and you're more likely to find a bottle of vodka than a bottle of bleach. She drinks lager mostly, the strong stuff, brown cans that she buys in fours down the off-licence. Only four's never enough. More often it's eight, ten, sometimes twelve. After the first four, there's no point talking to her. Two more and I know it's best to get out of the way, get Charlie upstairs and stay up there with him.

Once we're upstairs and Charlie's got his PlayStation on, there's nothing for me to do except listen. Tuesday's pay day, see? That's when she gets her money, so that's when she drinks most and when the worst of her mates appear. When I get in from school, I open the fridge to see if she's been shopping. There's a family pack of chicken goujons and twelve cans of special brew.

I realised ages ago that my mum and alcohol are a pretty exact science. Four cans and she's dancing around the kitchen, singing Madonna songs at the top of her lungs and burning the goujons. Eight cans and she could pass for an extra in *Casualty* – comatose and slumped against the wall, slurring or throwing up over the cushions. But twelve cans and she's a different animal altogether – twelve cans and she's pure evil.

She'd had twelve the night she chased me up the stairs and tried to pull me down again by my hair. I can't remember what I'd done wrong. I do remember trying to comb my hair the next day, the way it made my eyes water as I tried to pull the teeth through the matted strands where her nails had dug into me, flattening it down in the end and trying to make it look like I hadn't combed it at all. You can't see bruises on your head, but you can feel them. It was the week after that when I first went to Cadets. I took Charlie with me. He's a bit young and he didn't want to go. He would've much rather stayed at home on his PlayStation, but I told him I wasn't going to be home on a Tuesday night from now on, and he switched it off and put his trainers on. 'Where're we going?' he said.

I can't remember a time when it wasn't like this. Even when I was at primary school she was the same, swaying at the school gates, swearing at the other mums, forgetting to come at all. She loves us. I know that. But somehow that doesn't seem to make a difference. Sometimes she cries in the mornings, calls me into her room, sobbing as she hangs on to me.

'Sweetheart,' she says, 'you know I love you, don't you?' And I do. She's always sorry afterwards. But that doesn't mean I want to hang around here on a Tuesday night, and if I can stop Charlie getting pulled down the stairs by his hair once in a while then even joining the Sea Cadets is worth it.

The first time we went, I didn't know what to expect. There was this boy in my year, Matthew Sweeney, one of the really weird kids. I have to sit next to him in Maths because Mr Williams has a seating plan and you have to sit where he tells you. I didn't used to talk to the kid at first; I didn't want people thinking we were friends or anything. But then I thought, who are you kidding Jewitt, you're not exactly tripping over mates yourself? So I started talking to him one day, and after a few weeks he told me that he went to Sea Cadets and asked if I'd like to go. I laughed. No, I didn't want to go to fucking Sea Cadets. He shrugged like he wasn't bothered either way and we started talking about Dr Who. Then after half term he mentioned this trip he'd been on, how they'd camped in a wood and done abseiling and canoeing and stuff. I started to think it didn't sound that sad after all. 'How old do you have to be?' I asked him.

'How old?'

'You know, for Cadets.'

'Oh right. Twelve.'

I think about Charlie. He's short for his age. 'I'd have to bring my brother,' I say. 'He's eleven, but he'll be twelve in December.'

'Bring him then,' he said. 'Get there for quarter to seven and I'll take you to see the C.O.'

So now on Tuesdays we do drill and knot tying, and learn how to buff our boots until they shine like mirrors. It finishes at nine and we make sure we're always the last out, taking the long way home and dragging our feet so we don't get in before ten. She's usually passed out by then. We take our boots off in the hall and Charlie carries them upstairs while I go in the kitchen to see if there's anything to eat. When there is, I carry it up on a tray and we eat it sitting on our beds, still in our uniforms. When there isn't anything, I make us a cup of tea each and we drink it slowly, not bothering to say if we're hungry.

After a while, we get to like Cadets. The C.O. donates most of our uniform by asking the others to bring in old stuff that they've outgrown and stuffing it into my arms in a bin bag once everyone else has gone home. My jumper itches and I don't think I'll ever get used to wearing a beret. Charlie's trousers are too long and they slide on the floor as he walks, but he doesn't mind. Watching him on the parade ground, anyone would think he'd been born to march. He takes to it straight away, standing to attention, doing left and right turns, changing step seamlessly as soon as he hears the command. The C.O. says he'll make drill sergeant one day. I think he likes the sureness of it – there's no guess-work with drill. When the C.O. shouts attention we all know what he means. You stamp your feet together and then you stand still. Easy.

I watch my brother marching, chin up, his trousers trailing behind him and mostly what I feel is relief. He's happy, and at least here he's not getting the shit kicked out of him by our mum. It makes my stomach hurt even to think that – our mum, who loves us. But she's got her problems and, unlike Charlie, who still thinks she'll sort herself out, I've stopped believing she'll ever solve them.

For a while I'm really pleased with myself, thinking how clever I am to have found a solution to the problem of Tuesday nights. But then I find out that as soon as you solve one problem, another one comes along to replace it, because it turns out that the C.O. and I aren't the only ones who've noticed how good Charlie is at drill. We're not the only ones to notice how good he is at sailing either. When Chief Petty Officer Rawlins tells everyone about a week-long sailing course at Easter, I look along the line in time to see my brother's eyes light up. When Rawlins says it'll cost ninety pounds, I see how Charlie looks at the floor, not listening any more because he knows he can't go. Blood rushes to my face and I feel myself getting hot and angry. I think about the hole in the bottom of my shoe that's started letting in water, and how impossible ninety pounds is, and my face burns. I write my brother's name on the list on the noticeboard later, signing him up for the trip. Walking home, we talk about which puddings we'd put in our top ten and why school custard always has to have a skin on it even when it's watery, carefully not mentioning the sailing course.

I hand Mum the money and the bank card, holding my breath, forcing myself to look away as she stuffs them in her pocket without counting the money. The next day I'm scared to go home, sure she'll have realised. To waste some extra time, I call in at the pizza place on the corner and ask the man there if he needs anyone to do deliveries. 'You're too young, mate,' he says, shaking his head, 'but we do need some leaflets delivered.'

For the next five nights Charlie and I deliver leaflets

to every house in every street within a mile. At the end of the week the man gives me a twenty-pound note and tells me to come back in a month. I scrunch the note up tight in my hand, running home and hiding it under my mattress before even Charlie sees it.

I do two more lots of pizza leaflets and take small amounts from Mum's purse whenever she's really wasted, so that somehow, over the next two months, I manage to get the money together for Charlie to go to Portsmouth, forging Mum's signature on the form to say that he can go.

When I wave him off at Cadets, the first day of the Easter holiday, I still haven't told Mum he's going. She was sleeping when we left but the fridge was full of cans, so I decide to stay out of the way. I go round to Matthew's house and end up staying all day, helping him to fix an old bike his dad fished out of the canal. At tea time his mum comes into the garage and asks if I want to stay for dinner. I say I should probably get going, but I know we've no food in at home, so I let Matthew persuade me and when I see what it is, I'm glad I did: steak and onion pie with a big pile of mash, carrots and cabbage on the side with loads of gravy over it. It's so good it goes straight into my top-ten dinners list. Matthew's mum smiles at me as she spoons more mash on to my plate. 'You can come again,' she says.

The rest of the week passes slowly. Mum's in a bad

mood because I didn't tell her about Charlie going away, so I try to stay out of the house as much as I can. I deliver some leaflets for the man at the pizza place in exchange for a pepperoni pizza, but it's boring without Charlie and it takes forever to do just a few streets. I go over to Matthew's house a few times, but his mum's at work and his dad doesn't ask me to stay for tea.

When Charlie gets home, he's caught the sun and he's full of how great the course was, how all the people were really cool and he wants to go in the navy, or maybe even the marines when he leaves school. I tell him not to say anything about it costing ninety quid. If Mum asks, I say, tell her Cadets paid for you.

I keep the letter with me, unopened in my pocket. All day I can feel it, the thick cream envelope folded in half, hot against my chest. I wait until association after supper, hanging back, fussing with my blankets and pretending to make my bed.

'You go,' I say to Darren, 'I'll catch you up in a minute.'

I wait until the landing goes quiet before taking the letter from my pocket. I rub the envelope between my fingers a moment, feeling the thickness of it, the quality of the paper. I open it where it's already been torn open and take the letter out, smiling at the neat, familiar loops and curls of Charlie's handwriting underneath the prison stamp. I sit back on the bed and start to read.

I'm writing you this at the end of the proudest day of my life, he begins. *Mum didn't show, so no surprises there, but I did miss having my big brother here to see me pass out.*

I fold the letter in half, my eyes swimming. He did it then. I hold my palm to my eyes, snorting and fighting back tears until I'm calm enough to carry on reading. I open the letter again, reading it all the way through, twice, until I'm smiling so much it feels like my face might crack. I slot the letter back in the envelope, noticing the date at the top for the first time: the sixteenth of October. Tuesday.

I get up and rinse my face under the cold tap and dry it quickly, hanging the towel back over the frame of my bed. Reaching under the mattress, I push the letter right to the back, as far as it will go. At the door, I take a deep breath, holding the air inside of me and then letting it out slowly as I put my prison face back on.

I keep my head down as I make my way down the stairs and over to the pool table where Darren is watching two fat guys potting balls half-heartedly. He nods as I approach and I think about telling him my good news, but then decide to keep it to myself, to let myself enjoy it for a bit. We watch in silence as the men finish their game. As we watch, I think about that ninety pounds and how it seemed like such a lot at the time, and I don't know why it comes into my head, but I think about that thing people say; I've never really thought about what it means before – you've got to speculate to accumulate. I think about the ninety pounds and walking around with wet feet for two months. Then I think about my brother Charlie, the Royal Marine, and I think, yeah. This now, this is my Pay Day.

Documentary at Clareville Lodge

Susie Boyt

— When I first saw Marigold she was clutching a bouquet of marigolds. Wearing an emerald gown, satin, with lilac beading at the neck and on the hem. No one dressed like that in England then. She was like a mirage. It was the complete package. Golden hair from Regent Street. Beautiful shoes, gloves always. You have to understand the impression she created. I was in Piccadilly coming out of the underground and she was going into the Café Royale. The way she moved! Stopped me in my tracks. There was mystery, there was sex appeal. People thought she must be from America.

And then not long after Bob took me to a show and there she was again, only a smallish part, but she had one number and was wearing these striped cocktail pyjamas. There was a polka-dot pair later on and some with Chinese fringing that she wore with evening sandals. I think it was in the script. Recognised her straight away from Piccadilly. Don't know how she did it, but she had the whole audience in her pocket.

And afterwards I saw her come out of the stage door, with a beautiful young man on her arm, and she had on this breath-taking dress. It was black crepe – this was before America of course – and it was a Schiaparelli copy or Schiap-inspired anyway, bracelet-length sleeves with a big beating heart appliquéd on the bodice and arrows of love shooting out down the front. Can you imagine? This was when the other girls were all dimples and daisies. Her father was in the rag trade then, before that he'd had a bit of a career on the stage. Isn't that right, Marigold?

– Father worked in the sort of place where the chairman boomed, 'Kindly herblige the haudience with an hencore.'

– Whereas my parents thought the theatre was a cesspool of iniquity. Couldn't stand it. They never once even—

– *Carefree*, Gloria.

– What darling?

– *Carefree* – the name of the film with the heart dress. Dad modified the shape slightly over the hips.

– Not that she had any hips to speak of. Yes, and he had seen, her father had seen, Ginger Rogers wearing the dress in the film with Fred Astaire playing her psychiatrist. And on the poster they put that they 'Freudian slip and fall in love'. I think tap dancing formed part of the treatment.

– Sometimes we padded me here and there.

– That's right.

– You're terribly good looking, aren't you, dear? Isn't he handsome, Gloria? Such distinguished features. When the woman telephoned to set this up ... I thought you'd be a big florid man with a beard and a stammer.

– Did you?

– Seems so silly now. What on earth possessed me? I do apologise!

– Not a problem! And so you two became friends straight away? How did you actually meet, the first time?

– It was with friends of Bob's at the Café de Paris – he knew the maître d' slightly, got us a good table. And Marigold came and sat down with a friend of his. Bob's agent was there too. The nicest man in London people used to call him and if you were one of his he'd greet you like a long lost friend, a terrific slap on the back, sometimes a bear hug, made you feel you were the one actor in London he really wanted to see, and as he gripped you he slowly manoeuvred you towards the door all the time telling you how happy he was to see you and how fine you looked and how excellent the prospects were for you – next week – and by the time you said good-bye he had practically pushed you down the stairs. Why am I telling you that, there is a point to this story there is a— Oh yes, I simply couldn't believe that someone as beautiful as Marigold could also be so sincere. Usually with people, by which I mean with persons of both the female and the male, er, *genre,* it's one or the other.

– That is true.

– I don't know if I've quite communicated what it was like to be out with Marigold. Streams of men used to follow us down the street and women who wanted to look at her, really study her. When they were on the way to the factory or when they ought to have been collecting their little ones from school. The glamour that is today is simply nothing compared to what she had. The hats had to be seen to be believed, a gondola with a little waterfall of lace with a fish motif woven into it to represent the lagoon. Just on a Tuesday! There was another like an artist's palette, with splodges of paint made from rainbow paillettes and two crossed brushes sticking out with the dearest mink tips. A musical one that had a cascade of black velvet notes against ivory satin in a figure of eight. Stole it from the finale of *Melody Girl*.

– Do we still have that somewhere? We used to have it.

– Good question! When we were first in New York she got a Broadway show straight away, a small part, a thing called *Johnny Two-by-Four* – it was thirty dollars a week and our rent was twenty-three. She played the cigarette girl. We were living in a theatrical ladies' hotel. Some of those ladies were no ladies if you see what I mean. We only ate when people took us out. Befeathered, bejewelled and befurred we were after dark. We were eighteen going on thirty-five. All the girls lent us their best things, and we did too as soon as we got anything good enough to loan.

– And we were taken out a great deal, were we not?

– Oh we were, we were.

– And you know who else had a small part in that show? Betty Bacall! We used to jitterbug between rehearsals. But she contracted the measles, had it for most of the run. We thought it very unprofessional.

– So measle-free we took New York by storm. It was the Depression but as the song says, were we depressed? Nowhere near! All our money went into our clothes. It was an investment. She used to wear this shell-pink, silk-velvet, ombré evening skirt. A Dior copy from Paris, was it?

– I remember it like yesterday.

– Looked a tiny bit as though someone had thrown a barrel of pink champagne over you. And she used to pair it with – and this was terribly daring – a tiny white cashmere with a perfect, white, heart-shaped moth-hole just below the left shoulder. Can you imagine? It really was the end. Drove people wild. And later when she met Louis and went to Hollywood ... It wasn't our kind of town, naturally, but we made our little mark didn't we? And the parties that she had!

– Louis loved a full house. He loved everyone singing at the piano and everyone in beaded gowns. We were just happy to be able to eat every day. What luxury!

– He liked to serve mountains of pink and red crustacea on these mermaid-shaped platters. More like sculptures than plates. Turquoise and silver tails at one end with long golden hair at the other. Italian. And rivers of champagne. You could swim in it.

– Once I did.

– Once she did! They used to install these beautiful marble urns filled with flowers not just in the house but lit up with pink lights all the way up to the house from the gardens for a party – so elegant! I just adore tall flower arrangements outside. Used to have these white roses with a strong lemon scent and honeysuckle and tendrils of ivy trailing everywhere, and masses of stock, eglantine, hydrangea and narcissi, and in the spring-time silver ice buckets everywhere crammed with apple blossom.

– Lily of the valley . . .

– That's it.

– The flowers here disappoint me fifty times a day.

– I know, dear . . . and I am trying to address it. Janet says they're about as strong as the local florist can muster. Still . . . And there was this fashion then for very low-hung crystal chandeliers everywhere, very fluffy in appearance; French crystal, I think it was, and she put them in all the bedrooms, two feet off the ground, pairs of them next to all the bedsides in place of reading lamps. Can you imagine? She was more Hollywood than the natives! I came back one evening from London – my mother was bad and I had gone to see what could be done – and Hines let me in, and I remember hearing Marigold tell the decorator this was the Maple Drive House in this very certain voice, 'Oh, do use the red silk velvet, you know, that intense throbbing crimson, like in *Gigi*!' And I remember thinking, Lord we've come an awfully long way from the Dudley Hippodrome!

– Yes, I was going to ask about that.

– Remember they had that fancy sliding roof installed. Guaranteed to keep you cool on summer's nights and warm in the winter, or so they claimed.

– Oh, yes.

– But no one was happy when there were thunderstorms. Gallery had to put up their umbrellas! George made a joke about it. They used to call him the Prime Minister of Mirth.

– So many funny things. Remember you found that gardener called Ava. Marvellous hulk of a girl.

– She was so strong.

– That was when you were still with Louis, before we all came back from Calif and before he—

– Deborah, his third wife was it, the ballet dancer?

– Paulette, I think.

– Yes, Paulette. Why am I talking about her?

– Were you going to say about that thing she wrote about Louis in her memoir?

– She said – wrote in her memoir – let me get this right, 'Sometimes I think the only thing he ever gave me was athlete's foot!'

– But such a beautiful man.

– Yes, he was. When you were standing in front of him it was actually a little bit difficult to believe. He was like a— like an oil painting of a famous hero that everyone adored ... Is he still with us, do you suppose?

– No, oh no, he left us, sadly. Ten years ago I think, maybe twelve.

– Oh no. That's too bad.

– I'm sorry. Would you mind stopping the thing for a second? I just want to put a tiny bit of powder on her cheek – the lights you brought are very harsh on her face suddenly ... Thank you. There, all done, you can resume the thing now, whenever it suits. Are you ... is it on now? Good. Thank you.

– And ... and can you both tell me something about the book you've been writing together?

– Are we doing another book?

– Yes, that's right. Next year.

– Oh, I thought it was this year.

– We were doing that bit about your father yesterday. 'There's a little bit of good in the worst of us,' he used to sing. They used to say of her father that he had a wink that conveyed a wealth of meaning. And that he was a complete master of the unsaid. Can you imagine?

– Whatever did they mean, Gloria?

– Well, I know he took it as a compliment.

– Well, that's all right then, I suppose.

– We're not really allowed to talk about it yet, except to say it will blow off your socks.

– I look forward to it! Um ... um ... And now can you say something about how you find the routine here? Some of the other residents I spoke to said there's always something exciting going on.

– Oh, we don't join in on principle. Do we? We are not life's joiner-inners.

– That's right. We're in a world of our own making. It's SO much nicer. They call us 'the girls' here – it's what they called us when we were at the Empire, starting out. We're still 'the girls' now. It's how we think of ourselves. But we keep our distance. We are a little bit grand. A star is a star is a star.

– But we're gracious though, aren't we, Gloria?

– Oh yes, we're all about that. Unless, you know, we're provoked. Some of the gents who live here claim they knew us from the old days. They like to tease her. 'You wouldn't of even spoke to me back then would you, Marigold. Aloof? Forbiddin'? She wouldn't even of give you the drops from 'er nose, not that I'd ave 'em.'

– Yes! Oh yes! [clapping her hands wildly] Wonderful!

– Do be careful of the mic.

– I am sorry. Now, where were we? Did you say Louis was coming to visit?

– No, darling. He won't be coming, I'm afraid.

– He was always so busy with everything. Why are you so busy I used to say? What is it that is so important that you can't even—

– Yes, he did like to live a full life.

– I was going to ask more about your extraordinary friendship that has spanned almost six decades.

– Now this bit I do feel strongly about. You see Marigold was the first person I knew who really loved music the way I did. From the inside out, is how we always thought of the songs. She thought about what they meant, didn't consider them silly pieces of fluff, throwaway. We'd listen to old love songs and think about the girls in those situations, the girls on the records, I mean the American girls: Ella and Dinah and Deanna and Judy and Billie, looking for, and finding and losing, love.

– Oh, Billie took things very hard.

– I used to listen to the records like it was a novel, so in one song she's in love and then in the next it's all wrong, then it's wonderful again, then she seems to have shot 'im. Then she's waiting for him to come home. It made such strange sense! And then we'd think about those men they fell for. Why did they get into those predicaments? Why did they keep getting into them?

– Thing is, Gloria, if you fall for a playboy, fair enough, you're a fool to yourself, but it happens to us all at least once or twice and I'm the last person on earth to judge anyone harshly. You know how it is, wherever you go you see people looking at you pityingly as though you're a lamb to the slaughter, and you feel a bit foolish and confused and as green as a baby gem, and you know you're not the first or the last ... But do you really think you should try to get him to retire to a farm! If that's what you think's going to happen then you ought to be shot!

– Well, yes, but—

– Do you think that's why people move to the country?

– How do you mean?

– To keep their men folk away from you know ... harm?

– Well, when you put it like that it does have the ring of truth.

– Is that what everyone thinks I should have done with Jack?

– I don't know, my love. I don't know. Perhaps we never really know these things. Jack is ... Jack was ... It's such a long time ago. But we're all right. Did you remember this morning to take your [lowers her voice and whispers something inaudible].

– If you've ever waited for someone, in a way you wait for them always ...

– But coming back to your earlier question, everyone else I had met up till then thought the songs just didn't bear being gone into that closely, but I thought they could and so did, so does, Marigold.

– Yes, yes I do. Like in 'Making Whoopee', when it says, 'He doesn't phone, or even write.' Everyone knows phoning takes less effort than letter writing, so it should say and easily could say, shouldn't it, he doesn't write or even phone, and everyone else says, well, it's just like that on account of the rhyme, what's the problem, *dah di dah di dah*, but this is Cole Porter we're talking about – he wouldn't use the wrong word just because it rhymed. That sort of thing, you know? Why isn't it: 'Most every night, she sits alone/He doesn't write, or even phone . . .' Doesn't that make more sense? I used to sit wondering about that line for hours at the Cecil House. Sometimes it got dark without me realising it and I'd be sitting in the gloom. It just didn't make sense. Of course nothing about that time adds up. So often it's the one thing men don't tell you that makes sense of everything . . .

– I think it was the second time we met and Marigold telephoned me afterwards. I was actually washing my hair so water was dripping down my back and making a little pool on the landing. I was renting with three other girls, two typists and a dancer – two left feet she had, we all felt sorry for her – and there were never enough towels. Then without even saying, Hello,

Marigold says, Okay, me here, what do you think? In 'Thanks For The Memories' when the gentleman sings, 'And how I jumped, the day you trumped my one and only ace', to what is he referring? And I say, Well, evidently he's talking about playing cards, and the trump card of the correct suit will beat even an ace of a different suit ... and she says, Yes, obviously. I am not an imbecile – she was quite severe with me – but it's figurative, of course. The poor fellow tries one last crazy saving thing and it just doesn't work and it's curtains for their relationship. But what is it? What's the thing he pulls out of his hat, his best shot? Does he give her a huge diamond out of the bank that once belonged to his mother's mother and she drops it down a grille in the street the same day, or does someone else give her a bigger one that night? I need to know, she said. She was quite adamant. *So* we discussed all the options.

I said, Obviously she's run through all his money.

Well, yes, of course, she says. But what does it consist of, this last attempt? It's gotta be something financial. I think he names the biggest sum he can muster, or his father dies and suddenly he inherits the lot and she says, sorry, not enough, no dice.

It was so exciting to have that conversation. Can you imagine?

– But, Gloria, what do you think of this? I'm just thinking off the top of my head now, but imagine if it was a woman singing, what if she would say, 'Darling, I am expecting a baby,' and that would be her ace, hoping he would be over the moon, that it would seal in everything? But supposing he wasn't delighted. Not in the least. What if he just shrugged as though the whole thing was her problem and he didn't care one way or another and walked out of the door backwards, waving and apologising. So she would feel she had no choice but to get rid of it.

– I'll have to think about that. She's always had the most marvellous imagination, you know, like a novelist who takes three hours to read the newspaper every morning because he is imagining everyone in the news's feelings.

– Yes, I do do that.

– But, of course, William, the correct answer to what does he mean by 'how I jumped, the day you trumped my one and only ace' is this: nobody knows.

– There's so much that's maddening, Gloria. So much is wrong with the world. People always sing 'It's All Right With Me' as though it's a sweet enchanting thing, but actually it's very hard-hearted. There's a powerful man, predatory, trawling a bar or a party, trying to pick up a girl, any girl, because the one he likes isn't free. It's a song about someone looking for a quick— It should be sung hard, with hard eyes, worldly, menacing. But people don't do it like that. They sing it like a love song. Why do people who don't care about people pretend to be romantic? I can't stand it!

– That song always makes me think of Bob. He would show an interest in a pillar box when Joan was out of town.

– Well, yes. Yes he would. Or a lamp-post.

– A bollard!

– A Belisha beacon!

– He did always like flashy women.

– You're too funny, Marigold. Stop! You'll have me—

– Were there songs you were both particularly keen on?

– When I was dressing at the Palladium – it was a wonderful place to work – we didn't think of it as a theatre, we thought of it almost as a cathedral. And backstage it was like a labyrinth with all the stairs and passageways. Anyway, Marigold, she was in Calif and she would ring me up on Sunday nights – this was in the late fifties – and we would have the most wonderful 'chinwags', we called them then, in, in our day!

– Yes, and sometimes whole conversations made up of song lyrics.

– Marigold would telephone on Sunday evenings, it was terribly exciting, seven sharp, I wouldn't break the date for anything, not even when— In any case she would telephone and say something like, oh, I don't know, can't think of it now. I might be a bit down and say, 'I had that feeling of self-pity' and she'd say, 'Dinner for one please, James?' and I'd say, 'Picking on a wishbone from the Frigidaire,' and she'd say, 'I've got a little story I want you to know,' and I'd say, 'As the adding machine once said, you can count on me.' And she'd say, 'I'm in love with wonderful guy,' and I'd say, 'With nights of tropical splendour?' And she'd say, 'What made you think that I was one of those girls,' and I'd say, 'Is it more, don't throw bouquets at me?' And she'd say, 'My romance doesn't need a castle rising in Spain,' and I'd say, 'Derby and Joan who used to be Jack and Jill, kind of stuff?' and she'd say, 'I'm biding my time,' and I'd say, 'What is this thing called love?' and she'd say, 'Well, I don't understand the Parisians.'

– Except it was much better than that.

– Dinner here is at a quarter past six, can you believe?

– [Singing] I don't get hungry for dinner at six. I wear a ball gown with beige control knicks!

– Very good! There's usually some kind of show, a bit of singing. No one can dance any more but we say the name of the steps, mark the routine with the flats of our hands to show we still remember. A sherry or a martini at a quarter to, they bring us ... They allow only one, but it can be as big as you like.

– We like to shop for glasses in the vase department, don't we, Gloria.

– We do not, she is joking. Naughty! And if we're feeling Good Olde Merrie England, we'll have the sherry, but if we're in Broadway mode, if we're all I'll Take Manhattan, then it's a martini. And the funny thing is we never know which way we'll go until they ask us, do we?

– We never know. [Starts to sing] 'And when you came to visit, my parents said, "Good God! What is it?"'

– You are on a roll this afternoon, Marigold! The soap pays for all this. It's all right here. We provide our own glamour. Not too many low-slung chandeliers. We were awfully hoity about telly to begin with ... but you have to bend to the times.

– [Singing] 'I wasn't born to stately halls of alabaster, I haven't given many balls for Mrs Astor.'

– Isn't she wonderful? A hairdresser comes twice a week to sort us out. She does our nails if there's time and any other bits and bobs.

– She really is wonderful.

– And so after I stopped working so much myself, and I didn't want to be a dresser for the rest of my life because there were only so many times I could say, 'You were a knock-out, Miss Kerr,' I began devoting more and more time to organising Marigold's career, running the fan club, answering the mail, sending out the ten by eights and organising the personal appearances. We accept any charity requests involving children and animals. Especially if it's local, otherwise they must provide a car and driver. Requests come in all the time.

– And you know the thing about Gloria? Never in fifty-six years has she done a single annoying thing. She can't say the same in return, I know that, but there we are.

– She says that, but she's never, she's never been in a rehabilitation centre, she's had no issues with alcohol or, or with anything worse, there's been not one break-down, she has stolen no other woman's husband. There have been no suicide attempts. No neglected children to pen revenge memoirs. No shoplifting incidents. No dicey investments. Nothing that could be called any-thing approaching an episode. She's never even worn a bad dress. There is absolutely nothing on her. Not one thing. Tell me, who else, who on earth, of her calibre, of who else on this insane planet can one, in truth, say that? You tell me, young man!

– I do apologise about Gloria. She really is the end!

– Sorry, dear. I am too much sometimes. Anyhow ... Time is ticking on. A man's coming to do stretches with us in half an hour – he's eighty and wonderfully fit. There's literally a symphony of creaking bones in the rehearsal room but it stops us from seizing up. Luigi, he's called, an Italian.

– Both my hips are aliens now. Bionic or what have you. And one of my knees. The choreographers I could sue if I could only remember their names!

– And those of us who can no longer stretch do chairobics to the music.

– I wish I could still dance! You know, these days I can't even bear to look in the mirror.

– Marigold!

– I am afraid I won't stop weeping when I see what's

gone. I can't even sing in tune any more. Why did we have to get old? It goes against my pride so. [Begins sobbing uncontrollably.]

– Darling! Here, let me just ... Turn your head away, dear. Put your back to the thing, then they won't use it. Turn the camera off now, young man. Is that all right? *Right* now! Oh, good. Oh, thank you, dear. Thank you. Can you leave the room for a moment? Just so I can ... Pull the door behind, could you? Oh, that is kind. [Lowers voice.] It's all right, darling. I know. I know. You're tremendously brave about everything. And the wonderful thing is, everybody loves you. Just as they have always done and always will. You are a shining meteor who merely by existing has brought pleasure to millions and millions of people. How many people can say that? Please don't cry! Marigold, Marigold! Listen to me. Listen. You know, everything you've ever been, everything marvellous that's happened to you, every extravagant sunset, every beam of brilliant moonshine, every pearl, every duet, every sable, every dewy close-up, it's all still there, every last bit of it. All of it shines out of you like the most dazzling ray of starlight, lifting up the hearts of the world.

– Say it again, darling. Oh, oh, oh, oh, do please say it again.

Where Life Takes You

Dolores Pinto

The light here is brutal. It seeks out the smallest finger-print on the surface of a mirror, the smudge on polished wood. It finds me and I turn my head away, cowed by its radiance. I take the tea Spence hands me. He sits on the side of the bed cradling his mug close to his chest and we watch streamers of cloud race past the window. Gulls surf the air, their heads angled downwards like arrows.

'Come on, Rita,' Spence says, 'it's a grand day.'

I manage a smile but then falter; too muddled by sleep and resentment to talk.

He stands. 'I'll go and open up then,' he says, and there's a dying fall in his voice as he turns away. He goes downstairs and unlocks the café door. A neighbour calls to him and they talk about the weather, their voices loud in the quiet street. Everyone in Whitby talks about the weather; they listen to the forecast and study the clouds and the flight of birds, and discuss its vagaries endlessly.

I wash and dress, choosing my clothes with care. Flat shoes and black slacks, and a plain white shirt. Practical working clothes. Then I tie a red-polka-dot cotton square around my neck gypsy fashion, and encircle my waist with a broad leather belt. Now I'm a pirate, a film star, a tomboy. But no; too bold, too flamboyant. I take off the scarf and undo the belt.

Spence is clattering dishes in the kitchen, so I slip outside and lean against the harbour wall. The town is waking. A milk float hums and rattles over the cobbles, and the clash of machinery and the shouts of the men in the fish market reverberate in the stillness. Behind the quay tiers of houses, row upon crooked row climb up towards the dark silhouette of the abbey. Dracula's castle, the locals call it, a story for the tourists. At sunset when the ruined arches and spires show jagged against the horizon, you might think you see a cloaked man creep like a lizard down the walls.

A lone boat is coming in to harbour. It bobs and dips and the gulls follow. They wheel and dive and wheel again, as if to bring it safe home. Their raucous cries scrape the air. 'Why do they scream so?' I'd asked Spence.

'You'll get used to them after a while,' he said. 'You won't even hear them.'

I should have told him then that I don't belong here. That I want to walk unnoticed between tall buildings. To wake in my bedroom in Pimlico with its sloping ceiling and dark corners, and watch Louie dress in the light seeping through the curtains. Hear him scoop his keys and loose change from the bedside table. 'I'm off then, love,' he'd say, 'see you later,' and bend to kiss me.

This place is too stark, too unforgiving. The women in the town lower their eyes and the men nudge each other when I pass them in the narrow lanes, or on the stone steps leading to the church.

'The people here don't like me,' I told Spence.

'Give them time, they don't know you. They'll forget about you when the tourists come in the summer.'

'When they have someone else to gawk at?'

'They'll be too busy to gawk at anyone. They're curious about you, Rita. Give them a chance. Some of them have never been out of Whitby.'

'They resent me.'

'Don't start that again, Rita, please,' he'd said.

He's working at the stove when I go inside. I watch the play of the muscles in his forearms as he lifts the heavy pans and the slow methodical way he moves around the kitchen. I think of Louie's deft hands and quick movements as he set up his barrow in the market.

See him stand back and throw out an arm like an impresario, waiting for me to admire the pyramids of oranges and heaped apples, and the purple grapes arranged so artfully on plastic grass.

I leave Spence standing over his grill and push through the swing doors into the café. It's six thirty, time for the news, and I turn the dials of the wireless until I find the Light Programme. The plummy voice of the newsreader is familiar and reassuring. The Conservatives have got back in; Churchill is forgotten and Eden is the new man. It makes no difference to me. I hardly listen anyway. The men from the fish market will be here soon. I tie on my apron and wait.

The sound of their boots striking the stones and shouts of laughter herald their coming and they troop through the door. The fishermen come first, then the men who weigh the catch. The lads who swill away the stringy purple guts and gun-metal scales come last. They stamp their feet and rub their hands, and look at me from under lowered brows, as gauche and awkward as schoolboys.

'You're looking good this morning, Rita,' Donnie says. He makes it sound like an insult. He's Spence's best friend; they've known each other since school. The other men look at each other or at their shoes. But their eyes follow me as I trot between the tables to take their orders. I bring them their food, and they forget me and tuck into bacon, eggs, and thick slices of buttered toast.

Spence comes out of the kitchen, his tea towel over his shoulder. He leans his elbows on the counter.

'Keeping an eye on the missus?' a young lad says, looking at me sideways and winking.

Spence ignores him. He joins in the argument about the game on Saturday.

'He should have played two up front,' he says.

'He hasn't got one decent striker, let alone two,' someone answers.

I stop listening and start to fill the big metal teapots, one for each table. They like their tea strong, these men, and plenty of it. Spence clears the dishes. He pushes the kitchen door open with his hip and smiles at me over the laden tray. His smile is hopeful. Last night we'd slept with our backs to each other for the first time.

We'd met through an introduction agency. Spence had arranged for us to have dinner in a restaurant in Chelsea. I was late and he was already seated and studying the menu, his eyes straying towards the door. Not anxious, just alert. He's a big man. Craggy faced and broad across the shoulders. I liked the look of him and strode up to the table as bold and brassy as you like. He stood up, and his eyes never left my face, even as he clutched and caught at the napkin falling from his lap.

'It's not much, the café, but you'll love Whitby. What do you think?' he said a month later. We liked each other. Why waste time? His wife had died two years ago and Louie had been gone for over a year.

We'd been together for eleven years, Louie and me. I was twenty when I caught his eye; not long down from Sheffield, but long enough to learn that an eye for style, a lithe body and skin the colour of burnished copper wasn't going to get me far in London. He was standing outside Lyons Corner House in Piccadilly. My feet hurt from standing around, and I hadn't eaten all day. There was a ladder in my stocking, which I'd tried to mend with a dab of nail varnish, and my jacket let in the cold. He looked smart in a black overcoat and leather gloves. I smiled up at him from under the brim of my pert little hat and he tipped his trilby, as suave as any film star, and asked if he could buy me supper.

I was young and needy, and he was old, old enough to be my father. He wooed me with stories; threw a net of words over me and drew me in. He'd seen men dressed as women dancing in the squares of Marrakech, ' . . . and they wear the veil, as if they really were women,' and watched pelicans fly past the Golden Gate Bridge in San Francisco. Drank green sugarcane juice on the streets of Singapore, and ate chocolate-covered ants in Mexico.

'Paris,' he said, and reached for my hands on the table, 'you'd love Paris, with the shops and the jazz in the bars, the girls so trim and the men so slick. And you should see the women of Amsterdam, darling, posing in the windows, the light behind them.'

I imagined drinking cocktails with him on the veranda of a hotel somewhere warm. I would wear a pale silk dress, and he would wear a linen suit and carry a cane. By the time I found out he'd been a merchant seaman and all he really knew of foreign cities were sailors' bars and whores' bedrooms, it didn't matter. He was a good man and his flat in Pimlico was warm and safe. He understood that we all have secrets and never once asked me about my past.

'Tea up yet, Rita?' one of the men calls.

'Come and get it,' I reply, and they swagger up to the counter, bold now with their bellies full. The odour of fish clings to their fingertips. I wonder if they leave the briny scent on their women's flesh, if their children smell of the sea.

The wireless is playing an old song, 'Chattanooga Choo Choo'. It reminds me of the Yanks strutting around in fancy uniforms during the war. Pimlico took a beating in the Blitz. Thirty houses in Sutherland Terrace obliterated, hundreds killed. The worst of the bombing was over by the time I moved there to be with Louie, but there were still raids. Later there were the doodle-bugs. I stood in doorways and watched the search-lights crisscrossing the night sky, and listened to the buzz overhead. I held my breath in the silence before they fell.

Louie was too old to fight, and he was exempt anyway. He was cagey about that. Medical, was all he'd say. I know he had a dickey heart. He didn't let it slow him down; he forgot about it most of the time. He did his bit as a warden. Sometimes he couldn't talk when he got home. He'd sit and stare at the wall, his clothes covered in dust. They had a hard time, the wardens.

Then it ended. No more blackouts, no more sirens. Kids played on bomb-sites and fire-weed pushed up through the rubble where homes used to be. Demobbed soldiers roamed the streets, blank-eyed and jittery.

The café is quiet; the men have gone, tramping down to the boats with their clumsy, rolling gait. They'll pull on their rubber boots and fishing gear, sail out to sea, and leave all they know of the land behind them. Their wives will brush silver scales from their beds and wait for them to return.

Spence brings in our breakfast and we sit together to eat. We share the newspaper and listen to the wireless. Last night is still between us, and we're too careful with each other, too polite. He clears the dishes and looks at me expectantly.

'Just going to have a ciggie, then I'll be in to help you,' I tell him. He goes back to his kitchen reassured. He doesn't talk much, and I wonder if what I know about him is all there is. I know he's a hard worker and a good lover, and I know he likes to read and take photos of the harbour with a camera that his father left him. I know he won't speak about his war or his dead wife. I know he cares for me. It's not enough.

'Talk to me,' I'd asked him last night.

'What do you want me to say?' he'd replied.

My words then were vicious and childish. 'You're a coward,' I said, and 'you're ashamed of me,' and 'you let Donnie and the other men sneer at me.'

He smiled and threw words like 'disappointment' and 'paranoia' back at me. He said: 'You're too sensitive; you've got a chip on your shoulder.' We turned our backs on each other then.

Louie would never let anyone look at me the way Donnie does. He'd stare back with that dead-eyed, hard-man's stare he practised in front of the mirror. It made me laugh, but if you didn't know him, it was frightening. We were mates, Louie and me, partners. No one else mattered. We'd hurt and forgiven each other, survived the war and hardship together and now we were enjoying the peace. Weekends were special; we looked forward to them. Friday night we'd go to the pictures, see whatever film was showing. Romances, comedies, war films even, it didn't matter to us. On Sundays we'd go for a walk up on Box Hill if the weather was nice.

'Come on, slow coach,' he'd say, scampering up the hill, as fleet as a gypsy's dog. I'd pant after him carrying the bag with our lunch: egg sandwiches, crisps, and a bottle of stout for him, Tizer for me. We hiccupped and giggled on the bus going home, holding hands like kids.

Then he died. Just when things were getting interesting. Money in our pockets, colour coming back into our life. It was his heart. I found him in his chair when I got back from work one evening. I thought he was having a nap. His newspaper had fallen on to the floor, and I picked it up and went to put the kettle on. I dropped the teapot when I realised.

I couldn't get used to being alone. To coming home to an empty flat. To sleeping alone, waking alone. Having no one to talk to. I saw him in all our places for months afterwards. Walking in front of me on Turpentine Lane, his newspaper under his arm. Leaning over Ebury Bridge to watch the trains on their way to Victoria Station, or outside the cinema, lighting a cigarette. Then I stopped seeing him, he'd gone. I set out to find someone else and found Spence. But it was too soon. Grief returned just when I thought I had done with it.

I lay the tables then go to help Spence in the kitchen. 'How could you think I was ashamed of you, Rita?' he asks me. I turn off the flame under the pans on the stove. He locks the café door and follows me upstairs. We match our rhythms to that of the sea, steady and enduring, our naked bodies stark and marked by our years in the bright light.

Later that evening we walk along the cliffs. Spence points out the sites of wrecks, and tells me stories about vampires, and of Vikings and poets and bold explorers, and the men from the town that followed the whales. And the polar bear that swam in the harbour.

I lean against him and feel the ebb and flow of his breath. I want to tell him that I'll get used to the light and the shriek of the gulls and the taste of salt on my lips. That this is my home now. But I say nothing; just lay my hand against his chest to feel his heart beat against my palm.

Legs

Lynn Kramer

'Stop fidgeting, Anna,' said her mother, 'can't you stand still for once?'

They were waiting at the bus stop outside the Waldorf Dining Rooms where Yvette van Niekerk had her ninth birthday party the Saturday before last and Anna threw up in the lav over her black, patent-leather T-bars. Never again in her whole life would she order a lime cream soda even if Yvette drank three of them in a row, she was such a show-off.

'The bus will be here in a minute,' said her mother and took Anna's hand. 'It's not far, only Sea Point.'

Anna wiggled her fingers around so that she could feel the shape of the wedding and engagement rings through her mother's cotton glove. She once asked if she could have her rings when she died, and her shoes except for the plastic overshoes, and her mother had laughed and said she could, but that Anna's feet would be bigger than hers.

'Why are we going to Sea Point?'

Anna's feet were planted in first position: heels together, toes apart. Her feet were itching to try a pirouette. They longed to dance or skip or jump from one pavement square to the next. She shut her eyes for a second and wished she was inside the Waldorf, sipping a grenadilla float while the band played 'Rock Around The Clock' and people got up and jived, instead of standing here with the south-easter whirling dust and old bus tickets in her face. Except that if she wasn't here she'd be at school and Miss Smit would be shouting 'domkop' because she'd got her Afrikaans homework wrong again.

Her mother cleared her throat. 'To see a new doctor.'

'But I'm not sick any more,' Anna said.

'That's true.'

'So why are we going?'

'Because,' said her mother, grabbing the brim of her hat which was about to blow off.

Anna could see their reflections in the window of the restaurant alongside them. Her mother's straw hat at the top, then her navy-blue, button-through dress, and then her legs going on right to the bottom of the glass. Next to her, halfway down, was Anna's pink blouse with the puff sleeves, and her grey pleated skirt, and her legs which looked like pick-up sticks, except that legs were supposed to hold you up and pick-up sticks just fell down. She'd played it on the folding table that Sarie carried in from the lounge and set up beside her bed when she was sick. Only Sarie never had time for pick-up sticks because she always had to go and hang out the washing or polish the front steps or peel the potatoes for lunch, because Madam might otherwise give her the sack.

'Because why?'

'Because of your legs.'

'But,' said Anna, 'we've already seen millions of doctors and my legs are completely better now. I can walk and run, I can even do cartwheels like Yvette van Nie—'

'I know all that,' her mother said, and gave Anna's hand a shake as if she wanted to throw it away, except she didn't let go. 'That's the whole point.'

'So why are we going to a new doctor then?'

Her mother seemed to expel all the breath in her lungs at once. 'Will you please stop driving me crazy with your questions.'

The only parts of their bodies that Anna couldn't see were their feet because the window stopped at their ankles. So she couldn't admire the thick, white, crinkly soles of her new sandals, or her mother's high heels that matched her dress.

Sometimes she would try on those shoes. She'd wait until her parents had gone to work and Sarie was beating wet tea leaves into the lounge carpet as she sang along to pennywhistle kwela on the wireless. Then she'd open her mother's wardrobe and start with the red peep-toes hiding behind the shoe rack. But every pair she tried was always the same: her feet would slip about in them like fish. She stared at the window and kept her lips shut tight so no more questions could escape.

The bus arrived and they climbed on. The seats for white people were empty so they marched right to the front and sat in Anna's favourite place behind the driver. The conductor blew his whistle and the bus began to move. Suddenly a woman with a baby tied on her back in a red blanket ran across the road, waving her hand. The driver hooted and Anna swivelled round to watch the woman jump on as the bus gathered speed.

'Want to get yourself killed?' said the conductor, but the woman just laughed and gave him her money. All the seats by the doorway were full so she had to stand and hold on to a strap that hung from the ceiling.

'*Hoe gaan dit?*' said an old woman with a creased face. She got up, and the woman with the baby took her seat. They went on talking in Afrikaans but it was too fast for Anna to understand.

Sarie had said *hoe gaan dit?* when Anna dressed up as her friend and knocked on the door of her room in the backyard. She'd mixed cocoa and water in a saucer and rubbed it over her face, and tied her doll on her back wrapped in the old tablecloth that her mother had given her for dressing up. *Hoe gaan dit?* Sarie said to her. It meant: how are you?

'You'll rick your neck if you're not careful,' her mother said, 'and anyway it's rude to stare.' She tugged off her white gloves. 'I can't believe you brushed your hair this morning.' Turning Anna's face towards her, she unclipped her hair-slide, pulled the floppy brown hair away from her forehead and clipped the slide back in. 'Always untidy, just like your father. Shame you don't take after my side of the family; just think of Grandma's curls. Well, there's nothing for it but a perm when you're older.'

Grandma nearly got herself killed one day when her bus drove off while she was getting on. Anna didn't know if she had fallen into the road with her head cracked open like a walnut, and if the ambulance had raced up with the bells ringing, and if her blood had splashed into the gutter like the day the water main burst. Grandma lived in America so Anna couldn't ask her. And when she'd questioned her parents they said: don't be morbid. 'What is morbid?' she asked, and her father said it meant unwholesome or sickly, and her mother clapped her hands and told her it was time for bed. But when they wanted her to be careful about climbing on buses, or washing her hands after swapping comics at bioscope on Saturday mornings because you don't know where they've been, they would say: *Remember what happened to Grandma.*

The bus was slowing down in heavy traffic. Anna wiped the window to look at the flower sellers who squatted among the buckets of red and pink and purple flowers overflowing the narrow alley. A few yards further on, the bus came to a standstill outside OK Bazaars. Her father had bought a bag of hot chips in the basement which they ate with their fingers, and he said it was a poetic experience but don't tell your mother because she doesn't go in for poetry.

'That window is filthy.' Her mother clicked open her new tan handbag. It was made from the skin of an ostrich and had tiny pimples all over where the ostrich's quills had been pulled out. 'Clean yourself up now,' she said, shaking out a blue hanky, the spare one she kept in her bag for emergencies.

'It's not dirty,' Anna said, giving her hand a quick wipe on her skirt to be sure.

'What's this then?' Her mother caught hold of her wrist, spat on the hanky and rubbed it over Anna's hand and fingers.

Dirt was dangerous. Dirt made you sick. Flies could kill you. If you got polio you would die or end up with one of your legs shorter than the other and have to wear a black boot for the rest of your life. When she was sick her legs hurt so much she couldn't walk. She had to stay in bed and wasn't allowed to be a Raggle Taggle Gypsy in the school concert at the end of term. The doctor came every day. He stuck needles in her arms to siphon her blood into little bottles which he took away for testing. Her father bought her treats on his way home from work as a reward for being so brave: acid drops, iced zoo biscuits, little bags of sherbet with liquorice sticks to dab it up. She gave him her word of honour not to make a mess on the sheets.

'You see?' Her mother held up the smudged hanky in triumph. 'That's the proof. So don't you deny it, my girl.' She rolled the hanky into a ball and stuffed it in the pocket of her bag.

The ostrich bag, swaddled in tissue paper, lived inside the wardrobe when it wasn't being used. On the same shelf lay the birthday present from Anna's father: a silky black dress that looked like a petticoat which her mother never wore.

Anna had lingered in the passage after breakfast on her mother's birthday. Through the half-open bedroom door she'd seen her pull the dress over her head, and her father shake out a pair of stockings like golden shadows. Her mother sat down on the bed, the black ribbon straps of the dress slipping off her bony shoulders as she leaned forward to gather each stocking in turn and ease them on over her feet. Anna watched her smooth out the wrinkles to the tops of her legs, stand up and press the thickened welt into the little clips attached to her step-in. Then she straightened and looked across at the mirror on the wardrobe door, the folds of the dress she'd hiked up falling back over her thighs, all a shimmer in the morning sunlight. Her mother was staring at herself, it seemed to Anna, as if the woman in the mirror with precise, yellow-waved hair and sea-blue eyes was not her at all, but someone she had never seen before. 'You've got better legs than any of your precious ballerinas,' said Anna's father, who was standing close behind. He wound his arms around her mother and began to kiss the side of her neck. 'What do you want from me, Arthur?' she said in a low voice. 'Don't you know who I am after all these years?' He moved away, thrusting his hands in his pockets, and did not answer. She began to take off the dress. Her father started for the door and saw Anna standing in the passage. 'What are you doing here?' he demanded. She said that she wasn't doing anything. 'Then go and get ready for school.' She told him that she was ready already. 'In that case, go help Sarie clear the bladdy table, for chrissake.' Anna always took care to fold the petticoat dress exactly the same way her mother had folded it, and to set it back on the shelf in exactly the same place.

'It's enough to make you sick, the state of this bus.'

Anna's eyes followed the toe of the navy blue shoe which was pointing at each of the cigarette butts on the floor, and at the trail of wet left by a brown bottle rolling around under the seats.

'I've a good mind to complain to the City Council, but

will they listen? Ha.' The bus began to trundle forward again. Her mother frowned over Anna's head at the street. A couple of dronkies with battered felt hats jammed on the backs of their heads were staggering about on the corner, strumming banjos, crooning fragments of some long-forgotten, half-remembered song. 'No one cares about anyone else these days,' she said, 'they're all in it for themselves.'

When Anna was sick, her father cut holes out of an old grocery box and set it upside down over her legs like a bridge so nothing could touch them, not even the sheet. *Joko Tea Unequalled for Flavour and Strength* it said on both sides of the box. Her mother closed her eyes and murmured that this was the last straw. 'But,' said Anna, 'there isn't any straw in the box like there is when it's had peaches in it or guavas.' Her mother covered her face with her hands as if she was counting to ten for Anna to jump out of bed and run away and hide.

They reached the crossroads. The policeman in white gauntlets beckoned them on and they turned left. Anna's feet began to jiggle up and down as the bus rumble-grumbled out of the city towards the sea. The shops, the people, the slow-moving carts and lorries were all left behind, and suddenly they were going at such a lick she couldn't even count the palm trees on Beach Road.

'There's nothing to worry about. The doctor only wants to ask you a few questions.' Her mother's voice had gone all dry and papery, the way it did when she'd had it up to here and had to go and lie down in the bedroom with the curtains drawn.

Her mother wanted her to be a famous ballerina when she grew up, and the ballet teacher did say that Anna had useful legs. The teacher also told Yvette van Niekerk that she had perfect feet. The trouble with Yvette, said her mother, was that she had a vivid imagination. Anna's name was a compromise. Her mother had set her heart on Anna Pavlova, after the Russian ballerina, but her father was determined to call her Anna Livia Plurabelle who was a character in *Finnegans Wake*, his favourite book. In the end they settled on Anna Olivia Pandora. A compromise, her father explained, was what people ended up with instead of going to war.

Her mother inspected her watch, then delved into her handbag. She brought out a gold compact and fluffed powder over her nose and cheeks, ran a lipstick across her mouth. Anna wanted to press her fingers into that powder and make her cheeks all smooth and pink like her mother's cheeks. She wanted to turn her lips red with her mother's lipstick.

Soon she would see her favourite, her very best thing in the whole wide world and universe. They were getting nearer and nearer. Please don't talk to me, Anna thought, and she wished that her mother could see this thought inside her head. The bus slowed down on the next bend and there it was, shining like a castle in the sea.

The lighthouse. Her lighthouse.

Her mother squeezed her arm. She was holding out a twist of barley sugar. Anna crammed it into her mouth and turned back to the window to stop her mother spoiling everything, like when she burst into her bedroom in the morning calling, 'Anna, it's time to get up!' in the middle of a beautiful dream.

The lighthouse was her castle, her ship, her best friend; it was sailing round the bay right next to her; it was keeping her company.

'He says it won't take very long. Are you listening, Anna?'

Sometimes you could hear the foghorn at Mouille Point warning those in peril on the sea. This was also the name of a hymn sung in school assembly. The foghorn sounded like an animal with a sore throat, a great big lonely animal with a bellow so loud it drowned out the noises of people talking.

'Will you look at me when I'm talking to you,' said her mother, and her stockings hissed as she uncrossed her legs.

Anna turned away from the window and gazed at her mother's face and then at the ostrich handbag on her lap. Ostriches had thin legs and only two toes on each foot but they could run faster than anything. She used to run faster than Yvette van Niekerk but now Yvette could run faster than her. How did an ostrich become a bag with a pocket and a zip and a little mirror inside? She wanted to look out of the window again because any second now the lighthouse would disappear back down into the sea where it came from, even though her mother had once told her that buildings didn't move, it was impossible, just made-up nonsense in her head. But she couldn't look because her mother was watching her.

'Sit properly now,' her mother said, and smoothed Anna's pleats over her knees. 'This new doctor just wants to talk to you. It's about your legs.' She slid her gloves back on, pressing them down between her fingers. 'He wants to talk to you about why you couldn't walk. Because the hospital says all the tests are normal. Do you hear me? They said that every single one of those tests is completely normal.' She tore the gloves off and struck them against the ostrich bag. 'It's proof, Anna. It's proof there is nothing wrong with you.'

Roses are red, violets are blue, sugar is sweet and so are you. That's what her mother wrote on the first page of Anna's autograph book when her legs were hurting and she couldn't walk.

'Do you understand what I'm saying?' Her mother's blue eyes were tunnelling into Anna's grey eyes. 'When you were lying in bed with that grubby box over your knees you weren't ill at all. There was nothing whatsoever the matter with you.'

Anna stole a glance at the window. The south-easter was blowing the palm trees this way and that. It was blowing sea spray against the glass.

'Anna?' Her mother's eyes were watering. 'Anna, why won't you listen to me?'

It had gone now, the lighthouse had gone back down under the waves. Anna knew that, even though she was looking into her mother's sea-watery eyes and not out of the window at the sea. She knew it without checking because she didn't need to check. Because the bus had finished driving around the bay and was zooming straight along Beach Road; and soon it would be passing Rocklands and the swing park and the Pavilion, and then they'd be there.

The Elephant in the Suitcase

Deepa Anappara

Nirmal whistled as he shovelled, but he was not feeling cheerful. His head throbbed from the summer heat and his spine ached from bending down. He had hoped to dig a six-foot-deep trench around his house by nightfall, but a day's work had only resulted in blisters on his palms and a shallow ditch that even a child could cross. His mouth tasted of dust and disappointment.

A Malabar thrush picked up the feeble notes of his whistle, as if telling him not to give up. It was an old habit of his, this looking to the forest for signs. In his first year as a forest guard, a pair of mottled wood owls had kept him awake with their eerie howls one night and, the very next morning, the deputy ranger had turned up outside his quarters with the news of his mother's death.

He stopped digging to look for the whistling thrush in the canopy of trees surrounding the house. But the bird was nowhere to be seen. He aired his khaki shirt, which patches of sweat had plastered to his skin. A squawking flock of parakeets descended on the tree-tops. He wondered if he would be safer up a tree. His ditch would deter neither wild dogs nor elephants.

The shovel on his shoulder, he jumped over the ditch and headed back to the house, dry leaves crackling under his feet. His makeshift home in the forest looked grimmer than ever before. Paint peeled off its brick walls. The wooden shutters meant to cover the front windows hung loose like broken elbows. But what pinched his heart was the sight of the iron bars on the windows, which a bull elephant had bent out of shape the previous night.

Nirmal had just about fallen asleep when he heard the unmistakable crunch of branches being snapped into two. He tiptoed to the window, looked out and saw a lone elephant shaking the jack-fruit trees in his garden, its ivory tusks beaming in the moonlight. He crawled back to his folding bed, shivering in spite of the heat. Tried to be still. Prayed to all the gods he could name. But the elephant sought him out; charged against the walls of the house, and twisted the metal bars on the windows with its trunk, trumpeting so ferociously that even the always raucous crickets fell silent. In all his years in the forest he had never seen anything like it.

Was this too an omen? He drank some blessedly cool water from a mud pot and, on a messy table by his bed, looked for the letter from his wife. He had read it the day he picked it up at the check-post but he went over it again. As usual her real reason for writing the letter was hidden somewhere between the stories of their daughter's indifferent grades at school and the procurement of a new blender. *Call me as soon as you get this*, Shalini had written. *Ramesh has a job for you in the Gulf.*

There were no details about the job offer from his brother-in-law, a ploy no doubt meant to pique his curiosity. Shalini often badgered him about finding a better job, reading out recruitment advertisements in newspapers over the phone and, on his short visits home, making him entertain relatives who might know someone looking for a security guard or a clerk. There was a new urgency to her job search undertaken on his behalf, as if she had sensed his disquiet from miles away.

The two-room house was becoming dark. He squinted as he studied the letter, thinking of Shalini's face as she wrote it. She must have frowned as she tried to balance her threats with pleas. Her words carried the faint smell of coconut oil, which she applied to her curly, waist-length hair every morning.

Squirrels scurried on the roof above him. He lit a kerosene lantern and looked out of the window. The sky was dark blue, with rose-tinged clouds floating over it like the remnants of a pleasant dream. He decided everything would work out; it had to. Then came the high-pitched shrieking of birds, alarm calls rippling through trees and ringing in his ears. A deer fawn raced outside his window, followed by a pack of wild dogs, their red coats as bright and menacing as their snarls. Nirmal was used to these chases. This was the way of the forest. But today, the vicious whistling of the dogs hounding their prey made his hands tremble.

The elephant returned to his quarters that night, trampling his unkempt garden and his prayers. This time it tore off the window shutters and banged against the only admirable feature of the house: its thick, metal front door. Nirmal looked at his .303 Lee Enfield rifle leaning against a wall but it gave him no comfort or confidence. The gun was a colonial relic that jammed constantly. It should have been in a museum, not a forest. He wrapped its expired cartridges in a handkerchief and carried them in the pocket of his pants.

He crawled under the bed, closed his eyes and covered his ears with his hands. Mosquitoes hummed around him and sucked his blood. Only when the bites started to itch did he flap his hands; he dared not swat the insects as even a squelch might signal his presence to the elephant. He lay on the floor, his throat parched, even after the unruly sounds outside his door quietened down.

The next morning he inspected the ditch and found it was filled with leaves. Though he had expected the dismal result, predicted it even, it soured his mood as he set off on his patrol, the strap of his bag across his chest and his useless rifle hanging over his shoulder in a sling. Pavitran, a forest watcher who accompanied him on his rounds once or twice a week, joined him by a river a few kilometres from his quarters. In the monsoon the river was an angry goddess, spitting and frothing at the mouth, but now it was a gentle brown-green stream that occasionally disappeared between rocks. Nirmal told Pavitran about the elephant.

'Elephants can charge at forty kilometres per hour, I have heard,' Pavitran said. 'How fast can you run?'

Then he laughed at his own joke. Nirmal felt a rush of envy. Pavitran was still young enough to feel invincible. He scampered up mountain slopes, surefooted like a goat, unafraid of steep inclines and falling rocks. Just the thought of it made Nirmal's knees creak.

'Wait until it happens to you,' Nirmal said, heading in the direction of a watch-tower that he climbed every other day. 'See if you feel like laughing then.'

'Sa-ar, you have toddy in the house?' Pavitran asked, sprinting ahead. The 'Sa-ar' was offered without courtesy. Though technically Nirmal was his superior, Pavitran liked to treat him like a slow-witted uncle.

'What are you saying?' Nirmal spat out a bug that had flown into his mouth.

Pavitran skirted the chocolate saucers of a cluster of fungi growing under a branch on the ground. 'Elephants are great drunkards,' he said. 'They love toddy more than we do.'

'You know I don't drink. It's not that ... it's one of those things that you can't explain. This elephant, it's like he won't stop until he has stomped on my head.'

'You should ask for a transfer,' Pavitran said. 'Get a posting where you can stay with your family. In nice, clean quarters. Some place where there's a good school nearby for your daughter.'

The air was sweet with the smell of cinnamon but Nirmal felt bitter. Whenever he went home, his daughter smiled at him once or twice, then went back to the television or the phone or the stereo or whatever it was that caught her ever-changing fancy. When he asked her questions, Radha ignored him kindly, singing along to strange Hindi film songs, or pretending to develop a sudden yet keen interest in her books.

He paused to catch his breath. Pavitran stopped too, but he was restless. Like a monkey, he swung from the prop root of a fig tree dangling over their path.

'You think it's easy to get a transfer? You think I haven't tried?'

'All I'm saying' – Pavitran jumped down and wiped

his hands on his shirt – 'I haven't heard anyone else complain about an elephant.'

'Oh, I see, so I'm making it all up, eh? That's just great. And the best I could come up with was an angry elephant? Not even a bloody ghost?'

'Don't get mad at me, boss. I'm not your enemy.'

The steel watch-tower swayed in the wind. Nirmal gripped the rough railings to steady himself. The forest seemed deceptively empty. Not even a bird in the sky. Pavitran was looking through the binoculars a tiger-loving NGO had donated to forest guards in Kerala along with jumpers and blankets.

'You see anything?' Nirmal asked. 'Let me have a look.'

Pavitran held on to the binoculars. Nirmal nearly snapped at him, but stopped himself. He could not afford to alienate Pavitran, who having grown up in the forest, knew more about it than a trained guard like him. Pavitran still lived in a tribal settlement in the jungle, but unlike the other men in his community did not brew hooch illegally or help poachers. In return for his self-lessness the Forest Department gave him a khaki uniform like the one Nirmal wore, a daily, often-delayed wage of ten rupees and a scratchy blanket as bonus at Deepavali.

'No sign of any poachers,' he said, returning the binoculars.

'And elephants?'

'They're in the valley. Sa-ar, you know that. Once the monsoon starts—'

'Yes-yes, they will be back.'

'What I don't understand is, why do we even bother catching these poachers? The courts just let them out again.'

Nirmal did not respond but wondered if his own sense of disaffection had sprung from a lifetime of enduring such big and small injustices. Sometimes a leak in the roof could go unfixed for years before it caused the ceiling to sag or cave in.

Pavitran sat down on the floor, his legs hanging out between the metal rails. Nirmal zoomed in on a herd of sambar drinking at a water hole. There was a time when he had a hawk's eyes but not any more. He could once cover the entire stretch of the forty-kilometre beat he had been assigned, but now ten kilometres, even five, exhausted him. Was he old? When had he grown old? His short shadow mocked him from the ground below. His breath sounded hollow; his skin was creased. Tomorrow his body would shrink; his back would crack; bones would jut out of his skin, sharp as knives.

He put the binoculars back in his bag and tapped Pavitran on his shoulder. 'Nothing to see here. Let's go down.'

*

Nirmal, in his time in the forest, had learnt that the average elephant ate one hundred and fifty kilogrammes of plants, and drank one hundred litres of water every day. He saw no evidence of this scale of consumption on his patrols. His nocturnal visitor did not leave footprints, have dust baths, pass dung and urine, or scrape the barks of trees with its tusks.

He might not have looked for the elephant hard enough. He was short of time. The summer heat was beginning to strip leaves off trees. Small fires broke out in parts of the jungle, which luckily fire-watchers hired from Pavitran's tribal community managed to put out.

A week after he first saw the elephant, Nirmal visited the forest department office a couple of kilometres from the check-post. His officers told him to clear grass and shrubs around the area he patrolled to stop fires from spreading. He did not tell them about the elephant. (What if he had imagined it?) He did not call his wife, though another letter from her – this time with details of the Gulf job – had been waiting for him. (What was he to tell her?)

He scrambled back to the tribal village in the heart of the wildlife sanctuary, so he could speak to Pavitran about the fire line. Poachers started most of the fires in the forest, dropping matchsticks on grasslands to distract guards so they could escape with their kill. His department had no helicopters or extinguishers so Nirmal and others had to contain a fire by beating it with branches. The last time it happened his eyes had watered for days and it had seemed as if soot would never budge from his lungs. He stopped to pick up a couple of flowers lying on the ground under a red silk cotton tree and placed them at the feet of black rocks shaped like gods. *Not again, Lord Ganpati, Lord Vishnu, Lord Shiva. Not again.*

Above him a Nilgiri langur crashed from one branch to another. A herd of gaur crossed the track in front of him, scarcely paying him any attention. Nirmal continued walking, scratching his balls and spitting on the ground. He wondered if he could ever appease these cruel gods with his modest offerings. He was angry: with the poachers and the judges, and the government that did not care if guards like him had food to eat or a place to sleep. In ten years he had not even got a promotion. What was the point of it all? Would he not be better off doing something easier, like tending an Arab's or a Russian's garden in Dubai? He tried to imagine what his life would be like if he earned in dirhams. His daughter might respect him a little. They would have a house of their own so Shalini would not have to argue with crass landlords barging into her kitchen and peering into pans to find out what she was serving for lunch. But he would still be alone, in a land where only air-conditioners and sprinklers made life possible.

He reached a small clearing where a tour operator sometimes pitched tents for tourists so they could spend a night or two in the forest. The only semi-permanent features of the site – a bamboo table and a bench the operator had put together – had been smashed to pieces, perhaps by an elephant. Nearby was a grove of bamboos, whose shoots and leaves elephants favoured over most other plants. He made a mental note to ask his seniors to shift the camping site before tourists returned in September.

The snap of a twig near him. Must be a porcupine or a langur. He spied a black rock in the distance but— what was that, was it moving? Probably not. God, he needed a good night's sleep. No point looking. Pavitran would tell him to wear glasses and he would be right.

Thorns lanced his legs through his trousers. The birds on the trees around him were jittery, as if mirroring his unease. The staccato calls of giant squirrels filled the air. His feet ached. He heard a low rumble, then a high-pitched, brassy trumpet. Should he climb a tree or run? He ran, ducking under branches, flapping his arms as if he were swimming. His rifle thrashed against his back. His feet caught a gnarly root. He slipped and fell face down on the ground. A sharp pain pierced his jaw. Skin peeled off his blister-ridden palms as stones cut into them. Might as well give up. Might as well lie down. Let it end like this. He thought of Shalini and Radha. He thought of the brief, satisfying affair he once had with a tribal woman named Janu, which he had kept from everyone else. He closed his eyes and waited.

But there was nothing. Insects crawled on his skin. He slowly forced himself to stand up. Dusted his clothes. Felt a bit foolish. He bent down to pick up his rifle, which had fallen away from him.

'No need for that,' he heard a voice say.

The two poachers he and Pavitran had caught a month ago stood on either side, cornering him.

'How much does our government pay you?' a thin, bald man asked him. 'Nine thousand rupees? Ten thousand?'

'You should join us,' the other plumper man with wiry hair said, laughing. 'We may not get a monthly salary. But one kill and we can relax for two months.'

The men did not seem interested in killing him. They taunted him about his rifle and then poked him in the ribs with a slicker gun Nirmal could not identify.

'Don't come after us ever again.'

'Or we will kill you.'

'Not that we want to kill you.'

'But we won't have a choice.'

The thin man thumped him on his back as if they were friends. Then they walked away.

Nirmal bent down to pick up his rifle, his head sore, white lights flashing in the corner of his eyes.

Two days later, Pavitran visited Nirmal in his quarters. He examined the bent iron bars and the leaf-strewn garden, and said, 'But wasn't it always like this?'

'Forget it,' Nirmal said. 'Did those poachers come to the village looking for you?'

'Not yet.'

The sky turned black as they talked. A summer storm. A strong wind hissed through the trees. Birds huddled in the grooves of branches. White hailstones pounded the forest, followed by rain. Nirmal and Pavitran peeled off their shirts and stood outside, arms outstretched. Only the jagged bolts of lightning forced them inside.

Nirmal gave Pavitran a cotton towel to dry himself and made tea.

'I'm thinking of leaving,' he said as Pavitran sipped from his tumbler. 'I have spent ten years in the forest. Ten years, just imagine. A man can go mad in half that time.'

'Is this about the elephant? Because we will find that bastard, no problem. We will give him one of those injections that will calm him down.'

Nirmal stood near the front door and watched the rain pelting down.

'If you think about it,' he said, turning around, 'it's not the elephant's fault. What does it know? This is its territory. We're the trespassers.'

Pavitran scratched his head. 'I don't know what this elephant has done to you.'

'Actually, the elephant isn't real. Didn't you say that?'

Pavitran sulked. Water drops splattered on Nirmal's feet. He did not know how to tell the young man about the deterioration of his body; he did not think Pavitran would understand the exhaustion he felt, or the loneliness. For so many years, these forests, these quarters as paltry as his income, these conversations with those like Pavitran who lived in the jungle, had been enough. But no longer. He touched the bald patches on his head and thought of the receding treeline of the forest, chopped down to make way for dams or quarries. The forest was dying, slowly but surely, and so was he.

'But, Sa-ar, what will you do if you leave?' Pavitran asked. 'Where will you go?'

'To the Gulf. I could become a gardener. Or a guard. I don't know.'

'You won't like it.'

Nirmal walked with Pavitran to the check-post, his belongings squished into the two bags they carried between them. At 5pm a taxi would ferry him from the check-post to the nearest railway station, where he would sleep in a waiting room until it was time to catch the train home.

The summer storms had given way to an early monsoon. The croaks of frogs now joined the chorus of birds and crickets. Their feet sank into slushy mud as they walked. Water dripped on their heads from the gleaming leaves above them. Black leeches clung to their clothes and they stopped frequently to shake off the creatures.

'You should have taken all your stuff, Sa-ar,' Pavitran said. 'Such a waste.'

Nirmal, having left most of his meagre possessions behind for Pavitran to take home, said, 'It's alright. You will be using most of it, I suppose.'

A half-green, half-black frog sat on a rotting log by the track. It saddened him that he did not know its name. How many other creatures were there that he could not identify?

Everything seemed unreal to him, as if he was watching himself in a dream, up until the moment he shoved his luggage into the boot of the taxi. Then the smiling faces of his colleagues, wishing him well, putting a garland around his neck, presenting him with a small, wooden elephant as a parting gift, became sharp and clear. He felt like crying but grinned instead. It started to drizzle and people left. He asked the taxi driver to reopen the boot and put the elephant in his suitcase. Pavitran was still standing by his side, getting drenched in the rain. Nirmal embraced him, then got into the taxi, and told the driver, 'Okay, shall we leave?'

By then the sun had disappeared behind the clouds and the mountains. It was dark though it was not yet night.

'It's tricky driving in this weather,' the driver told him, flicking the headlights on. 'A bus rolled into a gorge this morning.'

'They were talking about it at the check-post,' Nirmal

said, scratching the taxi's stale-smelling upholstery. He felt bereft. He wanted to scream, knock his head against a rock. He wanted a sign. *Dear Lord, tell me I'm doing the right thing.*

'You have to be very careful on these roads,' the driver said, but then he drove too fast, the taxi's tyres veering towards the edge of the winding mountain road.

Nirmal clutched the dashboard but he was swung from side to side.

Negotiating a hairpin bend, the driver said, 'Looks like there's some trouble ahead.'

Through the windshield, Nirmal saw a truck that had stopped in the middle of the road. The taxi driver pressed the brake pedal too late. The car tyres screeched as the vehicle just missed slamming into the stationary truck.

'Maybe the road's crumbling,' the driver said, but he did not look concerned.

'Let me check,' Nirmal said and stepped out.

Two men on a bike honked behind them, revving their vehicle and shouting at the truck and taxi drivers for blocking the narrow road.

Nirmal walked ahead, passing a slanting sign erected on the roadside by the Forest Department: *Nature has everything to meet man's need but not his greed.* The thick, yellow headlights of the truck did not reveal any cracks on the tarmac.

'Get back in the car, you son of a dog,' a cleaner who sat in the front of the truck, next to its driver, shouted.

Nirmal felt fear gripping his shoulders but his feet would not move.

Perhaps tired of waiting for a landslide or an apparition to materialise, the men on the bike rode ahead having somehow squeezed past the bigger vehicles on the road. They had barely gone ten feet when they whizzed around. An elephant, its shape hidden until then by the blackness of the night, came charging behind them, a speeding mass of unbearably loud, terrifying trumpets. Was this his tormentor? Had it followed him?

The drivers pressed their horns and flicked the headlights of their vehicles on and off as if to scare the elephant away. The animal stopped running and sauntered towards Nirmal. He could feel its eyes on him; was sure its tusks would rip his chest.

The elephant snorted as if mocking the drivers' attempts to frighten him. Then he turned around and disappeared into the mountainside.

On wobbly legs Nirmal walked back to the taxi, where the driver stood leaning against the bonnet.

'What were you thinking?' he asked.

'Have a death wish, do you?' the excitable cleaner shouted from the truck.

Nirmal got into the taxi and wiped his forehead against the sleeves of his shirt. His heart was still racing.

The driver started the car after touching a small idol of Lord Ganpati affixed to the dashboard. 'It's good luck to see an elephant at the start of a journey,' he said. 'You're going to succeed in whatever you choose to do.'

'We will see,' Nirmal said. He stuck his head out of the window and looked at the forest above him, but it was too dark to see anything and raindrops fell on his upturned face.

Level and Nearly Unaffected

Carol Rowntree Jones

The second night, after you left, you didn't miss a thing. You know how we were trying to pluck up courage to join in and were really just enjoying watching his hips? Well, the next evening I went back and it was the ugly shift. No, that's cruel, but that guy would not have kept you awake at night. I didn't stay late; I had to pack and get an early train to the airport.

But I thought this salsa thing looked pretty good, and when some flyers arrived in the office about a class nearby straight after work, and I was feeling lardy around the middle, you know how it is, I thought I'd give it a try. I didn't want to go anywhere I would know anyone, didn't want to look a complete idiot, and it was a night no one needed lifts anywhere. It's getting easier now, isn't it – they're older and you get a bit more time. Still all the washing and you just have to stop yourself worrying about what they're eating. You make up for it other nights. It's like another friend of mine. She got a horse, was completely besotted, and the family had never eaten so well she felt so guilty.

So I went along. Random people – couples, other people straight from work like me. No one there for the lonely-hearts thing as far as I could tell. And I loved it from the start. You get the basic movements first – you know how the guy was showing the others at the session we saw, what we could see from the back of the bar – it's like three steps and then you pause, and as you get better it's what you do with the pause that counts.

This seems ages ago now, and for me to be having to spell it all out . . . but I just have to tell you. So I started to pick up the rhythm and it became the best thing in the week. The tutor, a married guy – he was local but he'd learnt it all in London, so he was good. Great hips, girl!

One, two three, tap. One, two three, kick. It was a different variation each week. Then you do clever things with the weight transfer – I know it wasn't salsa, but you know how Fred Astaire always looked like he was floating? Well, it's not like that, it's very grounded, but when you get it just right and the pause is practically electric it feels weightless.

I became the star pupil – yes, I know that's hard to believe – and the guy would use me to demonstrate. His hands were pretty nice on me but I felt immune; the absolute best thing was the dancing. By now I was going to another of his classes as well. More new people, but they were just bodies around me. Good partner? Indifferent? Totally rubbish and I'd blank them the next time. The music, the moves, took me high as a kite.

So how did everyone at home take it? Bit of a joke really. Nice for mum to be doing it, that kind of thing, a bit of a joke from him too. And that suited me, I guess – a bit of a laugh, a way of keeping fit.

It becomes odd, the significance of things.

I'd be in the supermarket trying not to three step and keep focused on the baked beans, but I'd be off to the rice, pasta and accompanying sauce; then aubergine, tuna and pulses. Even the shopping list was in time. I'd watch other people and see if they were salsa addicts – because that was what it was like, it was an obsession.

I started to think of all my relationships in terms of who was the lead and who following. I interpreted my daughter's tiffs with her friends as who was being open – still communicating, involving the other – and who was closed: shut down, restricted, taking no responsibility.

I heard there were salsa nights in town so I went

along with two of the girls I'd met at the second class. Every other Saturday, so our films still happened. These nights were dark, sweaty affairs. I've never drunk so much water. I tell you, I needed nothing else. And it's an art, what to wear. So that you can get out of the house looking fairly normal, but survive the evening on the dance floor without being a complete ball of sweat.

Then I danced with him. If we thought that guy we saw together had snaking hips . . . I hadn't seen this one at the club before, and that night the other girls couldn't make it so I was doing my own thing. He came up and asked if he could dance with me, and at salsa that's fine. It's all about the dance and you need a partner.

Did I mention electricity before? This was like we were burning a path through the room, like no one else was there. I didn't know how I was breathing.

I guess we danced together for a couple of hours, then the session ended and we said, 'next week?' And so it went on. We would dance there together all night – all evening – sweat together, love the music together, then leave. But I'd be dreaming it. I knew the weight of his hand on my back and how his hip fitted mine. I knew we looked good together. We improvised like we read each other's minds. Other people stood and watched.

But it made me feel so strange I had to stop.

All that stuff in the first class: 'the upper body remains

level and nearly unaffected'. Okay, a get-out clause in the 'nearly'. But I was certainly affected.

God, I miss it.

But putting dinner on the table, turning round the sports kit, being able to face people, clean toilets: I needed those as well.

But that sweet tension in my belly.

Life is calm now with no intricate foot-work. A kind of relief. It felt like a big thing that everything else might not survive.

So all is harmony here, that's me.

The Magic Toyshop

Angela Carter

Melanie swam like a blind, earless fish in a sea of sedation, where there was no time or memory but only dreams. Summer changed to autumn before she surfaced and lay palely on her bed, remembering. When she was strong enough, she went out one early morning and buried the wedding-dress decently under the apple-tree. Her breast felt hollow, as if it were her heart she had buried; but she could move and speak, still.

'You must be a little mother to them,' said Mrs Rundle. Mrs Rundle sewed black armbands to their coats, even Victoria's. Mrs Rundle's coat was black already; she was always prepared for mortality to strike. She was disappointed, even aggrieved, that the remains would not be brought home for a funeral. Since there were no remains to speak of. But even so.

Melanie started wearing her hair in stiff plaits, in the manner of a squaw. She plaited her hair so tightly that it hurt her, straining hair and flesh until it felt as though the white seam down the back of her head might split and the brains gush out. It was a penance. She chewed at the spiky end of a plait and kicked at a kitchen chair-leg. Through the open door into the hall drifted the murmuring voices of the auctioneer's men.

Everything was to be sold. There was no money left. Daddy hadn't saved any money because he thought he could always make more. In a vacuum, the children existed from day to day. There was still food for them to eat and Mrs Rundle was still there. She was a fixed point. Melanie stayed beside her, now, helping her about the house. She did not like to be alone. The mirror was broken and she hated the casual glimpses she got of her face as she cleaned her teeth or when she passed the hall-stand. But Mrs Rundle, the mother-hen, was looking for a new post and the house was to be sold over their heads, and the furniture, too.

'A little mother,' repeated Melanie. She must be a mother to Jonathon and Victoria. Yet Jonathon and Victoria hardly seemed to feel the lack of a mother. They had their own private worlds. Jonathon pressed on with his new model. Victoria babbled like a brook, chasing motes in the sunbeams. Neither referred to their parents or seemed to realise that their present life was coming to an end – Victoria too young, Jonathon too preoccupied. When prospective buyers came to look at the house, which happened more and more frequently, they stayed out of the way until they had gone.

'The burden is all mine,' said Melanie.

Mrs Rundle knitted a knee-sock. For Jonathon, a parting gift. She was turning the heel.

'They told me to tell you,' she said. 'The lawyers did. Since I am close. I have been waiting my time.'

'What is this?'

'You are to go to your Uncle Philip.'

Melanie's eyes grew wide.

'Your Uncle Philip will take the three. And it is not right for a family to be separated.' She sniffed emphatically.

'But we have never known him. He was Mummy's only brother and they drifted apart.' She dredged the name from a chance remark in the remote past. 'The name was Flower. Mummy was a Miss Flower.'

'The lawyer says he is a perfect gentleman.'

'Where does he live?'

'In London, where he has always lived.'

'So we shall go to London.'

'It will be nice, and you growing up. All London for you. Theatres. Dances.' From magazines and novels she recollected: 'Soirées.'

'How does he make a living? He used to be a toymaker.'

'And still is. He is married. There will be a woman's guidance.'

'I didn't know he was married.'

'These days,' disapproved Mrs Rundle, 'there is such a lack of contact within families! Fancy not knowing about your uncle's wife! She is, after all, your aunt!' Her steel needles flashed.

'It will all be new and strange.'

'That is life,' said Mrs Rundle. 'I shall miss you all and often think of the baby, growing up into a little girl. And you, into a young lady.'

Melanie bent her head and the plaits swung over her face. 'You have been so kind.'

'I shall help with the packing, of course.'

'When' – she gulped – 'when do we go?'

'Soon.'

October, crisp, misty, golden October, when the light is sweet and heavy. They stood on the step and waited for the taxi with black bands on their arms and suitcases in their hands, forlorn passengers from a wrecked ship, clutching a few haphazardly salvaged possessions and staring in dismay at the choppy sea to which they must commit themselves.

'I may never see this house again!' thought Melanie. It was an enormous moment, this good-bye to the old home; so enormous she could hardly grasp it, could feel only a vague regret. The rose wreath still hung in the apple tree, a little weather-beaten, already.

Mrs Rundle kissed them wetly one after the other. She, too, was leaving the house that day. She wore her good, black, cloth coat and her neatly darned cloth gloves and her sturdy, serviceable laced-up shoes. Her cat slept in a basket beside her trunk. Her new employer would pick her up by car. Their relationship was at an end. She belonged to another house, other people.

'Oh, dear,' said Melanie, suddenly. 'School.' The sight of the trunk reminded her. She had not thought of it till now. But she and Jonathon should be back at school and Victoria starting at the village junior and mixed infants democratically this term.

'Your Uncle Philip will see to all that,' said Mrs Rundle. 'Mind you look after them on the journey and buy them sweets and comic books for the train.' She dug amongst the bottles of aspirin and loose hairpins and tubes of digestive mints in her whale-backed black simulated leather handbag. 'Take this.' A pound note for a good-bye present.

Then the taxi came for them. Did the taxi-driver, the ticket-collector at the station, the other passengers standing on the platform – did they sense the difference about the children and, seeing the black armbands, nod sadly, knowingly, and smile in encouragement and sympathy? Melanie thought they did and froze at the first breath of pity, summoning all her resources to act coolly.

A little mother.

'I am responsible,' she thought as they sat in the train

and Victoria pulled up seat cushions to see what lay beneath them and Jonathon studied a diagram of the rigging on a schooner. 'I am no longer a free agent.'

A black bucket of misery tipped itself up over Melanie's head. Part of herself, she thought, was killed, a tender, budding part; the daisy-crowned young girl who would stay behind to haunt the old house, to appear in mirrors where the new owner expected the reflection of his own face, to flash whitely on dark nights out of the prickly core of the apple tree. An amputee, she could not yet accustom herself to what was lost and gone, lost as her parents scattered in fragments over the Nevada desert. A routine internal flight. An unscheduled squall. An engine fault. Two Britons are among the dead. We regret to announce the death of a distinguished man of letters. And his wife.

Mummy.

No, Mother. Now she was dead, give her the honourable name, 'Mother.' Mother and Father are dead and we are orphans. There was, also, an honourable ring about the word 'orphans'. Melanie had never even known an orphan before and now here she was, an orphan herself. Like Jane Eyre. But with a brother and sister whom she must look after for they had nothing left but her.

'London! London!' cried Victoria every time the train, a slow, halting, bucolic train, drew to a standstill, either at a drowsy country station where cow parsley foamed along the line or simply nowhere, among the fields, to have a little rest.

'They won't know us at the station, in London,' said Jonathon suddenly. 'We have never seen one another.'

'They will easily recognise three children travelling alone,' said Melanie.

The train was a kind of purgatory, a waiting time, between the known and completed past and the unguessable future which had not yet begun. It was a long journey. Jonathon stared from the window at a landscape which was not the one Melanie saw. Victoria, at last, went to sleep and did not see the slow beginnings of London nor wake when the train finally halted at the arched and echoing terminus. Melanie was stiff, aching and covered in smuts. She felt oddly cold and sick but bit her lip staunchly and gathered their cases together.

'Jonathon,' she said, 'you must carry Victoria.'

He considered this, holding a special parcel of his own.

'I would rather carry the model I am working on, in case it gets injured,' he said reasonably. She realised there was no use arguing with him.

'I'll carry her, then, and we'll get a porter.'

Victoria was a great, heavy lump of a child and Melanie's arms cracked under the weight of her. Buffeted helplessly by the crowd, Melanie peered around the platform. There were no porters to be had. And where was Uncle Philip?

Then her attention was caught by two young men who leant against a hoarding, drinking tea from cardboard cups with unhurried, slow, rustic movements. Their stillness attracted her. They created their own environment around them. Although behind them was a six-foot-high beer-bottle, with the red-lettered statement 'A Man's Drink!' across it, they superimposed upon it a silent and rocky country where there was always a wind blowing with a touch of rain on it and few birds sang. They were hard but gentle men. They were country people in a sense that Melanie was not, although she had just come from the green fields and they might have lived in London all their lives. They were brothers.

Obviously brothers, although startlingly dissimilar – two different garments cut, at one time, from the same cloth. The younger was nineteen or so, just a few inches taller than Melanie, with longish, bright red hair hanging over the collar of a dark blue, rather military looking jacket with shoulder flaps and brass buttons. He wore washed-out, balding corduroy trousers wrinkled with their own tightness. His clothes had the look of strays from a parish poor-box. His face was that of Simple Ivan in a folk-tale, high cheek-bones, slanting eyes. There was a slight cast in the right eye, so that his glance was disturbing and oblique. He breathed through his slack-lipped mouth, which was a flower for rosiness. He grinned at nothing or a secret joke. He moved with a supple and extraordinary grace, raising his cup to his mouth with a flashing, poetic gesture.

His companion was the same man grown older and turned to stone. Taller, wider in the shoulder, clumsily assembled, with a craggy, impassive face. A bruising-looking man in a navy-blue, pin-striped suit with trousers frayed at the turn-ups and a beige and brown shirt of the sort that is supposed not to show the dirt. His brown and blue tie was speared with a tie-pin in the shape of a harp. He had a half-smoked, stubbed-out, hand-rolled cigarette, disintegrating into rags of paper and shreds of tobacco, stuck behind his ear.

They drank their tea and did not talk to each other. They kept quite still, although all the commotion of the station swirled around them. They inhabited their silence and gave nothing away.

When the younger one finished his tea, he tossed the cup over the hoarding with a lyrical, curving, discus-thrower swing and wiped his mouth with the back of his hand. He seemed to be inspecting the train, raking the length of it with a slow, sweeping, lop-sided gaze. His eyes were a curious grey green. His Atlantic-coloured regard went over Melanie like a wave; she submerged in it. She would have been soaked if it had been water. He touched the other man's arm; at once he dropped his cup and they came towards her. And if one moved like the wind in branches, the other's motion was a tower falling, a frightening, uncoordinated progression in which he seemed to crash forward uncontrollably at each stride, jerking himself stiffly upright and swaying for a moment on his heels before the next toppling step. The boy smiled and stretched out hands of welcome; the other did not smile. Melanie knew they were coming for her and started.

She was dismayed to see these strangers accosting her when she expected to see an old man in a cowboy hat with a black and white photograph face. Half-remembered Sunday newspaper stories about men who haunted main-line London railway stations to procure young girls for immoral purposes ran through her mind. But the boy said: 'You'll be Melanie.'

So they knew her name and it was all right. She saw his mouth moving; he was still talking but a train was blowing its whistle and drowned his voice, which was extremely soft.

'I'm Melanie,' she said. 'Yes.'

Author Biographies

The Elephant in the Suitcase

Deepa Anappara is a graduate of the City University's year-long Certificate in Novel Writing course. Her novel in progress was short-listed for the 2012 Yeovil Literary Prize. Her short story *Easy to Forget, Easy to Remember* won first prize in the Asian Writer Short Story competition and was published in the anthology *Five Degrees*. Deepa grew up in Kerala, India, and currently lives in Essex.

Documentary at Clareville Lodge

Susie Boyt was educated at Oxford and London Universities and is the author of five novels and a much-loved memoir, *My Judy Garland Life*, which will be staged at the Nottingham Playhouse in 2014. Her latest novel, *The Small Hours*, a psychoanalytic black comedy about the best and worst of how we treat each other, was published by Virago in 2012 to great acclaim. Susie has been writing a weekly column in the *Financial Times* Life and Arts section since 2002 and has contributed to publications ranging from the *London Review of Books* to *Brides*. She has given talks on Henry James, music in fiction and the poet John Berryman among other subjects. She also works occasionally as a bereavement counsellor. She lives in London with her family.

The Magic Toyshop: an extract

Angela Carter (1940–92) was born in Eastbourne and brought up in south Yorkshire. One of Britain's most original and disturbing writers, she read English at Bristol University and wrote her first novel, *Shadow Dance*, in 1965. *The Magic Toyshop* won the John Llewellyn Rhys Prize in 1969 and *Several Perceptions* won the Somerset Maugham Prize in 1968. More novels followed and in 1974 her translation of the fairy tales of Charles Perrault was published, and in the early nineties she edited the *Virago Book of Fairy Tales* (2 vols). Her journalism appeared in almost every major publication; a collection of the best of these was published by Virago in *Nothing Special* (1982). She also wrote poetry and a film script together with Neil Jordan of her story 'The Company of Wolves'. Her last novel, *Wise Children*, was published to widespread acclaim in 1991. Angela

Carter's death at age fifty-one in February 1992 'robbed the English literary scene of one of its most vivacious and compelling voices' – *Independent*.

Duty-Free

Helen Dunmore is a poet, novelist, short story and children's writer. She was inaugural winner of the Orange Prize for Fiction with *A Spell of Winter*. Among other awards, her work has received the McKitterick Prize, the Signal Award for Poetry and first prize in the National Poetry Competition. Her most recent novel is *The Betrayal* and her latest poetry collection is *The Malarkey*. She has also published a novella *The Greatcot* and three collections of short stories – *Short Days, Long Nights*; *Ice Cream* and *Rose 1944*. Her work is translated into more than thirty languages and she is a Fellow of the Royal Society of Literature.

The Journey to the Brothers' Farm

Pippa Gough was born in England and spent most of her childhood in Zambia, Zimbabwe, Swaziland and finally Cape Town, South Africa. After leaving school Pippa trained as a nurse in Cape Town and then returned to England where she trained as a midwife and health visitor, and she has carried on working in and with the NHS in a variety of positions. In 2005 Pippa undertook an

MA in Creative Writing at Royal Holloway, University of London. She has the support of a fantastic writing group, which provides endless encouragement. In between times, she works as a freelance in organisational and leadership development with public services.

Departure Time

Tessa Green divides her time between writing, painting and part-time work in employment law, and between Newcastle and the Greek island of Hydra. As well as short stories she is currently working on a novel.

Legs

Lynn Kramer was born in Cape Town. She studied music and law and worked as a family law solicitor for ten years. Her story *Legs* is adapted from her recently completed novel *Body Language*. Other stories have been published in *New Welsh Review*, *Slow Dancer*, *Jewish Quarterly*, *Pretext 6* and *Ephemera*. Lynn lives in London and has begun her next novel, provisionally entitled *Domestic Violence*.

A Sense of Perspective

Penelope Macdonald completed a Diploma in Creative Writing at Oxford in 2002, followed by an MA at

Warwick in 2004. She says she then 'came to a stand-still' until her son started school, when she began writing again – poetry and short stories. She has recently begun a novel for young adults. This is her first story to be published.

School Run

Kate Marsh lives in Brighton and works as a book-keeper. She wrote short stories when she was younger, then stopped and wrote nothing for about ten years. Reading about the Asham Award gave her the impetus to write her first short story for over a decade. The 'journey' theme reminded her of family car journeys as a child – and the school run in particular.

Pay Day

Dawn Nicholson started writing seriously around ten years ago and completed a part-time degree in creative writing at Hull University in 2011. She wrote most of her first novel in the final year, while teaching English at a residential school for children with emotional and behavioural difficulties. She is currently working on her second book and looking for an agent and publisher. She lives in Lincoln with her husband.

Where Life Takes You

Dolores Pinto started to write four years ago after attending a weekend 'taster course' at an adult education college. Her tutor was a poet, and extremely generous with her time and advice and gave her the confidence to continue with her studies at Birkbeck University and the City Lit. She is in the final stages of editing a novel.

Birds Without Wings

Angela Readman completed her creative writing MA at the University of Northumbria. Her poetry has won the Essex Poetry Competition, the Biscuit Poetry Competition, Ragged Raven, and been commended in the Arron International Poetry Competition. In recent years, she began submitting her short stories. Her stories have since been shortlisted in the Costa Short Story Award, the Bristol Short Story Prize, the Short Story Competition and won The National Flash Fiction Day Competition. She is currently working on a collection.

Level and Nearly Unaffected

Carol Rowntree Jones started to write standing up on a busy London train. She lives in Nottinghamshire and works in media relations for The National Forest and, freelance, for MIEL books. A poet and writer of short fiction, essays and non-fiction, her work has been published by Leaf Books, and in the journals *Assent*, *Staple*, *The North* and *1110*. She is a graduate of the University of Nottingham's BA in Professional and Creative Writing.

Hwyl

Emily Russell started writing stories in her head fifteen years ago and then on paper ten years later when she ran out of room. She has a degree in journalism from the University of Sheffield. She lives in Sussex and is currently working on her first novel.

Leaving Her

Diana Swennes Smith was raised in a remote northern Canadian logging town. She attended the Iowa Writers' Workshop as a teaching-writing fellow, where she earned a graduation fellowship to lead a summer fiction workshop at Victoria University of Wellington, New Zealand. Her fiction has appeared in New Zealand's online zine, *Turbine*, and Canada's oldest literary magazine, *The Fiddlehead*. As a PhD candidate in creative-critical writing at the University of East Anglia, her peer-reviewed journal article on writing about character desire was published in *Reconstruction: Studies in Contemporary Culture*. Opening chapters of her debut novel, *The End of*

Steel, were runner up for the Summer Literary Seminar's Graywolf Press Prize. She took advantage of the tuition award to attend a two-week fiction workshop in lovely old Vilnius, Lithuania. Diana is currently researching a second novel and seeking a publisher for her first.

Acknowledgements

Acknowledgements

The Elephant in the Suitcase Copyright © Deepa Anappara 2013

The Magic Toyshop extract Copyright © Angela Carter 1967

Level and Nearly Unaffected Copyright © Carol Rowntree Jones © 2013

A cupboard full of coats

YVVETTE EDWARDS

ONEWORLD

A Oneworld Book

First published by Oneworld Publications 2011
This edition published by Oneworld Publications 2012

Copyright © Yvvette Edwards 2011

"Turn Around Look at Me", by Jerry Capehart (CA) ©1961
Warner-Tamerlane Publishing Corp. (BMI) All rights reserved

ISBN 978-1-85168-838-8

Typeset by Glyph International
Cover design by Ghost
Printed and bound in Great Britain by
TJ International, Padstow, Cornwall

Oneworld Publications
185 Banbury Road
Oxford OX2 7AR
England

A Cupboard Full of Coats

1

It was early spring when Lemon arrived, while the crocuses in the front garden were flowering and before the daffodil buds had opened, the Friday evening of a long, slow February, and I had expected when I opened the front door to find an energy salesperson standing there, or a charity worker selling badges, or any one of a thousand random insignificant people whose existence meant nothing to me or my world.

He just knocked, that was all, knocked the front door and waited, like he'd just come back with the paper from the corner shop, and the fourteen years since he'd last stood there, the fourteen years since the night I'd killed my mother, hadn't really happened at all.

I had imagined that moment a thousand times; Lemon had come back for me. He knew everything yet still loved me. Over a decade filled with dreams where he did nothing but hold me close while I cried. Had he come sooner, my whole life might have panned out differently and it might have been possible to smile without effort, or been able to love. Had he come back before, I might have been happier in the realm of the living than that of the dead, but he had left it too late and things were so set now I could hardly see the point of him coming at all. Yet there he was.

He stood there in the cold, wet and wordless. He offered no excuses or explanations; no *I was just passing through and thought I might stop by*. He didn't tip a cap or smile and enquire after my health, nothing. He stood there watching me as if he wasn't sure whether I might throw my arms around his neck with a welcoming shriek or slam the front door in his face. But I did neither. Instead I watched him back, till eventually he gave a small shrug that could have meant just about anything.

He had what my mother had always called 'high colour', a black man with the skin of a tanned English gentleman, and like a gentleman, he had always dressed neatly. In that respect, he hadn't changed at all.

His taste in clothes seemed the same a decade and a half later, or maybe he'd just found himself stuck with the wardrobe he'd purchased in his youth. He wore Farah slacks that day and a Gabicci suede-trimmed cardigan with a Crombie overcoat thrown casually over them.

Though the rain had stopped, he was thoroughly soaked through, from his hair – which he had always kept skiffled low but which was longer now: a silver-tinged Afro that was damp and forged into steaming tufts – to the lizard-skin shoes on his feet. But though his clothes were still the same, *he* had aged. There were changes around his face; the crow's feet at the corner of his eyes were wider fanned, the bags beneath them full and heavy, and his old skin bore new lines. His eyes were red-rimmed, the whites yellowed, the expression intense as he looked at me, already asking questions, talking of things that should be whispered even when alone, and it was me that looked away, looked down, wondering if my own eyes were as eloquent as his, afraid that they might be speaking volumes, scared of the things they might have already said.

I opened the front door wide as he wiped his feet on the mat outside. It used to say Welcome, but was so faded now, only someone who knew what it had said before would be able to guess the word had ever been there at all. He bounded over the step like a cat, lithe-footed. He had always been a good mover, the kind of man you could not take your eyes off when he danced, the kind of man you had to drag your eyes off, period. I closed the front door quietly behind him.

He was in.

He stood inside the hallway looking around. I had done a lot with the house in the time he'd been away. The green doors and skirtings had been stripped. The old foam-backed carpet had been replaced with laminated flooring. The last time he'd been here, the walls were covered in deep plum velvet-embossed wallpaper; now they were smooth, clean, white. I sniffed.

'You need a bath,' I said.

He nodded. I walked up the stairs to the bathroom and he followed. I turned on the taps and the tub began to fill.

'I'll get you a towel.'

I left him in the bathroom while I went in search of a towel and some dry clothes for him to put on afterwards. As guys go,

he wasn't really that big, kind of average height, medium
build, but he was bigger than I was, and I knew nothing of
mine would fit him, even if he had been prepared to wear it.
There was still some male clothing in the wardrobe in my
mother's room. Though I had considered it often, I hadn't
cleared out her stuff, and her room was pretty much as she'd
left it, but tidied, her things neatly packed away, as if she'd
gone travelling on a ticket with an open-date return and
might come back at any moment. I even changed the bedding
every couple of months, though I couldn't say why. It was
just me here, and while I often passed time in her room, I never
slept in my mother's bed, ever.

Inside her wardrobe I found a dressing gown, maroon with
paisley trim, and I took it back to the bathroom with the towel.
The door was still ajar, and though I knocked first, I found
him stepping out of his underclothes as I entered.

He turned around to face me, making no effort to cover
himself. The bathroom light was on and its bright glare
permitted neither shadow nor softening. Though only in his
fifties, he was headed towards an old man's body: thin and
hairy, and gnarled like a cherry tree. His pubic hair was thick
and grey. His penis flaccid. I could smell his body above the
hot bath steam: moist stale sweat, tobacco and rum. He
nodded his thanks for the clothes, turned his back to me and
stepped into the bath.

I heard him turn the taps off as I picked up his wet clothing
from the floor, and as he lay back and closed his eyes I backed
out of the bathroom, pulling the door shut behind me.

*

By the time Lemon came downstairs dinner was ready. Minted couscous, grilled salmon and cherry tomatoes, with spring onions, black olives and yellow peppers tastefully strewn across two large white plates. The dressing gown was knotted tightly around his waist, and his pale legs carried him soundlessly across the living-room floor.

'You hungry?' I asked.

He shrugged. 'You have anything to drink?'

I indicated the bottle of wine on the table, but he shook his head.

'Water? Juice? Strong?'

'Strong's good.'

'Help yourself. Cupboard under the microwave. Glasses are above the sink.'

In my mother's day, unless she was entertaining, the double doors at the end of the through-lounge were always kept locked, so that you had to go out into the passage to enter the kitchen. But I kept them open always, and he went through to the kitchen. I heard him opening cupboards, finding the things he needed. He'd always been good in the kitchen; tidy and able. I only just made out the sound of the fridge door closing and I shivered.

Most things, all they want is a little gentle handling.

I refilled my own glass for the second time from the bottle on the table, sipping this one slowly as I waited for him to return. When he did, he was clutching a tumbler filled with a clear liquid that was probably vodka, diluted with water per-haps, or perhaps not. I picked up my fork and began to eat as he sat down and took a couple of glugs from the glass in his hand. I saw him wince as if he felt the liquor burn on the way down. He glanced at me, read the question in my eyes, and briefly waved a hand in my direction, dismissing it as nothing.

His knuckles were bigger than I recalled, or maybe they just seemed bigger because they were so clumsy wielding the knife and fork as he grasped them tight and started poking around the food on his plate, investigating, unhappy. After a while, he looked at me and asked, 'Ah wah dis?'

My laughter caught me by surprise. He had come to England when he was still in his twenties, had lived here some thirty years since, and normally spoke slowly, his English tinged with a distinctly Caribbean drawl. He was from Montserrat; a small islander. That he had chosen to ask what I was feeding him in that way was an indication of the level of his disgust.

'If you were expecting dasheen and curry goat you've come to the wrong place.'

'I never expect that, but little gravy would be good.'

'You should taste it,' I said, as he pushed the plate away from him into the centre of the table, shaking his head.

'You want some pepper?'

He shook his head again.

I carried on eating. He liked the brown food; brown rice, brown chicken, brown macaroni cheese, brown roast potatoes, the kind of food my mother was so good at cooking, the kind of food I never prepared.

'My wife died,' he said.

'Did she?'

'Cancer. Five months back.'

'I'm sorry.'

'Wasn't ill or nothing. Just couldn't eat. Lost some weight. Went to the doctor's. Doctor send her straight to the hospital. They open her, look inside, then sew her back up. Wasn't nothing they could do.'

He swallowed a mouthful from his glass, closed his eyes as it went down, then took another quick swig. He dabbed the sleeve of the dressing gown delicately against the corners of his mouth as if he were using a napkin. He would have seen her hollowed out, skeletal, with even her gums shrunken so her dentures no longer fit. They would have used wax to plump her cheeks out, to give her mouth a fuller, more natural shape, and a transparent liquid tint to make her skin tone lifelike. In the right hands she would have looked healthier dead than when he'd last seen her alive. Though I knew he was married, I had never met his wife.

'What was her name?'

'Mavis.'

'What was she like?'

He shrugged. 'I took care of her myself. Never put her in no home or nothing. Had to give up my job and everything. Couldn't manage both.' He raised his glass again, this time to sip. 'Must be the first time I touch her, she fall pregnant. Her mum was gonna chuck her out in the street and she never had no place else to go. Must be three months from I meet her, sex her, baby on the way, and we done married off already.'

'Did you love her?' The words were out in the open before I'd even realized they'd been in my mind. It was the question

I had wanted to ask him when I was sixteen years old. All this time it had waited, as intact as if it had been embalmed, buried deep inside my memory banks, and I hadn't had a clue.

'Baby was on the way so fast, and she was sick, sick and vomiting till the boy born. Bills was coming like mountain chicken after rainstorm, one after the next after the next. Never had time to roll on a beach, or check a dance till dawn. Never really laugh much…hardly smile. But at the end, I was there for her. Cooked her pumpkin soup. I feed her from the spoon and wipe her chin. I change her nappy and clean her mess. I did that.'

'Did she love you?' I asked.

For a moment, he did not respond. When he shrugged it was as if he considered the question irrelevant. He said, 'She let me stay.'

It was my turn to share, to present my life's summary. His turn to ask random, intimate questions. I waited but he asked nothing. Finally, 'I have a son now,' I said.

Lemon looked around the room slowly, taking in the alcoved shelves filled with books, the comfy wicker chair beside them, the settee that ran the length of one wall, the stereo in front of the window, the TV on the stand above it. There were no toys to be seen. Nothing to indicate that anyone other than me lived here. I had photos but they were not displayed like fertility trophies on my walls.

'He lives with his dad,' I said too quickly. 'He's coming tomorrow. Comes every second weekend and stays.'

He nodded, then stared back down at his glass without the slightest curiosity. I was relieved. I was always braced for the automatic surprise to that statement, the judging people did of me, their revision of everything they thought they knew about me before, like knowing that one fact put me as an individual into context. He hadn't done that and I was glad. In all the years he'd been away, there were some things that hadn't changed. People always felt they could trust him. That had always been his gift.

'So is that why you came?'

He looked up, eyes narrowed, brow furrowed. I had lost him.

'Because of Mavis.'

He smiled sadly, and shook his head.

'We never talked,' he said. 'About you mum and all that.'

Though I knew we would talk about her, that it was inevitable she would come up, I panicked, standing up even though I hadn't finished eating, reaching for his plate, scraping the untouched contents on to mine, gathering together the cutlery and placing it on top.

'She's been dead for years. It's over,' I said.

'Is it?' he asked, then looked away, down at the floor, wriggling his toes as he spoke, alternate feet tapping the floor like the hands of a drummer sounding a beat. My heart began to pound, the wine spun inside my head and from nowhere nausea rose inside my stomach like a buoy.

'Berris came to look for me,' he said, then added, 'He's out.'

I did the washing-up. Then wiped down the cupboards and the worktop. I cleaned the cooker, emptied the bin, then swept and mopped the kitchen floor.

Lemon was in the living room. Smoking. I could smell it. It was something I had forgotten, the smoking. Him and Berris had both smoked back then and burned incense over it. Benson & Hedges and the occasional spliff. My mother had provided the incense. She had never been a smoker herself. The only other man she'd ever lived with was my father and he hadn't smoked either. Yet, like everything else, she accepted it without a murmur, throwing the windows wide, pinning the curtains back, waving the joss stick around in circles. I closed my eyes and for a second I saw her: small and slim and perfect, arms raised, dancing.

He's out.

He had served fourteen years of a life sentence, a fixed-term punishment with rules and walls that had now ended, and I envied him. Able to begin his life anew, his crime atoned for in full. Blamed and punished, he had served his time, then been freed. Free to visit Lemon so the two of them could talk. Now Lemon was here to talk to me. I inhaled deeply, leaning against the wall, eyes closed, willing myself to calm down, unable to stop the question echoing inside my head: how much did Lemon already know?

I took a saucer from the cupboard and carried it back into the living room. He'd been using his hand, his cupped palm, to flick the ash into.

'I don't have an ashtray. I don't smoke,' I said, handing him the saucer.

He was sitting in the middle of the settee. I moved to the wicker chair opposite and sat there, watching him, waiting for him to speak. He held the cigarette pinched between forefinger and thumb, took a long, slow drag and opened his mouth to allow some of the smoke to curl lazily upward into his nostrils, before finally drawing it down into his lungs. As he blew out, his rounded lips shaped the smoke into rings and he pulsed them out, one after the next, till the smoke was gone.

The nausea from earlier was still there, like my mother was being exhumed, and in the silence it was getting worse. I was desperate to know what he knew, yet at the same time petri-fied he would blurt it out before I was ready. It was that fear which drove me to speak first, to start the conversation from the outside edge, the farthest point away from the core that I could find.

'So how'd he look?'

'He's changed.'

I raised my eyebrows, looked up at the ceiling and pursed my lips to contain a snort.

'Don't believe it if you want, but it's true.'

'I've heard that before...'

'He's not the only one.'

I felt the familiar stirring of anger, and I embraced it. Had he expected to find me the same after all this time, after all that had happened? 'I've grown up,' I said. He didn't respond. Instead he concentrated on putting the cigarette out. 'So what did he want?'

'To say thanks for me being his friend.'

'How touching.'

'And he asked after you.'

'Ahh...sweet.'

YVVETTE EDWARDS

'And to say sorry.'

'Fuck him!'

Lemon raised his eyebrows. His was the old-school generation. It was all right for them to *rass claat* and *pussy claat*
and *bomba claat*, but children were expected to be seen and
not heard. Even though I was an adult in my own right, I was
still a clear generation younger than him. He considered my
swearing disrespectful.

'It's a bit late for apologies,' I said.

'It's never too late to try and undo the wrong a man's
done.'

'That's rubbish and I don't want to hear it! She's dead.'

'I take it you're without sin?'

Though there was no suggestion of sarcasm in his tone,
I felt myself struggling to read between the lines, trying hard
to gauge what he knew; flailing. 'I don't need any belated
apologies from him. Or lectures from *you* on sin.'

'That's not why I came.'

'So why did you come? What is it you want?'

He looked away from me, down at the floor. Now it felt
like I was pressuring him, but it was already too late for me
to stop.

'He cried, didn't he? I bet he bawled his eyes out. He was
always good at that.'

'He wasn't the only one.'

'And you listened and nodded and said, "I forgive you"?'

He didn't answer. Nor did he look at me.

This time I made no effort to hold the snort back. 'I need a
drink,' I said.

I went back into the kitchen, took another glass from the cupboard and filled it with more wine I did not want. My heart was pounding inside my chest, my throat dry; the hatred I had spent so many years suppressing was back with a thud as hard-hitting as a train. All the walls, the structure, the neatness of my life, and he'd smashed through them with two words casually tossed.

He's out.

I left the wine untouched and stormed back inside the living room.

'You know what, I don't want you here,' I said. 'You'd better go.'

And he said, 'Not yet.'

'You just don't get it, do you? I don't care that she's dead!'

He didn't even glance my way, merely shrugged. 'And me? I never gave a damn that she live.'

I had been running for the last four years. It had come upon me one day, a few weeks after Red had left me. I hadn't worked since I was six months pregnant. That probably had a lot to do with it, because when I was working I was *feeling*. Outside of the cold room, I felt nothing. That particular day, I had finished repainting my bedroom white. It had been cream when I'd started, cream and burgundy, because Red hated white. He said it was sterile, that he wanted to be comfortable kicking off his boots in the bedroom, to feel cosy and warm. Once he had gone, I had no further need for compromise, so I changed it.

I had thought that when it was finished I would feel something; satisfaction or pleasure, even uncertainty or dislike, *anything*, but I didn't. The job was finished, that was all. It was done. I washed the brushes, cleaned out the bathtub, packed the cans away into the garden shed and went upstairs to look at my handiwork again. My relationship had ended and Red had taken my son. My life was my own and I could do anything I wanted, yet I felt nothing. As I stood staring at the walls, searching inside myself for some kind of emotional response, the nothingness suddenly welled up inside me, like a physical mass, so vast and empty and infinite I was terrified. The very first time I went running, it was from that terror, from the possibility of being sucked down into emptiness for ever, and as I ran I discovered I *was* able to feel; pressure in my lungs, pain in my legs, my skin perspiring, the pounding of my heart.

My routine was erratic, I ran when I felt like it, usually five or six times a month. So was my style. It was nothing like that of the runners I grew accustomed to seeing, the ones who regulated themselves, jogged two or three times a week, who did a warm-up first and stretching exercises afterwards, the people for whom the activity was a hobby. I ran like my life depended on it, as fast and as hard as I could. Sometimes, passers-by would look beyond me as I ran towards them, with fear in their eyes, trying to see who or what was pursuing me, trying to work out whether they should be running too. As long as I was feeling, I didn't care.

But that night, with Lemon smoking in the living room, my mother dancing in the kitchen and Berris out, it felt like my circuits were overloaded. I found myself feeling too much at once to be able to process any of it, and the only thing I could think to do was run.

I left him sitting on the settee, pulled on jogging bottoms and trainers and took off. The moment I closed the garden gate behind me, my feet began pummelling the pavement and I found myself headed towards Hackney Downs in a sprint.

I turned right at the park, intending to follow its perimeter, and raced along Downs Park Road, with the park on my left and the Pembury housing estate on my right. The evening was as dark as night, the weather drizzling again and windy. Icy cold.

I felt it.

Felt the breath in my throat like pure eucalyptus, the liquid droplets in the air against my face and neck, my calf muscles screaming. I focused with all my might on the things I could physically feel, hoping to cork the memories Lemon had stirred up about a time I had no desire to remember, and it worked for about twenty minutes, till I had run more than halfway around Hackney Downs. Defeat came in the form of a piece of paper, a mere scrap, tossed on a wind to land against my hand with a wet slap. I flicked it off immediately and increased my speed, but it was already too late. Suddenly it was impossible not to think of her, my mother, and the choices she had made, to wonder how any woman could ever be so pathetic, could become so weak and passive that she would not raise her own hand to defend herself, even in the final moments when she must have known that if she didn't she would surely die.

*

15

Too beautiful. Everyone said she was and it was true. With baby-wide eyes and long thick lashes in a perpetual flirt-flutter, and purple-blush lips that parted in a half-moon over even ivory teeth, and high colour so flawless it was as if she had been slow-dipped in a vat of chestnut gloss, lowered and turned and raised by a patient doll-maker, his hands clenched tight around the ebony mass of her kink-free coolie hair – my mother had been a beauty.

She was the only child of a poor, uneducated Montserratian land worker and his semi-literate wife. In an era when it was normal for Caribbean migrants to leave their children behind with relatives as they headed out to the Motherland to make their fortune, with the wild card Hope flapping hard against the ribcage, my grandparents took their daughter with them. Between the three of them, they bore a single cardboard grip, and most of what was inside it belonged to her. Everything I know about them I learned from her, and the sum of everything she said was that they could not have worshipped God himself more than they worshipped the ground she walked on. Full stop.

She was too beautiful to make her own way to and from school at a time when every other child in the country was doing it, or to cook or clean or shop or carry, or even to amass a single useful life skill. So when she was seventeen and my grandparents died, it is hard to imagine what would have become of her were it not for the benevolence of my grandfather's friend Mr Jackson.

Mr Jackson was fifty-three when he took her in. *Fifty-three.* Fair with the tenants who rented the rooms in his house, he was a shrewd Jamaican migrant who had somehow landed soundly on his rickety old legs. He was gaunt from the diabetes that would eventually finish him off for good, and though half blind from glaucoma he still had vision enough to see that my mother was too beautiful to weep broken-hearted, forlorn in her single bed, *alone*.

Within a year, they were married and she was rescued. It was Mr Jackson who taught her how to be a woman, how to pick good vegetables, the best pieces of meat to buy, how to cut chicken, gut fish, where to shop for everything you needed to make a jug of Guinness Punch.

He took her shopping. Bought her jewellery and underwear, dresses and jackets and shoes that she chopped and changed like a child with a dressing-up box and nothing to do but play. She was too beautiful for anything but the very best and that was all she had because Mr Jackson doted on her.

My mother talked about herself all the time, told me everything about her life as though she were telling fairy tales, talking while she played with my hair or I played with hers, whispering in my ear as she tucked me into bed at night, or on cold nights in her bed as I snuggled into her warmth. About her and my father, how they had been married nearly three years before conceiving me, how by then he'd lost all hope of ever fathering a child. When my mother told him she was expecting, he was both overjoyed and convinced I would be a boy. It was Mr Jackson who called me the name they went on to enter into the *Register of Births and Deaths*, as if it were a real name they had given a lot of thought to, a normal name, borne of love. He said it suited me, not just a girl, but one who, instead of looking like his wife, resembled *him*; small and dark and demanding, too greedy for my mother to keep on the breast, too noisy for my father to want in their bedroom. After I arrived, he gave up the tenants and bought the house I still lived in, with a bedroom for them, one for me, and a third just in case, then kept me and my mother locked up tight inside it. Away from church and work and parties and shebeens and hard-assed younger men and life.

She whiled away a few more years till Mr Jackson died, cheating me of all memory of him bar one: me sitting on the bed beside him, rapt, listening as he told me a story. What it was about, I do not know. I can barely see him in the memory or recall any detail of the room. The most vivid thing I remember was my excitement, the sheer thrill I felt listening as he spoke. I must have been about three. By the time I was four he was gone.

I had completed a full circuit of the park and was too shattered to run the rest of the way home, so I power-walked, on shaking legs, past the estate and the garages, past the houses and gardens of normal families, back to where I knew Lemon waited. I opened the garden gate and, at the front door, felt my left calf beginning to cramp, so stopped and stretched it, trying to stave off the worst of the pains.

The one thing my mother always said about Mr Jackson was that he was a decent man, that he took proper care of things, including this mortgage-free house that he left to her, which she then left to me when I was sixteen and she was dead. Decent enough to ask no more of her than that she occupy it and dedicate her life to raising me, forsaking all other men till I had grown up. 'Grown up' she interpreted to mean when I was sixteen. It was ironic that I actually *had* grown up then. Sixteen and overnight my childhood was over.

Maybe everything that happened was Mr Jackson's fault. Had he married someone his own age, he might not have been so obsessed with the idea of other men sleeping with his wife after he was gone. Maybe had she had the chance to live in the real world, she would have picked up a few strategies to stop it killing her. Or maybe if I'd been given a name like Peace, it would have been a self-fulfilling prophecy of a different kind.

But I was making excuses and I knew it. The fact was, I had done what I had done. Made up my own mind and committed myself to a course of action. My blame was my blame and my blame alone. I opened the front door and entered the house, then slammed it shut behind me, as if in doing so it was possible to lock a world's worth of excuses outside it.

Inside the shower cubicle I scrubbed. Scrubbed my arms and legs, my neck, stomach and breasts. The scent of bergamot shower gel had begun to subside, and my skin reddened in response to what had become an abrasive rub till, eventually, it began to sting. I stopped scrubbing then, standing beneath the coursing water till the hot water went warm, then tepid, then cool, and the sting became a tingle and goosebumps swelled. I withstood the cold till I could bear it no longer, before finally turning the water off.

I slid open the glass door, reaching for the white thick-pile bath towel, becoming gentler with my aching body, slowly patting it dry. With the towel wrapped around me, I unlocked the bathroom door and stepped out on to the landing, headed towards my bedroom. As I passed my mother's room, the door was slightly ajar. I paused outside it, listening to the silence within before slowly pushing it open and entering.

Inside her room there was a cupboard full of coats. The cupboard had been built into the alcove and was probably as old as the house itself. I went over and creaked open the door. The coats were suspended inside it on large wooden hangers, each one an expensive and beautiful work of fine tailoring, protected individually by transparent dustcovers. I ran my fingers across the tops of the hangers lightly before settling on one, which I then withdrew.

Carefully I raised the cover and examined the coat underneath. It was made from nubuck suede, a long, ankle-length, close-fitting garment, grey-blue like cloudy sky, with diagonal slit pockets lined in cobalt-coloured silk.

A gift.

A small tug, a dulled pop, the button was forced through the hole and the coat was off the hanger. I pushed my arms into the sleeves and stepped out of the towel nest around my feet. Deeply, eyes closed, I inhaled the stale scent of years infused with leather. A surreal dizziness mushroomed inside my head and I swayed slightly, then surfed the remainder of its wave.

I did up every button. My body was a little fuller than hers and the coat moulded my naked shape as perfectly as a second skin.

I walked to the mirror where I examined myself, turning this way and that, moving my legs to emphasize the long slits at the buttonless bottom of the front and the vented back. I studied my reflection side on, unhappy. I sat on the stool before the dressing table, pulled my damp hair up into a ponytail, picked up her brush and a powder foundation, and started dusting it on.

This was the one thing she had taught me to do well, applying make-up with such proficiency I could even make the dead look like they were dozing. She had let me brush her powder on, allowed me to practise coating her long lashes in sooty mascara, her full lips in glossy plums, while she sat hardly blinking, still as a doll. She had preferred Max Factor, and as I used up the items on her dressing table I replaced them with the same, though for my workbag I chose an assortment of brands that were just as effective on brown skins.

Apart from the foundations, her other cosmetics suited my colour as much as they had hers. I picked a red-bronze rouge, a golden eyeshadow, and painted my lips a metallic mocha brown. Finished, I examined my reflection again, still dissatisfied, knowing the picture was incomplete. I pulled my hair out of the ponytail, pushed my fingertips beneath the surface, down to the scalp, and tousled it from the roots to create more body. I pulled the sides and back up, leaving the top mussy and wild, and held the glamorous style in place with one hand.

I tilted my head slightly, exposing more of my neck, and mirrored in the glass I saw Lemon, just inside the bedroom door, and I froze, watching him watching me. He looked as shocked as if he had seen a ghost. My attention returned to my reflection where I expected to see myself posing, but instead, after all the years she'd been dead, I found myself face to face with my mother.

I gasped and stood up too quickly, knocking the stool over behind me, then tripping on it as I stepped back, releasing my hair and stumbling. I might have fallen but for Lemon who was inside the room now, close enough behind me that I could feel his heat. He grabbed my arm and held it firmly, steadying me. I turned around to ask whether he'd seen what I had, but when I looked at him, his eyes were as hotly fired as a kiln, and everything I had to say lodged as thickly inside my throat as grief.

'She was beautiful,' he said, slowly raising his hands and smoothing the sides of my hair, cocking his head as if to get a better angle for the view, smiling, but not at me, at something he saw in the distance. Someone. 'I never seen anyone as beautiful in my life.'

He held my head between his hands like a ball, moving only his thumbs, stroking my eyebrows from thick end to thin with a slow, hypnotic repetition.

'They have a rock down by Carr's Bay back home. Huge. 'Bout the size of a small house, off the beach, in the water, with some small rocks leading up to it, good size but small-looking alongside the big one; like a bridge. When you on top of the big one, it's like you out to sea. Most times the sea down there was rough, with big waves – if you was in the water could knock a man down clean.

'Don't exactly know how to describe it, when I used to climb out there and sit down, how I felt, 'cept "good". She was the only person to ever make me have that feeling on dry land. Just to look at her. That was all. Just to see.'

Leisurely, he ran his palms down my neck on both sides, thumbs around the front – if he changed mood they could strangle me – and out, across my shoulders, before returning to my neck. Then his hands moved downwards, over the front of the coat, tracing the swell of my breasts beneath the coat's peach-skin nap. I stepped back.

'No,' I said.

It was his turn to step back. He sat down on the edge of the bed and looked around the room, the floor, the walls, everywhere but at me.

'She wore that coat that night,' he said.

'I know.'

'She was looking out for him the whole night and I was looking at her, feeling like I was on the rock, thinking what a fool he was, knowing he was still but a small fool compared to me, the Fool King.'

So much time had passed since then, almost a decade and a half, yet the details were all there, as vivid as if everything had happened only yesterday.

'He was so angry,' I said.

Lemon nodded. 'I knew he would be.'

'I couldn't talk to him,' but even as I said the words I knew that was not the truth of it. I had not spoken when I should have done, and then when I did, I had lied.

'He woulda never listen. Not them times. Kinda man he was then.'

I pushed hard and the words tumbled out of my mouth. 'I didn't think about her; just me.'

'You was young. You was scared.'

It was the compassion in his voice that made me bristle, the understanding. 'How the hell would you know? You weren't there!'

'You're right,' he said. 'I wasn't.'

'No one was! So don't you ever try and tell me how I felt because I am the only person who knows.'

I turned my back to him and started unbuttoning the coat. Though my hands were shaking, I was impatient to be done. I knew now that he did not know. He was making excuses for the little he thought I was responsible for and he could not have done that if he had even the slightest inkling of the truth. But instead of relief, I felt disappointment. I had been let down. Again.

'We need to talk,' Lemon said. 'There's things I need to tell you. About me. What I done.'

'Save it for *Trisha*!' I answered, securing the towel around my body before taking the coat off. I retrieved the hanger from the bed and fed the coat back on to it, pulling down the cover, putting it back into its space inside the cupboard. 'She's got time and sympathy. Have you not noticed I'm a bit lacking on the touchy-feely front?'

'Yes,' he said, 'I have.'

Another day, different circumstances, and the sincerity of his voice to my rhetorical question might have made me smile. I had hoped he had known and had still come anyway.

It had to be him. He had always been the only person who might understand; my only hope.

'You can sleep in here,' I said. His eyes moved around the room, with its flower-patterned walls and old-fashioned furnishings in sharp contrast to the other rooms in the house. I'd had to replace the original carpet because the stains had been impossible to remove. Otherwise, her bedroom had been as carefully preserved as a crypt. 'Unless you're scared of jumbies?'

He gave a single nod and suddenly I was exhausted.

'My son's coming in the morning,' I said. 'You're gonna have to give me space. I can't do that and...this. It's too much.'

He nodded again.

'My son comes first,' I said and felt a blush rising. I wondered why I had added those words and whether he had seen through them. 'I'll see you in the morning,' I said, and left.

2

They arrived at ten on the dot, punctual as ever. Red rang the doorbell once and Ben banged the flap of the letter box over and over again non-stop, up until the actual moment I opened the front door. To hear him you would have thought there was some kind of emergency, that it was urgent he get inside, that maybe having had no contact with me since his last visit a fortnight ago, he was desperate to see me again. Yet the instant I opened the door he became shy, twirling one finger round and round inside his mouth, leaning against Red, the other hand wrapped around his father's long leg as though it were a life-support system. Ben looked down at the floor, stealing glances at me with those huge eyes and thick dark lashes he'd inherited from my mother. Red nudged him with his knee.

'Aren't you going to say hello to your mum?'

Without taking the finger out he said, 'Hello, Jinx.'

I bent down and picked him up, cuddling him clumsily, trying to ignore his passive resistance as I kissed him yet irritated by it;

hardly one step through the door and he was already being difficult. He was clean, shiny as a new chestnut, and I inhaled deeply the smell of the cocoa butter on his skin and the coconut oil rubbed into his hair, sweet and at the same time cloying.

'Hello, little man,' I said and kissed his cheek.

'Urgh.' He wiped the kiss off. 'I hate lipstick.'

I laughed as if he were joking and kissed him again. 'You'll love it when you're older.'

'When I'm older,' he asked, 'will you be dead?'

Though there was nothing in his tone but interest, the question floored me completely. Stunned, I opened my mouth to reply, but could think of nothing to say.

'The mum of one of the kids in Ben's class is dead,' Red said, his tone neutral. 'Ever since he found out, he's been obsessed.'

'Will you?' Ben pressed.

'Mummy will die when she's old,' his father answered, and I had to bite my tongue, because I knew better than anyone that death did not pre-book appointments decades in advance. Its approach was random, based on whimsy, often violent. I came from a line of women who bore a single child and were dead before its eighteenth birthday. 'You've got nothing to worry about,' Red said.

I turned and carried Ben into the living room, giving Red an eyeful of my bared legs. I had been up for hours after sleeping badly, head full, muscles aching. My legs were freshly shaved and creamed from the heel up to the high hemline of the fitted black skirt I had worn for his benefit, so short that it was a wonder it covered the icebox he believed hummed between my legs. I heard the squeaky friction of his trainer soles against the flooring as he followed me in.

'So how *is* school?' I asked my son. He would be five next month, had started school last week. It was incredible to me that his nursery days were at an end when I was still getting over his birth. He was growing up fast, getting heavy. I put him down.

'Okay,' he said, twisting and bending his head and shoulders and hips in a writhe.

I looked up at Red. Even in my heels he was still a clear foot taller than me. Smelling of shower gel and aftershave and skin cream freshly applied. He was dressed casually in a tracksuit, hands tucked deep inside the pockets of his trousers. His body language was, as always, relaxed. It was one of the first things that had attracted me to him, the perfect proportions of his body, the grace in his movements, the flawless lines.

We had met over his father's corpse after he had died from a stroke, his face contorted. I had spent the day working on him: inserting eye caps to close his eyes, small pieces of foam in his cheeks to recreate symmetry, suturing his upper and lower jaws to bring his lips together naturally, then using a mouth-former to fix them in a position inclined towards a smile. I had shaved him and trimmed his hair, and applied a layer of make-up that was virtually imperceptible but restored his colour and gave his cheeks a healthy flush.

I had almost finished dressing him when Red returned to view him in his casket. Having been the person who had discovered the body, he'd had to brace himself hard against seeing his father again to say goodbye. When he saw what I had done, he was speechless, just stood there staring down at his father for the longest time, then finally cried. Days later, he told me he had been too horrified to cry when he had found his father. The tears he'd shed in the parlour had been sheer relief. Laid out, his father not only looked dapper, but also completely at peace.

I had been attracted to Red straight away. Grief-stricken, with his height and grace and raw vulnerability, to me he was irresistible. It was ironic that the same things I'd been attracted to, now made me feel mocked.

'Is he settling down okay?' I asked.

'Yeah. Fine. You should've phoned him. He would've told you himself.' His tone was even for Ben's benefit. 'School was good.' His voice became gentler as he stepped over to stand beside Ben, rubbing his enormous hand over the small boy's skiffled head. This was where he always won, hands down. He was a good dad. Naturally good.

'You were *so* grown up, weren't you? Come on, gimmee a hug. I've got to go.'

'I wanna come with you,' Ben's voice was tiny. He glanced up at me as though he would have preferred it if I wasn't listening.

'Come on, don't start that again. We've talked about this, haven't we? Your mum *wants* to spend time with you...' – he threw an angry glance at me – '...and I'll be back to get you tomorrow.'

'But I'm not feeling well. My tummy hurts. Feel my head.'

Red put his hand on Ben's head. 'You're not hot. You'll be fine.'

'I wanna come with you, *please*, Daddy...'

He stooped to hug his son tight, to kiss him, and I watched Ben's desperate response, claw-cuddling, kissing *him* back, trying to lift his legs from the floor to force Red into picking him up.

'Come on,' I said, going over and lifting Ben up myself. 'Your dad has to go. He has things to do.' I imagined they involved another woman, on her back, legs wide, wet. 'We're gonna have fun.' My smile felt tight.

Ben stopped struggling, resigning himself to my hip and his staying. His lower lip trembled.

'You've got my number. Any problems, ring,' Red said. 'I'll pick him up tomorrow about four.'

'Fine,' I answered.

A moment later I heard the metallic click of the front door as it closed behind him and, simultaneously, Ben began to cry.

He didn't want to eat or drink or watch TV or play. He followed me around like a dog, not speaking or interacting, with a wretched expression on his face as if his small shoulders bore the weight of the world in grief.

On my part I made small talk, trying to engage him in a conversation of some kind: *How's school? Do you have many friends? Are they nice? Would you like me to make you something to eat? Please tell me, is your mouth going to stay like that for the rest of the day?* Often his reply was a single word consisting of just the one syllable. Occasionally it was not even that, just a nod or a shake of the head. It was as exhausting trying to get a conversation going as giving birth itself. He had only been with me an hour when I found myself working out that it would be twenty-nine hours more before his dad came back to collect him.

So far, Lemon had slept through everything. There had been no sounds from upstairs, no indication he planned to get out of bed at any time today, but the fact he was here, the things he had stirred, the *feelings*, put me under more pressure than usual, which I hadn't realized was even possible. Since Lemon had arrived, I'd found myself engaged on some kind of voyage of discovery. The failure of my relationship with Ben was something I simply accepted. I had no friends to speak of, there was no family to visit on my side, there were no observers. But with Lemon here, after my silly boast about Ben's needs being my top priority, I felt ashamed, as though for the first time I was on the outside of our relationship looking in, trying to gauge how it might appear to someone else, and from that perspective, things looked pretty grim indeed.

'I know,' I said, 'let's go out and do something.'

Though I wanted to change into something less dressy and maybe head for the park, I was reluctant to go back upstairs. I didn't want to wake Lemon just yet, or to introduce him to Ben while he was looking so unhappy, accusing me with his expression alone of being the world's worst mum.

So I decided to do something with him I didn't need to change for, and also that he would enjoy. Something nice together, something different, something fun.

'You've never been to the cinema before, have you?' I asked.

He shook his head.

'In that case, you'd better hurry and put your coat on. You're in for a real treat.'

We drove to the Rio on Kingsland High Street where, luckily, some kids' film or other was just starting, so we quickly bought popcorn and Coke and sweets, then hurried into the cinema before we had missed too much of the beginning to be able to follow the storyline.

He wanted to sit in the very front row and as I was determined not to spoil the occasion, I conceded. There, he faffed and fiddled, picking up his drink every fifteen seconds for a sip, putting it back down, then somehow finding yet more reasons to continue fidgeting. He stared around behind him regularly, as though the people sitting there were more interesting than what was on the screen in front of us, and asked a hundred questions about what was going on in the film, every one of which, had he been paying proper attention, he would have known the answers to himself. Finally, after about twenty minutes, he needed to go to the toilet.

'What, *now*?' I asked.

'Yessss,' he moaned, 'I can't hold it.'

We had to leave our seats, disturbing everyone else in the process, and crossed the foyer with me trying to explain that he shouldn't wait till the last minute to ask for the toilet, but should mention it in good time so it was not an actual emergency to get him there. As I spoke he was doing what looked like some kind of monkey dance, legs bowed wide, one hand cupped over his crotch, index finger and thumb in a pinch, as if he was holding the end of an inflated balloon and was trying to stop the air inside from escaping.

At the women's toilets I opened the door and stood waiting for him to enter.

'What's the matter?'

'I don't go in the girls' toilets,' he said, 'I go in the boys'.'

'We're not going into the men's,' I said.

'My daddy doesn't take me in the girls'.'

'I'm not your dad. I'm your mum and I'm not allowed in the men's toilets. We don't have a choice.'

'I can go on my own.'

'No you can't.'

He began to cry. 'I'm a boy,' he said.

'It's just a toilet, Ben!'

'But I go in the boys' toilets with Daddy.'

'Well, he's not here so you can't,' I said.

He didn't move, so I picked him up, ignoring the tears. Then he wriggled and howled as I carried him in, wrestled him into a cubical and undid his trousers. After he had emptied his bladder there was wee all around the seat and on the floor. There was even a little spray on the walls. I cleared up, then coerced him over to the sink so we could both wash our hands.

Outside in the foyer I had to calm him down because he was making too much noise for us to go back into the cinema. Even then, when we went back inside and took our seats, he was still sniffing, but mercifully subdued and quiet enough for us to be able to carry on watching what remained of the film. But just as I had begun to relax and think it might yet all come good still, he began to cry again.

'What is it?' I asked.

He shook his head.

'Shush! People are trying to watch the film. What on earth are you crying for now?'

His response was to cry yet louder. I stood up.

'Come on,' I said, but he shook his head. Other people in the cinema had had enough of us and were making their feelings known. I had no choice but to lift him up, put him on my hip and carry the reluctant boy out. As I put him down in the foyer, I felt the wetness of my skirt against my hip, then saw the telltale patch on the crotch of his pants.

'I can't believe you've wet yourself,' I said. 'This is bloody ridiculous!'

'I'm sorry, Jinx,' he said, and to his credit he did actually look as though he felt bad. But I was too far gone to be able to respond to his belated remorse.

'Don't give me that!' I shouted. 'I *know* you did it on purpose!'

Ben didn't speak to me on the drive home. He stared out of the passenger window all the way so that even when I could bring myself to glance at him from time to time, there was nothing for me to see but the back of his head.

I was angry, not just with him, and the wet pants, and the whole disaster of the trip, but with the entire and complete fiasco of our relationship. I felt like I was always a hair's breadth away from losing it with him, like I was out of control, like the capacity to hate and hurt was bigger inside me than any capacity to nurture. Instead of loving him, I was messing up his head. He would grow up to be the thing I wanted least for my son: to be like me. But though this was crystal clear, I did not know how to change it. It felt like something needed to happen inside me. But I was not a magician. There was no quick-fix abracadabra available to change me into anybody else.

At the traffic lights by the junction of Amhurst Road and Shacklewell Lane, in a car that pulled up alongside me while we idled waiting for amber, there was a woman with two young kids in the back, and she was pulling faces in the mirror and laughing with her offspring, and they were happy back. Though I couldn't hear a word of the exchange between them, it was not necessary. It was so obvious, her pleasure in them, in being with them; she was beaming. Her car was full of happy family sounds that I could only imagine. And I was jealous. I wanted what she had for myself.

My fortnightly sessions with Ben were a chore, a series of exasperations that drove me to despair. They always made me feel like I was on a treadmill pounding away without making the slightest iota of progress. And I hated it. Hated it all, the false hope, the wasted energy, the inevitability of failure it presented every time.

He could not get out of the car fast enough when I pulled up outside my house. Still tangled up inside the seat belt, stumbling in his haste, he leapt for freedom the moment I turned the ignition off. Then he ran up the garden path. By the time

I caught up with him he had ripped three or four heads off the crocuses planted along the thin bed that ran the length of the path from the gate to the front door.

'Ben, don't do that please,' I said as he started tearing off another. Ignoring me, he yanked it off anyway, adding it to the collection in his other hand.

'Will you bloody stop!' I said.

When he looked at me, those enormous eyes were filled with tears. He held out his hand. His voice was tiny. 'These are for you,' he said.

And I looked at the small, fresh, squashed bouquet held out to me, and for a second I could have taken his gift and smiled, then cuddled and whispered to my son, *Forgive me. I love you.*

But the words that came out of my mouth instead were: 'Great! Why don't you kill every single flower you can see?' And I looked away, into my handbag, searching for the keys as he opened his hand and let them fall, then rubbed his palms together to dry them.

I opened the front door and held it wide for him to enter, following him inside and closing it behind me with a deep sigh. He walked into the living room, stopped, gasped, then looked at me. I passed him. Inside the room, Lemon was sitting on the settee where he had been watching TV. He was wearing his trousers and a string vest, with the maroon dressing gown slung casually over the lot. He looked comfortable. *Too* comfortable.

'I forgot to say, Ben, I've got a friend staying with me.'

'Is he your boyfriend?' Ben asked.

'No, he's...' – *my man friend* is what came to mind – '...a family friend. Lemon, this is Ben.'

'Howdy,' Lemon said to Ben, slowly scratching his head with a single forefinger.

'Hello, Uncle Lemon,' Ben replied in the monotone of a child answering the class register, and I wondered who had taught him that old-fashioned rule, to call adults 'Uncle' or 'Auntie' out of respect, and whether he had begun that lesson by calling some woman 'Auntie' in his father's home.

Lemon held his hand out and Ben took and shook it. Then he started to laugh.

'Hey! Who give you joke?' Lemon asked.

'Lemon's a funny name.'

'That's for sure.'

'I don't like lemons. When I lick them my eyes go squeezy squeezy.'

'Next time, dip it in sugar first. Then taste.'

'Is that how *you* eat them?'

'Always.'

'Lemon likes lemons,' Ben said and laughed again.

Lemon looked at me. 'I see there's more than one comedian in the family,' he said.

Though I could not think of a single joke I had cracked with Lemon, I gave him a tight smile and answered, 'So it seems.'

Ben walked over to the settee and was about to sit down. 'Come on, Ben. You need to come upstairs with me so I can change you.'

'Are you going now?' Ben asked.

'Not as far as I know,' Lemon said. 'I'll be right hereso when you come back.'

Then, as if he had just been given the best news he had heard in a long, long time, like maybe his team had just scored the goal that would assure them the cup, Ben punched the air and grinned.

'Yeah!' he said.

If Lemon had been wearing a skirt, Ben would have been up underneath it. He followed Lemon around like he was a beloved relative who after having been missing for years and presumed dead, had miraculously been found alive and restored to the bosom of his family.

The two of them played with their lunch, chicken nuggets, ketchup and chips – the only meal Ben was guaranteed to eat a bit of – as if they were both five-year-olds. Lemon laughed his head off at everything Ben said and, inspired by this, Ben hardly paused between words for breath.

I listened as he told Lemon about Max in his class whose front tooth came out when he bit into the apple in his packed lunch. There were anecdotes about his Power Ranger toys, Thomas the Tank Engine, and Shaggy's exploits in *Scooby-Doo*. He talked about his new teacher, Mrs Smith, and how impressed she was with his reading. Lemon gave him a piece of paper and a pen and Ben proved once and for all that he could write his name himself without any help from anyone.

I was in shock. I had never heard my son like this before. I had simply thought he was a morose child, because morose was how he always was when he was with me. I had never seen this side of him, this laughing chattiness, the non-stop outpouring of everything going on in his life, the pleasure he took from his accomplishments, such as they were. And I felt hurt. Really hurt. Wounded to the core just listening to how natural and happy he could be with a virtual stranger, when I had been trying for nearly five years to have a relationship with him and had come up against brick after brick after brick.

He made me feel how he had made me feel when he was a baby. Like no matter what I did or how much time I put in or how hard I tried, anyone could walk into his life and they were immediately more important than I was. Like I did not matter. My existence meant nothing. And all the while, as I sat on the periphery of their conversation, I could feel myself getting angrier and angrier, and though I tried to rationalize my way out of it, I just couldn't stop myself.

So I left them to finish lunch together and I did more cleaning. Upstairs, I entered the smallest room of the house, Ben's. I had painted this room while I was pregnant, a pale yellow that had darkened over the years to a colour similar to the skin on a bowl of cold custard. I had chosen yellow because it was a perfect colour for a girl's room, and neutral enough in case the baby had been a boy. It contained a single bed covered in a yellow quilt, which ran the length of one wall, a small wardrobe and a tiny desk with drawers below. On top of the desk was Ben's bag for overnighting, his dirty clothes folded neatly beside it. A large car was parked in one corner, left behind when Red had left four years ago, too cumbersome to carry with them at the time, then just forgotten.

Since then, Ben had grown so much he could no longer fit inside it.

To be honest, there was nothing inside the room to clean. This was a space that merely needed the occasional airing. I had left my son downstairs and gone upstairs into his empty bedroom to connect with him. It was ridiculous, but true. I sat down on the bed and held my head in my hands. For the umpteenth time, I wished with all my might that things between me and my son were different, but they had been this way for ever.

I never wanted a boy. All the way through my pregnancy it was a daughter I prayed for. A living doll to dress up and cherish, who I could sing to and fuss over and love with abandon. Then along came Ben, after a difficult birth; two days' hard labour, episiotomy, forceps and suction cup, the boy had to be dragged from my body in a screeching, splitting, bloody gush, huge dark balls and willy in disproportion to the rest of his body.

Red was over the moon. As ecstatic as my father might have been had I been born a boy. He returned to the maternity suite that evening grinning and bearing a blue-ribboned bouquet of long-stemmed white lilies – my mother's favourite; flowers that would have been perfect for her grave.

But Ben wasn't fooled by any of this. For the first day he didn't feed, just lay there watching me, an unhappy frown creasing his dry, scaly brow, disapproving even then, as though he knew the numb, dumb shock I was going through was as much to do with him as the experience he had put me through, like he was already aware he couldn't count on me.

He had an air of resignation about him, acknowledging me as his biological mother and also, his certainty that I would eventually let him down. I wondered if he wanted to die.

The second day, as if some reasoning had altered the course of his mind, he started to cry, a shrill, angry catcall to feed, mouth opened wide to be filled with the breast and when I gave it to him he clamped down on it like a vice, not just drinking milk but consuming *me*, like some starved pygmy cannibal, sucking so hard I could have stood up and let go of him and he would have swung like a pit bull, suspended in mid-air by the sheer power of his jaws and the vacuum forcing my nipple deep down his throat.

Within days my tender flesh was reduced to raw, weeping meat and he had to go on the bottle. I harboured hopes then that with my body back I might begin the process of recovering, but no. If it wasn't hunger or nappy rash it was colic, night and day, unsettled and unhappy, he cried and cried and cried, calming down only in his father's arms, sleeping only on his father's chest, rejecting me so completely the only thing I felt was resentment.

That was when the advice started, from the man able to get away for ten hours every day and have a break from the relentless whining: how to hold him, how to feed him, how to wind him, not to shake him, and in between regularly reminding me that the six weeks of abstinence the midwife recommended had long passed. That was when I bought the costume, when I realized he was thinking about sex while I was thinking about ways to kill myself, when I knew without doubt we had run out of middle ground.

Having Ben changed me into something I had no idea how to be: a mother. I had expected it to come naturally, but for me it didn't. And the fact that parenthood came so easily to Red made it worse. He stepped into the role of father as if his whole life had been leading to it, as if it were the culmination of everything he was and had ever wanted.

Finally, a few days before Ben's first birthday, Red had had enough. He said it was the swimming costume, that it made him feel bad.

Like a rapist.

When I realized his suitcase was already packed, sitting on the floor beside the door, that he was not raising the issue as an agenda item up for discussion, that what he was actually doing was informing me of the decision he had already made, I tensed, the anger coiled up inside me as tight as in a cat psyching up to the pounce.

Then he picked up Ben.

If a proper mother should have argued, should have insisted that the offspring remain with her, I was not a proper mother. My experience was that motherhood was a façade, a fabrication that sometimes took sixteen years to unravel, but occasionally just the one single year was adequate. I held the front door wide for them both to leave and I felt two things. The first was disappointment. About all the time I had invested, all that energy wasted. As a woman, both as a mother and a partner, I had failed. The second feeling was sadness, sadness and disbelief, that a single elastic garment could be held to blame:

Exhibit one, your honour!

As if that one tiny item had ever been large enough to bear responsibility for everything.

From downstairs I heard laughter. I stood up and got started. I plumped and straightened the bed, wiped down the window ledge, moved Ben's car to the passage outside the room, then swept the floor and mopped it. Finished, I could see no point returning the car to the same spot it had occupied for years like a memorial, so I picked it up, carried it downstairs and left it by the front door.

They were watching TV when I went back into the living room, on the settee together, with Lemon's arm around Ben's shoulders and Ben's head virtually wedged up into Lemon's armpit, watching one of those patronizing children's programmes where there was a huge focus on covering guests with snot-like goo, and the presenters shouted every word they spoke and leapt about like they were high on E. The kind of senseless show I detested, and they were laughing their heads off. Both of them. As though it was the funniest thing either had seen in some time. And they were oblivious to my presence. They noticed me twice; once when I swept the floor in front of the TV, and the second time when I mopped the same spot.

Ben was in his element. Normally I never allowed him to watch stuff like that, but that day, everything was out of control. Berris was out. Lemon was here. The cinema had been a disaster and now my home was filled with a cacophony of screams from the TV and its audience of two, locked into each other's arms like old mates. Finished, I sat down at the table pretending to read and, at some point, Ben stood up to go to the toilet. On his return he spoke to me for the first time since lunch.

'Why's my car in the passage?'

'I'm throwing it out. It's too small for you. That's why.'

'But that's my favourite car.'

'Really? When's the last time you played with it?'

'But it's mine. I don't want you to throw it away.'

'Look, I don't want to have a full-blown discussion about it. You don't play with it any more and it's too small for you even if you did want to. It's pointless keeping it. It's going in the bin.'

He was silent for a moment. He glanced over at Lemon, probably hoping for some support from that quarter. When none was forthcoming he looked down at the floor. 'I wish you was dead,' he said, his voice so low I thought I had misheard.

'What did you say?'

He looked up at me, eyes full of tears. 'I wish you was dead!' he shouted. 'I hate you I hate you I hate you I hate you I hate you!' and fell upon me, kicking and punching and biting and scratching and wailing at the top of his voice, deranged and hysterical.

For a moment, I was completely immobilized. He could have said anything else in the world to me and it might have been okay. But those words were too terrible. What had I ever done to him that was bad enough for him to wish that? I pulled him away from me with one hand and with the other I slapped him hard across the face. There was a moment of shocked silence, a deep sucking in of breath on Ben's part and then he let loose one mighty piece of screaming.

Lemon jumped up from the settee and ran over to him, picking him up and cuddling him. Ben locked his arms around Lemon's neck and his legs tight around his waist. He threw back his head and howled at the top of his lungs.

I too was stunned. It could only have been a few seconds that I stood there, mouth open, to say what, I have no idea, but at some point I realized the phone was ringing. On automatic pilot I walked over and picked up the handset from on top of the TV.

'Hello?' I said. Over Ben's screams it was impossible to hear what was being said. I put my free hand over the other ear, listening hard.

'... see if he's okay...Look, what the fuck is going on over there?'

It was Red.

Thirty minutes later he arrived and took Ben from Lemon without a word. The moment Ben saw Red the sniffs grew worse and as soon as he was in his dad's arms he began to cry again, letting loose the proportion of distress he had deliberately held back for the moment of his grand finale.

Cuddling and kissing Ben as though he too was close to breaking down, Red took him out to the car, where he mollified him for another five minutes before returning to collect his bag.

He was as angry as I had ever seen him. An involuntary tick pulsed at the edge of his left eye. He picked up Ben's bag, then turned to face Lemon, who stood beside me.

'Do you mind?' he asked.

'Sorry,' Lemon said, but instead of leaving the room, he went and sat down on the settee, as if he was suddenly fully engaged in watching the TV and by some miracle was giving us the privacy Red had been too subtle requesting.

'I know how it looks,' I said, 'but Ben...'

Red's hand came up in a Stop sign. 'Just don't! Don't you dare blame him.'

'I wasn't going to *blame* him...'

'I don't wanna hear it,' he said. 'This is the end of the line. I'm not doing this any more.'

'If you would just let me explain...'

'But I don't care what your reasons are. He's been here for five hours. You haven't seen him for a fortnight. How could things get this bad so quick?'

'Red, if you would just listen...'

'But it's just more rubbish. He's a little boy. Four years old! Don't you think he's already got enough on his plate?'

I didn't answer, because what was on his plate was me: absent mum, useless mum, bad mum. I knew it and I didn't want to discuss it in more detail in front of Lemon, but Red was on a roll.

'You don't visit. You don't phone. You don't do anything. *I'm* the one going round mopping up, making good, lying to him so he thinks, despite everything you do and every word you say, that you care. Well, I'm done with it. No more.'

All I wanted to do was wrap the discussion up as quickly as possible. 'It's obvious there's no point trying to discuss this with you, so where do we go from here?' I asked.

'I'm not bringing him any more. You want to see him, you come to *our* home and see him there. You wanna talk to him, pick up the phone and ring.' He glanced at Lemon lounging on the settee in his dressing gown, like a sugar daddy. 'Assuming you can make the time.'

'You seem to have forgotten something; he's my son too!'

'Really?' Red asked, looking at me, waiting for more, but I could see no need to elaborate. The fact that I was Ben's mother was irrrefutable. He shifted the bag to his other hand and turned around to leave. He was almost through the living-room door when he stopped and turned around. The anger was gone, replaced by an expression I could not identify.

'Do you know he cries for you?' he asked. 'Did you know that?'

He watched me for a moment, waiting for a response, but it was so inconceivable I could think of nothing to say. Then he waved his hand as if I were a waste of space, dismissing me. He left the room and a moment later the front door slammed shut.

And then, in case the whole thing wasn't already bloody obvious, and only Lemon had been endowed with sufficient insight to recognize this was not a positive development, at that moment he turned around to look at me, shook his head slowly and said, 'Hope you don't think I'm minding you business when I say that did not go well at all, at all, at all.'

3

Although it was not yet three, and early in the day even by my standards, I poured myself a glass of wine. I did not offer Lemon a drink. The rational part of me knew that the episode with Red and Ben was not Lemon's fault, but another part of me held everything that had happened firmly against him; if it had not been for him I would have changed my clothes and gone to the park instead of the cinema, so there would have been no wet trousers and no scene. If he had not been here when we returned, Ben would have been paying attention to *me* and because I would have been paying attention *back* there would have been no cleaning done upstairs and the old car would still be sitting in the corner of the bedroom gathering dust. If it had not been for him, my head wouldn't have been so filled with Berris that I could hardly think properly, never mind function. No matter which angle I approached from, Lemon sat squarely in the way, and however much I tried, it was impossible to push the blame beyond him.

He helped himself to a vodka on the rocks anyway, watching me all the while, giving me a look that asked: *Well? Are we going to talk about this or not?* It was a look I pretended not to understand; my private business was nothing to do with him. Instead, I fixed my face into an A*sk me any questions and I'll chop your head off* look to keep him at bay. And so for a while he said nothing.

He looked comfortable leaning on the counter, glass raised, examining the contents as though it were the first time he'd ever had the opportunity to study the clarity of vodka at leisure. It wound me up that he dared to look relaxed when my life was breaking down around me. Then I realized that whatever he did would wind me up because it wasn't the things he did that pissed me off so badly, it was *him*. Why had I asked him to stay? I had succumbed to a moment of weakness, a desire to confess the unspeakable, had believed that somehow this man could deliver me, as if such a thing was possible, as if life had not already taught me that the only person I could ever truly depend on was me, and I felt as angry with myself as I did with him, that I had been stupid enough to believe that anything good could ever come from bringing history into my home. It was as much my fault as it was his, and not talking to him was childish and ridiculous. This knowledge, though obvious, instead of making me behave differently however, simply increased my resentment.

I carried my drink into the living room and he followed. I sat on the settee and he sat down beside me. I shifted over a bit towards the end, so we were further apart. He reached over and switched the telly off. When he turned around to face me, I could tell from his expression he intended to stall no longer and I began gathering a few openly hostile responses in my mind to bring to any discussion concerning me or anything I considered to be My Business.

'You know I'va son, don't you?' he said.

'Yes,' I answered.

'You know how long I never see him?'

'Nope.'

'Guess.'

'I'm not really in the mood for guessing games...'

'Thirty-two years,' he said. 'From the day me and Mavis came to England till the day I took her back home to get bury. Left him behind with Mavis' sister, the oldest one. She was still living with Mavis' mum. There was plenty space for the boy to run round, 'nough people to watch over him. Was only supposed to be for a year or two, now here we are.'

He sighed, as though he had finished talking. I waited for what felt like a long while before saying, 'I'm assuming there is actually going to be more, that you were actually endeavouring to make a point?'

'I wrote to him, after Mavis pass,' he said, his tone neutral, as though he hadn't heard me speak and was continuing of his own accord. 'First letter I ever write him. Mavis used to write all the time, think sometimes two, three letters a month. We never had no more kids after we come here, and well, I wasn't around much, working working working, come night-time out with me friends, as you know. Think she was probably bored most the time. And lonely. But she never said a word. Never said, "'Isn't it 'bout time you start stay in?" or nothing. Can't remember her complaining about a thing, all the years we was married, 'cept the cold of course, always the cold. Never could get used to it, no matter how long we live here. Couldn't stand it at all. Anyway.

'Though I was never one for writing and such like, I wrote him when she died. He moved to the States 'bout ten years ago. New York. Married an American woman out there. You might think it strange I never just ring but after all the years I never ring when she was alive, was a habit hard to suddenly break after she pass. So I wrote him, told him 'bout the funeral arrangements, etcetera. Mavis always say she never wanted to be bury here in the cold ground for all eternity, so I took her back home, like she wanted. Wrote and tell the boy the date and time. He came over on the day. Never brung the wife but he came – thirty-two years I never seen him till then – and he brung the grandkids.'

He put down his glass and ran his palms over his trousers as though trying to smooth out any creases. I had seen people do this in the undertakers, occupying their hands as if doing so straightened out the thoughts in their minds and made it possible for them to say things they could not otherwise say. I remembered an elderly Jamaican woman, widowed two days, who stood beside her husband's casket twisting her handkerchief between her hands for half an hour, then saying, 'I'll never forgive him for this.' I looked down at the floor and Lemon carried on.

'Course I knew they was born, Mavis tell me and I seen the pictures John send, but at the funeral was the first time

I actually laid eyes on them in the flesh. Two boys and a girl. The girl...'

He was grappling for words though I didn't know why. He was a natural storyteller and, angry as I was with him, I was entranced.

'At the graveside, I was crying, man, couldn't stop. Anyway, I felt something and I look down and she was holding my hand real tight, and she smile at me. You know, if Mavis wasn't six foot under by then, that's exactly what she woulda done, hold my hand and smile. No words, nothing extra, just a little simple something for me to know she was supporting me, standing by me, like she always done, even all them years when I give her no reason for it, never give her nothing back, but she done it anyway. Now I'm not a man to go with all the jumbie business – though me nah say a word against Jack Lantern, you understand – but I when I look into the girl's eyes, was like looking into her grandma eyes for true and the thing shock me.

'That night, couldn't sleep, just up pacing this way and that till after dawn when there wasn't any point trying to catch sleep again. And I wondered, how could a little nine-year-old girl know to do that, that that was the best thing she coulda done, that nothing else in this life coulda comfort me more? Just a hand. One tiny hand. How could she know? S'impossible, innit?

'I never felt so shame. Every time I think 'bout it, water come to me eye. To know she live nine long years and not once I ever did a thing for her, not a biscuit, not a ginnip, not a bean, and she still give me her hand. Man, it make me feel small.

'John never stop in Montserrat. Went back to the States same night. Had some urgent business to attend – or so him say – so off he went. Didn't get a chance to speak to him or nothing.

'Anyway, I wrote him. Asked after the family and such like, then ask why he don't come up to London. Said I would pay the fare and they just come up and stay by me for a few weeks. He wrote back real polite, not angry or nothing, say he long find comfort in the Church and he have all the father he need right thereso. And you know what? The worse thing of all? I couldn't even say nothing, because the man was right. His whole life I never put myself out even the once. Why should he raise a finger to do something for me now?'

The tale was done, his point made and I bristled.

'Look, no offence right, it's nice of you to share this with me, but my situation is not the same as yours.'

'I never said it was.'

'But that's your point, isn't it? You've messed up with your son, I should try not to mess up with mine.'

'All I'm saying is sometimes you know things need sorting but you don't do it. Someday you might find you dallied so long, the time's passed and you don't have the choice no more.'

'But I've been there for Ben. I've bought him birthday and Christmas presents, and every Easter I get him an egg...'

'And tomorrow?' he asked.

I knew he wasn't asking about the one day, he meant the future; tomorrow and the day after and all the tomorrows thereafter, but I responded literally.

'Tomorrow, I'll go and take some advice. In law, Red doesn't have a leg to stand on. He can't stop me seeing my son. It's my legal right.'

'You legal right,' he repeated slowly, like he was feeling the words in his mouth, exploring them, rolling them around. As though he had been talking about rum and I had brought up rhubarb. When he looked at me, his eyes held something in the way of contempt.

'I need some decent food,' he said. 'I'm gonna go do some shopping and when I get back, I'll cook.'

'Fine. Whatever.'

'I take it when I get back you gonna let me in?' he said.

He was offering me a choice. When I looked at him his eyes were speaking again, mocking me: *I know you*, they said, *know the type very well. You're a runner. A duck-and-diver. Scared.*

'You can take my key,' I said, getting up. 'That should reduce some of your worry, shouldn't it?'

Having given him the key so he could go shopping to buy the things he needed to cook, I naturally expected him to have the money to pay for them, but he did not. When he asked me for money, I collected my purse, grudgingly pulled out a couple of twenty-pound notes, and handed them over without meeting his eyes.

I gave him a curt nod on his return home. He was laden with so many carrier bags it looked like he had done the whole week's shopping. Though I wondered when I saw the mass of food he had bought, I could not quite bring myself to open my mouth and enquire just exactly how long he planned on staying. Nor to mention, though it hadn't escaped my notice, that he hadn't had the courtesy to hand back any change.

It was not my intention to make him feel self-conscious – it would have been pointless anyway; the man was immune to subtlety – but I sat on the high stool in front of the breakfast bar scowling as he hummed and unloaded some of the bags, then began searching the entire pot cupboard for a suitable vessel in which to bubble up his concoction.

As soon as he had hoisted the pumpkin out from inside one of the bags, a piece that was about a quarter of the size of a large one, burnt-orange flesh oozing moist white pips, I knew what he was making. What else would a Montserratian man shop for and cook on a Saturday? It was such a stereotype that on another day, in better humour, I might have chuckled. He was making soup.

I watched as he exerted himself, thwacking the skin off the pumpkin, reducing the flesh to fine-slivered squares, then chopping the cucumber and onions while the kettle boiled. Everything went into the pot on the stove and he lit the fire beneath it.

My mother had cooked pumpkin soup on Saturdays, virtually every Saturday when I was young, yet I had forgotten. Somehow, it had slipped my mind. Lemon had eaten here, eaten *that* here, years back, laughing and blowing hot spoonfuls with Berris. He was contriving to look innocent, but I damn well knew the only reason he was cooking soup now was to take me back to then.

Without asking he turned on the kitchen radio. It was set to Classic FM. Bach's *Magnificat* ceased abruptly as Lemon began to retune the station, turning the volume up in an effort to hear the faintest illegal transmissions of reggae pirate-radio stations, and the static crackling and hissing, the tuning in and out of stations he had no interest in, went on at length, stretching my poor nerves till I felt like a passenger travelling on a fast train beside an open window.

He found a station of his choice finally, an old-style giggip-giggip channel, playing the weary, slow reggae of singers long dead. To raise them, he whacked the volume up as high as it could go.

My eyes followed him back to the sink where he washed the lamb, lifting the pieces out, and trimmed off the fat and bloodied edges with fingers that went about their task deftly. Compared with how clumsy his handling was of the table knife I gave him last night with dinner, he wielded the meat cleaver with the finesse of a pro.

All the while, he kept a lit cigarette poised in the right-hand side of his mouth. He kept the smoke out of his eyes by keeping the right eye half closed and his head tilted slightly to the left.

I watched.

He put the lamb into the pot and emptied another kettle-ful of hot water over it. He selected a few choice branches of thyme, ran the water over them at the sink, shook the excess off as though he were shaking down the mercury in a thermometer, then tossed them into the cauldron as well. He rummaged in the cutlery drawer for a ladle, positioned himself in front of the cooker and, with his back to me, as uninhibited as if I was not sitting there watching him and scowling at all, as he stirred the pot, he started to dance.

Instantly, the room was filled with the aroma of soup beginnings, the earliest stage when all the ingredients still retained their own fresh and heightened smells, an aroma that was a group or sequence of different scents that assailed individually, till the fragrant thyme finally rose to dominate. Then, on the back of the record before it, from the radio came the instrumental sounds of 'Mr Bojangles', and John Holt's smooth vocals began to croon about the very first time he'd met him.

There were things I no longer believed in. God was one; a pretty straightforward process of elimination had clarified that issue once my mother was dead. And all the stuff she believed in, that they all believed in, their generation, the spirits and jumbies and obeah, the miscellaneous hocus pocus, all of that nonsense I had thrown out years ago. I was not a spiritual person. I did not believe in karma – of which I had seen little evidence – or fate or destiny or anything along those lines. It goes without saying that listening to someone explain an out-of-body experience would have produced little more response from me than a sneer.

Yet I don't know how else to describe it. The combination of the soup and the music and Lemon throwing down moves like he was Mr Bojangles himself, and I had a feeling, like déjà vu, as if the whole universe and every sound and atom of air inside it had curved sharply and was blasted back on rewind at warp speed, and suddenly the kitchen was full of glamorous bejewelled women, and sharply dressed men, the air filled with the smell of party foods: lamb curry, rice and peas, beef patties, goat water, salt-fish fritters and fried chicken. There were drinks galore, the hard stuff, rum and vodka and whisky and brandy, and everyone had a glass, drinking and chatting away in voices that sounded like they were cussing each other, drowned out by loud and regular laughter.

Over in the corner stood Berris on his own, sucking on a toothpick, immaculately dressed even by his standards, dripping gold from every part of his body that could sustain it, sipping whisky chased with water, red-eyed from the marijuana he had been smoking, green-eyed with petty rage, staring through the open double doors between the kitchen and the living room.

In the living room, calypso blared, Arrow's 'Hot Hot Hot', and a sea of bodies bobbed and swayed, arms raised, backs bending, hips bumping, waists winding, and in the midst of them all, my mother, the best dancer of all the women there, and Lemon, the best man, bouncing off each other's bodies in a perfect passion of rhythm and style.

Finally, Berris put his drink down on the counter closest to him and removed the toothpick from his lips. He dropped it into the glass and began making his way towards them. His gait was brisk and sure, like a bulldog on muscular legs slightly bowed, his shoulders moving as if they too were strolling, left right left right left. In his expression there was no trace of anger or malice. Instead his features were set hard into the focused expression of a man who had repulsive but necessary tasks to perform; the man responsible for garbage disposal or sewage clearance, the person charged with vermin exterminations.

Only his eyes blazed.

All but two of the people in the house that night were aware of him as he walked, and the wave of bodies across his path parted as if he were Moses himself. For a man who danced badly, there was grace in the fluid swing of his arm, and my mother spun across the room in a clumsy pirouette for one who danced so well. She landed on the floor in shock and it was only after she touched her nose and saw blood that she even realized what had happened. By then, Berris had passed her en route to the record player. There he dragged up the stylus in a loud and permanent scrape across the LP. In the quiet, no one spoke. Berris looked around, like a proud father at his daughter's wedding, just checking he had everyone's attention, about to commence his speech: *ting ting ting*. It must have been a trick of the dark, but he appeared taller, his chest fuller. He had but the two words to say to the people watching, and when he spoke his voice was loud but calm.

'Party done.'

When I came to I was lying on the settee. I felt dizzy and confused. There was a pillow under my head and a blanket over my body. It was dark outside and the living-room lights were on. Kneeling on the floor beside the settee was Lemon, his hand on my forehead, like he was checking to see if I had a temperature. There was a pain towards the back of my head, above the left ear, like I had taken a hard blow. I looked around the room, trying to get my bearings. It was the decor that was out of place. My mind was in the wrong era. She was not here and had not been for years.

'What happened?' I asked. My throat was dry and I cleared it.

Using his thumb, he pulled back my eyelids, first one then the other, examining my pupils, looking for signs of concussion I guessed.

'You passed out. But not to worry. I gotta strong feeling you gonna live.'

'Super,' I said.

I tried to sit up, but the effort required was too much. I flopped back down and Lemon adjusted the blanket gently.

'You have somewhere to go?' he asked.

'No.'

'Then rest up. Relax. S'about time you start take care of youself.'

I thought about my life, tried to think of a single good thing in it, just the smallest reason to want to live, to care enough either way, and found nothing.

'Why?' I asked. 'What's the point?'

'What no kill you make you strong.'

'Spare me the cheery sermons, please.'

He looked at me like I imagined I looked at Ben sometimes. As though I was a difficult child and he was doing his best to not rise to it. He picked up a bowl containing water and a flannel from where he had placed it on the floor beside him and I realized while I had been unconscious he had obviously been using it to wipe my head. It felt like the greatest act of kindness anyone had done for me in years, that simple functional task: dipping, squeezing, dabbing. To my horror I felt tears prickling the surface of my eyes.

'I'd really prefer to be left alone,' I said.

He stood up. 'Let me get you some soup.'

Oohh, that soup, that soup, that soup; it was heaven. Not too runny, not too thick, the consistency was perfect. Saffron-coloured and bursting with flavour, with small, soft pieces of yam and sweet potato and green banana and tania seed, and chewy torpedo dumplings. The lamb was not overcooked till it fell from the bone, but had retained its elasticity. Every mouthful bore deliciously delicate treats: carrots and pearl barley and christophine and lima beans. He sat beside me on the settee and fed me like he must have done his wife, slow, careful, spoonful by spoonful. I recalled the story of Rapunzel and her barren, unhappy mother who, having tasted the salad pilfered from the witch's garden, decided she must have more of it or die. With every swallow, how I identified with her.

And as I ate in wonder, Lemon spoke non-stop, voice low, as if I were too infirm to converse back and it was incumbent on him to keep the conversation going single-handed. The most important ingredient was the pumpkin. Once the pumpkin was good, you were halfway there. And you had to know the difference between what you wanted boiled into the soup for flavour and what should be kept back and added later. And you needed to know when the lamb was cooked, the point at which it should be removed from the pot, to be later returned. Timing was everything. To cook a perfect pot of soup, you had first to learn how to tell the time.

When the contents of the bowl had been polished off, I offered up the three words that best expressed my feelings.

'I want more,' I said.

He looked at me and smiled. It was the first time he had smiled since his arrival. I had forgotten how charming it was, how attractive it made him. He had one of those smiles that engaged every feature on his face, his wide mouth, his lean cheeks, his eyes, the creased skin at their corners. When he smiled at you it was as if you had his fullest attention; no one else existed for him anywhere. It was irresistible. I felt myself smiling back as he rose and left to bring me seconds.

I felt different. In the centre of my feelings, like the eye of a tornado, the anger held its ground, but around the edges I could feel it giving way to something softer that made me feel uncomfortable. Vulnerable. I wished I had the capacity to just enjoy the moment, to embrace the pleasure of having things done for me, but it was not in me. Instead, I found myself wondering what was in it for him, why he was doing this, and just how bad the sting would be that brought me back down to earth.

When he returned I was happy to see the bowl was almost as full as it had been last time. Carefully he settled on the floor beside the settee, moving slowly, careful not to spill a drop. I reached out and took the bowl from him, turning to lie on my side so I could feed myself.

'You sure you can manage?' he asked.

'Yes. Why are you doing this?'

'Got nothing else to do.'

'That's not a good enough answer.'

'It's the best answer you gonna get.'

'I don't want the "best answer", I want the truth.' I waited, but he didn't reply. 'You visited him, didn't you, in prison? That's why he came to see you.'

He shook his head. 'Me and Berris go back a ways. We had unfinished business, things that needed to be said.'

'About my mother?'

He shrugged. 'And other things.'

'Like?'

'You asking me to number and reel them off? Most stories are like that bowl of soup you eating now, a whole heap of ingredients put together at the proper time. You can't pick up one thing on its own, piece of dasheen say, and study it then walk and tell people you gotta understanding of soup. You have to start with the things that need to go in the pot first. You want the truth, I gotta start at the beginning.'

'So start at the beginning then,' I said, wondering where the beginning of my own confession lay. Not the night of the engagement party, *ting ting ting*. By then things were already in full swing. The beginning was back further. Months back.

'Now?' he asked.

'Yes now.'

'I need a drink.'

'So? Get one.'

He was slow to stand, unsure but going along with it. He rubbed his hands together, psyching himself up.

'You want one as well?'

'Sure,' I answered. 'Why not?'

*

'We growed up together, me and Berris both. In Cudjoe Head. North Montserrat. People say his father never want to know him from when he born. Don't know if it's true but it don't matter anyhow, 'cos Berris believe it to be so.

'His mother put him to board with Mistress Jolly when she went to Curaçao. Visited a few times but never come back to get him or send ticket for him to come. Wasn't no work in Montserrat then. Yeah, there was the odd cleaning job in one of the hotel or rich people house, but you couldn't live off what you earn there. Folks had to go to the other islands. At that time was mostly Curaçao they went. Had sugar and coffee and oil there. Was work to be had, and money.

'They went off. Send back whatever they could to keep the kids. Pretty sure his mum done that, same as everybody else, but Berris say if she did, he never see a cent. Mistress Jolly tell him his mother never send a bean. Type of person she was, can't see she woulda keep him for nothing. But that's what she say and that's what the man believe.

'We was raggedy. All the kids was raggedy then. Had but the two pair of trouser, one for church and one for school. You never wear you church trouser to school 'less you want you arse cut, and you school pants you take off soon as you reach home in case you wear those out before time and have to go school with you arse outta door. Must be only a handful had shoes and them what did was lucky if they fit. I remember Orlando Weekes, schoolteacher son. Boy used to bawl fire because the shoes be biting him all day and his mother make him keep them on. Boy used to limp like a dog with a crab on him paw. Girl, we were raggedy then. Raggedy. Times was rough and all of us together was poor.

'But it come like Berris was worse off. Don't know if it was the hair or what. We used to go down by Mas' Cook. Mas' Cook was a handicap. Had short legs but might as wella had no legs and done 'cos they never work. Used to pull hisself 'long on him backside with the hands. Come like after a while you hardly even notice 'cos he move so fast. He's the one person I know them times make a good living. Man used to make mat and basket from reed and they was always by the gate for people to see and buy. And he used to cut hair. He cut all our hair. Would chap you in the head if you move once he start cut. Most times you get a skiffle you hadda lump on you head you never start out with.

'But Berris never have his hair cut. Or even plait. Used to look nasty. Kids being kids they take the piss outta him bad. Must be that why he learn to fight so hard. Got so no one tease him any more 'cos when he fight you, it's like say he wanna kill you, even the girls...'specially the girls. Always had to be someone there to stop him, 'cos from when we was boys till we come men, I never once seen him stop hisself.

'All of us was living with family, the grandparents, or an auntie or some such. I live with my father's sister then, and girl let me tell you that woman was a devil. But she was nothing next to Mistress Jolly. Berris' mum family never want no truck with her bastard pickney, so she *had* to leave him with Mistress Jolly, never had no choice the way I see it, though to hear Berris talk you'd swear she had 'nough. Mistress Jolly take in a whole heapa kids, 'nough jingbang, collect a whole heapa money, but she keep near 'nough every dollar for sheself.

'That woman was always vex for something. You might as well say "switch live in her hand", 'cos it was there from sunrise till sunfall. Only time she put it by was Sunday morning when she go church and odd time the parents come. Barring that, them kids get some licks you see. 'Nough licks, man, 'nough licks.

'None of us had much food then. Was mostly vegetarian but not from choice. If there was piece a meat in you house and you lucky, you peas might catch little the flavour, but the only time you had a solid chance of meat on you plate was Christmas Day and Easter, and even then was no guarantee.

'Mistress Jolly was always walking and talking 'bout how the orphans was eating her out of house and home, but they must have been some serious slow eaters, 'cos the house was always being fix: new roof, extension, big old comfy chair. And that woman was fat! She was fat till fat roll when she walk. To look at her you would never say she was someone who live far from the kitchen.

'But Berris was small. All Mistress Jolly pickney was small. We never have much but I still save a dumpling for Berris from my soup, or little dasheen, small piece of yam. Up to now don't know why. 'Cept I seen him cry. Something pitiful. When he thought was no one there to see, I saw. See him put down some piece of bawling, never seen nothing like it in my life. Guess I felt sorry for him or something. Anyways I did it, give him a little food regular like. According to him was that little something save his life. Think that's how we growed up to be so close.'

He paused for a moment and lit a cigarette. With a grimace, he swallowed a mouthful from his glass, then took a deep drag and exhaled.

'He call me a fool when I marry Mavis.' His voice was quieter now, tired. 'Think that was the only time we nearly come to blows. Said she was easy, I wasn't the first to fuck her, that she take me and make jacket to give her bastard a name. She never forget that. Never forgived him neither. After we come to England I still use to see him, we was still tight, but he couldn't visit my yard. Was his fault for true and probably serve him right, but he still hate her for it. Hate her bad.

'Course Mavis tell me all was lie, Berris jealous, the kinda thing she *had* to say, if you think on it, and I listen to what she have to say, but I study my son when he born, study him hard to see what he have for me. Like you, he favour his mum bad. Never could see me in him 't'all. Think that was the reason I never send for him, even when we get settle here and we coulda.

'Deep down in my heart, all that time, I never knowed, never knowed for sure…was he mine?'

'Are you telling me all those years you never had a relationship with your son was 'cos of what Berris said?' I asked.

The soup was finished. I replaced the spoon in the bowl as he took it, nodding. 'Yep.'

'So he said one thing and your wife said something completely different and, of the two, you believed *him*?'

'You wanted the truth, that's what you getting.'

'Just so I'm clear, *you* messed up but it was Berris's fault?'

'I'm not making excuses...'

'Yes you are! So what that he said it? So what?'

'I did what I did. Can't turn back the clock. All I'm trying to do is tell it like it was,' he said.

He raised his brows, his hands, his shoulders in a shrug, and all at once he looked old. How many lives had Berris trashed in his lifetime, I wondered? How many? And yet Lemon still stood by him, still visited, still had him round for talks on old times. Even though I felt like a bully, like I was beating someone up who was making no effort to defend himself, I couldn't stop.

'She was your wife.' To my surprise, my voice was choked. 'Why couldn't you just believe her?'

'You think I didn't want to believe her? You think I never try? Girl, you can't even begin to imagine my misery, the ways I let her down. What I told you ain't nothing.'

'What, there's more?'

'Always more. But I need to get a refill first. You want one?'

I shook my head. I had been concentrating on eating. The glass of wine he'd brought me was still full.

'Think I better have some soup first; line me stomach a bit.'

'Okay,' I said, and he went.

There was a time when I would have been overjoyed to know just how dissipated Lemon's family life was. Clearly, since then, I had grown up. Now I just felt angry with Lemon, angry he had given Berris free reign to manipulate his thoughts, then done little else other than sit back and accept the resulting unhappiness, like a willing victim patiently poised, awaiting a fatal stab in the back.

I asked him why he had come to see me and he had started from the beginning, with his childhood, and Berris was there. Berris was at my own beginning too. Everything had begun with him, literally begun from the first moment I laid eyes on him here in this very house. Up until then, my childhood had been spectacularly humdrum. It had chugged along with the monotony of a fairy tale; the odd discomfort here and there swiftly resolved and resulting in a happy-ever-after. It had been solid, unwavering and predictable. Like my friendship with Sam, my best friend from the day I started secondary school and found myself in the formroom sitting beside her. Samantha Adebayo. She was also at the beginning. My life changed on a day that started with Sam, the day we counted virgins and netball practice got cancelled.

Considering it was the moment that signalled the beginning of the end of my childhood, you might have thought something dramatic had marked it out; a blazing comet crossing the sky or thunder pounding like a roll of drums. Instead it was a usual day, completely normal, a day so ordinary that I hadn't suspected a thing.

4

I waited for Sam on the corner of Amhurst Road and Dalston Lane, outside Easton Chemist's, at the bottom of Pembury Estate where she lived with her family, the whole of the Adebayo posse; her mum and dad, herself and three younger brothers.

Her family was the complete opposite of mine, where it was just me and my mum and everything was quiet and in its place. Her dad was kind of okay but Mrs Adebayo could be a bit weird. Because of her, I didn't visit them much, but on the occasions I had, Sam's house was as noisy and crazy and manic as the school dining hall at lunchtime. Compared to hers, my house was like a morgue.

From where I stood I could see through the courtyard, almost to the middle of the estate. The Adebayos lived in the block right at the top, overlooking the park, and there were several exits between that end and where I stood, but I knew Sam would come out this way because she always did. This was where I met her every morning; a short walk down from where I lived and across the road from Hackney Downs Station where we caught the 48 bus to take us to school.

I was digi because it was a Monday and on Mondays after school we had netball practice. About half the time, Sam forgot her kit. She was pretty scatty, forever leaving something behind or just forgetting things completely. I was digi because I didn't want to end up at practice on my own. But the minute I saw her, I relaxed.

She was running from the moment she came into view, racing through the estate in the disgusting maroon uniform we hated so much, satchel flapping, blazer and cardigan undone, the carrier bag with her kit in it held between her teeth, her hands busy pulling her auburn hair into a ponytail; late as usual and still not finished dressing.

'Jay, you gotta stop letting your mum do your hair, man,' she said as she reached me, slowing down to a walk, which I picked up alongside her. My mum had washed my hair the day before and spent the evening cornrowing it into fine plaits that ran from my forehead to the nape of my neck, like Leroy's from *Fame*.

'I'll take them out for you at first break,' she said.

Up until then, I'd quite liked the style, but if Sam thought it was dry, it would have to go.

'Okay.'

'You done your biology?' she asked.

I nodded.

'Man, I can't do shit at home. You don't know how lucky you are. Once I've finished my O levels I'm out of there. My family's seriously fucked.'

We were five months away from our O levels and the end of our school days for ever. It was kind of strange knowing that, like the end of school was supposed to mark the beginning of being grown up, but I didn't feel grown up at all. I didn't have the first idea about what I wanted to do with my life. The only thing I was good at was writing stories, but that wasn't much use when you were trying to work out what kind of career you could end up with. That was another difference between me and Sam. She always knew exactly what she wanted to do and no matter what, she went ahead and did it. Her mother was English and her father Ghanaian and she was totally against mixed relationships. She was sick of her parents arguing all the time, sick of being in a two-bedroomed flat and not having her own bedroom, sick of being the only girl in her family and having to slave behind her brothers, and sick of being told what to do. As soon as our exams were over, she was leaving home.

'You should've come over the garages on Friday,' she said.

She was talking about the car park underneath the tower blocks on Nightingale Estate. There were always loads of guys hanging out from the estate down there, renters mostly, trying to get the girls who passed through into the empty garages on a one-to-one. I didn't like the scene as much as she did and it wasn't just because the boys all seemed so immature, or even because the second they laid eyes on Sam it was like I'd suddenly become invisible. I had a deeper personal problem: French kissing. I'd never done it. You couldn't count the hours spent practising on oranges; cutting them in half and gouging out the fruit using only my tongue.

Good French-kissers left the pith clean, but I was nowhere near that level of proficiency. Usually, I just ended up with an exhausted tongue, and sore bits at the corners of my mouth so that when the juice touched them it stung like hell. I was terrified my inexperience would make me look ridiculous, and over the garages, that fear made me mute.

'Was it good?'

'It was wicked. I got asked out again.'

'Who by?'

'Donovan, innit! Jay, if I tell you something, you gotta promise me you'll never tell anyone as long as you live.'

She was so dramatic. 'Like *I'd* tell anyone,' I said, rolling my eyes.

'You have to promise me. Swear on your mother's life.'

'I swear, okay?'

'I saw his wood.'

'Liar!' I shrieked.

'I swear.'

'I don't believe you.'

'You think I'd lie about something like that?'

'How did you see it?'

'He took it out. He wannid me to touch it –'

'Ergh! Gross.'

'But I said "no", of course,' she added, but it sounded kind of lame, like maybe she had only added that last bit because of how I'd reacted, and I wondered whether she really had touched it.

Donovan was in the sixth form at Homerton House. He had been asking her out for months, and the way she told, it was like he was some renter and she just wasn't interested. But I knew she had *some* interest, because I caught them kissing once, one evening when all the kids were playing out on my road and we decided to play Knock Down Ginger with the old fogies who lived on the first floor in Bodney Mansions. But when we took the corner into the dark stairwell, Donovan and Sam were already there, doing some serious kissing and grinding up. She looked well shamed when she saw me, and they both tried to play it like nothing had been going on. But it was blatant. I'd caught them cold.

'So what did it look like?' I asked.

'Like a saveloy when the skin's peeled back.'

'Ugh! I am *never* gonna eat saveloy ever again,' I said.

'When I'm older, I'm only gonna go out with white guys,' Sam said.

'Why?'

'Coloured people are more sexed than white people. That's what my mum says. That's why they shouldn't mix.'

This was news to me and I was quiet as I digested it. Because she had one black and one white parent, Sam was an expert on everything to do with colour. I was lucky to have her as a friend. I learned a lot from her.

The bus stop was crowded with people, including two African boys from Shoreditch School, who were usually at this stop in the mornings. One of them fancied Sam. He tried to pretend he never saw us, but he was just styling it. His friend gave him a butt with his elbow in the stomach, then started to laugh.

'Stupid bubus!' Sam said, loud enough for them to hear. She called all Africans 'bubus', even her dad. Then, turning to me, she whispered, 'Ugh! Can you imagine me and one of those bubus doing The Nasty?'

For an instant, my imagination ran riot. I stared at Sam, she stared at me. There was silence. Then we both cracked up.

I started taking the cornrows out during biology and by first break they were gone.

'I wanted you to look like Farrah but it ain't happening, man,' Sam said, as she teased my hair into large curls that fell out as soon as she let them go. According to her, Farrah Fawcett-Majors wasn't just the best looking of the three Charlie's Angels, she was the most beautiful woman in the world. *She* was the woman who should have played Lois Lane opposite Christopher Reeve, the world's best-looking man.

We were in the girls' toilets. It stunk of wee and cigarettes and the manky smell that was always in the changing room after we'd finished PE. My hair was frizzed from being plaited straight after being washed. The Electrocuted Look. I hated it when it was like this.

'I need a hairband, man,' I said.

'You're telling me? One thing I do know, you can't do Farrah with a bushy Afro.'

She pulled a thick elastic band off her wrist where she always had a stash of them and I took it, pulling my hair back into one, smoothing it down as much as possible.

'You better put some water on that, Kizzy,' she said.

I did that, splashed water on it, without looking at her. Sometimes her comments stung, but it wasn't cool to show it. Kizzy was the daughter of Kunta Kinte, the African slave in *Roots*. Sam pushed her face close to the mirror, examining it.

'Shit, Jay! Look at this,' she said, but I blanked her. 'I think I'm getting a zit. Right on the end of my nose as well. That's just fuckry, man.'

Sam had a permanent patch of scarlet mounds on her forehead. The spots that came up on her were always red. Her skin was very pale, whiter than most of the white people I knew, and she had hazel eyes that were just beautiful, and thick hair that was a kind of auburn now but, in summer, bleached in the sun so she had blonde highlights at the front and around the edges, and it was kink-free, like her mum's.

They were a strange bunch, her and her family. They all had the same mum and dad, yet none of them looked alike. Only one of her brothers looked proper half-caste. The middle one was nearly as black as me and the youngest one was as pale as Sam was, but he had red bushy Negro hair. It was like every child in that family had had their parents' genes put into a Coke bottle, shook up, and then a separate burst of spray had been collected to make each of them. They were as different from each other as a litter of kittens.

'I'm gonna squeeze it,' she said, and she did. A few moments later, the site where the teeny pimple had been was ablaze and swollen, as if someone had boxed her.

'Do you know how you can tell for sure if someone's done The Nasty?'

I shook my head without looking at her and she was quiet for a second, clocking me.

'Look, my whole family's doing my head in. At least you know who you are and where you're coming from. A whole of something, not frigging *half* of nothing. I swear, I'm never gonna marry any boy who ain't coming from where I'm coming and put this shit on my kids...' Her face had gone red, like she was blushing badly. The way she always looked when she was about to cry. The silence was broken by the bell. Break was over. I took one last look at my hair, picked my bag up off the floor, then turned to face her.

'How can you tell?' I asked.

She smiled, blinking quickly, relieved. She linked her arm through mine as she hitched her satchel back up on to her shoulder. Though it was only us in the toilets, she glanced around like there might be crowds hiding in the cubicles, ear-wigging. Her voice was low. She began to explain.

We counted the virgins at lunchtime, not just among the other pupils and the whole of the teachers, but the ones walking around the streets too. We saw an old lady on a Zimmer who was about ninety million years old and still hadn't done It, and I cracked up so bad I actually wet myself a bit.

It was so simple, I couldn't believe I had only just found out how to tell. Virgins walked with their toes pointing inwards and those who had done The Nasty, when they walked, their toes pointed out.

On our way into the chip shop at Haggerston Square we passed a group of seven or eight guys from Shoreditch School acting like they thought they were sweet-boys. We queued for ages and took turns drowning our chips with salt and onion vinegar, then carefully tore the bottom off the chip cone so the warm vinegar, instead of ending up dripping out slowly all over our clothes, could just trickle out the one time and done.

The Shoreditch Massive were still loitering a few shops down and, laughing our heads off, we concocted a plan. We came out of the shop and walked past them with our toes pointing so far outwards, we were waddling like a pair of penguins. When we were far enough away to outrun them, Sam turned around and shouted, 'Renters!' and we legged it.

I felt heady with knowledge, the power to look at total strangers and know for sure what they'd been up to. I even found myself studying my own feet as I walked, and Sam's when she wasn't looking. My feet seemed to naturally point inwards, which made sense. But Sam's didn't. Her feet were more or less parallel with each step and I wondered what exactly that meant.

At home time, we discovered netball practice had been cancelled. Sam wanted to go over to Nightingale Estate and mess around in the garages for a while because her mum wasn't expecting her home for another couple of hours, but I was hungry and couldn't be bothered.

Unlike me though, Sam didn't need the company. Once she'd made up her mind about what she wanted to do, that was it. I said I was gonna go home and she decided to go over the garages on her own.

We'd already spent the remainder of our money, what should have been our bus fare home, on rhubarb and custards and pink bon-bons, so we had no choice on the journey home but to trod. Nightingale Estate was just on the other side of the park from the top of my road, so Sam walked with me to my house. We joked about outside for about ten minutes, then she carried on, and I watched her skipping till she disappeared out of sight round the bend at the top of the road.

I let myself in with the key I wore on a shoelace around my neck, having lost the last three keys my mum had given me. Inside, the house was warm and steamy with rice and peas and the smell of curry recently cooked, which was good. I dropped my bags on the floor inside the passage, opened the door to the sitting room and walked in.

My mum was on the settee with a man I'd never seen before. They were kissing so hard that it was a moment before they even realized I was there. I took in a zillion things in a second. His wet red tongue poking into her open mouth. Her blouse undone. His hand inside it. His flies undone. My mum's hand inside the gaping hole there, moving. Sounds, I think from her, like someone who'd been gagged still trying to speak. And her hair, it looked like she'd been in a fight or something! Of the three of us, I don't know who was the most shocked.

She leapt up and turned around so her back was to me and I could tell she was buttoning up her blouse. The man kind of leaned forward with his arms crossed over each other on his lap, as if that was supposed to make me believe his flies were done up now.

'You're home early!' my mother said over her shoulder, but it wasn't a question she was asking, it was an accusation.

'Netball got cancelled,' I said.

She turned around. Her shirt wasn't tucked in properly and she'd left a button undone, just above the waistband of a short black skirt that I'd only ever seen her in once, at the shop, after she'd tried it on. She'd asked me what I thought and we agreed it was too short to wear on the street. She must have gone back without me and bought it. She hadn't needed to keep it a secret, and the fact that she had, though it was a small thing and silly, made me feel hurt. She smoothed down her hair like that smoothed everything over and said to me, as if it were a perfectly normal occasion and that man had just knocked at the front door, 'There's someone I'd like you to meet. This is Uncle Berris.'

When I looked at him, he was staring down at the floor, but he nodded his head at me in a quick flick, smiling in the foolish way the kids in my class did after they put up their hands to answer a question, got picked, then gave the wrong answer. I looked back at my mother. She was wringing her hands together now and smiling at me in a *whatever you do, don't make a fuss* kind of way. Looking at her made me feel like I'd shrunk, then I realized I hadn't, it was her that had grown. I looked down at her feet. She was wearing red clogs with the highest heels I had ever seen her in. And I tried really hard not to notice but it was just blatant that while her heels were neatly together, her toes were definitely pointing out.

*

'He makes cars, toy ones, for children to play with; makes them out of metal, and he fixes things. He's really good with his hands…' – she laughed then at a joke I did not get. 'He's just so nice…and so good-looking. Go on, admit it,' she said, 'he's good-looking, ain't he?'

He was kind of okay for an old guy. He was tall and looked strong. He was dark though, not as dark as me but nowhere near as light as she was, with broad features so sharply shaped it was as if his head had been chiselled out of a smooth piece of dark wood. His hair was skiffled low with a side parting etched on the left-hand side of his scalp, and he had a neat beard that joined his sideburns so that his whole face looked like it was in a black velvet frame. But he was no Superman. And for all his good looks, there was something I didn't like about him, something in the slant of his eyes and his way of not really looking straight at you, but snatching glances instead, which was what he'd done as he was leaving.

Almost as soon as I thought this, I wondered if I was being fair. The fact was I wasn't happy, but I did not know if I was unhappy with him. I really couldn't say what exactly it was that I was unhappy about. All I could think about was what they'd been up to and how many times he'd been here behind my back. And above all of that, I couldn't stop thinking about the position of her toes. Reluctantly, I nodded.

'I'm so glad you like him,' she said, even though I never said that. 'Jinxy, I think I'm in love. I never thought it woul happen again. I never thought anyone would make me fee like this…' She laughed again, closing her eyes slowly, smi ing like she was remembering something wonderful that ha nothing to do with me and I wondered if it was to do with what they were doing inside each other's clothing, her and that man.

'Why did you say he was my uncle?' I asked.

She waved away my small and insignificant point. 'He's a big man and you're a child.'

'I'm not a kid, I'm sixteen. And we're not related.'

'I know that, but you should still call him that out of respect.'

'But I don't even know him. How can I just start calling him "Uncle"?'

'You can't call him "Berris", like you and him are big alike. I want you to call him "Uncle" for now.' She laughed. 'You never know, if things work out maybe one day you'll call him "Dad".' Then came the killer. 'Jinx, Berris is having some problems where he lives. I told him he could stay here, with us, for a while, till he sorts something out.'

I'd been starving when I came in, famished enough to eat the whole dutchpot of curry on my own. But I'd been playing with my food as she spoke and somehow, even though I'd hardly eaten anything, my appetite was getting less and less the more she spoke.

'What, live here?' I asked.

'Yes.'

'Where? In the spare room?'

'He can sleep in my room,' she said with yet another laugh. 'In my bed. With me.'

I put my cutlery down as she rose from her side of the table and walked over to me. She bent down and cuddled me, then kissed me on the head. She was playing me, and I knew it. This was the kind of thing I normally did to her when I wanted money or clothes or for her to grant me a favour of some kind. What kids were supposed to do to parents, not the other way round.

'Don't worry, it's only for a while. You won't even know he's here. Okay?'

I was very unhappy about it. Very unhappy indeed. But what could I say? And it wasn't really like she was asking me because she had already told him he could stay. It was a done deal.

'Okay.'

She smiled at me and kissed me on the forehead again, smoothed my brows and flicked something from my hair.

'Good girl. Now eat up.'

There are many different types of rain, and England is famous for all of them. There are showers that start with a light drizzle, then build up to a steady pour. Then there's rain that begins drip drip, gets heavy, then stops then starts and stops and starts again. Then there's sudden rain that falls quickly when it's sunny, like its only ambition is to make a rainbow and once it's done that, it stops. If I had to describe Berris as rain, he was none of those, and the words 'You won't even know he's here' turned out to be the understatement of the year.

He moved in within days of my mother telling me and it was like he'd taken over completely, starting with the bathroom. There he spread his man-wares, things alien to our house till then: razors, shaving cream, Pearlwhite toothpaste,

Stud, Bay Rum, Brylcream and masses of bottles of after-shave too numerous to count. And he left bits of his jewellery everywhere. There were pieces around the sink, on the edge of the bath, on the cistern at the back of the toilet, the win-dowsill; Krugerrands and sovereigns on fat rings and heavy belchers, and his collection included some of the chunkiest chaparritas I'd ever seen in my life.

He had a toothbrush that was only a fraction smaller than the toilet brush, as though he needed an industrial cleaner or something to get rid of the gunk growing inside his whop-ping male gob. Even worse was the toilet seat that either had drips of his wee all over it that you had to wipe off before you could sit down, or was left up, in which case you had to try not to touch the wee on it when you were putting it back down so you could sit.

In the shower he had more lotions and potions than me and my mother put together: bottles of shower gel, Brut and All Spice, and an 'intimate wash' for his willy alone which was too gross to even think about. There were scrapers for the heels of his dry feet, tweezers for plucking the Yeti hairs from his nostrils, and a huge scratchy strap type of thing that was apparently the only thing in the universe that cleaned his back properly.

And clothes? There were masses of them. He was the living boutique. I swear he owned about twenty coats in every colour you could dream of and it seemed like every single one had a hat or cap to match it. And shoes? He must have had fifty pairs: leather shoes, suede shoes, patent shoes, lizards, snake skin, crocodile skin, *ostrich* skin for crying out loud, all of which I was forbidden to touch, and cleaning them seemed to be his number-one hobby.

The first thing my mother bought after he moved in was a huge wardrobe just for his stuff, but it wasn't enough. They spilled over into the wardrobe in the spare room and, over time, spread till they covered the bed completely. In fact, after a while it was like the spare room had become his personal walk-in wardrobe. Had we had a guest, there wasn't a space inside that room they could've sat never mind slept.

But the changes were much vaster than him and his clothes. They included the things I was used to and virtually everything I'd come to take for granted in my home. For example, before he came, my mother cooked what *we* liked, and that was chicken. Chicken and rice and peas, chicken curry, roast chicken, chicken soup, fried chicken. After he came, she was cooking for him: hard food instead of rice, boiling oxtail and butterbeans for hours on end, fried fish, fish soup, cow-foot and evil bubbling mannish water.

And suddenly, but kind of casually, like it had been happening my whole life, my mum began to serve up puddings after dinner. I was accustomed to puddings after lunch at school, but puddings *at home*? Before he came it would have been like chucking money down the drain. But suddenly, every meal had a pudding to follow it; apple pie and custard, rhubarb crumble, trifle, butterscotch-flavoured Angel Delight, treacle sponge pudding and home-made rum-and-raisin ice cream with cinnamon finely grated over the top.

Unused to a big meal followed by a hefty pudding, half the time I couldn't eat it. But Berris, he ate like it was his last supper every time; wolfed down those puddings like he had never tasted anything finer. Probably he hadn't. I wouldn't think many people had.

But the worst thing, the thing that got me most, was the evenings. Before Berris moved in, me and my mum would often stay up late watching TV: *Soap*, *Dallas* and *Dynasty*, *The Love Boat* and *Fantasy Island*. We were addicted to our weekly ration of other people's lives and dramas and even if one of us fell asleep, the other person made sure they stayed awake so they could fill in what had been missed. But after Berris came, the three of us would settle down in the living room, and all would be fine for about an hour or so. Then Berris would get up and say he was going to bed. About twenty minutes later, my mother would yawn loudly, as if suddenly overcome by fatigue. She would stretch and get up and say something about how tired she felt and go off to bed too. One time Berris actually went to bed at seven-thirty and she was just so exhausted she just couldn't keep her eyes open any longer come eight!

Everything changed when he came. *Everything*. I couldn't sleep in my mother's bed any more, because he was in there every night. Suddenly, I wasn't allowed to 'just bust' into her room, I had to knock first, and not just knock, I had to wait till it was convenient for them to *invite* me in. In my own home.

Every day I waited to hear that he'd sorted his situation out and would be moving on. I even checked his stuff for signs he'd started to pack, but there was nothing. It felt like it was *his* house and *I* was the visitor.

Berris wasn't a gradual drip drop of rain, an off-and-on downpour. It was like on a sunny summer's day there had been a sudden thunderclap, followed by a lightning flash and monsoon rain that poured without break, heavy, depressing, persistent, with no end in sight.

About six weeks after he'd moved in with us, one night after he'd gone to bed, when she yawned and stretched and stood up, that night, I'd had enough.

'How much longer is it gonna take him to find somewhere to live?' I asked. He was always 'him'. I would not call him 'Uncle' and I could not call him 'Berris' and I preferred to die rather than call him 'Daddy', so I called him nothing. She seemed surprised, as though living with him was just The Bomb for everyone.

'Why?' she asked. 'What's wrong with him being here? We've got the space. He's no problem...'

'No problem for you!' I shouted. 'I don't actually want to spend all my time in bed.'

I heard the crack of a slap before I realized she'd struck me, and I was stunned. There was a delay of a few seconds before I felt the sting across my cheek, and in that moment I could tell from her face, her surprise was equal to mine. She had never slapped me before. Never. And to do it over that man! I was more upset about that than the pain. I began to cry.

'I hate him. I don't want him here. This is Daddy's house, not his.'

An even more amazing thing happened then. I knew she'd surprised herself with the slap, so I was expecting her to comfort me, to turn back into the person I knew. Instead it was the opposite, she went further, becoming a stranger before my very eyes. Maybe she'd been changing for weeks and this was the first time I'd noticed, but I realized then. Suddenly I saw a strength in her I hadn't known existed. She pulled herself up to her full height, and looked at me steadily, coldly. The movement of her mouth when she spoke was exaggerated, like she was determined that even if I couldn't hear the words I would be able to lip-read them.

'This is *my* house,' she said. 'I say who comes and goes, and when. Berris lives here now. I hope I never have to have this conversation with you again.'

5

'S'funny thing to watch a person die. When you mum died, was out of the blue and there was things I shoulda said but I never, things I wished I'da told her but I didn't, and I have to say for years afterwards, man, that troubled me.

'I kept on saying if only I had the time back, and the knowledge I have now, I woulda done this for certain, I woulda said that for sure, woulda come clean for true and if I hadda done, maybe I coulda been happy. But Mavis taught me different. You don't just need the right time, have to be that in you mind, *you* in the right place too. And that's where you start in on the problem.

'When Mavis was ill, when we knew for sure she was gonna die, when I watched her getting smaller by the day no matter what I cooked and fed her, that was the time to talk, to clear my mind of the worries I'd had the whole of my marriage, put them straight once and for all, but I couldn't. It was the right place, but it felt like the wrong time. Hardly slept at all them last three months, tossing and turning like a fishing boat on top a rough sea, wondering what the best way was to put it; the best way to ask you dying wife, after you marry thirty-three years, if her thirty-two-year-old son was truly mine, just how to phrase it so's it wouldn't upset her.

'Upset her so much during her lifetime, did so many wicked things no other woman apart from Mavis woulda tolerate, yet she did. Knowing she was dying, I had no right to say a thing to add to the pile of all she already forgived me for, not a shred of right, not a ounce or drop. I wanted to ask more than anything. I *needed* to know. But I just couldn't do it. Couldn't bring myself to hurt her a single time more. In the end I swore to myself I would let it lie, leave all alone. I promised myself them words would never pass my lips. I would only do, I said, what needed to be done and say what she needed to hear me say and that was that.

'But that question ate at my belly same way the tumour ate at hers. Never give me no rest, man. We talked some talk. Most of it about back home. Talked about them twenty-odd years we growed up there. Talked about everything under the sun, even down to lipstick.' Lemon laughed, looking relaxed for a moment, swept along on the stream of his memories.

I lay there, watching him as he spoke without a glance in my direction, staring out into space. He could have been talking to me or to the room or to God. At some point, he picked up the tail end of what he had been saying and carried on as if there hadn't been a pause at all.

'When we was young men, boys really, when I first met Mavis, her lips was red. They had a flower back home, don't recall the name of it, but kinda like hibiscus. Folks used to call them "yellow flower". The girls used to take time to open them, peel back the petals careful like, one by one, fretting and watching in case was a bee inside. You ever see a black bee? I'm not talking about no bumblebee. Them black bees don't bumble, they fly like dragonflies, fast you see. And I tell you, them would soon as look at you as sting you. They was always round the yellow flowers, so the women had to be careful for true.

'Inside the petals was what we used to call "the male part", covered in a thick red powder. You rub you finger over the power then you rub it over you lips and that was lipstick. That was what all the girls wore then. That was the lipstick Mavis did have on the first time I clap eyes on her: yellow-flower red. When I try to remember her then, seems all I can see is her mouth and her teeth, pretty man, well pretty. She talked about yellow flowers, and school and the licks we used to get, and going to river, and mangoes. Man we eat some mangoes growing up. Eat mango till we have to go lie down. This is the kind of talk Mavis talk, recalling every tiny detail, while I feed her ice chips and press the flannel with little cool water on top her head, and all the while inside, that question was gnawing and gnawing away: *Tell me, Mavis, did someone else kiss those yellow-flower red lips before me? Did you pass off another man's child all these years? Is John truly my son?*'

He lit another cigarette and inhaled deeply, settling back on the settee beside me. I was getting used to his way of just stopping in the middle of the tale as if he were finished.

I resisted as long as I could, then, 'So?' I said. 'Did you? Ask?'

He shook his head. 'Couldn't. Wanted to so bad, but I couldn't do it. Them last weeks, she hardly spoke at all. Just *thank you*. And *I love you*. Then, two days before she died, she said it. Two words. Opened her eyes – was the only part I could still say for sure was her, the eyes, the only part the cancer couldn't manage and left behind. Seemed like she was calling me, and I put my ear to her lips and she said, "He's yours." That's all. *He's yours*. Didn't need to say who she meant 'cos we both knew. I never said a word to her but still she heard me, heard me asking. With her dying breath, she told me what I wanted to hear but was never man enough to voice...'

'Oh my God,' I said. Maybe the alcohol had made me hypersensitive, because this had to be the saddest tale I had ever heard.

'I couldn't even speak, was so choked. Just cried. And held her hand while she close her eyes and slept again.'

My head was woozy. I was listening to him, listening to the inflection in his tone, and though I wasn't sure my judgement was sound, it seemed he was not yet finished. He had wanted to know the truth, after thirty-three years no less, and she had told him. So why didn't it sound like the story was drawing to a close? Why did it not sound like the end?

'But?' I asked.

'The thing is this: I know Mavis love me. Can't say why but she did. Have to accept that, 'cos she never give me reason to doubt it. Was times when I rave all night Saturday, pass the day in other women's yard and come home late Sunday night after I know she gone a bed. And my dinner was always there, dished and cover up on the side waiting; no questions, no blame, not a word. She k*new* me. Like a mother know her child. And no matter what blame was mine, she still go out of her way to make things all right for me, to please me. That was the problem.'

'I don't get you,' I said.

'I know Mavis woulda never said anything to me to upset me because she never did. Never. So even though she said it, I know she coulda say so *not* because it was true, but because she know it's what I needed to hear, and she give me with her dying breath what she give me with her living life, a plaster, a kiss to make things better and stop me bawling. In hospital, them call it a plessi-bow...'

I shook my head. 'I don't want to hear any more...'

'I knew Mavis would give me that lie 'cos she knew I needed it.'

'Why couldn't you just believe her?'

'And I took it. And wept. The last time she open her eyes, I gave her back a lie from the depths of my heart, I searched and found it and gave it back. The last words to ever pass from my mouth to her ears, the killer lie to beat all lies, one last big one to grease her passage to Calvary. She open her eyes and saw me where I sat 'side the bed waiting with her. I pick up her hand, looked her straight in the face, give her one last kiss and I said, "I believe you".'

He looked at me. He wanted something from me. Wanted it bad. But I was too overcome by sadness to work out what it was.

'Was I wrong?' he asked.

'I can't judge you,' I answered. 'It's not my call.'

'You know what you think though, don't you?'

'What I think doesn't matter.'

He wouldn't let it go. 'It matters to me.'

I was surprised to find I felt so strongly about this woman, his wife, a total stranger. Whether he believed her or not was his business. Yet even though I knew that, I was angry with him. That he had taken Berris's word over hers. That he had allowed Berris to ruin his marriage and offered no resistance whatsoever.

'You should have believed her.'

Instantly, his eyes were filled with tears and he sniffed, looked away from me and sniffed again. A speck of blood appeared on the floor at his feet, then another. He cupped his hands below his nose as the blood began to pour.

'I need a tissue,' he said, and I jumped up and ran.

He was a difficult patient. He refused to lie down in bed and insisted he would clean up the settee and the floor himself as soon as the bleeding stopped. I helped him up the stairs to the bathroom, and when we got there he closed the door and locked me out. I cleaned up anyway, and when he came back down, holding a wad of toilet paper beneath his nose, and realized, he kissed his teeth.

I had to virtually force him to sit down on the settee (again he refused to lie) and to lean his head back to slow the flow. He seemed unsurprised; clearly this was not the first nose-bleed he had ever had, and he was adept at dealing with it, in an obstinate kind of resentful way. He refused tea and coffee and paracetamol, insisting the only thing he needed was another drink.

I made it for him, fretting, convinced that more hard liquor, which he appeared to have been drinking non-stop since his arrival, was probably the last thing he needed. And when he took a mouthful, with his customary wince as it went down, I wondered whether he had some kind of alcohol-related illness or whether he was drinking more because he had some other medical problem and was of the opinion it no longer mattered what he did. Had he come to see me because he was putting his house in order while he still had time? As I had learned, the fact a person was too young to die did not buy them any more time. Was he dying?

I sat away from him, in the wicker chair opposite, watching, gauging that the bleeding had almost stopped, thinking his skin colour looked less natural, more like the pallor I was accustomed to working with, stupefied by the realization that the thought of Lemon dying hurt, genuinely hurt; that there was a chink in the armour of indifference that I'd been enveloped in for years.

I felt it.

But I was no closer to telling him anything. He had told me heaps. More than I had asked for. Much more. Yet, so far, I had shared nothing. He was right, you couldn't just pick up a piece out of a story and present it on its own. Alone, it was worthless. But I had not spoken to anyone ever about that night, had never trusted anyone enough to tell them the truth about what happened with my mother. I hadn't wanted to.

And now that I did want to, it seemed an impossible task. He didn't need to know about Sam and her family and the garages and Donovan. I wasn't his kind of storyteller, taking everything back to the dawn of time, slowly building up to the point chapter by chapter. This man was indecent. The choices he had made were beyond understanding, but the heinousness of them, the shamelessness, his disgraceful honesty, made him the one. It was either him or it would forever be no one. It *had* to be him. Maybe the beginning was wherever I chose it to be. It did not have to be Sam's spots, or meeting Berris. Maybe it had nothing to do with feet and where toes were pointing.

'I'm an embalmer,' I said.

'What's that?'

'I prepare the dead, so their families can see them. I work on people who have died, black people mostly, as a freelancer. Most of the funeral parlours round here use me. Probably because of the hair. They never know how to manage our hair. So they get me in and I do it, fix their hair and repair their faces, make them look comfortable, give their families back some peace. That's what I do for a living.'

'What kinda job is that?'

'I enjoy it,' I answered. I could not explain that it was the only thing I truly enjoyed, that among the dead was the only time I felt happy, that I was able to feel while I did my work: pride, vanity, grief, sadness, loss, *something*. That while I worked on those cold bodies, sometimes I found myself humming.

'Can't you get a job in some kinda beauty parlour instead?' he asked, and I laughed aloud.

'I could, but I don't want to.'

'Seems a strange way to make a living.'

'Someone has to do it. Someone did it for Mavis. Bet you appreciated it then.'

'It's no kinda life.'

'It's the only life I have.'

'It ain't...normal.'

'It suits me.'

I wanted him to link my work to *her*. It was an obvious link, but I needed him to make the connection himself. Then I could explain it was some kind of atonement and tell him why. I waited.

'You better not be planning to get them hands on me,' he said.

Despite my disappointment, I laughed again. 'I can wait.'

'Good,' he said, but he shook his head slowly for a long time afterwards and I knew he was disappointed too. He wanted more for me and I knew it would have been impossible to make him understand that for most of my adult life there had been nothing more that I wanted, nothing more that I needed, nothing more.

I put the TV on, sat back down beside him, and watched it in silence. Or at least I acted like I was watching it, face fixed resolutely in the direction of the screen. It felt strange, the close proximity, the sharing of the sofa, the evening. It reminded me of the years I'd spent watching TV in this same spot on another settee, with my mother, just us two; easy years, carefree times. I found myself more relaxed than I could remember being in a long time. And when he casually slipped his arm around me, over my shoulders, and pulled me closer so I was leaning into his warmth, I didn't resist or pull away. I snuggled up against him as my son had done, and felt just like a child.

In silence he held me, gently rubbing the top of my arm with his warm palm and I felt safe. For the first time since she had gone.

I felt it.

Though I was no closer to telling him the terrible truth, I felt okay and I was grateful. I knew it was merely a lull, the calm before the storm, yet his being there with me made me feel like maybe, somehow, there was a chance, the smallest suggestion of a hope, that things might turn out okay.

She made saltfish and Johnnycakes for breakfast. We'd never had it for breakfast on a weekday before, because the saltfish needed to be soaked overnight and boiled two or three times before it was ready to be used. And her Johnnycakes were a slow job, requiring sifting and kneading and frying on a low flame, to ensure that the outside didn't cook while the middle was still doughy, and by the time the middle cooked, the outside wasn't burned. It was a Special Treat, one we'd normally have for breakfast on Christmas Day or at Easter, and always on my birthday because, as we both knew, saltfish and Johnnycakes was my favourite breakfast.

We both also knew she'd cooked it because of the slap.

She must have gotten up at the crack of dawn to have it ready before I left for school, and I was glad – glad she'd recognized that what she'd done was weird and wrong, and even more glad that it had kept her awake, gnawed away, forced her out of the warm bed she now shared with Berris and into the kitchen at a time of day when those with clear consciences were still hard and fast asleep.

I ate without speaking, swallowing bulky mouthfuls slowly, pretending not to watch as she packed up Berris's precious portions into a couple of Tupperware containers for his lunch.

She kept up a perpetual flow of conversation, about the quality of saltfish on sale down Ridley Road Market, how it was best to buy a whole fillet rather than the pieces cut to fit the small packets they were usually sold in, because after you boiled what saltfish was inside them, then skinned and boned it, there was often hardly any actual fish left and by the time you finished cooking, there was nothing in the pot but onions.

She was wearing a dressing gown, slinky satin, in a dark gold colour, one I hadn't seen before. Underneath, she wore a matching nightie that was so short, when she moved and the gown opened over her legs, it looked as though she was completely naked till you caught a glimpse of the hemline, high up, more like a piece of underwear than something to keep you warm at night. I wondered where it had come from. Had *she* bought it or had *he*? What had she done with all her old nighties and pyjamas? When you started living with a man, did you need a whole new wardrobe of bedwear?

When Berris came in to collect his packed lunch, he was dressed casually in jeans and a black polo neck, hurrying because some other guy who worked with him at the Lesney factory gave him a lift in the mornings and he couldn't make him late. He still found time though, when she kissed him goodbye, to put his hand on her bum, run it over the irresist-ible silky smoothness and give it a squeeze that made her jump and then style it out like no one knew she'd swallowed a shriek. She laughed and wriggled away from him, glancing over at me where I sat staring at my plate like it was the telly. A moment later he was gone and I felt my confusion begin-ning to clear. She owned this house and he owned her. The only thing I needed to get my head around was where exactly I fitted in.

'I thought maybe we could go out later,' she said. 'After school. I'll come by and meet you and we can go down Kingsland Road, do a bit of shopping. Would you like that?'

She knew me and she knew I would like that very much. To me it was kind of like I knew she was sorry for slapping me and that she was doing her best to make up for it, but while I knew that and felt sorry for her, I just couldn't bring myself to act like it hadn't happened or I'd forgotten or things were cool, so I shrugged as if it was no big deal.

When she tried to put her arm around my shoulders I stood up quickly, lifting my plate and stepping away from the table. I turned my head to the side when she went to kiss me so that she almost kissed the air beside my cheek.

'See you later,' I said, without looking at her.

Walking up the road to meet Sam, I wondered why it was that *I* was the one who'd been left feeling bad.

'Only reason it even seems like anything big is 'cos you don't get regular beats,' Sam said. We were in the toilets at first break, in front of the mirror. She had both her mouth and her right eye opened into an O and, when she talked, it was without moving her lips. She held a tube of mascara in one hand and was using the other to apply the make-up to her lashes. 'If you lived in my yard, you'd know something about beats.'

'Yeah, but ain't it worse if you never get hit, to then get slapped for no reason?' I asked. Sometimes she was so annoying. It was like whatever was going on with you was always small fry. She'd already experienced it on a much bigger scale and your titchy problem was nothing compared to what she'd been through.

'Yeah, but what did you think she would say when you started going on about sex?'

'I never said nothing about sex!'

'Oh? Like they're really going bed that early 'cos they're just so tired. *Every* night. I've told you, black people are more sexed than white people. What did you think they were doing?'

Suddenly, it was clear to me that she was right. No wonder she sometimes talked to me like I was some kind of idiot. Had my mum thought when I'd said 'bed' that I was talking about sex too?

'Sam, just forget it,' I said.

She was blinking fast in front of the mirror now.

'They're at it big time, boy, night after night, like rabbits...'

'Puh-lease!'

'I know for a fact your mum ain't wearing no costume at night.'

'Why would she be doing that?'

'S'what you have to do if you don't want more kids. Especially if you're with a black guy. My mum's got three.'

'Your mum's got *three* swimming costumes?'

'Yep. She always wears them. Under her nightie. Every night. You telling me your mum ain't got none?'

I sifted through her wardrobe of nightwear old and new in my head, and shook it.

'Then don't be surprised if any day now you hear the patter of little feet.'

I didn't want to talk to Sam about my mum having sex. I didn't even want to think about it.

'Sam, I beg you, shut up right now or I'll kill you!' I snatched the tube of mascara out of her hand, whipped out the brush and brandished it at her, slipping my feet into a fencing position, like d'Artagnan from *The Three Musketeers*. 'With this!'

She looked at the brush, looked at me, and raised her eyebrows.

'Jay, you're really scaring me, man.'

She snatched it out of my hand as the bell went. We began to make our way back to class.

'I got asked out again last night,' she said casually, like she'd only just remembered. She'd gone to the garages after school yesterday on her own again. For years everything we'd done we'd done together. Every interest we had was shared. We'd talked about boys, but they were outside of us and the things we did. But recently, something had changed in her, like us being together wasn't enough any more, playing with our hair, running jokes, passing notes, swapping

Mills & Boons, all those things we'd done a thousand times, that I wanted to do a thousand more, she now called 'dry'. She wanted excitement, the unknown, more. Increasingly, it felt like she had a double life, the one she shared with me, and another separate world over the garages. At first she used to tell me everything that went on there. Now she specially selected bits to tell me and I found myself endlessly trying to work out how much of what she'd told me was true and what had been left out. For some reason it all felt kind of seedy to me. According to Sam, that was because I was too stuck-up, or to use her word, *stush*.

'Who by?'

'Donovan, innit.'

'And?'

'Blatantly it ain't happening.'

'Why are you so wicked to him?'

'I ain't ready for no big-time relationship. I'm young, man. I've got my whole life ahead of me and I wanna have some fun. I ain't tying myself down. I'm gonna be a air hostess or a actress and I don't want no big ole black ole weight holding me back, bawling every time I'm getting on a plane, breeding me down.'

'Did you tell him that?'

'I said I'd think about it. He's gonna be over the garages later. You have to help me decide how I'm gonna blow him out. You *are* coming, aren't you?'

'I can't,' I said. 'My mum's meeting me from school.'

'Jay, you know what? If you let them, parents will fuck up your life for good,' she said.

*

Of course, there was no sign of that opinion when we walked out of the school gates to find my mum leaned up against the barrier waiting for me. She looked good, slim and attractive and well dressed, young in comparison with the parents of the other kids. Even so I felt kind of sheepish, but Sam was straight in there with *Hello, Mrs Jackson. I'm very well, thank you. Yes they're all fine. I'd love to come with you, but I've got my own chores waiting for me.* Then with a quick wink at me and a pat of her hair, she was on her way.

My mum and I went shopping down Ridley. She bought me two pairs of leg warmers and a wicked pair of Levis. Then we went to a café near the bottom of the market and ordered dinner, just us two, like in the old days, before Him.

Normally, it would've been a real treat being there, but I felt awkward sitting opposite her. It had been easier not speaking while we were moving and the market was bustling around us, but now it was just us and the silence that came from my end and drowned out her attempts to make up.

Then out of the blue she just said it.

'I shouldn't have slapped you. It was wrong and I'm sorry. I was angry, but that doesn't make it okay. I won't do it again.'

For some weird reason my eyes filled with tears.

'Jinxy, I know this is hard for you. I know that. You've had me to yourself nearly your whole life, and now you have to share. I understand that. But you have to try and understand as well. One day, you're gonna leave...'

'No I won't.'

She smiled. 'You will. You'll grow up and fall in love with someone wonderful and you'll want to be with them and you'll go. Would you have me sitting on my own in that big old house, lonely and crying? No one to talk to, no one to laugh with, no one to hold me?'

I did understand, although the 'hold me' bit was embarrassing. I knew what she meant and I knew she wasn't being unreasonable, but I still said, 'It's not fair.'

'Talk to me,' she said. 'Tell me what I can do that would make things okay for you.'

What came to my mind was: *Chuck him out! Tip his stuff into the street! Let him go be tired in some other woman's house! Make everything as it was before!* I shrugged my shoulders and she sighed.

'I love him,' she said, when I had most wanted her to say she loved me. 'I love him and he is a part of my life now...part of *our* lives. But it doesn't change anything between us, me and you. I will always be here for you. Do you believe me?'

My throat was so choked I thought my voice would break. 'Yes.'

She reached over the table and held my hand, squeezing it firmly enough to make me look at her, but not enough to hurt. 'That is my promise to you for all time. I will always be here for you.'

'I believe you,' I said. She let go of my hand as our plates arrived. I wiped my eyes as though I was just flicking off a speck that had randomly landed on my lashes. 'This looks good,' I said and smiled at her. She returned the smile and we ate.

*

It was after seven by the time we returned back home. I was happy we'd gone out together, that we'd managed to sort things out. I was determined to try harder to be understanding of Berris even though I didn't want him there, because she *did* want him there and she was my mum and he made her happy, and somehow I had to find a way to make the best of it.

But he was vexed.

He hardly looked at her when we came in. He was in the living room, just sitting on the settee, not playing music or watching TV. I wondered if he'd been standing at the window watching out for us coming down the street. He acted like we'd done something wrong, but I didn't know what that was. My mother didn't know either, I could tell. She made light of it, pretending she hadn't noticed his mood, kissing his cheek and making jokes like he was happy and joking back with her. When he looked at me, I saw something in his eyes that I understood, and it surprised me. It had been the first time since he'd moved in that she'd spent any time with me on my own, two or three hours on one occasion in nearly two months, that was all.

And he was jealous.

To me he was acting like a child who was angry with his friend for liking someone else as well. His lips were pursed, he wouldn't meet her eyes or speak. He met mine though, and the message in them was clear: he was upset and it was my fault. I couldn't do the chirpy acting my mum was styling out like she was aiming for an Oscar, and in the end, after all the complaining I'd done about the two of them going to bed early, I ended up leaving them in the living room, for the first time the first to go to bed. I said that I was tired and went upstairs to my room.

I lay in bed, on my back, a Mills & Boon propped open against my knees, and I would have been reading it if it had been possible to concentrate. But I couldn't. I could hear them. Arguing. I couldn't hear the details, but I could hear the pitch of their voices. His was angry. Accusing. Hers was placatory. Pleading. At some point I was sure she was crying.

I got off the bed and went over to the door, opening it slightly, still standing inside my room, able to hear a bit better, alarmed but unable to decide if I should go downstairs or stay in my room and carry on pretending I couldn't hear a thing. Suddenly I heard my mum cry out, loudly, as if she'd been hurt. It went quiet then for what felt like a very long time and my indecision felt like a pressure building up inside me. I heard someone come up the stairs and go into the bathroom and close the door. The footsteps were hasty and clumsy.

Berris.

I waited a few minutes longer, scared he would come straight back out and catch me, but he didn't. Finally, I forced myself to move my feet and they carried me down the stairs.

I walked into the kitchen and, to my surprise, he was sitting there, at the table on his own, eating leftover Johnnycakes and saltfish; waxing it off.

He looked up at me in that strange way I was still getting used to, not actually meeting my eyes, just kind of focusing on me in bits; firstly my hair and then my breasts, then nodded in the direction of my feet before his eyes went back to his plate. I didn't know whether he'd been greeting me, or if I'd just been dismissed.

There was something about him at that particular moment which disturbed me, but it was hard to put my finger on it exactly. It was as if he had a glow around him, not the visible one around the kids in the Ready Brek advert, more of an aura I couldn't see but felt instead, something physical and static and scary. I didn't like him, I knew that. But it wasn't just dislike I felt, it was fear, the kind of fear you experienced passing a digi group of bullies when you were on your own. His eyes had that same look about them that I'd seen in the eyes of bullies, not just threatening, but smug too, like he knew something that gave him power over anyone who was weaker. It made me feel afraid.

'Where's Mum?' I asked, looking around the kitchen, though it was obvious she wasn't there.

'Upstairs in her room,' he said and he flicked his head towards the ceiling, like he was saying *Up there* and at the same time telling me he couldn't care less. I waited for a second, but he didn't look back up.

'Thanks,' I said, relieved to be leaving the room and more worried than I had been before I had entered.

She was still inside the bathroom and though the door was closed it was unlocked, so I tapped first and when she didn't answer, opened it and saw her, bent over the sink with the cold tap running. She was splashing water on to her face.

'Mum?'

She turned her head to look at me.

'Oh my God,' I said and she turned away quickly and started squeezing out the flannel in the sink, carefully folding it and gently dabbing at her face. I took a step closer, watching her movements through the mirror above the bowl. The left side of her face was bruised, from the eye – puffed up so bad it could hardly open – to the cheekbone. Against her pale skin, the bruising was a riot of colours, a deep maroon giving way to dark red giving way to crimson round the edges. And in the centre, a gash about an inch long bled.

'It's all right,' she said in a chatty kind of tone, talking well fast, 'it looks worse than it feels. Don't start fretting, Jinx. I'm really fine.'

Downstairs the front door slammed. I assumed it was Berris, leaving. As if that was her cue, she sagged to her knees, covered her face with her hands and I stood dumbstruck beside my mother as she started to cry.

He'd done it. I knew in my stomach it was him, but when I tried to ask her about it she fobbed me off, and when I pushed it she started getting angry, so I ended up backing off and though it was the most traumatic thing that had ever happened in our house, we didn't discuss it.

But even though I wasn't putting my thoughts into words, I couldn't get the questions out of my head. Like, what could make a big man like Berris punch my mother in the face? How could he have looked at my beautiful mum and done that, then calmly sat downstairs and eaten? From what I saw, she did everything he wanted, tried her hardest to be perfect for him. I could think of nothing she could've done or said that made sense of how he'd manhandled her.

Maybe she was right when she said I was too young to understand. Maybe that was true. But the way she cried, the level of her upset, I was sure she was no clearer on the answers to those questions than I was.

We stayed up together till late that night, like old times, me sat beside her on the settee watching TV, her arms around my shoulders, kissing my head from time to time, silently wiping away the tears that just refused to stop coming, while I acted like I never saw them. She wasn't watching the telly really and neither was I. We each pretended for the other's sake that everything was perfectly normal, ho hum, when it was clear the whole world had violently tipped and life as we knew it was upside down; each of us pretending neither had our ears cocked for the sound of his return, that neither of us was dreading it.

It was after twelve when we finally went to bed, yet late as it was I couldn't go to sleep. I felt too confused, as if I'd been battered myself. Confused by all the feelings inside me that had nowhere to go, but still boiled and bubbled furiously like mutton inside a pressure cooker.

I wanted to kill him. I'd been angry before in the past, but nothing on this scale ever. I wanted him dead. My heart bled for her, but for him I prayed for a double-decker bus to mow him down that very same night, to splatter his carcass across the high street in a dead, flat mass. I hated him.

Yet beneath that, to my shame, and I would have rather died than admit it to anyone, beneath that, I was glad. It was clear to me he'd messed up big time. The single bright light that shone for me that night was that he'd gone too far. He'd hurt my mum in a way that was beyond understanding. What he had done, she'd never forgive. I'd wanted him out of our lives and, with his bad-tempered self, he'd handed it to me on a plate. After what he'd done, the relationship was over; I knew beyond any doubt that now and for all time she'd never take him back.

It would probably take a while for her to get over it, but once she did, things could return to normal and I would, as I'd wanted all along, have my mum back to myself. We would be happy, the two of us, the way we were before he came. And it was that comforting thought alone that made it possible for me to relax enough to finally get some sleep.

I brought her breakfast in bed. Tea and toast with scrambled eggs, arranged on a tray beside a love heart I'd cut out and coloured in myself to cheer her up. With him gone, I didn't have to knock. Still I entered her room on tiptoe, so as not to wake her. But on that score, I needn't have worried at all.

She was lying under the bedspread, on her side, eyes open, staring at nothing, and I wondered if she'd managed to get any sleep at all that night, because she looked wrecked.

She smiled and sat up, trying to act like everything was still cool, but it wasn't and I knew it. She was treating me like a baby, like I wasn't old enough for her to tell me stuff, so young and stupid in fact that if she pretended hard enough, I wouldn't be able to guess there was anything wrong at all. And it struck me as weird really, because not only did I feel older, but it felt as though everything was reversed and somehow I'd become the mum and she was now the child.

'Aren't you going to school?' she asked.

'It's just revision. It's okay. I won't miss anything.'

Normally there'd have been no way she would have let me skip school for no good reason. But I think she was too tired to make an issue of it. She must have known there was no way on earth I was going to go to school and just act like it was some regular, random day. How could I leave her alone in the state she was in?

She didn't eat much. In truth, I'd done a bit of a bodge-job. I'd been concentrating so hard on stirring the eggs that I forgot the toast under the grill and it had burned. By the time I scraped off the black bits it was cold and somehow, all the black bits managed to get into the butter, which didn't melt into the toast like it was supposed to, but just sat on top looking filthy. She was kind of humouring me with the few nibbles she had, but she didn't fancy it and I could hardly blame her. She drank most of the tea though, and smiled at me between sips, and picking up the heart, she looked at it, blinking fast, and touched my face and kissed me and said thanks.

Her eyes kept welling and spilling, despite the smiles. It felt like her heart was broken and the knowledge broke mine. I wanted her back to normal but I didn't know how to make that happen. I looked at the pathetic heart I had made. It had been childish of me to think a scrap of paper could change everything in a flash. How could it be possible for a tiny piece of paper to accomplish a massive thing like that? That day I learned a new kind of fear.

I ran her a bath and she lay in it for over an hour, hardly moving. I had to encourage her to get out and then all she wanted to do was just lie down and rest, like she hadn't already rested for most of the day. When I went to check on her at lunchtime to see if she wanted me to make her something else to eat she was fast asleep and, I had to admit it, I was relieved.

While she slept I cleaned up downstairs. I moved quickly, trying to keep ahead of the fear that dogged me. Not of Berris, but of her, how she was. It was like someone had shaken everything out of her, every ounce of hope, every decent memory, everything good she'd kept stored inside, and left in its place a sack, one that could still be shifted from place to place, propped up, made to lie flat, but no matter how hard I searched, was empty inside. It did my head in to see her like that, really did it in. What would happen if she stayed like that for good? Was it possible for someone to never recover from something like this? It was sick and it was selfish, but still I wondered, if she didn't recover, what would happen to me?

I took out some food and made dinner. I'd been watching my mother cook for years, marinating, seasoning, frying, boiling, stewing. In a baptism of fire, I went from scrambled eggs on toast to rice and peas and chicken. I discovered that what I had taken for granted, fine meals beautifully presented and tasting like heaven, was actually an art form my mother had perfected. It was tough, not just the chicken and the rice, but the whole process. Watching and doing were two different things. That was the second thing I learned that day.

I underestimated the time it took the red peas to cook and even though I'd boiled them for about an hour before I put the rice in, they were hard, rubbery edged with crunchy centres; and the rice was way overcooked, soggy as pudding. I turned the fire up under the pot to dry it out a bit and it burned at the bottom, leaving a distinctly smoky flavour, not yummy-smoked like sizzling bacon, more like the singe of overheated iron combs on hair.

But the chicken looked okay. I'd taken it out of the freezer and defrosted it under the running tap before seasoning it and putting it in the oven to roast. It looked a lot better than the gravy, which was pitch black from an overdose of gravy browning, and tasted well weird, more like a chemistry experiment gone wrong than anything I'd ever come across before on a dinner plate.

When it was ready, I carried her dinner up to her on a tray. I was relieved to see not only that she had gotten up but she was also dressed, sitting on the edge of her bed, painting her toenails. She broke into a smile when she saw the plate, which was good, though the laughter that followed was like the right sign in the wrong place. I went to get my own plate of food and we ate together in her room, something else we hadn't done in yonks.

I have to say the meal was despicable, and after the consolation I took from the chicken, which was the only thing on the plate that looked *nearly* okay, as soon as I cut into it, it began to bleed.

'Next time it will be better,' she said. 'Don't worry. When I was your age I didn't even know how to make a cup of tea.'

We took our plates back downstairs and emptied them and she helped me tidy up the mess I had made of the kitchen. She gave me some money and I left, headed for Kentucky's to buy us some finger-licking food it was actually possible to eat. She was up, she was moving, she was talking. I was so happy I wanted to fly. I bombed it all the way to Mare Street and then, so our food didn't get the chance to cool too much before we ate it, I bombed it back.

The round trip took about half an hour and I was out of breath as I opened the front door, calling out to her. She didn't answer. When I stepped inside the living room she was sitting on the settee looking down at her lap, demurely. Beside her sat a man I'd never seen before, tall and light-skinned, really good-looking for an old guy, and very smartly dressed. He smiled at me as I entered, real friendly like. It was so contagious that I smiled back automatically and the smile froze on my lips when I realized that Berris was in the room too, standing beside the window, his weight on one shoulder pressed hard against the wall, as if his legs alone were not strong enough to keep his body upright. His other hand was wiping away a stream of tears.

He looked at me. I think it was the first time he had ever looked me in the eyes for more than a few seconds, like he was so distraught he didn't care who saw him or what they thought, as if being that upset exempted him from pride and shame.

'This must be Jinx,' the other man said. 'I'm Berris' friend, Lemon.'

Looking at Berris, I experienced a feeling that I despised for years after. I'd never seen a grown man cry before. Never.

Up till then it was something I hadn't even known was possible. I must have read about forty Mills & Boon books all in all, and in not a single one had any man cried or even come close, whether they were sorry for what they'd done or not. And Berris looked like he had been crying non-stop for twenty-four hours straight. His eyes were red, the skin all around them puffed and swollen and blotchy. Even though his skin was dark, his nose was still blatant Rudolf.

I'd hated that man so bad for weeks, wanted nothing else in that time but that he pack up and get out of our home, yet he looked more wretched than any man, woman or child I'd ever seen in my life. Like he knew he'd done the worst thing a person could ever do and was truly, to the heart, sick and remorseful and sorry. He couldn't look at her and he couldn't stop himself from bawling like a baby. It was the most pathetic thing I'd ever seen.

In that moment, because I knew what he'd done, how he'd smashed in my mother's face in temper, because the memory of him polishing off his dinner and the look of pure satisfaction in his eyes was still fresh and vivid in my mind, my feelings shocked me. I looked at the man who had caused our family so much hurt, so much upset, and there was no denying it; I felt sorry for him.

I felt sorry for him.

6

It was the smell that woke me. Heaven scent. Both alien and familiar at the same time. First it permeated the air, then pervaded my nostrils, then made its way down to my gut where it took hold and wrenched hard, and I found myself simultaneously hungry and awake.

I lay where I had fallen asleep the night before, on the settee still. Lemon had put the blanket over me, wedged a pillow under my head, and I had slept like a babe. I didn't know where he had slept himself, but he was up now, in the kitchen, frying fish.

I could smell it.

Snappers maybe or red mullet. Traditional fare. The kind of fish my mother had fried, the kind of smell this house had not contained since that time. Maybe he intended to feed me to death, kill me with West Indian food, serve me every dish my mother had ever cooked and given me, bring back into this house everything that made me remember her and all those things I had foolishly thought I had been so successful in forgetting.

It smelled delicious.

I threw back the blanket and stood. It had been a long time since I'd had the pleasure of waking to a meal I hadn't prepared myself. I breathed in slowly, relishing the wonderful odour, realizing what I felt was more than mere hunger, it wasn't just a desire for something to pick at or nibble on: I was famished. Not only did I want to ingest the aroma, my mouth was salivating, my stomach contracting as though I hadn't eaten for weeks. The only time I could ever remember having that kind of physical response to food was when I had been pregnant with Ben, as though all sense of smell and taste had risen a plane, gone up a level, a hunger that was elevated to the realm of the supernatural. For a moment, my longing for the breakfast Lemon was cooking was so intense I actually felt afraid.

I folded up the blanket and took it upstairs with the pillow and had a shower. A fast one. And brushed my teeth and dressed and went back downstairs where I found him waiting for me, sitting on the second to bottom step. He stood up as I approached and nodded his good morning.

'I cooked breakfast,' he said.

'I know.'

'You ready for it now?'

'Yep.'

'Then come. We eat.'

I followed him.

I was right, it was red mullet, perfectly fried, crisp and salty on the outside, moist and steaming on the inside, served with a fiery salsa of onions, sweet and scotch bonnet peppers, tomatoes and garlic, and on the side of the plate, a small pile of cucumber, sliced wafer thin and smothered in lemon juice, pepper and salt.

'Is good?' he asked, watching me, his cutlery in his hands, his own plate as yet untouched.

My mouth was full so I nodded. I was eating slowly, exploring the tastes inside my mouth and the experience was as erotic as foreplay. I swallowed.

'Bloody good,' I said.

'You look like you could do with little meat on them bones.'

'Are you trying to fatten me up?'

'I'm just saying you don't need to be on no diet.'

'You're hardly Barry White yourself.'

'But I eat proper food.'

'*I* eat proper food.'

'Decent food.'

'Marinated overnight then cooked down for five hours?'

'With taste.'

'I have to admit, this is delicious, Lemon.'

'You look so much like her.'

'Don't spoil this for me,' I said.

He made sorrel. First sorting through the dried hibiscus flowers and discarding the bad ones, filling and refilling the kettle and pouring the boiled water into a mixing bowl that had been unused for almost a decade and a half. Then he tipped the flowers into the bowl, where they floated. He used a ladle to press them down into the water, where immediately they began to bleed.

I sat on the high stool and watched him.

The radio played soca in the background. Different parts of Lemon's body danced at different times; his bouncing shoulders, his nodding head, his tapping toes or winding waist or swivelling hips. At no time while he worked was he ever detached from the music. Even when he was grating fresh ginger into the mixture, he kept perfect time with the beat.

He threw in whole cinnamon sticks and a couple of cloves. With a knife he peeled the skin from a large orange in a single coiling strip and let it fall in. Then he halved and juiced a couple of lemons and added them as well. Last came the cane sugar and he poured in almost half the bag. The air was spicy and zesty, filled with the promise of tasty future treats.

'I can't remember when's the last time I had sorrel,' I said.

'I made this for Mavis once sometimes twice a week. Was one of her favourite drinks. And mine.'

He used a ladle to stir till the sugar was dissolved to his satisfaction. Finished, he turned the volume of the radio up and danced his way over to where I sat. He took my arm and tried to pull me to stand and dance but I resisted.

'I don't do calypso,' I said.

He continued dancing as if I had gotten up and was dancing with him, holding both my hands and moving them in time to the beat as he jumped and pranced and bounced his body against my legs and knees and thighs. It was impossible not to laugh, not to be swept upstream with him on the current of his exuberance, and as soon as I did he pulled me off the chair, and because it was pointless trying to resist any longer, I joined in. I couldn't remember the last time I had danced.

Afterwards, we put the telly on and he asked me to get the hair-grease and comb. He sat on the settee and I sat on the floor between his legs. Working in sections, he greased my scalp, then combed and plaited my hair in tiny perfect braids that were better than any I could have done myself. The last person to have done that was my mother. He was unhurried and so gentle. At one point I had to struggle to keep my eyes open it was that nice. And unexpected. I sipped sweet sorrel on a warm, full belly and found myself content.

'You did her hair as well, didn't you?' I asked, and he nodded. Then all was silent till he finished.

'You have any clippers?' he asked.

'Upstairs,' I yawned.

'Bring them down, and some cream.'

'What, *now*?'

'Unless you busy.'

I went upstairs to my bedroom, searched quickly, then brought them to him.

He clipped my fingernails, and filed them down. Then rubbed cream into my hands, slow and meticulous around the cuticles, so gently it was almost impossible to believe a man was doing it. Finished with my hands he did my feet. The nails first and then more filing. He took longer over creaming them, rubbing and squeezing and pressing and massaging them on their way into foot heaven. I sat on the settee looking down at him, watching as he worked, studying the careful precision of his fingers, marvelling that I had ever thought them clumsy, relaxing till it seemed I might slide off the settee into a shapeless, boneless heap of melted contentment at his feet. And still he rubbed.

With his fingers.

I was aroused.

He looked up at me and I wondered, did my breathing change? Had my temperature suddenly soared? I couldn't say precisely how, but I knew he knew exactly what I was feeling; he had always known, always. The words tumbled out of my mouth involuntarily.

'I love you.'

The movement of his hands slowed, almost to a stop.

'You don't know me.'

'I know enough.'

'You got no idea who I am, the things I've done.'

It wasn't what I wanted to hear. On the verge of tears I said, 'I don't care.'

He released my feet and stood. 'I shouldn'ta come.'

'Why won't anyone love me?' The tears began to fall and I hated them for coming now, for the indignity, but I had no more control over them than I had over the words queued up inside my throat. 'Not her! Not him! Not you! Not even my son! Why?'

'She did love you.'

'She didn't.'

'I know she did.'

'She loved him, only him. After he came there was nothing left for me. Nothing.'

'How can you think that?'

'I was there! I saw!'

'From what I seen, I know she loved you.'

'And you?'

'I don't have the right.'

'I give you the right.'

'You don't know enough to say that.'

I was shameless in my begging. *'Please!'*

'I'm sorry,' he said and reached his hands out as if he wanted to hold me, to embrace and comfort me. I chopped at his outstretched arms with one of my own as hard as I could, and with the other I wiped my face.

I said, 'In that case, keep your fucking hands to yourself!'

I felt like an idiot, a silly adolescent child. Like I was sixteen years old again. What was the point of time passing if nothing changed? I cleaned the bathroom. Wiped out the bath and the bowl and the shower. Then the mirror and every surface. And swept and mopped then dried the floor.

I was fuming. At myself. For wanting too much, for asking. For forgetting that I had loved him once before and had already been hurt. Furious that what I wanted to say was still bound tight inside me and I was blurting out the things that were better kept hidden. It was the food, and the drink, and the comfort, peeling back my armour to leave me naked. Instead of loving my son, I was loving this man who had already let me down, doing what my mother had done to me. I studied my face in the mirror seeking any sign that I had changed, or worse, seeking signs that I had changed into her.

He was in the kitchen when I went back downstairs, funnelling the last of the sorrel into empty bottles he must have retrieved from the recycling box outside. When he looked at me I wondered what he saw. *Who*. I wanted to say sorry, but unlike the declarations of love mobilized to burst their way free of my lips, the apology merely smouldered.

He smiled.

It was as simple as that.

He smiled and we were friends again.

'These will keep for weeks,' he said, indicating the bottles.

I nodded slowly as if that was an extremely useful thing to know.

'If you keep them in the fridge. They can prob'ly even freeze.'

'I'm sure I'll drink them before then.'

He looked away from me for a moment, to the side where his drink sat. He put his finger into the glass and swirled the ice around. He took the finger out and rubbed his hands together to rid them of the moisture.

'If you want me to, I'll go.'

'I don't want you to.'

'I don't know what I'm doing, why I bothered to come. I told myself it was for you, but that's not true. I never did nothing I didn't do for myself.'

'Join the club,' I said.

'I should be strong. What I have to tell you don't really make no difference after all this time. Only reason for telling you is that it might do some good for me.'

'Okay.'

'Thing is, I don't know where to start...'

'You've been talking for days. You've already started, haven't you?'

He smiled again. 'That's true. You right. Think I'm just stalling. I brought things to make Guinness Punch. You like it?'

'I do, but I'm running out of space in my fridge.'

'We'll drink it when I'm done.'

'Okay.'

He held his palms out towards me and said, 'I just need something to do with these hands.'

'Okay.'

'Only, I forgot the Nutrament. I'm gonna pop out and buy some. I won't be long.'

'Fine.'

I stood aside to let him pass, but he didn't move. My eyes met his and communication started.

'One last thing. You know you said nobody loves you?' he asked. Instantly my vision was blurred by tears and I nodded. 'Just think I prob'ly need to say that that's not true.'

7

The mirror I held in my hand was bigger than my head, yet it was too small to be able to see everything I wanted to see, to see all the things I needed to see in order to get my head around the things in my life that it was impossible to get my head around. Still, I looked.

Though it was a Thursday morning and I should have been leaving for school, my mum was pressing my hair. I could hear the iron comb sizzling, could smell the scorch as it passed through my nappy locks, magically transforming them into silken tresses that were straighter than when she'd started, closer to the coolie hair on her own head that she was able to take for granted.

The comb had to be blazing to do its job properly – not red hot, which would burn the hair off my head, but – in my view anyway – not much cooler. I sat on a chair beside the cooker, adjacent to the low flame of the front burner, watching her section and comb and press, holding the towel tight around my shoulders so my uniform wouldn't get messy, and each time the rising smoke cleared, I found myself examining her face.

If anything, that morning, the bruising looked worse. Overnight the redness had settled to black-greens and purpley-browns that glistened beneath the Vaseline she'd smoothed over it. I was trying to focus on watching what she was doing with my hair, tensed for the sear of the iron comb against my scalp, or worse – and more likely – the top tips of either ear, but my eyes and my thoughts were on *her*, trying my hardest to understand how it was possible for anyone to look so beat-up and yet so happy at the same time. And boy was she happy. She was so full of joy that day, she was glowing.

He was back.

It had been inevitable from the moment he dragged his sopping carcass into our living room. Even though I knew it was a waste of time, I had still harboured the faintest of hopes that he'd brought Lemon around to help him pack, but of course, he hadn't. Lemon had come to beg on Berris's behalf for my mother's forgiveness. His presence was needed to stop her phoning the police in a panic, thinking Berris had returned to the house to finish her off. He was there to act as a peacemaker, to keep the discussion calm, to hand Berris the occasional tissue, to keep me occupied so that the two of them could have privacy for their Big People Talk.

In the kitchen, Lemon asked for a cup of tea and I made it. He drank it while I slowly picked at the chicken and chips I'd such a short time ago been so excited about. I ate with indifference and Lemon talked all the while, real friendly like, friendlier than Berris had ever been, asking about school, my lessons, my teachers there. My answers were short, you could even say abrupt. I couldn't really concentrate enough on what he was saying to have a full-blown conversation. It's very hard to have a normal discussion with anyone when you have one ear cocked and your whole body braced to charge out of the room at the first sound of a scream.

I'd made my way through about half the box when my mother bounded into the kitchen.

Beaming.

When we'd left her, she'd been all eyes downcast, on the verge of tears herself, utterly miserable. When she came into the kitchen, neither of us needed to ask for a summary of how their talk had gone. She was happy and laughing, even as she winced from the pull of sore skin over bruising.

'We've sorted everything out,' she said, virtually singing the words, and I felt so many things that even if anyone had actually bothered to ask my opinion, I wouldn't have had a clue what to say.

I felt sorry for her because I'd seen first hand how much he'd hurt her, not just physically, but her spirit, her mind. I was glad for her that he was back in her life and abracadabra, she was happy again. And Berris? I hated him, hated what he'd done. At the same time I felt sorry for him, for the low level his wrongs had sucked him down to, and in a way relieved. His suffering over the last day had obviously been on par with hers. Maybe it really was true love. I felt relieved for him that things had been sorted out, that he could now fix himself up and carry himself with a little more pride.

Every time I thought of how he'd looked, how wet and snotty and pathetic, I squirmed inside.

But for myself, I was wretched. I wanted him here, I wanted him gone. I wanted her happy, I wanted her to myself. Round and round it all went inside my mind like a merry-go-round, till my head began to feel like it was me that had taken the pounding.

And afterwards, Lemon had left briefly, then come back again. He'd stayed late, the three of them laughing and drinking and eating and joking till after midnight. Must be as soon as the front door clicked closed behind his back, they were ready for bed. Then this morning she was up early, fixing Berris a hearty breakfast before he went to work, hugging me, fussing over my hair, pressing it on a Thursday morning before school, a process that took ages and was normally done on a Sunday night. She had a strange smell about her that I'd noticed before but couldn't identify, like the smell on her hands sometimes, hours after she'd been chopping onions. Not quite that smell, but like it. I felt again as I had yesterday, like I was the responsible adult and she was a kid who'd been naughty and was going to extra lengths to smooth things over.

'I don't want you to worry,' she said. 'All relationships have their ups and downs. And anyway, Berris never actually meant to hurt me. If I'm honest, what happened was more my fault than his. But I don't want you to worry about this. It's never gonna happen again...' She laughed. 'I think we must've stayed up the whole night talking.' She was quiet for a moment. When she spoke next, her voice was like ultra casual. 'Jinxy, I don't want you telling anyone at school about this, okay?'

'I won't.'

'Because it's our private business. You understand that?'

'Yes.'

'If anyone asks, I just tripped, coming down the stairs.'

My whole life till then she'd gone on about how important the truth was. 'Better a thief, than a liar,' she'd always said. Now she was actually instructing me to lie. I didn't know what to say to that and I think she was embarrassed, because she was quick to add:

'But I'm sure no one will ask you anything, so don't worry.'

As if that suddenly made everything okay.

'Guess what?'

Maybe she was speaking another language? I felt like I sometimes did in French, listening to tapes with French people talking on them, straining my ears for the odd word or two that I was actually able to understand, that put together with another word might make some sense of everything I was hearing. I was so confused it was beyond me to guess anything.

'What?'

My mother laughed again and, for a moment, she reminded me of Sam. It was the laugh the girls at school did sometimes when someone told them some guy they liked fancied them back, kind of surprised and giggly and blushing all in one.

'He's asked me to marry him.'

'Uh? Ow!' The comb seared the top of my left ear.

'That's your fault. You need to sit still.'

'That hurt!'

'I'll put some Vaseline on it, okay?'

'No it's not okay. It's not okay...'

'Come on, Jinx, you're being a baby. Don't you want your hair to look decent?'

'I was happy how it was before.'

'You want me to stop? I've only got a little bit left to do and we're done. Can I finish it?'

I nodded.

'Then stop crying. And sit still.'

I wiped my eyes as she continued. Other than the hot crackling of the comb it was silent. Then she asked, 'Well? What do you think?'

It was just too freaky. Even though he lived here, I still felt like I hardly knew him. And she'd only just taken him back last night. And that would mean he'd be with us for ever. This was my dad's house, but once they married it'd be like it was his. But she loved him and I knew it. She'd been happy since he'd been in her life and although she was asking my opinion like she genuinely wanted to know what I thought, I also knew she wanted me to *want* her to get married to him. She wanted me to say, *Yes, do it. What a great idea. We'll all be one big happy family*. I knew that.

'Isn't it a bit quick?'

'I'm not getting any younger. If we're gonna have our own kids, we need to get a move on.'

'Kids?' I felt dazed. Like she'd boxed me.

'You've always said you wanted a little brother or sister.'

It was true. I had. A million times. And the times I'd said it, I had truly meant it. Being an only child sucked. That was one of the things about Sam I was most jealous of. But this reality terrified me. And the words 'our own' made me feel sick, because I wasn't, was I? I didn't belong to them both. I was only hers. And a silly thought came into my mind, really childish but I couldn't push it away: do you love kids more if they belong to you and the man you're with? Is there enough love to go round? Or is there just a certain amount of it that gets divided up more ways so that somebody ends up with a smaller share?

'Have you finished?' I asked.

'I have. Shall I style it for you?'

'I'll do it myself.' I stood up.

'Well, what do you think?' she asked again.

I wanted to say, *I was here first!* Those were the words in my head that repeated themselves over and over like a stuck record, but it was too childish, too ridiculous to say.

'Do what you want. I don't care,' was the answer that came out instead. And before she could respond to that, I ran upstairs.

Sam was in a serious strop. She was vexed, her face was screwed up hard, and she did little more than grunt back when I said hello to her.

'What's up?' I asked.

She raised her hand in a Stop sign and shook her head. She was blushing badly. I didn't ask anything else, because I knew if she had said a word about whatever it was, she would have started to cry. If I was honest, her mood suited me. Though I couldn't get anything that had happened out of my head, I couldn't talk about it either. And it wasn't because of what my mum had said, the reason was even weirder: I was ashamed. I couldn't understand why I felt that way about what Berris had done to my mum, but I did. It was as if somehow what he'd done reflected on us, on my mum, as though in some way we deserved it or it was our fault, *her* fault. I felt embarrassed to hold my mother, with her outward-pointing toes, up to Sam's scrutiny. So even though I could have burst with the words stuck deep down inside me, I said nothing.

When we got to the bus stop, she carried on walking and I followed without question. She was doing some kind of funky walk, kind of like she was kicking imaginary leaves out of her way with every step and, at the same time, didn't really care if they were kicked out of the way or not. It took nearly fifteen minutes, till we were nearly at Dalston Junction Station, before her walk returned to normal and she finally spoke.

'So what happened to you yesterday?'

'I came on. I had really bad cramps so I stayed home.'

'Lucky you,' she said.

'*Bloody* lucky,' I threw back.

Though the lie came easily to my lips, I didn't look at her as I spoke because I was sure the fact I was lying my head off would be painted across my face. Desperate to get off the subject I asked, 'So did you speak to Donovan?'

'I've got better things to do than waste my breath on that renter,' she said. I took that to mean the talk hadn't gone well.

'Bet your mum bought you loads of stuff,' she said, but it came out sounding kind of resentful and for some reason made me feel embarrassed.

'Just some jeans,' I said.

'Nice.'

'I'da preferred it if she hadn't needed to suck up to me in the first place.'

'*My mum smacked me! And now she's bought me jeans,*' she whined. 'You're acting like you got the worse problems in the world, man. Grow up!'

She cut me deep and the rest of the way to school we trod in silence.

As if God had been listening and had not approved of my lie, halfway through double French I really *did* come on. With it came period pains so strong I felt nauseous. I hadn't packed any pads, so I had to go to the office to borrow one. I didn't want to go back to my lessons and I didn't want to go home. I returned to the office to ask for a couple of paracetamols and asked for permission to lie down in the sickroom till they took effect. The secretary gave me both.

The sickroom was the best place on earth for a person as wretched as I felt. Small and sterile, empty of everything, even medical supplies. It was like a broom cupboard painted white, with a small camp bed inside it, and on top of that a pillow, and on that a small, thin blanket folded neatly. Just the bed and a chair from one of the classrooms, and in the corner by the window, a small sink. No pictures on the walls, nothing to distract you from the objective of being there: getting well.

That morning, the dry, bare space felt like a sanctuary. I was angry with my mum, I was angry with Berris and now I was angry with Sam. For the first time in my life I felt completely alone. And old. Way older than sixteen and I wondered if my childhood was over, if the best and most carefree years of my life were already in the past, and how it had happened that out of the blue my life had become so full of confusion on every front.

At first break Sam came looking for me. She was shame-faced, like she knew she'd been well out of order. After a quick enquiry about how I was feeling, she flopped down on the chair with her arms folded across her stomach, and I swear she looked as unhappy as I felt. It was like the thing with my mum, like again I was still angry, but at the same time I knew she was sorry, and even if I'd wanted to, it was impossible to keep up a stand-offish front, because she looked so miserable.

'Are you gonna tell me what's up?' I asked.

'I found out Donovan's been two-timing me,' she said.

I tried to get my head around that. How he could be two-timing her when she hadn't told me she was going out with him in the first place and, secondly, I thought she wanted to blow him out, so what difference did it make if he went out with someone else?

'Oh,' I said. Even to my ears my response sounded a bit inadequate, so I quickly added, 'That's well weird.'

'All the while he's been going on like *yeah, baby, I love you*, and the whole time he's been saying exactly the same thing to some girl Paula, blacker than my bloody dad, with big old doo-doo plaits and buck teeth...'

I started laughing.

'It's not funny! He's been using me, all this time. Just using me,' she said and, *click!* just like that, it wasn't funny any more. I went from being a kid to understanding everything: that she'd felt more for him than she'd ever admitted to me; that like my mum, she was heartbroken, that she'd done It. With him.

'The bastard!' I said. Her face was getting redder and redder. I reached out and held her hand. She pulled it away.

'Don't or I'll start bawling my head off! Oh God…' – she stood up. 'Just thinking about it's making me feel sick.'

And she was. Sick. A combination of sobbing and vomiting that took us through the rest of the break. It was a lucky thing we were already in the sickroom with the sink right beside her, because if she'd had to make it to the girls' toilets, there would have been a trail of vomit through half the school all the way behind her. Although she'd come to see me because I was the one who wasn't well, I ended up having to get up and take care of her. Then, when we went to the office to tell them Sam had been sick and asked if she could stay in the sickroom as well, we ended up getting bawled out and were told we both had to get back to our classes, like we'd been lying and trying to skank our way out of our lessons.

Later, when we were supposed to be revising logarithms in maths with Mr Botha, between my stomach and my thoughts I couldn't concentrate on a word he was saying. I was lost, trying to get my head around relationships, how different they were in real life to Mills & Boons; how disappointing and seedy and unappealing. And I vowed I would never be like Sam or my mum, never cry over any man, never take their shit, never hand over the reins of my emotions, and I'd kill any man with my bare hands who ever tried to beat me. If what I was seeing was true love, I wanted no part of it. Any man who ever loved me would have to do it on my terms.

And they were: he would be light-skinned and sensitive and gentle and caring. He would be as good-looking as Superman himself, and like all the men in Mills & Boons, he would be mature. And experienced. Most of all, he would never hurt me or use me or do anything to make me cry. If he didn't match those criteria, he might as well forget it.

And for some very strange reason when I'd thought all that through, it was Lemon who came to my mind; Lemon, with his friendliness, his wide mouth, good looks and laughter.

The older, more sophisticated man.

And I shivered.

They'd been shopping. From the number of bags in the living room, it looked like they must have stopped and bought something from just about every single shop they'd passed on the way to the jewellers. My mother had mentioned marriage only this morning and by the afternoon, there it was.

The ring.

She'd also mentioned babies. Though he'd only been with us for two months, I wondered whether Sam was right, that any day now I'd be hearing the patter of little ostrich-shoed feet. Everything was moving too fast for comfort. It felt like I was playing catch-up.

She showed it to me.

Bling bling!

A white-gold band with a row of gems that twinkled and glittered every time she moved her hand, but no matter how hard they struggled to compete, they were overshadowed by her smile.

Berris said nothing. He sat on the edge of the settee, watching her watching him, the two of them playing games with their faces. It was like a whole language had evolved between them, one I could not speak or understand; whole statements made in the lift of an eyebrow, the puckering of lips, the cutting of eyes, the smiley mouths. Before, they'd had to go to bed to make me feel ignored. Now they were managing to achieve it even while I was in the same room.

He'd bought her a skirt, long and flowing, crinkled silk fit for a gypsy princess, and two pairs of shoes, pointy winkle-pickers I would have liked to have owned myself. She'd picked him out a bottle of aftershave because he only had like twenty bottles or so in his personal collection so far, and an LP by Roberta Flack, whose voice was strumming my pain with her fingers track by track as it played in the background.

And he'd bought her a real fur coat, a long one that fell from her shoulders to below her knees in thickest, darkest, sleekest brown. It was, without a doubt, the most luxurious and glamorous item of clothing she'd ever owned. It looked like mink, although he said it was just lame old cony fur from rabbits. Fur jackets were the cutting edge of cool and not only had I seen other women in them, but I'd longed for one myself. Hers was the first full-length one I'd come into close contact with, and it was by far the most beautiful coat I'd ever laid eyes on. In it, even I had to admit, she looked like a movie star, and she acted like one too, holding her hand in front of her mouth like a runway to launch the kisses she blew in his direction. All very Marilyn Monroe.

Finally, my surprise was brought out, in a green drawstring bag that identified it immediately. My instinct was to snatch it out of her hands, and it was only the fact that I remembered my age that stopped me.

'You bought me Dunlop plimsolls,' I said.

'Not me,' she said. '*We*.'

There was a time when if my mother had said *we* she'd have meant me and her. Now it was them. She was still a part of *we*; it was me who wasn't. *They* used to be other people, those who lived outside our home. Now *they* were inside; it was *me* and *them*.

In my view, it was a blatant case of curryfavouring. The fairy-tale king was becoming a fairy-tale father, so generous he was even prepared to treat the stepdaughter like his beloved own. I'd wanted those Dunlops for nearly a year, yet following fast on the back of the *we* comment, taking them out of the box made me feel ill.

'Try them on then,' she said, all excited. 'See if they fit.'

I toed a moccasin off one foot reluctantly and replaced it with a pristine white plimsoll.

'Perfect,' she said, though I wasn't sure if she was talking about the shoe or this fabulous new life of hers. She paused and waited, then quietly asked, 'What do you say?'

She'd hoped, I knew, that I'd have said it without the prompt. The words were there all right, clogging my throat, but I had to use the biggest force to get them out.

I glanced at him quickly and feigned a brief smile. 'Thank you,' I said.

I felt gutted, like everything in my life was wrong; somewhere I had taken the wrong turning and ended up lost. It was as if my mother's happiness was in direct proportion to my unhappiness, and any joy I had inside me was being sucked out to double her portion. I was running out of avenues in which to turn, and somehow she'd become oblivious to what I was going through.

Later that evening Lemon came round and, incredibly, I was as happy to see him as if he were *my* friend come to visit. He brought with him a bottle of Appleton's rum and some sweets in small white bags; a quarter of aniseed twist, a quarter of Tom Thumb pips, and a half-pound of pear drops, which he was particularly partial to; big ones encrusted in sugar, which cut the roof of your mouth if you got a bit impatient while you were sucking them.

I appreciated the sweets more than the plimsolls I'd so longed for. To me it was as if he'd actually been thinking of me and had made an effort to *not* make me feel left out, and it was ironic, because of everyone in the house at that moment, *he* was the outsider, the one I should have felt furthest from. Instead I felt closer to him than either Berris or my mum.

Lemon was the perfect house guest. He took no liberties. He didn't walk in with his bare hands swinging, dishing out demands. Not only did he not expect to be waited on, but he seemed to be on the lookout for chances to be useful. Why couldn't my mother have gone out with him instead? How much easier was he to get on with, to be around?

After dinner, he offered everyone drinks and it was Berris who told me to get up and give Lemon a hand, as though he was too busy to do it himself, and I was some sponger just sitting around scratching my backside. I went with Lemon to the kitchen where he made himself busy, collecting glasses, pouring liberal swigs into them and topping them up with the chaser.

'You just worry 'bout the ice,' he said with a smile, and I went to the freezer and pulled the tray out of the drawer. It was the gentleness in his voice and the smile that really did it to me.

I held it out to him and he took it from my hands, then asked, 'What's up?'

There is a moment when there is so much stored up inside it's like you could burst, when anger is the only way you can hold it together and just about keep it all in, when even the smallest act of kindness will push you over the edge, into the abyss of the bawlers. His question caught me in that moment. It was impossible to answer, way way way too vast. And everything that was wrong welled up in my throat and eyes thicker and faster the harder I tried to regain the smallest driest dregs of self-control. Suddenly all was lost and the tears spilled and I started to cry. Not any normal kind of crying, but the kind where once you start you need to cry up everything inside you, and nothing short of exhaustion or dehydration will allow you to stop.

He didn't say, *Hey, stop that*. Or, *Don't you worry, it'll all be okay*. Or, *What is it? Why are you crying like this?* He didn't even seem uncomfortable. The way he pulled me into his arms was natural. Like a father might have done, and he didn't need me to say a thing, as if my tears themselves were a language he understood and I didn't have to say a word.

I cried buckets. It was like I'd started out as a rain cloud and when the tears stopped, I'd become a fluffy white one hanging in a pale blue sky, basking in the light of Lemon, the sun. He released me then, went and pulled off a strip of kitchen roll and handed it to me to blow my nose. It was abrasive, scraping the rims of my nostrils like a scourer as I blew and blew, then wiped. Finally, testing my choked voice box, I uttered the word 'Nothing'. And he laughed.

'Well I'm glad it's nothing,' he said. 'If it was *something*, we woulda need to call out the coast guard.'

I sniffed and involuntarily smiled.

'That's better,' he said.

And to my surprise, I actually did feel better.

'Thank you.'

'S'no big deal. Most things, all they want is a little gentle handling.'

He put the last touches to the drinks and dropped in the ice cubes, then tidied up behind himself, putting everything back in its rightful place. He even wiped the cupboard sides down and when he'd finished, if you had come into the kitchen afterwards, you would never have known he'd been there at all. I don't know why, but that impressed me. Berris was meticulous about grooming himself. His shirts and trousers were ironed to perfection and at the point of his putting them on they were faultless, the seams brought to the zenith degree of sharp, which he admired in silence while running his clothes brush over them back and forth, removing microscopic specks that were invisible to every eye but his own. But on a domestic level, he seemed to expect – and my mother was happy to oblige – that everything was done for him. He sat like a god, entertaining himself with his music while she cooked, coming to the table to find his plate awaiting him, and when he was finished he just leaned back to let his food go down, and shortly after, as if by magic, she'd appear and take it away. Perhaps because Berris was the first man in my life – I couldn't really count my dad because I didn't remember enough about him – I'd come to think that maybe that was just how men were. But Lemon was different.

'Grab those,' he said when he was done.

He picked up two of the glasses on the table and I picked up the other two.

'The full one's yours,' he said. Then, 'You ready?'

I nodded and we carried the drinks back inside where we handed them out. I sat on the settee and watched Lemon settle himself on the floor in front of the stereo. A moment later, he was transformed into the music maestro.

Music was his passion. It was obvious. He selected records impeccably. He seemed to know exactly what tunes followed perfectly from the one before and his particular skill was setting and maintaining a mood and masterly judging the moment to change it.

He played and they danced.

Berris was a reasonable dancer. Not completely crap, but nothing special either. He had rhythm and he could hold a decent two-step, but nothing that made you want to watch him. On the other hand, my mum was wicked. She was compelling viewing anyway because of her looks, her high colour, her long legs and her perfectly rounded bum that made the back of her jackets fall into the soft curve of a duck's tail. She had been born to be beheld, and never was she more compelling to watch than when she danced.

She used Berris like he was a maypole, a baton in the hand of a marionette. She used him. In physics, we'd learned about malleability, the property of being able to take on different shapes, of being easy to form and reform, and that was what she was when she danced, malleable. As if her body was the sea, a wave, honey, the wind.

As I watched, I was suddenly overcome by jealousy. I wondered why so much had been given to some and others – specifically me – had been given so little. I discovered that I was even more jealous that she was dancing in front of Lemon, and he rocketed upward in my estimation of him when I realized he was purely focused on the music, glancing at them from time to time, but not with the hangdog open-mouthed adoration that Berris exhibited always. Lemon looked like he had even less interest in her than he had in watching Berris dance.

Four or five tracks later, she'd worn Berris out, and Lemon changed the tempo, brought it right down with Esther Phillips, 'Turn Around, Look at Me'. My mum and Berris melded into one intertwined dancing being, eyes closed, every part of the front of their bodies touching the other some-where; her head in the curve of his neck, his head folded downwards as if she were his favourite pillow, her arms around his waist, his hands flat against her hip and back, both of them moving so slowly, they were but a fraction of a movement removed from standing still completely.

I was so engrossed in watching them I hadn't seen Lemon get up, hadn't realized he'd come over till I felt him tugging me by the arm to stand and, when I did, he pulled me in his direction and we danced.

It was the first time I'd danced with a man. I'd danced with my mother many times, up close, eyes closed, but this was dif-ferent. Before, I hadn't thought about my body, hadn't been aware of it, had instead been consciously counting the beat in my head, like I was at a dance lesson aiming to learn something. With Lemon, however, I was aware of nothing but my body, the shape of it, the quality of every movement and how it would look to him; the jellying of my knees, the drumming of my heart, and the heat that blazed inside my body and intensified on the surface of my skin at every place I felt his slightest touch.

Most things just want a little gentle handling.

He held my waist lightly with one hand, scorching a hand-print there for ever, and his other held my free hand, pointing outwards as if we were dancing ballroom, with a respectable distance between our bodies of about a foot or so. His eyes were open, as were mine. It was the first time I'd seen him dance and it was obvious straightaway that he was good. Good enough to be the perfect partner to my mother. The knowledge made me feel even more ungainly.

All I kept thinking was, *This is it. The real thing. I'm danc-*
ing my first dance with an older, more sophisticated man and
I'm in love, yes I am, oh my God, I love him. At the same
time I was stricken with embarrassment because I knew the
way he was dancing with me was because he thought of me
as a child when I wanted so badly for him to hold me close
and treat me like a woman, to lay my head against his chest
and have his arms wrapped around me tight for the rest of
my life.

I died a thousand deaths wanting to watch him move,
dreading he would catch me doing it, knowing he was watching me and laughing, not out loud, just with his eyes, not at
me but *with* me, because he was my older, more sophisticated man and the only person on earth who understood my
suffering.

'Pull up, Mr DJ, come again,' Berris said and Lemon
released me, lifted the needle back to the beginning of the
track, turned the volume up a little more, then took me in his
arms again, a fraction closer. Though it was a record we'd
played many times before, for the first time, as we danced, I
found myself listening to the lyrics.

There is someone watching your footsteps,
Turn around, look at me...

He looked through my eyes and into my soul. Though the
words came from the stereo speakers, it felt like Lemon was
talking to me aloud.

There is someone who really needs you,
Here's my heart, in my hand.
Turn around, look at me,
Understand, understand...

He knew me. Knew my anguish and how much I was hurting.
A witch doctor of rhythm remedy and he was fixing me.

Look at someone who really loves you,
Turn around and look at me...

Releasing my waist he spun me around like a ballerina, with
his other hand raised high above my head, holding my hand,
then caught me in his arms at the end of the second revolu-
tion, closely enough against him for me to feel his heat, and
my breath caught in my chest and I felt a rising dizziness that
seemed connected from my head to my groin and I don't
know how, but he knew it. I saw in his eyes that he did. And
for one totally crazy mind-blowing moment, as our gazes
locked, it was inevitable; he was going to kiss me then and
there. My real-life Superman.

'This ain't no cradle-snatching business, Lem,' Berris said,
and the moment disappeared like a balloon popping, vanishing into the space between us, as Lemon firstly stepped
back, then let me go. 'You better remember you's a big old
married man.'

I hadn't known he was married till then. The thought
hadn't even crossed my mind. In my fantasy he'd been single,

bowled over by the beauty he suspected lay beneath the darkness of my skin. Passionately in love with me. Ridiculous as it was, I felt like he'd cheated on me.

'Ease up Berris. They're just dancing,' my mum said.

Lemon walked back to the stereo and began flicking through the LPs leaned up against the stereo.

'You better go buy a guard dog,' Berris said to my mum and they both laughed. Lemon laughed too, without looking at me, but it was the kind of laugh you laugh when everyone's laughing at a joke and you don't want to make it seem like you're the only person without a sense of humour. I, on the other hand, wasn't laughing at all.

'I'm a big old married man,' he said drily. 'You don't need no guard dog on my account,' but it was me he looked at when he added that last bit and, like my mother, I went crashing from cloud nine straight on to the asphalt.

I'd made an utter fool of myself.

'I've got my biology revision to do,' I said lamely. 'I'm going up.' And as quickly as I could without running, I left the room.

Everything had been inside my head. He'd been laughing at me, not with me. I'd been a total idiot.

Upstairs, with a burning face, I relived the dance while a quiet bass vibrated softly from downstairs and I wondered what his wife was like, how old she was and whether he loved her. Though I felt like the world's biggest prat, it struck me that the difference in our ages was still smaller than the age gap between my mum and my dad, and that I was only a little younger than she had been when she'd gotten it together with Mr Jackson. Had she felt as I did now? Had she wondered what it felt like to be kissed by him? Had he known and laughed, then taken her? Was it possible that there had been nothing between us, that Lemon had felt nothing for me at all?

His wife had to be a witch, a fat old hag with a crooked nose and feet big as the susquatch, reeking of BO, her chin covered in coarse dark hair. Without a doubt, she was liquorice Mojo black, with pink rubber lips, alopecia and stinking breath. How could he not love me? How could he not?

And what evil, what merciless cruelty existed in the world for the only man I'd ever loved to be already married to another?

Forgotten was my earlier vow; how all would be on my terms, how I'd never let any man make a fool of me. I lay on my bed and sobbed and wept and crushed my hand against my breast in anguish. In the few hours since I'd sworn my vow of strength in love for ever, not only had I fallen head over heels, but I'd also managed to have my heart irreparably torn asunder into the bargain as well.

8

'When we growed up, back home, that was when things was all right and then things went all wrong. No matter how many times I go over it in my mind, that was where it started.

'First I give him food, then he become my friend. Then we was like twins, everywhere you see one, the other had to be close by. If it hadda been anywhere else on the planet but for that little island where everybody knowed everything about everyone living there, sure people woulda think we was brothers. Or poofters.

'We neither of us had brother nor sister to our name. In a way we was the only family the other one had, even thicker than blood. He scratched my back, I scratched his. The more we growed, the tighter we got, and everything was working out cool and dandy. Up to the day I meet Mavis.

'Up until then, we'd had women. Wasn't hard to have if you was a working man back home them times with little money in you pocket. I had my share. Shamed to say now was even a couple of times we had the same woman, wasn't nothing serious, you see. Was like lending you brother a wear of you shirt, allowing you spar a quick spin in you car, nothing serious. Them times in fact it was a laugh. Can't think of a single woman Berris really like if I'm honest, up until you mum. He was always talking 'bout how is money them looking for, man to take care of them jingbang, all of this kind of thing, on and on till it was like there wasn't a single woman on the island who had in her body but an honest drop. Every woman for some reason was out to trick. Not sure I believed it all, but didn't really matter anyhow because up until Mavis, I never found a woman that I felt something for above the waistband, you understand. When she come along, that was the first time I even come to consider what this word was all about that people call "love".

'Berris used to say that Mavis musta visit some obeah man; he musta give her some kinda potion that she slip ina my drink when me back turn, because he never see a man turn fool-fool so bad over one woman in him life. And I have to say it was true. Was the first time I ever wanted to spend time with anyone more than I wanted to spend time with him. Before that, even when we had women, they was with us, me and him. When Mavis come along, I suddenly find myself annoyed with Berris. It's like I only then realize how demanding he was. And he wasn't no more demanding of me than I was of him, but I'm just trying to tell you how it felt at that time to me.

'Mavis used to try persuade me to spend more time with him. He blamed her for not seeing me, but if it was down to her, chances are, me and her woulda never have a minute on our own. And I wanted her for my own. I didn't want to share her with Berris. Yes, it was selfish, but I was young and when you young, you know how it is; the thing you want most, be it a new pair of shoes, or to go to a particular rave, or to spend time with your new girlfriend, that thing is the most important thing in the world and nothing else even come close. So I didn't share. End up spending so much time just we two on our own, that was probably the reason she end up pregnant so fast.

'But the other thing was, I *knew* the man. He was already making comments, already telling me things he hear about goings-on with women who match Mavis description and the suchlike. He was jealous of her. Jealous bad. And he's always been the same, once he's in a temper, can't calm him down, have to act out the whole thing and pick up the pieces the next day or the day after, salvage what he can from the little rubble left over. I know two women got involved with Berris round them times and both of them, money or not, refused to sleep with Berris a second time. Truth is, I never want him anywhere near Mavis, because if he started in on his fuckry with her, how I was feeling then, I woulda had to kill him.

'Anyway, she end up pregnant, he say what him have to say 'bout the chances of the pickney being mine, etcetera, and I marry her. Think I was so vex with him I marry her to teach him a lesson; that from time to time it's necessary for a man to keep his mouth shut. Afterwards, when she find out what he was walking and telling people, she refuse to have him around her or in our yard. And I can't say as I blame her, because the man make up all manner of story and he tell two people: Who Ask and Who No Ask. Even so, I still kinda liked her, but because of what he said, it's like any trust we coulda had was killed stone dead. In a way, that helped things to work out okay. Me and Berris still used to hang round together all the time, work together, rave together, pick up the odd woman here and there and in truth, it was just like old times, 'cept I had the good luck after to come home when night done to find me dinner cook. Know this don't paint too decent a picture of me them times, but it's a true one and that's what I'm aiming at: the God's honest truth.

'Everything was fine and running to plan. Even after we leave Montserrat and come to England. He find a little place, then he keep an eye out for another little place for me near by. I get one foot through the door at Lesney's and I work till I open another door for him. Fine and dandy, everything was running smooth and sweet. Then one day, Berris met you mum.

'I thought I had it bad when I meet Mavis, but I tell you this: I know I said it before and I doubt you believe me, but I'll say it again anyway – Berris was in love. In a way, I think what he done and how he acted was kinda like what I did, except with him it was more, much much more. For example, I knew he was seeing someone because he was taking days off work, the odd one here and there, no reason for it, and afterwards telling me he done some old dryness with his time that I knew for sure was an out and out lie. Never said he had a woman, kept it, kept *her*, all to himself, but suddenly smiling all the while, always in deep thought, miss half of what you had to say to him so you had to go over everything a second time; smartening hisself up – was always pretty smart anyhow, but went that one step further – and I knew what it was even without him telling me, but it pissed me off something that he never came outright and just said so. What was I gonna do if he told me? Sex her? The whole thing was a mockery! Didn't do a single thing but stir up some bad blood even before I come to meet her.

'Anyway, was out in a bar one Friday, on our way to some shebeens they used to hold down the top of Amhurst Road, and I speaking speaking speaking, repeating everything to him two, three, four times, and I finally lost it.

'"Me nah repeat myself again. If you can't keep you thoughts off the woman for long enough to hear what me a say, maybe you should go home to her," I said.

'I was vex, but Berris laugh like is joke me making with him.

'"Lemon," he said, "there is women and there is *women*. All these years, couldn't tell the difference. But I got me a *woman* now. Got me a woman to beat all women, I'm telling you."

'"I take it she just happen to be the one woman on the planet not after you money?" I said, and he laugh.

'"She no need my money. She own she own house, not a drop of mortgage on it, not a drop."

'"She must be a old bird then. Never thought you woulda prefer boiler fowl over spring chicken."

'He laugh again. "She's young enough. She married some old man died years back and leave her the house and a good pile of money."

' "And she fit?"

' "Lem," he said, "up until you see her, you don't even know the meaning of the word."

'I knew I was talking crazy, childish really, trying to find some kinda imperfection in this woman out of the blue he suddenly love, but I couldn't stop.

' "A widow, huh? So no virgin then. She have pickney?"

' "One. A girl child. Fifteen or sixteen or some such. Ain't met her yet."

' "Never figured you was one to go raising other men's kids," I said.

' "You know what, Lem, sometimes you have to weigh these things up. At the end of the day, I know what I'm getting straight up. The girl ain't mine and no one's trying to convince me to give up my money and freedom swearing she is. I know where I stand and that's all I want. I know for a fact there's 'nough man out there who would be glad for just one tiny bit of that peace of mind."

'It was the first time I really thought hard about the business with him and Mavis. Yeah, of course it come up in my head from time to time, but I never stopped before to dwell on it. Never really thought about why Berris acted like he done, but when he first met you mother, come like all of a sudden the foot was in the other shoe and I didn't like it one bit. In a way, how he done it all made me feel like he was cheating on me, which was rubbish of course, but that was how I felt. Then them little comments he made, always referring to Mavis and the boy, well they didn't help nothing at all.

'Truth be told, felt like I hated your mum long before I got a chance to meet her, and I know how childish that makes me sound but that was how, at the time, I did feel. Man, I dwell. Imagine all manner of corn on she foot, wig on top her dry head, hump on her back, the works.

'Even after she ask him to move in with her and he did, even up till then he never introduce me to her or nothing. I think he held it like a grudge, like he was saying "I can't visit your yard, you sure as hell ain't gonna visit mine." But really, it wasn't fair. He was the one who made hisself out-cast from my yard. Whereas me, I never said nothing for him to go on them ways. Anyway, I bristle up, vex-face out, let him pay for his own pint down the boozer, little things really that shoulda been below me, but I stooped to them anyway just to make the point.

'And things was different. Before he moved in with her, I was round by his place most nights, even when we wasn't going nowhere, playing music and the such. After, was like a drought, me stuck indoors bored to tears, and Mavis so excited you woulda think it's honeymoon we on. I never willed the relationship no good, simple as that. I wanted it *not* to work, so things could go back to the way it was before. And above all, I *knew* the man, knew he could be charming, smil-ing all the while things was good, but that when things went wrong, he'd explode the way he always done. I knew all I had to do was be patient. My day would come. I wasn't happy but, still, I just settle back. All I had to do was bide my time.

'One day, I open up the front door and who should I see standing there, bawling, girl, bawling, but Berris?

' "Philemon! You have to help me, man!" he said.

'First thing come to my mind was the police must be after him. He musta rob a bank, thief something, kill someone. I even take a quick look up the road to see if my yard was under surveillance and the like as I quick time pull him inside and shut the door.

' "What happen, man? Talk no!"

'Even Mavis come a hurry out to look-see what a go on. Soon as she see is Berris, she push up she mouth and gone back upstairs.

' "Me mash everything up. Slap her down over some little stupidness. Knock her down like a man. I know she nah go want me back. Lemon, I blown it, blown things bad. I know I shoulda control myself. But I love her."

'When I realize is little domestic bring the man to pound the front door like hurricane warning, I had to laugh. And straight away him tense up, looking like he want to fight me too, only start to calm down when I explain to him me think he turn fugitive or something, though that wasn't the whole truth of it; I was happy. Knew things would sour after enough given time. They did and I have to say I wasn't just expecting it, I was glad.

'I beg him fix up himself, give him little brandy, and he explain to me what was in truth a little stupidness that he flare up for and smack her two smacks, etcetera. I wanted so bad to say to him that he had made a point of showing me this relationship was nothing to do with me, but I never could kick a man too tough when he was already down. So I did the only thing I could, I listened. And when he finished, he begged me to talk to her, to explain to her how sorry he was, 'cos he was sure if he went back to the house she woulda probably have him arrested, which was exactly what the man deserve.

'On and on, first begging then threatening, man recall every favour he ever done me in me whole life, if you listened too hard you woulda think the only thing he never done was born me. In the end couldn't take no more, had to say, "Yes. Yes I will go round and speak to her. Leave it with me. I will do what I can."

'When I clap eyes on her I couldn't believe it. Had to admit Berris was some kind of lucky bastard all right. Even with half her face looking like someone mash black grapes into it, she was beautiful. All that "beauty is in the eye of the beholder thing" seem like it never had the first bitta truth to it. Only person who coulda say she wasn't beautiful had to be a man walking with his shirt button inside out and his hands them holding on tight to a white stick. I wanted her for myself. Don't know which part of the house she woulda fit into on account of Mavis doing so good a job of using up every piece of free space I had, but I wanted her. Don't know which country I woulda have to go hide for Berris not to find me, still I wanted her. Made no sense to me. All I could think was maybe I was suffering some kind of male menopause, or mid-life crisis or some other kind of craziness you only even know exist because you can't sleep and end up watching foolishness on the TV in the early hours of the morning. I wanted her.

'I did my bit. Cuddle her and tell her how he never mean nothing, just a little temper, needing only a little understanding to change him, straighten him out. And it worked.

'After, when I speak to him, wasn't expecting no tough thanks, maybe just a "cool, man" or something, nothing big, you know what he turn round and said?

' "Pass back later for dinner, man. Make me teach you 'bout the kind of woman man supposed to marry."

'Serving up compliment with the uppercut as usual, and as usual it never miss the mark.

' "You better ask her," I said. "Make sure it's okay. She might not feel for no visitors, might not want to be bussing no big cooking tonight."

' "I make the rules where I live, and tonight I say we eat."

'I growed up with the man from youth, knew all the things he'd done in the past, and my mind shoulda know him for the type of person he was, but I never. Somehow, up till then, I think I believed what I told your mum, that he needed some love and some caring, that enough of that would bring about his change. But when he said that to me, *in his situation*, something in me changed for the worse.

'Feel shame to say this, poor Mavis probably still warm underground, but even though I feel shame, in my life I told so many lies, to her, to others, what a liar I was, so good I even manage to lie to myself, but no more. I vowed to myself I would try my hardest to be true, so I have to say this: I was like a dog.

'Man, I used to visit this house and watch Berris and you mum, mouth adrip, like watching another dog eat the wickedest, tastiest bone, watching the floor mostly, waiting for the odd scrap to drop, working out how to move on in without ending up in a serious brawl. I did some watching.

'Used to wonder what you mum see in him. Sure he was good-looking, but no more so than any other five-limbed man, no more so than me. Had fine clothes and shoes to kill, but not a drop of generous blood, not a single aim to please anyone other than himself. Used to see her beat up afterwards and wonder, what is it this man have over her? Often ask her, what is it about this man you love? Only conclusion I could come to was that having never really lived – you can't call what she did with your pops, old as he was, 'life' – having never had a young man naked in her bed, someone she could walk outta street with and see other women watching and wanting, downright made her lose every droppa common sense in her head.

'Even started to get vex with her when I see her all mash up. Couldn't say wipe your face and come with me to my house, not 'cos I couldn't get the words out. Fact is they was always so close to the tip of my mind and tongue it was more of an effort to keep them words in; that wasn't the problem. Problem was I know she woulda never do it. Was so wrapped round him, round his boot, his fist, his little finger, I know she woulda said no.

'At the time, I told myself I was frightened for her, frightened he would hurt her bad, but on its own, that wasn't the truth at all. I was jealous. Couldn't see why Berris, who I'm sure never even *liked* women, why him of all men should have a woman like that, what he'd done to *deserve* her.

'That was the first thing that went wrong, really. My feelings for her. No healthy place to put them, yet at the same time couldn't shake them off. That was the first thing. Second thing what went wrong was you. Don't know when and how I noticed you. Think it was the day we was dancing, definitely not before. Up till then, think I never really saw you, 'cos was only looking at the skin colour and thinking you was dark; I never noticed before then that you had her eyes and her mouth, that mouth always put me in mind of Brazil nuts, the shape, still does, and seemed like as soon as I noticed that, I noticed you was looking at me the way she was looking at him. Talk about from the pan to the fire. But I'm getting off the point.

'The thing is, bit by bit I was growing to hate Berris. Started out a little resentment, but it just kept getting bigger and bigger. Got to dwelling hard and carrying feelings. Thinking about ways to put him in his place came like my number one hobby after a while. That was bad enough, but it got to the point where that was the strongest of all the feelings I had, and I started saying things, small things at first, but things I knew would vex him. Started with the odd little comment in private: *Yeah man, she look good. Look like she happy to show it off too wearing skirts like that.* Soon, was doing what I told myself was only tick for tack pretty much every chance I got; slipping in a little honeyed uppercut myself, and leaving it with him to fester.

'Working on him alone was enough to cause middling upsets, can't deny it. Used to upset me something rotten to begin with that them upsets ended with your mother getting hurt. But after a while, think I musta started getting used to it, or maybe I somehow got a taste for it, don't know, but I took things to the next level, and that involved not just working him, but working her as well.

'So I started in on her. Small piece of advice, that was all it took. Mention to Berris that seems her blouses getting tighter and tighter. Mention to her that Berris always boasting to his friend them 'bout the way she dress, the way she look, especially in the chest department. If you have it flaunt it, etcetera. Little things aimed at causing minor controversy. Nothing big, mixing into every whopper some little truth to keep things real. Knew things were working because it got to the point where I was sure Berris couldn't sleep at night. Had him so wound up, looked like he pretty much wanted to fight the world and everyone in it one time.

'And even that was drowned out by all sense when they came home late that night, talking about what kind of wedding they was gonna be having and Berris boasting about how he was gonna be a daddy. I was rocking and acting like I was just listening to me music, but inside I was eaten up, eaten up bad. Woulda still been all right if he hadda stopped there, but Berris being the kinda man he was couldn't stop there, no. Had to go further, had to laugh and say the baby would finally give me a chance to be a real father, even if it was only a godfather.

' "But better a godfather than a jacket," he said, and I wanted so bad to knock him down but I just smiled. Smiled and thought what I could say to this man, living in his perfect kingdom, with the perfect wife and daughter and no doubt a young prince on the way, perfect as a tale out of a story-book. I went too far and I should've stop myself, but it's done now and that's that. Can't put the clock back, nor change anything that's gone before. Went too far the night of the engagement party as well. Was laughing to myself as I rubbed up on her 'cos I knew Berris, with his lead-foot self, woulda been stiff-up somewhere, vex-face watching. Knew I was playing with fire but convinced myself that everything I did then was justified, all was right and above all else, Berris deserved it.

'There's only three times I knowed for sure I'd gone too far. Every other time felt like I had the right to do what I did. Now I don't know. Feels like the one person who did deserve some comeuppance was me and I reckon I'm getting it now, reckon I'll probably be getting it till they put me under as well. Maybe after. Like to think I'll have done enough to join Mavis, but can't be sure of that, no matter how much I do. I'm sure wherever she is she don't have no worries, that the place she's landed is filled with light. That's the only place, the right place for someone like her who never did a living soul a scrap of harm.

'Whereas me now, I'm trying hard to build up the merits. Trouble is, the place I'm starting is so low, there's a whole heap I need to get hold of just to break even. I'm not even talking about getting ahead.

'But I'm getting off the point again, rambling like an old man. What I'm trying to say in this long, winding roundabout way is this: the space between love and hate is small, very,

very small indeed. And sometimes, a man can find hisself stuck there, like I did, and I tell you this much, you don't have room to move or turn, and it ain't exactly a menu, you don't have no choice at all. Your mother staying with Berris was love. What Berris did to her was love. And what I did to them both, I did 'cos of love.'

He had been making Guinness Punch, in the biggest pot I owned, an inherited one; mixing together the Guinness and whipped eggs, sugar, milk and Nutrament; grating in the cinnamon and nutmeg, lacing it heavily with rum. Methodically, using a tea towel folded in half, he crushed the ice placed inside it with a rolling pin. Slowly, he picked the pieces out and used them to fill the two glasses on the counter in front of him, then shook the remaining splinters off the tea towel into the sink.

'Told myself for years all was Berris' fault; everything I did was 'cos of him and the way he stay, but it wasn't true, I accept that now. Comes a time when a man has to do some reckoning with hisself, raise his hand for all he own and say, *Yep, I did that*. Never used to think like that before, but lately…Let's just say that's changed.'

'So what is it you're doing? Putting things right?'

'S'too late for that. Only thing I can try to do is put the record straight.'

'Well, you've done that.'

Why hadn't she told me?

'I'm not finished,' he said.

Using the ladle he poured his concoction into the glasses till they were full, then picked them both up and handed one to me. I took it, raised it to my lips and filled my mouth.

'I want you to forgive me,' he said.

Inside my mouth was a riot of flavour: savoury Guinness, creamy bitterness, aromatic spices, intense sweetness and, undercutting the lot, the alcohol's fiery warmth. My tongue moved about the mixture slowly. Wallowing.

I believed in honesty to a point and no further, as much honesty as a person needed to get to where and what they wanted, enough dishonesty to hide what should be kept private, like Family Business. Lemon was clearing up his past and his honesty was like bleach. He had been the Pied Piper, the music man. He'd set the tempo and they'd danced as he had mixed and changed the rhythm, then sat back to watch them pick up and follow the beat. And he wanted me to forgive him? I could not.

And yet, I had my own skeletons. Instead of decomposing over time, they'd fossilized. He had his share of responsibility and I had mine. He had manipulated and he had schemed, but I was the one who had murdered.

'I hardly know what use it is for me to say this, but I forgive you.'

He had been watching me, but he looked away then, down to his own glass, which he raised quickly in cheers before knocking it back.

'This is good,' I said.

'Thanks.' His voice was thick with feeling.

It was too much. Everything. I put down my glass and covered my face with my hands and began to cry. Inside me raged the anger of the betrayed, the shock of the double-crossed. Lemon came over to where I sat, pulled me into his arms and, holding me close, rubbing my hair, asked, 'What?'

The words were so big I could hardly get them out, but I pushed.

'How come she never told *me* she was pregnant?'

9

Over the next couple of months I came to feel like I'd been duped. She felt it too, my mum, though she did her best to try and style it out like everything happening was normal, and her and Berris were just fine and hunky-dory. But that man had tricked us good and proper, and I knew it.

Those first few months he'd lived with us had all been some huge kind of act. Somehow, he'd kept all his aggression locked up tight where my mum wouldn't spot it, concentrated on worming his way in so tight that now, not even a crowbar could shift him. Or maybe it was her taking him back that did it. Maybe after that first incident he thought that whatever he did she would always take him back and forgive him. Or maybe he'd just gotten the taste for it back, and I mean *back*. Him vexed, him angry, whatever it was inside him that made him want to hurt others, hurt her, that was his genuine character, how he was when he was relaxed, how he looked when you caught him in unguarded moments; *that* and not what we had seen at first was his true nature and

I just knew, I don't know how, but deep down inside, I knew he'd done this before to other women, that after months of pretending to be something and someone else, that after the first time, he'd gotten the taste back. And I was terrified.

While he was at work she was home all day. As far as I could make out, she was at home doing nothing except thinking about him: shopping for him, cooking for him, moving the furniture around into different positions she thought would appeal to him; that was pretty much it. But to listen to him in his rages you'd think she'd been out on the prowl constantly for the attentions of other men, that she was thinking of nothing else but attracting them, that her head was filled from morning till night with being with them, doing things with them. And Berris was obsessed with catching her at it.

Sometimes he'd pop home unexpectedly in the middle of the day, or he'd get in from work hours before he'd told her his shift was ending, or he'd return home shortly after leaving for work saying he'd made a mistake and was actually off work that day. These things he appeared to me to do with the express intention of catching her red-handed.

Only the day before he'd given her a rocketing slap. In front of me. Because his dinner wasn't ready when he came in and she was wearing fishnet stockings, and she couldn't explain quickly enough to his satisfaction why she was wearing them *and* was late cooking. I couldn't even fathom a connection between the two things, they were that unrelated in my mind, but for that he'd split her lip. Though it was the first time he'd done it in front of me, it wasn't the first time he'd busted her mouth.

It was puffed and swollen the evening he gave her the black suede three-quarter-length coat, with a sheen like richest velvet and a black leather trim that might have been hand-stitched it was so delicate and divine. And her hip where he'd kicked her was livid with bruising that made it painful for her to stand when she first tried on the sheepskin: camel-coloured, with a deep-pile chocolate lining that pushed its way out and over into a dense plush collar that was soft and warm and luxurious. And he'd had to help her to put on the yellow leather box jacket, patiently standing behind her and holding the right side low enough for her to get her hand into the sleeve, because her mashed shoulder prevented her raising her arm, or even moving it much. Up until then I'd never even imagined you could get leather in colours like that: a pale yellow with the slightest tinge of green in it that reminded me of a fiery French mustard. Every one of those coats was so beautiful they made a person ache just to look at them. Truly ache.

And the tears, the ones that had set us up the first time, the ones that had seemed so much like the real McCoy, that had made me feel sympathy when I should have felt fury, made her take him back when she should have banished him for ever – those crocodile tears were history. He no longer stormed out, or bawled, or looked ashamed or even sheepish when he did what he did, or when he gave her the coats after-wards. He would watch her as she struggled to smile despite the pain, watch her twirling and spinning inside them, as if every gift she'd ever been given in her life had followed on the tail of a roasting and she expected no different, and his own face would be set with a smile that was smug and satisfied; his eyes when they met mine were challenging, daring me to say a word.

And Lemon came and spoke to her every time. With Berris and me she acted like everything was cool, nothing was going on that was ugly or crazy or way too wild for any mortal being to understand. For us she continued churning out those yummy platters of dishes marinated overnight and slow-cooked over low heat for hours. But alone with Lemon she cried. After one of them had given me food or drink or sweets and banished me to my bedroom so they could get on with their talk without having to worry about the big ears of little donkeys. But I could always tell when she had been crying because she was like Sam. Maybe all people with high colour were like that when they cried; all red eyes and noses and blotchiness that made it impossible to pretend that they'd been doing anything else. In private with Lemon she cried, and sometimes just knowing that was enough to make me cry as well.

But the evening of the day after the slap he gave her in front of me, I crept back downstairs and listened. I needed answers too. It felt like Berris was going further every time. He'd been hurting her in private. Now he'd progressed to doing it in front of me. What was left? Would he start knocking her down in public? *Then* what? I was scared because I couldn't work out just where all of this was going to end. So I crept halfway back down the staircase in the darkness, sat on a step, pressed my face between the spindles of the banister, and listened to them.

She sounded like a poor swimmer trying to speak while doing doggy paddle, talking too quickly, spluttering her words in gasps between wet breaths.

'Tell me, tell me what I'm doing wrong,' she said. As though what was happening was her fault, not his. As though maybe Berris was the victim.

'It's not you, it's him,' Lemon answered. 'The way he is. Never had nobody to trust before and it takes time to learn that. You gotta give him time.'

'*If* he comes back...'

'He'll be back.'

'I don't know if I can take it.'

'But you love him?'

'Yes.'

'Then you don't have no choice,' he said, and for a while all I heard was her crying.

'I'm so scared,' she said finally.

'I know.'

'Of being alone.'

There was a rustling noise, then I heard her blow her nose. It was his turn to be silent. I thought that, like me, he must have been digesting her fear of Berris *not* coming back, when what any sensible person should fear most was that he *would*. But when he answered, I realized he must have been thinking about something completely different.

'Look at you. How could a woman like you be afraid of being alone? You think Berris is the only man alive who can see?'

'But I was. For years. More than ten years. I can't go back to that.'

It felt funny hearing her describe her life with me as though I wasn't in it. Funny hiding outside on the stairs, unseen, hearing her say that.

'Because you love him?'

'Yes.' It was quiet for a bit. Then, 'He's all I have. I can't go back to how it was before, being a single mum again, every decision mine, night after night with no company, just me on my own with the ticking clock. I'm not one of those women who don't want to cook, who don't want to listen. He tells me to do something and it's done. But *this*? I can't understand why it's happening. Why is he doing it? Why?'

When Lemon spoke, his voice was so low it was a strain for me to hear it. 'Look at you with you crying and you bawling and you moaning and complaining. You think Berris want a woman to walk over? The man don't need no doormat. You want respect you gotta earn it. Show him your own mind. Let him see you can do for youself. Let him know you's not some kinda bups he's dealing with.'

She laughed, loud and disbelieving. 'I think he'd probably kill me.'

'Remember I known Berris his whole life. Don't need no private investigator to tell me what he want. I heard it myself, straight from the horse's mouth.'

'Berris told you this himself?'

'Would I lie?'

'And you really think it'd work?' For the first time during their discussion there was hope in her voice.

'I *know* it will,' he said.

This time when she laughed it sounded like a proper laugh. 'Look at me. I'm a mess. I think I need a cup of tea,' she said.

'Let me get it.'

I stood up as the living-room door opened and Lemon stepped out into the hallway. He looked surprised to see me. I was styling it for dear life, like no way had I been earwigging, just coming down the stairs naturally, and he looked kind of puzzled, like he was trying to see through my act.

'Hi,' I said.

'I'm making hot drinks. You want one?' he asked.

'Please.'

On his level now, I paused outside the living-room door.

'Give you mum a few minutes,' he said. 'Come and keep me company.'

In the kitchen, I sat at the table and watched him. The male equivalent of my mum. Everything he did was so graceful; the way he stood, the stretch of his legs as he reached into the cupboards above the sink, the line of his arm as he lifted the kettle, the way they folded across his chest as he leaned against the sink, watching me and waiting for the water to boil. Again, that crazy certainty; he knew everything I felt without me saying a single word. Still, though, I said them, the words uppermost in my mind, the ones that had kept me awake the night before.

'He's going to kill her.'

'No,' he said, 'he's teaching her a lesson.'

'What lesson?'

'To respect him. It's how we all came up: respect the teacher otherwise you get you arse cut, respect you grandmother or you aunty or you mother otherwise you get you arse cut; respect you man…It was a lesson in respect.'

In the silence he put his hand against the kettle, felt its clammy coldness and, realizing his mistake, pressed the button, turning it on. I didn't know what to say to that. It felt like 'respect' was the wrong word but I didn't know what the right word was.

'Is she gonna be okay?' I asked.

'Depends what you mean by okay,' he said. 'Nothing's broke. Her face will heal.'

'This time. But what about next time?'

'It'll be fine,' he said after a long pause. I waited for him to elaborate but he didn't. He concentrated on the cups, putting the tea bags in, pouring the water, stirring. Finally he asked, 'Sugar?'

'Two,' I answered.

He was trying to change the subject, treating me like a child, like it was that easy to make me forget, to get me focused on sugar and sweeties instead of murder.

'How do you know?'

He sighed and stopped stirring. 'Jinx, Berris is a very particular man and he likes things a very particular way. You mum just need to mind when he speak. If she can do that, she won't have no problems with him.'

He had just said the opposite of what I'd heard him saying to her and I was shocked. I wanted to say something, but didn't know how to without exposing the fact that I'd been hiding on the stairs listening to them. Why would he have said such different things to the two of us? When I thought it through, knowing what I did about the type of person Berris was, what he'd told *me* made more sense. And almost immediately, it came to me. I knew why he'd lied to her and I wondered how I'd missed it before. He liked them being together no more than I did. If my mum followed his advice it would make things worse, not better, possibly even break them up for good. For a second, looking at Lemon was like seeing my reflection. He and I were one and the same and we wanted the same thing. I felt that unidentifiable stirring in my lower belly again. He must have been such a sweet boy when he was young. He was, even for an old guy, one of the most attractive men I'd ever seen.

He handed me my cup of tea. Embarrassed, I took it, then looked away.

'Thanks,' I said.

'Any time.'

I missed Sam badly. I should have told her about what was going on at home from the beginning, but I hadn't and it was like the more things that happened, the further I kept getting from the possibility, as if my whole life was a dark, dirty secret that was getting harder to explain the longer I left it, and at the same time all I could think about was discussing it with her.

I needed her.

I needed someone to talk to so bad at times it felt like the pressure of keeping everything inside would drive me crazy. But she'd stopped coming to school. She'd been off for nearly three weeks straight, even though we were supposed to be doing our O levels in two months' time. I'd been to her house but I didn't get past the front doorstep. Mrs Adebayo had acted so weird I hadn't dared go back; so weird that only some kind of enormous shock could have made me go back, something that freaked me out to the max. And that's exactly what I got.

For the three weeks Sam had been off, things had chugged along predictably at school. Then one morning, during registration, when our form tutor called the register, he missed off her name.

The class register was like a poem we'd been memorizing for five years, with the odd change here and there, but otherwise pretty much the same, and during that time Sam's had always been the first name called. From day one. I was so accustomed to the rhythm of the register that Mr Botha had made his way through the following five names before I even realized it was being called.

'Sir, you forgot Sam Adebayo,' I said.

Mr Botha paused between names and looked at me. You were supposed to put your hand up if you wanted to speak, and I hadn't.

'Samantha is no longer a pupil here,' he said. 'I'm surprised you of all people didn't know that.'

I felt like I could hardly breathe with the hammering inside my chest. He resumed his call and I sat and tried to think of a single spin I could put on what he'd said that would make those words mean something else. At break time I went to the office, but the secretaries wouldn't give me any more information than I already had. Sam was no longer a pupil.

Why wouldn't she be coming back? What was going on? I stayed through physics, but as soon as the bell went for lunch I left. The only thing I could think about was going to see her, going to see and speak to the only friend I'd had for the last five years.

By the time I reached Pembury Estate it was a little after one. All the way there I hoped the rest of Sam's family would be at school and work, because if her mum answered the door I might as well forget it. Outside their flat I rang the doorbell, then knocked the letter box, then rapped on the pane of glass in the front door first with my finger, then my key, but there was no answer. No one was in. She was my best friend and I would never see her again. My eyes smarted from the sheer unfairness of that on top of everything else going on in my life.

Then, for a split second, I thought I saw someone or a shadow shift past the kitchen window and I threw myself at the door, hammering and pounding away and calling her name. I felt reckless with desperation. I didn't care any more if it was Mrs Adebayo inside, I just needed to see someone, anyone who could explain to me what was going on. There was someone in the house and if I had to pound all day I would. I swore I would not stop till the front door opened. And it finally did. What felt like ages later. And there stood Sam.

'Oh my God! Where have you been?' I asked her.

I wanted to hug her, but her body language was kind of hard to interpret. She moved back as though she knew the instinct was in my head, stepped back out of reach, and she shrugged.

'I've been sick.'

'For so long?' I asked, studying her. The amount of time she'd been off I would have expected her to look half dead or something, but she didn't. She looked normal. A bit pale, but that could have been the shapeless black jumper she wore. It hung on her like a baggy dress. Dark colours always made her look a bit anaemic.

'Yeah,' was all she answered.

'Where's everyone?'

'My dad's gone down the market. You can't stay long. If he catches you here I'll be in even more trouble.'

'You don't look sick.'

She shrugged again. 'You coming in?'

I stepped into the hallway and waited while she shut the door behind me. She passed me and I followed her into the living room. There I found a state of chaos. There were towels and dresses and T-shirts, masses of clothing and underwear strewn about the settee, and in and around a couple of suitcases that were opened and being packed on the floor.

Some of the stuff was obviously newly bought, but the older stuff I recognized as Sam's. When I met her eyes, my own were questioning.

'They're sending me to Ghana,' she said with a slow blush rising.

I was terrified. 'For a holiday?'

She shook her head. 'For good.'

'But why?'

'Guess.' But she didn't sound like she had the slightest interest in playing games and I didn't either. It was too serious, too final for jokes.

'I can't.'

'I'm pregnant,' she said.

'Oh my God...Who for?'

She rolled her eyes in exasperation. 'Donovan, innit.'

'Does he know?'

'Yep. Does he care? Nope.'

'When's it due?'

'Six months. S'what the doctor reckons.'

'But what about your O levels?'

'School's saying I can't sit them. I'll be showing by then.' Her face was beetroot now. 'Please don't tell anyone,' she said, and the first tears fell.

'I won't,' I answered and, moving forward, finally hugged her.

'Swear on your mother's life.'

'I swear.'

'I don't want everyone laughing at me.'

'No one's gonna laugh.'

She pulled away from me. Went and yanked a tissue from a box on the table, flicked it out then carefully folded it in half. 'Why not? I've been so stupid.' She blew her nose.

'You don't have to go. You could run away.'

'And go where?' she asked in a voice that was completely flat. 'It's not just me any more.' Years she'd been talking about leaving home, getting her own place, doing her own thing, as soon as our exams were over. All that bravado had gone. It was like she had no more choices now. Like all options had been brought down to this one unimaginable one. What had her parents done to her to get her to this point? How had they broken her? Could this really be the last time I'd ever see her? I wondered why I wasn't crying myself.

'You better go. Before my dad gets back.'

'I don't want you to go,' I said, and as if someone had pulled the chain, my own eyes filled.

'Can you imagine me as a mum?' she asked.

I nodded. 'You'll be the best.'

'I'll write to you,' she said. 'Send you pictures and that.'

'Okay.'

'Promise me, Jay, you won't make the mistake I did. If you end up with a black guy, get a costume. My mum told me enough times. I wish I'd listened.'

'Okay.'

'If you don't, you'll end up wasted. Like me.'

'You're not wasted.'

'Promise me,' she said.

Even if Sam had worn a collection of costumes to bed every single night of her life, it wouldn't have stopped her getting pregnant, because she hadn't gotten pregnant in the night-time lying in her own bed, but in the daytime over the garages under Nightingale Estate. She was such a drama queen. Would there be anyone in Ghana to love that about her? 'I promise,' I said.

'He could be back any minute. You have to go.'

But I threw my arms around her instead and hugged her for the last time. I didn't want her to leave me on my own. She was the last person I had left. In the end it was her who untangled me and literally pushed me out the front door.

It was too late to go back to school and too early to go home without a thousand questions, so I walked up to the high street, went into the library, found a quiet corner to hide in and sat there for hours. Everyone I cared for was vanishing before my eyes, moving out of touching distance, leaving me behind to face the emptiness alone. I felt like I'd been boxed into a tight place with too little air to breathe and I didn't know just how I was supposed to make it through the rest of my life.

They were dancing to Randy Crawford when I came in. High day in broad daylight, and the two of them had their arms wrapped around each other, dancing in the middle of the living-room floor, locked away in their own private world, oblivious to everything. Neither of them heard me enter the room. More spookily, they didn't even sense me as I stood watching them. It felt like it wasn't just my life and the people in it that were vanishing, it was my very person, like if something didn't happen soon, I would cease to exist.

She was wearing the red high-heeled clogs again and a black coat I had never seen before that fitted her so close it was like it had been tailor-made. It goes without saying it was beautiful: leather, falling over her body almost to the ground, with a red satin lining that shocked every time the split at the back shifted to reveal it. When the track ended, it was Berris who opened his eyes and saw me standing inside the doorway. He stiffened and his smile faltered. He tapped her on the back with his fingers, lightly. Slowly, she opened her eyes and, as the haze lifted, finally realized I was there.

She smiled and winced and instinctively her finger went up to her face, touching the bruised lip and checking her finger for signs her mouth had begun to bleed. Then she remembered Berris and glanced at him quickly, curling the finger along with the others into her palm, giving him a small smile and touching him with that same hand as if to say, *It's okay, honey, it's healing*. She whirled away from him, coming to a sultry pose in front of me even though that coat required nothing whatsoever from her to look good.

'Do you like it?' she asked. 'Berris bought it for me. Isn't it gorgeous?'

'It's wicked,' I answered, and it was. 'Hi,' I said to Berris.

When he smiled at me his eyes were mocking, but swiftly, they returned to her, because nothing else of importance existed for him anywhere.

'What's for dinner?' I asked.

'I'm taking you mother out,' Berris answered, looking at her as if she might be one of the items on the menu. He asked, 'Did you tell her?'

My mother looked a bit embarrassed. 'She knows we're getting married,' she answered.

'I'm talking 'bout the party,' he said.

Her colour rose a fraction higher. 'Did I say we were having a party?' she asked, as though she couldn't quite remember, when we both knew blatantly she hadn't.

'No.'

'For the engagement,' Berris said.

'Oh.'

'On Saturday. You can invite as many of your friends as you want,' she added.

I couldn't think of a response to that. 'What time you going out?'

'About eight. Lemon's coming round to babysit –'

'I'm not a baby.'

'I know, I know. He's just gonna be here till we get back, just in case...,' she said.

'Of what?'

'Come on, Jinxy, don't be difficult.'

'I'm sixteen. Stop treating me like a kid.'

'I've fried you some chicken and plantain,' she said too fast. 'And some coleslaw and potato salad and rice. I know you've got revision and stuff to do, I just didn't want you to be here till late on your own. That's all.'

'Fine,' I said. Then Berris took hold of her hand and pulled her into his body and they picked up the beat of 'Secret Combination' first with their feet, then their hips and thighs, then her head was against his chest, and their eyes closed.

When they left hours later, the top of the house smelt like a whirlwind had passed through a cosmetics factory: Skin so Soft and cocoa butter and Dax and hairspray and Brut and Soft & Gentle and Chanel No. 5, a dense cloud so cloying it threatened to suffocate those of us who remained behind.

I stayed in my room. In the pre-Berris era, my mother would have sought me out and given me a kiss before she left. That night, however, she remembered me only as an afterthought on her way down the stairs, chuckling at something Berris had said, shouting goodbye through a throat full of laughter. I doubt she even realized I hadn't answered, like she was nowhere near noticing how miserable my life was, how much I needed someone to be there for me and how wretched I was that there wasn't anyone.

Though I hadn't yet seen him or said hello, I knew Lemon was downstairs. I could hear the low music playing. I didn't care if it came across as rudeness; he could go hang. I was sick to death of concerning myself with other people when it was clear that no one was concerning themselves with me.

For a couple of hours I sifted through textbooks and notes, trying to revise, taking nothing in whatsoever. She'd been with me, Sam, in all of these lessons, and everything I touched reminded me of her, of notes we'd passed and jokes we'd cracked, and the billion things we hadn't yet done that we would never have the chance to do now.

It was ultimately hunger that drove me out of my room and downstairs to where the curry-favour banquet was that my mother had prepared, all of it stuff I liked. I virtually tiptoed down the stairs, stepping in time to the bassline of 'I Shot the Sheriff', hoping I wouldn't encounter Lemon, then for some weird reason when I didn't, feeling disappointed. I paused outside the living-room door, holding my breath, spying on him through the crack on the hinge side. He was lying on the floor with a cushion under his head. His arms were folded over his chest, his legs crossed at the ankles. Eyes closed. His fingers and his feet danced.

It was the first time I'd had a chance to study him unobserved. For a moment, I forgot my stomach and just looked. He wore a pale cream cotton shirt, the wrists folded over several times loosely. His forearms were hairy, or maybe they seemed hairier than they really were because the hair on them was thick and dark and contrasted hard against the paleness of his skin, which was maybe even slightly lighter than my mum's.

The older, more sophisticated man.

He wore navy slacks that fit him snugly and it was easy to imagine him naked, so perfectly sculpted were his legs inside them. I bet they were covered in hair too, like his arms were. His trousers were especially tight and raised high over his wood and I wondered whether it was just his wood that filled out that part, or was it hair as well, a thick Michael Jackson Afro of pubic hair? It was so tantalizing and at the same time so ridiculous that I laughed out loud.

His eyes opened.

My dash to the kitchen was clumping and clumsy and, to style it out, I was doubly noisy, banging the cupboard doors and crashing my plate on to the table, rustling through the containers in the fridge, desperately trying to compose myself, willing my breath back to normal. When I closed the fridge door and straightened up, he was standing just inside the doorway, watching me like he was trying not to laugh. The bowl of coleslaw in my hands felt heavy. I put it down on the table, beside my plate.

'Thought it was some kinda stampede going on in here,' he said.

'I'm just getting something to eat 'cos I haven't had my dinner yet,' I said, praying that the blush I felt could not be seen, while at the same time positive it was just blatant. My hands were shaking as I peeled the clingfilm from the bowl. I couldn't meet his eyes.

'You need help?'

I shook my head.

'You sure?'

I nodded.

'You think the fridge door likely to ever open again?'

'Funny!' It was a feisty answer for me, but instead of making me feel embarrassed, it made me feel bolder. Not bold enough to look at him, but my hands were steadier as I forked out some coleslaw on to my plate and smoothed the clingfilm back into place.

'I'll sort myself out,' he said, as though I'd offered to dish up food for him as well.

'Right,' I answered, putting the bowl back into the fridge and making a show of closing it in slow silence.

'You sure there's nothing you want?' he asked, and it felt as though his voice had plucked a string. Low down in my belly, even lower, something went *twang*. I couldn't look up. I couldn't move. My legs felt like jelly beneath me and I didn't trust them enough to even shift my weight. I nodded.

'I'll be inside if you change you mind,' he said and then he was gone.

I was too wound up to eat. Too wound up to even know what it was that I wanted to do instead. I put a dish over my plate and put the whole thing in the fridge. I went back upstairs, ran a bath and sat in it. It was Lemon's body I thought about lying there in the warm water, feeling my own body, so familiar and at the same time so different, sensitized in new places to the heat, the lapping, touch.

Out, I dried myself off, creamed my skin and put on deodorant and a clean pair of knickers. Wrapped in a towel, I padded back to my room and put on a dressing gown. I thought it might cheer me up putting on a little make-up, that looking good on the outside might make me feel good on the inside. In my mum's room, sitting in front of the mirror, I put on mascara and blusher, then carefully, with hands that were insufficiently steady, a dark plum lipstick. I examined my reflection, trying to decide whether I looked sexy or silly, then because I truly couldn't make my mind up, I wiped it all off. I reapplied the mascara in the hopes of making my lashes look fuller and my frog eyes smaller. I didn't know if that worked either, but I left it anyway.

I felt brazen. I was a little girl playing at being a grown woman and the thought that Lemon could have even the slightest interest in me was ridiculous. Not only was he married but I knew without ever having set eyes on her that his wife was gorgeous, like my mother, light-skinned and graceful, with long coolie hair and a deep husky laugh, and him finding me sexy was as likely as any man preferring corned beef to T-bone steak. I abandoned the whole scenario in my mind, the Mills & Boon fantasy, images of Lois Lane and Superman. I realized I was hungry again and, following the sound of music, went back downstairs.

When I walked into the kitchen he was sitting there eating, and when he looked up at me I froze and he stopped chewing. I no longer felt brazen, I felt naked under his eyes, my Superman. Did he have X-ray vision? Could he see through my dressing gown? Did he know how little I wore beneath it? I fought to keep on moving, to look natural. My legs were trembling so bad, I wondered if I was going to fall over in front of him. If that happened, he'd have to call an ambulance because I wouldn't be getting back up. I would be too shamed. I'd have to pretend to be unconscious. If my legs buckled and I ended up on the floor, I'd actually prefer it if he thought I was dead.

'I left you plate in the fridge,' Lemon said, and his voice sounded different, but I couldn't be sure if it was really his voice that was different or whether the blood pounding in my ears just made it sound different to me. I felt a stirring low inside my stomach, kind of like a rumble but different, more tense. He was eating a piece of plantain, sliced and fried. The oil on his lips made them shiny and, as I watched, he licked them.

'I'm not hungry,' I said, and dragged my eyes upward to focus on his. He put the cutlery down.

'Don't look at me like that,' he said, and I knew it wasn't the blood in my ears then, that his voice really was choked, because he cleared his throat.

I didn't know what to say, how exactly you did this kind of thing. I wanted to say 'I love you' but if I said it and he laughed I would die. More than anything, I wanted him to tell me he loved me. But I couldn't ask that, the words wouldn't come, so I just said, 'Please.'

He stood up and walked over to me, standing close, reached out his hand and oh so gently slowly touched my face, my mouth, with a fingertip, tracing its shape, watching himself as he did it. I wanted more than his finger there, I wanted his mouth to crush down hard on mine, my older, more sophisticated man, I wanted his tongue inside my mouth, to breathe him in and swallow him. I wanted him to possess me. I said it again, 'Please.'

He said what I already knew in my heart. 'You's just a child.'

Even though I knew it was the truth, it was like a physical blow, a super-punch, winding me. All I wanted was someone to love only me, not even for ever, just for a moment, just to know how it felt to be desired, to be the only person wanted by another human being, and he was the only person left to ask and he'd said no. I started to cry. He'd called me a child and it was beyond me to do anything more than act like one. The tears made my humiliation complete. When he tried to pull me into his arms, it was too late. I pushed him away and I ran.

He chased me, calling my name, shouting *Wait!* but I couldn't stop because I was running away from everything in my life, not just him. On reaching my room, I burst through the door and tried to shut it behind me, but he was already too close, half his body already through, and he flung it open and took me in his arms, kissing me, small pecks, over and over, and when he finally kissed me on the lips I realized

I had never lived, that I'd never known anything, that up until that moment I truly had been a youth, that what I'd been doing with oranges had been child's play.

His mouth possessed me.

His hands, hot hands, found their way inside my dressing gown and he groaned to find my skin bare, like a man lost, his palms gliding over my nakedness, branding trails that in the darkness would have glowed like kryptonite.

There was a hollow near the base of my neck, like the eye of a tornado, which tried to burst through my skin when his teeth scorched that spot and I gasped. Pulling the gown apart his mouth found a place to feed, and as he sucked I thought my legs would finally give, felt a hardness where before only softness had existed, every nerve in my body concentrated in the single nipple parrying his thrusting tongue.

And slowly, oh so slowly, like he didn't want to scare me, his hand made circles on my stomach, moving lower and lower till he touched me there, through my knickers, where he pressed his fingers and, as if he'd flicked a switch, an electric current surged upwards through me, escaping my mouth in the shape of a moan.

'You're beautiful,' he whispered. 'Beautiful.' Then he stopped and sank to his knees and pulled my underwear down. I lifted a single shaking leg to free them, and they fell around the other like an ankle bracelet. He shifted my feet so my legs were more apart, then his fingers touched me there, doing more parting of their own, and then his mouth.

The only thing that kept me standing was the door against my back and I braced myself against it as my heart moved from my pounding chest to the part of me he licked like a lollipop, till it throbbed as if it would burst. Then he stood and undid his belt, and his button, and his zip, and pulled his clothing down and his privates touched my privates then he was in me, filling me, then stuck.

'Oh my God!' he groaned. 'Oh my God!'

He pushed again and something gave and I knew what it was to be filled. He stood perfectly still, his hardness pulsing inside my tightness, his body pressed against mine.

'I don't want to hurt you,' he said. Then he kissed me again, sucking my tongue deep into his mouth, one hand under the cheek of my bum, forcing my hips up against his, and the tension in my body rose higher and higher till it burst in a spasm of pleasure so intense that for a moment there was nothing else in the universe. As I came down from the clouds I felt him pull himself out of me, then crush himself against my belly, rubbing himself in the sticky wetness he spurted there, with a grunt. Then we were done.

His body was still against mine for a moment, then he kissed me on the forehead one last time. He didn't meet my eyes as he hitched his clothes up and tucked away his privates. For some reason, he looked kind of defeated, and I pulled the edges of the gown around me, covering my new body, every part he'd touched, every slippery spot sensitive now to the feel of the fabric over it. He paused on his way out of the door as if he had something to say, but then said nothing. His going left me changed.

I was a woman now and I understood everything. Sam and the garages. This was what happened in the darkness, why everyone kept returning. My mother and Berris. This was why they went to bed early. This was what he was doing with her. Not having this was what she meant by being alone. I understood.

I went to the bathroom and this time I showered. My body felt different to me. I felt different. I stood in front of the mirror afterwards examining my face, trying to see if I could see a physical change, wondering whether others might be able to see it even though I couldn't. After I put on my pyjamas, I went downstairs to get my dinner. He'd taken it out of the fridge and left it on the table for me.

I thought about carrying it into the front room, where music played still, where he was, but I couldn't. Something stopped me. Like instead of what we'd done making me feel closer to him it made me feel we'd done something wrong, *I'd* done something wrong. Instead I decided to eat at the table in the kitchen on my own, and I did it as quietly as I could.

He came in while I was still there, and I think he felt the same. He smiled, but it was brief, tight, forced. He hummed as he poured himself a drink, as if everything was normal, but he was styling it and I knew it. He moved quickly and was out the room before I'd had a chance to think of a single thing to say to him.

I wondered whether he was, like me, thinking of what we'd done. Did he see me differently now, and if he did was it different good or different bad? And would we do it again? Should I let him? Then I remembered his wife and I felt gutted. All the things that stood in the way of our love struck me at once: he was Berris's friend, he was much older, he was married, I was still, for two months anyway, a schoolchild. He was probably thinking of these things too, not me, not love, just the wrongness.

Though all of these thoughts should have reduced my appetite, I waxed off the food on my plate as if I hadn't eaten for days. Afterwards, I scurried as quietly as I could through the passage, up the stairs to my room, and for the rest of the night I stayed there, lost in my thoughts, marvelling at my life and all the things that just kept coming at me, at what felt like the length and breadth of the world's experiences, all concentrated inside the smallest possible amount of time.

10

I had to get out. To clear my head. I washed my face and threw on some clothes, desperate to escape the place that for so many years had been my cocoon against the world, the safest hiding place until he came. I shouldn't have let him in, allowed him to weigh me down with his stress-filled tales, his protracted exhumation of all things buried deep. I pushed my purse into my jacket pocket, pulled back the hundred tiny braids he'd plaited into a ponytail, wrapped a scarf around my neck and left. I felt like a tightrope walker who'd been carefully balancing for years, suddenly given a hard boot in the back.

It was Sunday, still early, and the streets of Hackney were quiet. In a few hours they would be as busy as any workday rush hour, but at that time of the morning it was almost peaceful. It was typical English early spring. From inside, through the window, the day looked bright, but what I stepped out into was a biting cold. The sun played without warmth or humour against crystallized car windscreens and on every exhalation, my breath smoked.

The only other people on the streets were sedate, the churchgoers, outfitted in their Sunday finest, on their way to pray. I had never gone to church as a child, never had religion. But that morning I envied them. How I wished I had faith, that I believed in a greater, grander plan, that everything was part of some clever design and for a purpose. More than anything I wished I had it in me to pray.

I walked towards Dalston, my pace brisk yet still too slow when what I wanted to do was run. I turned off Dalston Lane, right on to Ridley Road where the great clean-up was underway from yesterday's market; the road filled with the noise of motor-powered vacuum cleaners and the relaxed chatter of shopkeepers leisurely straightening things up. There would be business done today, Sabbath or not. My pace increased.

This was where she had shopped, my mother, rummaging through cardboard boxes of moist compost for the freshest cassava, the least blemished christophine, delicately breaking ginger root with her fine, slim fingers, pressing and testing the ripeness of the choicest green sabaca. The men here paid compliments to the women who bought from them. They flirted and rounded prices down to numbers divisible by ten.

My route took me up to the high street, past the pound shops with their cheap wares piled high and broad in primary-coloured plastic baskets, past Cash Converters and the charity shops, the bookies and the fluorescent off-licences with their neon-lit signs, past the distinguished undertakers with their high-shine wood and stone exhibited through speckless, pristine glass.

She had told Berris and he had told Lemon. Why had I been left out of the loop? How was it that even dead she still had the power to make me feel insignificant?

Inside the supermarket I took a deep breath of air, chilled and void of odour. The tension in my body began to abate. Here, the produce was set out in orderly rows, the fruits and veg and meat sanitized and attractively presented in neat polystyrene packages. I found the symmetry calming, the parallel aisles and shelving, the neat-stacked rows, the square labels and barcodes, the clean smooth walls.

I took a trolley, not because I intended to buy much, just for the feel of the roll of the wheels as I wandered round. I stocked up on the essentials; a litre-sized bottle of vodka, a bag of ice and four more bottles of wine. Even to my eyes, the contents of my trolley looked like they belonged to someone with serious alcohol issues, so I had a wander around the store in case there was anything else I needed. In the bread aisle, I put a loaf of brown bread into my trolley before noticing the hard dough bread on the shelf below. I knew Lemon would prefer hard dough, so I took the brown bread out and the hard dough in. As soon as I had bagged and paid for everything, I knew I'd bought too much. Or maybe I should have brought the car with me. In any case, like the ongoing story of my life, it was too late for regret.

Outside it was drizzling. Lightly at first, gradually getting heavier the closer I got to home. I walked slowly, feeling oppressed both by the weight of the shopping and the weather, yet still reluctant to get back to where I lived. It felt like my distress was in direct proportion to the distance from home, and the closer I came to it the worse I felt. I so wanted to cry.

But it was impossible to say what I should cry for. For Mavis? For Lemon and Berris and Ben? For murderers who went to jail or those who lived on the outside in jails of their own making? For the brother or sister I could have had, whose loss was no less for the fact that I hadn't, till today, even known they'd existed?

By the time I took the corner into the road I lived on I was drenched. On the doorstep I put down a bag, searching my pockets for the key. Unexpectedly, the front door opened and Lemon was there, standing inside, awaiting my soggy entry with red-rimmed eyes so shiny it was evident he had been crying himself.

I passed him without a word, through the door, the hallway, into the kitchen, where at last I was able to put the carrier bags down. He followed close behind me, then as I turned, he half stepped, half fell towards me, hands going up and around my back, crushing me hard against him. He buried his face in the bowl of my collar bone, heaving and snorting, adding his wet distress to the rain on my neck. My body was stiff as he clasped me tight. And over and over and over again, he just kept repeating, 'I'm sorry.'

I laid in the bath for hours, topping up the cooling water regularly, unpicking the plaits he had been so patient putting in. I finished when the hot water ran out. I stood then and stepped out. I was slow to dry my skin and, for the first time ever, I could not be bothered to wash the bathtub out afterwards, so I left it.

He was sitting there, obediently, on the floor outside the bathroom door, like a faithful hound; had maybe been there the whole time I was in the bath, just waiting. I didn't look at him as I walked past and he didn't speak, but I heard the rustle of his clothing as he began to move, following behind me as I entered my room.

He sat on the bed as I towel-dried my hair, discarded the towel, creamed my skin, combed through and then blow-dried my hair. He watched in silence, with an expression I was unable to fathom, but which was not anger or madness or lust.

I felt removed. As though my spirit had vacated my body and broken free to glide overhead, observing my life from a detached perspective, seeing my bedroom, the bed, a weeping man's arms wrapped tightly round himself, a naked woman on a stool, two fingers deep inside a hair-grease tub.

And when I had finished, there was nothing left, not even the energy to find a nightie or a pair of knickers, I just crawled into the bed and he covered me and sat down beside me, gently rubbing the back I had turned on him as I closed my eyes and willed sleep to take me, willed eternal sleep to take me, please. I slept.

He was gone when I awoke naked beneath the quilt. The room was fresh and I pulled the bedding closer around my neck, trying to make sense of what was happening to me. I couldn't recall ever sleeping in my birthday suit. In fact it was so out of character for me that the more I thought about it, the more certain I was that I was having a nervous breakdown, and the possibility didn't surprise me in the least. What did surprise me was that it had taken so long to occur.

My son.

I slipped out of bed and went over to the dressing table, into the least used bottom drawer, where I took out a box and carried it back to the bed. I leapt into the warmth beneath the quilt, took my nightie from under the pillow and pulled it on. I opened the lid of the box and there he was, Ben, two months ago, at Christmas, in a photo taken by his dad at his house, in front of the tree, surrounded by presents, eyes round with wonder. Red had invited me to join them but I hadn't. I told him I had already been invited to a friend's, then spent the loneliest day of the year on my own.

His eyes.

Looking into his eyes had always disturbed me. I dug deep down into the box and found a picture of him when he was six months, and there they were again.

Her eyes.

His skin was a shade darker than hers had been, his hair a short crop of shiny jet curls, cheeks fat as hamsters', but there they were, my mother's eyes, love-me eyes, so big you could get lost just staring into them. Was that what kept making it so hard for me to love him? Her?

I went back to the Christmas photo and touched his face. Though not as fair as her he was still way lighter than I was. I had never been able to judge whether he was a good-looking kid or just light-skinned, like some people thought all blonde women were beautiful when in fact they were just blonde. I would stare at him, trying to judge as a parent with some objectivity, not wanting to be one of those people who treated lightness and blondness as some kind of independent beauty criteria. There was no doubt his eyes were compelling, but did they alone make him handsome? I still couldn't say. Looking at him, all I could say for sure was that in that photo he looked happy, utterly happy. And complete.

Was this how my brother would have looked?

Would I have found it easier to love my brother than my son? Or a sister? *Their* daughter. How was it possible to experience grief for someone I couldn't even be certain it would have been possible to love?

And Ben; what was I really doing with him? I hadn't rung him or his dad, hadn't felt outrage or loss or grief at the thought I might never see him again. Instead I was making plans to go to Citizen's Advice. For what? It wasn't as if I actually *wanted* him, wasn't as if I longed to have him here with me full time. If it were that simple I could have gone to the police, accompanied them to Red's and collected Ben, as per my legal rights. But I didn't want that. What I wanted was what I'd had before, nothing more and nothing less: for Red to look after him and for me to have him every second weekend, here, not there, like some paedophile having supervised contact, Red breathing his advice down my neck while taking notes, judging. Because I had given birth to him and I had the right. What kind of reason was that for me to base a relationship on? With as much emotion as you'd find on a yellow legal pad. My feelings had nothing to do with love and everything to do with ownership. What kind of person was I?

I put the photos back inside the box. When I replaced the cover it fell into place as securely as a coffin lid. I pushed the box under the bed and lay back down. The tears came fast and unstoppable then. On a roll.

He'd cooked oxtail and butter beans for dinner, with small round dumplings the size of marbles, brought it to me in my bedroom on a tray, waited while I adjusted the pillows behind my back and smoothed a level space on the duvet for him to put it down. He sat on the bed near my feet and watched as I ate. The meat was so tender it fell from the bone, melting inside my mouth, the gravy spicy and so compelling I found myself unable to stop eating even when the plate was empty, sucking out every crevice of the bones, using my mouth like a bottom-feeder, my tongue like a young girl French-kissing an orange.

I thought I had been creative about food in the past, ensuring a balance of texture and colour and nutrients, attractive to the eye, contrasting on the palate, on inspection, perfect in every respect. But everything he had cooked since his arrival had been divine. I could not recall any dish I had ever prepared that had an impact like this, that was such a dizzying, seductive, overwhelming experience that the more I ate, the more I wanted. Even how I was feeling, with all the emotions I was carrying inside – the confusion, the distress, the impact of new hurt piled on top of the old – my appetite was so great it surprised me.

Like gorging at a funeral.

He watched.

'You want more?'

I shook my head.

'Then we should talk.'

'No more talking. Please. I can't take any more.'

'What no kill you, make you strong.'

'I think it will kill me.'

'You's so like you mum. There's nothing you can't cope with.'

'She didn't cope. She's dead.'

'I can't understand why she never tell you.'

'It doesn't matter.'

'How can anything upset you that much not matter?'

'I don't wanna do this. It's too late. There's no point raking up ancient history. What difference can it make?'

'I have to say it make a big difference to me.'

'Because you *loved* her?' The words were sneered. He *had* loved her, loved her in one of the many forms his love took, love that he chose not to distinguish from envy, or anger, or madness. 'You both did, didn't you? Loved her to death!'

He flinched.

'You's just like him,' he said. 'How he was them times...'

'Don't compare me to him!'

'Cept he use his foot and his fist where you use you mouth.'

'I am nothing like that man!'

'Talking down, talking hard, using love like some kinda dirty word...'

'He was a monster! I am not a monster.'

'Like something nasty stuck to you shoe...'

'You take it back!'

'Like you never loved her too.'

It was my turn to be dumbfounded. Then I laughed. Aloud. In disbelief that anyone could be so stupid. But it wasn't funny and almost immediately I stopped.

'Lemon, you've been good company. Thanks very much for the food. You've outstayed your welcome. I want you to go.'

'You gonna sit here in front of me and say you never loved you mother?'

'I need you to go *now*!'

'Say it. Say, "I never loved her." Then I'll go.'

'I told you I didn't want to do this...'

As I sprung up from the bed, the tray on my lap and its contents spilled to the floor. He didn't glance at them, just reached out and grabbed my arms preventing me from moving any further away. It was the first time since his arrival that I had felt his strength. His hands closed tightly around my wrists and, though I struggled to free them, I was held fast.

'Go on. Say it. You don't have no problem opening you mouth to broke a person down, so open it now and tell me you never loved her.'

As I struggled harder, his hands tightened around my wrists.

'Let me go!'

'Say it first!'

'Fucking let me go!'

'Say it!'

I screamed the words: 'I hated her!' He let me go. 'I hated her! I hated her! I hated her!' I sank to my knees on the carpeted floor in front of him, the strength in my legs vaporized, the rage spilled, exhausted. I didn't look at him. I knew what I would see. Contempt. He wouldn't understand. No one could. It was impossible for anyone to understand the impossible.

'Why?' he asked. 'What you mum ever do to you?'

'Nothing. She did nothing.' When she should have said *Stop*, she was silent. When she should have fought, she ran. I felt his hands, slipping under my armpits, pulling me up, into his arms, enfolding me into his body. He laid his head on the top of mine. I repeated, 'She did nothing.'

'She loved you,' he said.

'She loved him more.'

'Differently!'

'*Instead*. Even Berris knew. It was him who told me.'

'He was wrong.'

'For telling the truth?'

'He said it from spite. Spite is a wicked thing. I don't just say so because I think it, I know because I been there. I sunk to the depths where you do a certain thing you know is well out of order, but you tell youself at the time you was within you rights to do it, how it was exactly what the other person deserve.

'S'where my head was the night he told me 'bout the baby. All I was doing was rocking and listening to me music. For years after, I told myself I wouldn't of said nothing if he did only stop there, that it was his fault, his fault for laughing and going too far. But it wasn't true. I shouldda kept me mouth shut but I let spite open it.'

Suddenly, I felt sick. I pulled away from him and stood up. 'What did you say to him?'

'I went too far.'

I put my hands on either side of my head, squeezing them tight, locking the train of thought inside it. 'You told him!'

I almost thought he had not heard me but then he looked up and I saw in his eyes that I was right. He wore a child's expression: *No matter how badly you think of me, it's nothing compared to how badly I think of myself.* 'Oh my God, it's true. You really did.'

'I never told him everything…'

'What did you say?'

'That you came on to me. That you asked for it…'

'Did you tell him what you did?'

'I told him I said *no*.'

Then I did laugh. Now that really *was* funny. Genuinely funny. I laughed my bloody head off and he watched me in silence till I had calmed down enough to say, 'So you came out of it stinking of roses. That was good. You were good.'

'That was the second time I went too far.'

'So let me just get this straight: you went too far the night of the engagement party, and too far when you slept with me…'

'No! I *shoulda* said no but my head was so full already, there wasn't a drop of space left to think. Any full-blooded man woulda had a hard time saying no to what you was offering on a plate, and having you was like getting back at Berris and having some of you mum at the same time. Then afterwards, separate, was the rest of the feelings that might've come first and natural to any other man in the same spot. What I said to Berris after was where I went too far. Not before.'

I closed my eyes. There was nothing sacred, nothing decent, nothing pure and good and innocent left. Not even the giving of my virginity to the man I loved. He had taken what I had offered and while he did, he'd been thinking of her.

'And the third thing? What was that?'

'Her last night. That was the third and the last time I went too far.' He was quiet for a moment. 'Told myself for years all was Berris' fault; everything I did was 'cos of him, the way he stay, but it wasn't true, I accept that now. When I say spite is a wicked thing, believe me, I know what I'm talking 'bout.'

The words came out of my throat sounding crushed. 'I thought he saw something in me. That I was marked. That somehow, somewhere, there was a sign on me that other people could see. Do you know what he did? What *you* did? With those words?'

Now his eyes were filled again and I was glad. I felt my anger returning and it was like having back a misplaced comfort blanket. I had long ago vowed never again to be wrong-footed by the cruellest of all hoaxes – grown men's tears.

'He hurt me.'

He was ashamed but he did not look away. 'I'm sorry,' he said.

And I could see he was, could see it with my own eyes, but what difference did it make? He had said what he'd said and Berris had changed me, changed me into a person I could no longer recognize, except in my similarity to him.

11

She was in the living room when I entered, sitting on the settee next to Berris, eyes downcast hard. That was the first sign that should have alerted me to the fact that things were not normal, but I missed it completely.

For the whole day my head had been filled with Sam and Lemon. In my mind I'd travelled with Sam: into the car with her and her cases, tagged along on the airport run, watched as she checked in her luggage for good, as she boarded the plane and carefully belted herself into the seat that would take her away and out of my life for ever. And in the moments I hadn't been thinking of her, I was thinking of him, what we'd done, and what the difference was between being a lover and being in love, whether those two things were as jumbled in his head as they were in mine, whether he was thinking of me, and if so, *what* he was thinking.

It had been impossible to concentrate at school, and after lunch I hadn't bothered going back. I went to the library again. Somehow, being surrounded by books made me feel more secure, like there were a thousand stories with a thousand alternative endings, any one of which might be the truth. There I'd spread my textbooks on the table in front of me, trying to make it look like I was justified in being there, giving the impression I was someone with their head cleared enough to be able to study, to focus on the future, though there was so much going on inside my head it was a wonder I could think at all. After, I left and walked around Pembury Estate, then round and over Hackney Downs, and even over to Nightingale, as if everything might have been some huge mistake and I'd see her there, chucking down her bag, laughing and flirting like she owned the place, hooking on to my arm as naturally as if it were some part of her own self, glancing at a single thing, then me, and both of us cracking up without a word being said, because we two shared the same mind.

Emotionally, I was everywhere but in the present. Even so, I still clocked it as weird when I said, 'Sorry I'm late,' and she didn't answer.

'Sorry, is it?' Berris asked.

He was looking at me, genuinely looking, meeting my eyes and holding the contact. As usual, he looked like he knew something no one else did, and kind of smug, like he did when he'd hurt my mum and was challenging me to say something. But there was something else there as well that was out of place and unnerved me, an expression I couldn't put my finger on then and there. Even before I had a chance to try to work it out he spoke again and the steadiness of his gaze and the tone of his voice chilled me through from the outside in.

'Where you coming from this time of night?'

My fear was like an enormous stress. I'd seen his work, what he was capable of doing to her, and I was smaller than my mum. How much easier would it be for him to do that to me? But below the fear, constant and expanding inside my chest, was anger. Just who did he think he was? He was already living free of charge in my father's house, pounding my mum and treating her like dirt. If she wanted to accept that it was up to her, but he had no right to ask me anything or to expect me to explain myself to him. He wasn't my father. If anyone should be asking me anything it was her – and she wasn't. She wouldn't even look at me.

I said nothing and, because I knew the anger would be blazing in my eyes, I looked down at the floor. He walked over to where I stood and stopped in front of me, too close. His feet were planted wide apart. He was wearing maroon leather brogues, with cream socks to match his jumper. Though I couldn't see the sides of them, I knew those ones had large maroon diamonds up the sides. His shoes were immaculately polished.

'You hear me ask you a question?'

I nodded. His shoes moved a fraction closer and I stepped back.

'School done three hours ago. You out looking for man?'

'No!' I said.

He was close enough to slap me and that's what I was expecting. I was tensed hard, expecting to feel the blow any moment, but it didn't come.

'Look at you, with you short skirt...' – his hand skimmed it lightly – '...you blouse open up, everything hanging out.' He flicked my blouse, above my breasts, and I flinched. The top two buttons were undone, nothing big, not like you could see anything unless you came and stood right next to me and looked down it. 'You been out with you man-friend?'

I blushed and shook my head. If he'd said *boyfriend* it might have been okay, but *man-friend* made me think of Lemon. Suddenly it became clear to me and I was terrified. The signs I'd sought in the mirror, signs I'd changed, that I'd become a woman, though I hadn't seen them, Berris could. Maybe not just him but others as well. How could I have expected to change so much on the inside and for there to be no outward sign of any difference? I looked at my own feet and was horrified to discover my toes were pointing outwards. I shifted quickly, turning them in. I wanted to look up to see if he'd noticed, but I didn't dare.

'Liar!' He stretched out the fingers of one hand so they were splayed wide, then examined them. Using the fingers of the other hand he rubbed the skin between his fingers. The rest of his hand looked fine, but the skin there was chapped and in want of creaming. It looked better when he'd finished, but only a little. He rubbed a particularly dry spot one last time. He was like a man out strolling, in no hurry at all. He flexed his fingers then finally spoke. His voice was as gentle as I'd ever heard it. 'Go upstairs to your room.'

*

I began to cry as soon as he walked into my bedroom and closed the door behind him. He held a maroon leather belt in his hands, one that he'd probably picked out especially that morning to match his shoes, and it did. Perfectly. It was doubled over in his right hand, and his left played with its length, running up and down, touching and caressing, as though the feeling it gave him was nice. He said if I told the truth he might not have to use it, but I knew he was lying. I couldn't have put into words how I knew but it was to do with his eyes and the thing I'd seen in them downstairs; the aliveness in them, the thrill, like the look Lemon might have seen in my eyes when he stood still inside me and pressed me against him. If he'd looked into my eyes then, he would've seen what I saw in Berris's eyes as he stood in front of me fingering his belt.

Passion.

No matter what I said, he was going to use it on me and that's why, even before he'd started, the tears had already begun to fall. More than anything, it was the inevitability that really got me.

To *who you been seeing* I answered *no one* and he let fly the first lick. Same question, same answer, the second. The third time he asked, I panicked. I'd never been beaten before in my whole life, ever. Never with a belt. Never felt a crack across my back explode through my body like a lightning bolt of pain. I lunged at him, caught the belt mid-swing like a length of fire against my bare hands and held on, trying to wrestle it from his grip. My mistake was painted across his face in the darkest colours of rage. He fought me for it and won. And that's when the beating really began.

There may be people so brave they would have struggled and done their best to show how tough they were, who would not have given him the satisfaction of hearing them yell at the top of their lungs, who might have been mortified for the whole street to know they were getting a roasting.

I was not one of those people.

I screamed my head off as loud as I could. I called for help, for my mother, for him to stop. I made so much noise, I fully expected to see any moment my mother bursting into the room fighting him off me, that the neighbours would pound the door, then race up the stairs to see what was going on, that someone would call the police and they would kick the doors down and charge up the stairs to arrest the bastard. By the time he'd finally finished with me, out of breath and panting, covered in a light sheen of sweat from his exertions, my throat was as raw as if he'd beaten that part of me as well.

But no one came.

The whole street must have heard.

But no one came.

The whole world must have known what he was doing to me and not a single person did anything to stop him. If I'd thought I felt alone before, it was nothing to how I felt after, lying on my bed, body aflame, full of disbelief and fury, unable to do a single thing about what he'd done to me but cry. Lying there, I vowed I'd never make the mistake ever again of counting on anyone in any circumstance to help me. I'd never expect protection. I had thought Lemon had made me a woman, but I was wrong. I'd been a little girl who'd had sex. It was Berris who'd taken me from the realm of childhood into adulthood, made me like one of those people in the Before and After adverts; the person before the beating, the person I became after. Lying there I promised myself whatever happened in my lifetime, I would always remember I was in it on my own.

And as for my mother, everything I'd ever felt for her, the envy, the confusion, the sympathy, the annoyance, the admiration, the frustration, the love, that man removed every one of those feelings. I had a single feeling left, so thick and complete it would be with me till the day I died, so strong I couldn't even speak it. She'd stood by and let the man she had chosen, the man she brought into my father's house, wear himself out on my skin, without lifting a finger to stop him, not even a word or gasp or whisper. She'd cast me aside and out as if I were nothing. No matter what she said, I would never forgive her, and I promised myself that no matter what came after, I would never forget it.

Ever.

12

In glorious high-definition Technicolor, complete with stereo-surround sound, the memories in my mind played out like the trailer of a film: a baritone roaring, a soprano scream, the ripping of a paper sheet into a hundred tiny pieces of confetti. My mind kept stepping back, trying to keep to the shadows around the edges, resisting, avoiding, terrified, and all the while my heart hammered inside my chest as hard as if it were tunnelling up for air.

I drank.

Enough to have taken me beyond the point of recall, lucidity, or even consciousness. I should have been legless, passed out in an unthinking slump over the toilet bowl, beyond even vomiting. Instead I was awake, alert, drinking more.

And feeling.

He had known she was carrying his child, known that, in killing her, he would also be killing his own flesh and blood, yet that hadn't been enough to stop him. Not just the taking of a single life, but two.

His son.

Their own daughter.

While he was plunging, had the thought even crossed his mind?

Or was it for their baby he had cried? Head back, mouth wide, a primeval creature processing a single emotion: grief. As if he'd just come across her body unexpectedly, and its expiration had nothing to do with him. Tensed veins were raised hard beneath the underside of his skin, corrugating his neck, his arms, his face, and his vocal cords strained to pierce the silence that had followed in the wake of her screams.

Her screams, *those screams*, I still heard them at night. In dreams where I crouched on the floor beside my bed, face squashed into the centre of the pillow, the sides pressed so hard against my ears it made my wrists hurt; in dreams where my eyes were squeezed shut, jaws clenched hard, my lips pulled tight over my teeth; in dreams where I actually prayed for the screams to continue, because the only thing worse than the sound of her screaming was the silence when she stopped.

That night, in my bedroom, the sudden silence had been louder than what had come before, almost static, raising the hairs on the back of my neck, sending a tingling spray of pins and needles over my skin, which took their energy from the strength vacating my knees.

The silence had been like a vacuum. It drowned out the sounds I made as I rose on weakened legs, drowned out my footsteps, the creak of the bedroom door opening, every normal household noise I should have heard as I crossed the landing – the click of the boiler, the whirr of the fridge, the blare of a lorry horn in the distance – drowned everything out. I heard nothing as I opened their bedroom door, not a peep, just felt a shift of air, like a draft brushing upwards, as my legs finally gave and crumpled into a heap beneath me.

There was hardly any mess at all. The room looked so ordinary; everything on the dressing table was in its place, the bed still neatly made. It bore an impression, so innocent, as if someone had sat there earlier to ease their shoes off, or clip their toenails, maybe rested there briefly before drawing the curtains against the night. The normality of the room created a spotlight effect on the bloody splattered couple at its centre, on the floor.

Berris was on his knees beside her, cradling her head in the crook of his left arm tenderly, as if she were a baby, raising her shoulders from the carpet as he pulled her floppy torso against him. The other arm cuddled her around the waist, supporting her back. As if he had forgotten it was there, his fingers were still closed around the handle of 'exhibit one', the knife responsible for blowing away any chance of a lesser manslaughter conviction. The fact that he had taken it from the kitchen drawer, carried it up the stairs and waited for her to come in; 'The very premeditation of his actions,' the prosecution said, 'belie the defence's claim that this was a crime of passion.'

Her floor-length velvet dress bore a harsh rip just above the hem, where she had trodden on it in her haste to flee.

And tripped.

The heel of her right shoe had snapped, and though I didn't notice at the time, the coroner would later note that in the fall she'd bruised both knees.

Those bruises were not the cause of death.

She died from four stabs to the back, deep and clean. He bore not a mark, not a single bruise or cut or scratch, because there hadn't been a struggle. When she should have been fighting for her life, she'd tried instead to run.

He cuddled and cradled her, with his head thrown back, mouth opened wide, emitting a mighty roar that the vacuum swallowed up along with every other sound. Apart from the grotesque horror and absence of music, the whole thing was like a scene from a silent movie.

She let him beat me, and I made him kill her.

Lemon was right. There was no difference between Berris and myself. I had turned into the man I hadn't even wanted to call 'Dad'. I almost laughed at the irony of that cold, steely fact, the truth of it. He had lived with us for around four months, that was all, just over one hundred days out of the thousands I had already lived by then, days I had spent with her, loved her, been fulfilled in her company, even while she had one ear fixed fast on the ticking of the clock. Even now, at thirty years of age, I could no more understand that level of desperation than I had then; the crazy logic that any company, even the company of a man like Berris, was worth dying for, the knowledge that she must have been dying for love for years before he came.

A woman like her.

There were as many different types of love as there were people, Lemon was right about that as well. And my love was like Berris's, to do with ownership and rights, legal-pad-yellow love, camouflaged and cold-blooded and destructive; fine and dandy if you were a single man on the pull for a pretty, rich widow, but I was a mother.

It was, had always been, beyond me.

Throwing back the covers I rose from the bed.

My bladder was full.

I wanted him.

First, I visited the bathroom. Then I went into her room and turned on the light. I opened the cupboard and selected a coat. The floor-length black leather one that flashed a scarlet satin slit. Still inside its dustcover, I placed it gently on the bed. The briefest whisper of settling cellophane, then all was quiet. I went over to her dressing table and sat down on the stool. I pinned my hair back so it was off my face, picked up a powder brush and began.

She had sat here that last night and made herself beautiful. My hatred had been too fresh and consuming for me to watch her, to watch the slow care she took at every stage of the process of transforming herself from merely beautiful to divine. I had seen her when she came back from the hairdresser's, hurrying to be ready in time, rushing to her room, heard her feet going backwards and forwards between here and the bathroom. I'd been downstairs, acting disinterested, feigning an interest in watching the TV, so I hadn't been taken through the transformation detail by detail, in small and tiny steps that made the end result less unbearable. Instead, she appeared before me when her metamorphosis was complete and even I, my head fresh with the memory of skin that stung and welts that wept, with my heart full of rage as piercing and murderous as a blade, even I was stunned.

She was beyond beauty.

Literally, she took my breath away.

She who would soon be dead was dressed to kill. She wore a dress, off the shoulder, in black velvet, with a black satin trim that framed the tops of her arms and fell in waves to sweep the floor, and she held it up, raised it from the hip with a finger and thumb, like some southern belle or an aristocrat, someone totally at ease with fashions that needed assistance to make it through the world intact.

I had seen it then.

Her shine.

I thought it was the contrast of the midnight fabric she was draped in like an exquisitely wrapped treat. I thought it was partly because she knew her body so well, knew how to maximize every essence of the beauty she'd been born with, but that night it wasn't just that, it was more.

She shone.

It seemed her skin shimmered, she truly was glowing, as if for her whole life her beauty had been building up to this moment. The hairdresser had put her hair up at the back and sides, and the top was an explosion of curling gleaming ebony tresses, and a few fell to frame her face, which was fuller, *she* was fuller, with softness and a secret that swelled inside her womb. She had never looked lovelier or more perfect.

But Berris was late.

He should have been home by six at the latest. The party was in south London and they were being picked up by friends who would drop them there and bring them back. They had collected Lemon first, and when he arrived at the house, when he saw her, I know now he must have wanted her to himself for a while, to have her on his arm, to be the one introducing her around, knowing other men were watching with envy, thinking she was his. For such was the nature of his love, drooling and waiting, making do with crumbs, stealing a slightly bigger morsel whenever chance provided an opening.

'You ready?' he asked.

'Berris isn't back yet. I don't understand it. He should've been home long time.'

'Shit. The people them ah wait outside.'

'Invite them in, let them have a drink till he comes.'

'But he need to fresh and dress and everything. I can't ask them to wait for all that.'

'Then what should we do?'

He paused a moment, thinking. 'Come, we go.'

'And leave Berris?'

'Berris is a big man. He can make his own way. He know the people them due here at six. He can cab it and catch us up down there.'

'But he don't have the address.'

'I'll write it down. Jinx, get me piece of paper and a pen.'

A car beeped outside as he wrote.

'Maybe I should stay,' my mother said. 'Wait for him...'

'Don't make no sense me leaving you as you're ready and all,' Lemon said. He tore the sheet off the pad and handed it to me. 'Give this to Berris. Tell him I said we'll see him when he come.'

'Okay,' I said.

'You sure you gonna be okay on your own?' my mother asked.

I couldn't speak to her or meet her eyes. I nodded, looking away.

'I'll make it up to you tomorrow,' she said and she went to kiss me but I turned my face so the kiss missed and flew off into the empty air. She looked at me kind of disappointed, saddened. For a second it was as if she were about to say something, but then she straightened up and the moment passed. 'Don't lose it,' she said as Lemon handed the sheet to me, A4 sized, with hastily scribbled words set out in the centre, like an oversized envelope. The party address.

Don't lose it.

The last words she said before leaving and they expressed nothing but concern for him.

'Make sure you put it somewhere safe,' Lemon said.

'Okay.'

The sky-blue suede coat was draped over her arm. She handed it to Lemon. He smiled as he opened it wide so she could step inside, slip her hands into the arms and ease it on.

He guided my mother out of the door with a hand placed gently in the small of her back, and a moment later, in a mixed aroma of hairspray and aftershave, musky perfume and animal hide, they were gone.

*

I floated down the stairs. I heard music playing, always music: Gladys Knight and the Pips. At the living-room door I paused and peeped though the crack by the hinges, experiencing a frisson of déjà vu.

He made me come and when I did he'd been thinking of her.

He was sleeping, upright on a chair, sitting side on to the table, chin in palm, the elbow supporting his chin on the table, peaceful as a person who had died while dozing. Silently, I stepped inside.

Able to see all of him now, I noticed that his ankles were crossed, one on top of the other, and the top one tapped out the bass line, dancing. He opened his eyes wide. Abruptly the movement stopped. Hastily he stood and looked me up and down. As if it had been handpicked for this precise moment, 'Help Me Make It Through The Night' began to play. He stepped towards me, took me in his arms and smiled.

And it was as it had always been, that this man, this maestro, could always find the magic words through music, the ones that spoke what I needed to hear that moment, or to say, or to have said to me, and there was no more perfect place to be as the track played on than in his arms, his hands inside the coat, playing with the bare skin of my back, my head resting on his shoulder, his own folded over my neck, inhaling the dizzying scent of my mother's perfume as it rose from my body.

We danced.

It was as it had been when I was sixteen, the same headiness, the surprising want I hadn't known I had the capacity to feel. I felt a pounding against my ribcage and I truly could not say whether it came from my heart or his.

We kissed.

It was for me as if it were the first kiss. As if we had risen a few inches from the ground, and the world continued to revolve around our stationary bodies as they hovered lip to lip conjoined.

I felt him.

He moulded me against him, forcing my heat against his hardness, danced that part of his body against mine there.

He danced.

And when the track ended, I began to unrobe him, tugging with desperate hands that shook as I struggled to untie the knot that held his dressing gown together and me outside it. But he put his hands over mine and stopped me. He leaned his cheek against mine and I felt the hot air from his lips fill my ear as he whispered, 'Not here.'

He turned the lights off, asked me to keep the coat on, and we lay down on the bed in the room where my mother had slept and died. The drag of his tongue scorched my skin, and despite the fact that I drenched them, his fingertips burned. In the darkness his mouth found my lips. He kissed them and said a single word, 'Beautiful.' He manoeuvred himself into position above me and when I gasped, I found my lungs filled with her scent. As he repeated the word over and over again, my need grew too desperate for patience, and my release was both swift and intense.

And after, when I thought I was done, gently, he eased me onto all fours on that bed. I felt him shifting himself, shifting me, and in spite of the heat I shivered. Then finally, he took me on my knees like a dog, and I threw back my head and I howled.

13

'Was a friend of a friend's do. A fella from work. Was me who invited Berris and your mother to come. Those days was different, you see, not like now. The chap having it was from Montserrat and them times, any party hold by someone from back home was a open invitation for any Montserratian to pass. You just needed to know where you was going, pick up you bottle on the way, and reach.

'Man, I was like some kinda crazy dog. In some kinda stupid love. Knew full well she was his but I wanted her anyhow. Knew full well she wanted him and I hated him for it. I told Berris the details, but I told him we wasn't gonna leave till eight. Was such a silly lie, because all it took was for you mother and Berris to talk on the subject and they woulda known I give them different information. Was a bit of a gamble, and I already had my excuse to hand in case that happened. Woulda just tell Berris ah no me tell him eight, that I'm sure it's six me say. Woulda say his mind too full up of love for him to think straight. But it never came up. In a way seemed like the gods was on my side. Finally that night it seemed the gods was on my side.

'Man, I felt like Cinderella for true. She spent the night watching out for Berris and I spent the night watching her. I kept thinking this was how it would be if she was mine, if something happened to Berris and it was just me and her. I knew, I knew for a fact, that us leaving without him woulda piss him off something chronic. Knew clear as day that someone was gonna pay for the few hours of pleasure I stole. But I've often wondered since, if I hadda known, truly known how things woulda turn out that night, could I have done different? Would I have waited for him and missed the chance to spend a whole night with her, just we two? And I tell myself of course I'da waited, of course I woulda, over and over, like if I said it the right number of times it would be so, and in my head the answer wouldn't be followed up by the same old question that always mocked me after: *For true?*

'I danced with her and I danced with her and I danced with her. Had Berris've reached, I woulda end up dancing on my own while the two of them cootch up one side holding up the wall, 'cos he couldn't dance but the two steps and she woulda stood up stiff alongside him to keep the peace. But with him gone, man we put down some piece of dancing that night. Wasn't a man alive who wouldna killed to be in my place. Not one.

'How I kept my lips off her, I can't say. All I know is that two o'clock, when our transport was ready to drop us back, I never walked to the car, man, I floated.

'On the way back she started getting worried proper. She knew Berris would be vex. Knew it. She'd had licks for a lot less, and she knew he wouldn't see her going raving without him in any kind of happy light. Me, I played stupid. The man wasn't there on time, so what could we do? We leave him the address, didn't we? I'd had a bit to drink that night anyhow and by that time the dancing was done. I just wanted to get home to my yard, take out on the wife the little excitement that I couldn't take out on you mum. She wanted me to come in with her, but I told her she was being foolish. He would understand, she would see. At the end of the day, she never done nothing wrong, is it? Then don't act like it! But the truth is, I had my own reasons why I never wanted to go inside and face him.

'I knew I had stirred things up, bare-face lie to the man and all, that what I had done to him that night had nothing to do with friendship. I'd been coveting my spar's woman, that was the bottom line, and what with the drinks I'd already had, I didn't wanna fuck up any explanations. Knew he woulda give her a couple of licks, but I thought that woulda been that, afterwards, everything cool as usual, and the three of us just move on. This was what was on my mind as I ease her out of the car and pat her on the shoulder, like *there there, off you go*, then got back in the car and let my man drive me home to my yard.

'Other funny thing that strikes me: I ask my man to wait till you mother got herself inside the house, watch as she root down her handbag for the keys, till she open up the door, turn on the passage light, and give us a wave before she close it back then lock up behind her.

'In my mind, you see, it wasn't safe for a woman to be on her own on the street, late at night. Anything coulda happen to her. You take a woman out, you see her back safely inside her yard, that's the way I was brought up, that's what I was thinking.

'Knowing what I know now, I realize I knew about Jack shit. She woulda been safer on the street. She mighta been alive today if she'd slept the night over Hackney Downs, or in some alley, or on the floor of a shebeen. I waved back to her from where I sat in the car, *grinning*, my mind like a camera, taking her image for ever to visit again and again in the time thereafter; this was how she looked after I drop her home, smiling and waving *at me*. I never hadda inkling, no idea at all, that inside this house was the most dangerous place she coulda ever have step that night. Not a clue.'

He was quiet in the darkness, holding me spooned tightly against him, the leather of the coat between our skins, part of us, rubbing my bare stomach gently with the soft, warm palm of his hand. When he continued speaking, his voice was filled with the utmost weariness.

'And sometimes, over the last fourteen years, some nights I can't sleep and she's on my mind, and I'm wide awake tossing and turning, because the one thing I've always said was that I *knew* Berris. Knew him well, knew exactly how he thought and what he might do. And I find myself troubled, because I think that maybe, when I was wiggling my fingers

in the air, and feeling the rock between my legs on the journey home, maybe I knew exactly what woulda happen the
moment he got hold of her and there was no one around to
help. Maybe I knew.'

He blamed himself. All these years he had been thinking he
was responsible. He thought it had all been down to him and
what he had done. I knew how that felt, the dark places that
kind of thinking took a person. It confirmed for me again that
he had never come close to guessing, he had no idea of the
part I had played, the responsibility I alone bore. He blamed
himself, this man I thought I could love, and it was precisely
that reason I was able to tell him the truth, to speak it for the
first time since she had died, to say the words aloud that I had
swallowed and held down, then spent over a decade pretending they hadn't existed at all. The darkness helped too, the
fact that he couldn't see me and I wouldn't have to see his face
turn over in disgust. He felt the sudden tension in my body
and when his hand stopped moving, it was like a question.

I said, 'I'm the one to blame. It was my fault.'

He actually laughed. 'You was a child. Nothing that happen
that night was down to you.'

His mind would not allow him to go there, yet I needed it
to. Needed someone else to share my terrible secret, to
understand me, needed him to know, this man who'd always
known me better than anyone else, who had, like me, made
a banquet of jealousy and grudge. I needed him to know
exactly who I was and what I was capable of. And I said it.

'I never gave Berris the address.'

*

From the time they shut the front door behind them, my mind was made up and closed to any other alternative. I didn't want Berris around me or in our home or in her life. I wanted him gone and I was prepared to do what I had to do to make that happen.

What right did she have to be happy, to have so much? How did she earn the right to glow like that? What about me and what had happened to me? What about that man and what he'd done? Maybe he had a right to do what he did to her because she *chose* to tolerate and accept it. But he had no right to do what he had done to me, with her knowledge, in my father's house. In my mind, they had both gone too far.

The address.

I looked at the sheet of paper without reading. I had neither interest nor curiosity in the details. It was enough for me to know it existed, his passport to join her on her merry night. Slowly, I ripped it neatly and longways in half, then quarters, then eighths, then into the smallest pieces I could manage. *That* was the act that made the whole thing irrevocable. From then, we were all committed to playing out the scenario I had set up for us, as compromising as a tram track. I would pretend I had lost it, that was the initial plan, or what I told myself at any rate. When Berris came home, I would tell him I'd lost the note and couldn't find it. And that would be that.

I knew him, knew him as well then as I thought anyone could, knew he was crazy. He would drive himself into a rage by the time she came back and when he saw how she looked he would be even angrier. He would imagine men had glanced at her, that they had wooed her, that she had danced with them, rubbed up against them. He might even think she'd thought of leaving him. Such was the train of his thoughts, the landscape of his imaginings. Even though I was only sixteen, the way his mind worked was so elementary a child could work it out.

And I did.

He'd give her the hiding to beat all hidings. Hopefully it would knock a bit of sense into her and she would finally chuck him out and we – as in us, her and me – could move forwards with our lives and Berris would be nothing more than a bad dream we reflected on from time to time. That was what I thought. Or what I told myself I thought.

Then I had to decide what to do with all the pieces. I didn't want to leave the remnants in the bin in case he found them, so I ended up flushing them down the toilet. It must've taken ten flushes to get rid of it all and I still had to pick three floating bits out and roll them into papier mâché pips that I flicked to the bottom of the bathroom bin. After that there was nothing more to be done so I went to my room to do some chemistry revision while I waited. I was calmer than I'd been in weeks and the revision went well.

He arrived back about an hour after they had left, slamming the front door hard as he came in. I felt the reverberations upstairs and that moment was the first time I questioned the unchangeable course I'd embarked on.

Even though he'd just come through the door and had no idea what awaited him, he was already pissed off. I knew the space between him being pissed off and in a rage was gossamer thin.

It was already a thousand times worse than I'd anticipated and nothing had even happened yet. I wished I hadn't torn that piece of paper up and, what's more, flushed the pieces away for ever, but it was too late. I hadn't even read it, so it wasn't as if I could knock out a few of the details myself. At that point my mother hadn't crossed my mind at all. He had come in and I felt afraid, but not for her. Every fearful thought I had, I had for me alone.

He called her. Shouted her name at the top of his voice. If it had been written down, there would have been no question mark to follow the word. He wasn't making an enquiry, it was a demand. Twice more he shouted into the silence. His footsteps pounded up the stairs heavy and quick. I heard the sound of her bedroom door being thrown open and then he swore.

He walked back along the landing to my room and, without knocking, walked straight in and marched up to me so fiercely I thought he was going to grab me or knock me down, but he didn't. He looked like he wanted to though, like it was an effort not to give in to the urge. He paused between each word.

'Where. Is. Your. Mother?'

If there had been a moment when I wanted to come clean it was then, and if I hadn't torn the note up I would have. But with the note gone for ever, it was impossible. If I mentioned it, I'd be expected to produce it, and there was no explanation I could come up with to explain why it had been torn up and flushed away, no explanation that spread the responsibility for that act to include anyone else along with me.

And while all this was going round and round inside my head, the way he was poised, as if any moment he would let loose a cuff or slap or punch, made me feel pressured to respond quickly, to say something, *anything*, and my mouth moved of its own accord and the words simply tumbled out.

'I don't know.'

'*You don't know?*'

'I don't know.'

'What, she never tell you where she was going?'

I shook my head, everything compounding, getting worse the more I spoke, and desperately, I tried to find a way back, but I was already hemmed in by the solid wall that had sprung up behind me, its foundations in my footprints.

'But she was dress up?'

'Yes,' I said. 'She went out with Lemon.'

'Dress up in her fine clothes and covered in perfume, she gone out with Lemon and she never leave word where them a go?'

If only he had stepped back beyond arm's reach, given me just enough space to draw from the air the courage I needed to confess, but he didn't. His voice was in the realm beyond calm, like when he came to my room before to beat me. Like when he spoke after turning the music off at the party. I didn't think about what would happen later, when she did get back and told him she'd given me the address to give to him, had no idea what I would say to him then – if he gave me the chance to speak. Sitting on my bed looking up at him, I knew only that there was no one in the house but us two and that he would hurt me bad. I looked down at the bed as

I shook my head. I sensed him move and flinched, bracing myself for a blow that never came. Instead, he stormed out of the room, slamming the door behind him so hard that it rebounded open with a crash, and with my heart somersaulting inside my chest, I realized I'd been holding my breath and began again to breathe.

He cleaned the house. I could hear him from my bedroom, scraping the bath and the shower out, the wet cloth slapping against the tiles and floor, using so much bleach and disinfectant that even with my door closed, the smell was gagging.

Then he was downstairs, in the kitchen, doing something similar; in the living room, covering every surface with furniture polish and wiping; sweeping the stairs, cleaning down the banisters, then the Hoover was out and he went at it hard, upstairs and down. I'd never even seen him take his own plate to the sink before. I wondered if cleaning was some kind of therapy, a thing you did to contain your anger. It struck me as very weird. But then *he* struck me as very weird. In that respect alone, what he was doing made some kind of sense.

The only room he didn't clean that night was mine and maybe that was because I was in it. Maybe if he had tried to clean my room he wouldn't have been able to keep his hands off me. Maybe he was concerned that, as before, he would have ended up tiring himself out on me, and was making a conscientious effort to preserve his strength for when she finally came back.

I couldn't revise or read or sleep. My head was so full, the only thing I could do was think. I had no idea how I was going to get through the night in one piece, what exactly

I was going to say when she told him, as she certainly would without a shadow of a doubt, that the address had been left with me, in my hands, with clear instructions to pass it to him. Not only hadn't I done that, I'd lied and said I didn't know where they were.

What had possessed me? Why had I done it? The short time I had spent living with Berris had taught me much about fear, how infinite its heights were. Even so, the level I experienced was beyond anything even I could have imagined. Maybe that was why, as the hours slowly passed, it did not even cross my mind what he would do to her, how what I'd said might impact on her. I knew too well how efficiently he could hurt me, and the beating I'd had before had been because he had a suspicion about me, nothing concrete, not a fact. How much worse would my punishment be for this, this lie so terrible it had driven him to clean the whole house?

I heard him making food in the kitchen. Opening cupboards, clacking plates, putting a pot on the cooker, opening and closing the fridge door. My mother had cooked saltfish and ackee before she'd gone out. He gave out coats to say *sorry* and she made food. I could smell it warming up, and when it was ready he called me. Despite the fact that it was late and I'd had no dinner, I had no appetite. I had even less desire to eat with him. But I thought if I didn't go down it would make things worse, which was ridiculous really, because things were already as bad as it was possible for them to be.

In the kitchen, he'd set up two places at opposite ends of the table, the hot food steaming on both. I sat down in front of the plate that had the smallest portions and waited for him to sit down as well. She'd also baked Johnnycakes, and he'd given me two. He brought a bowl of cucumber salad to the table and put it down in the middle of us both. He didn't look me in the face. I thought it was because he was embarrassed.

He'd been crying. Like the day he'd come back with Lemon. His eyes were red, the bags beneath them swollen. His nose was red and he looked as though he was exerting a superhuman effort not to break down and carry on bawling his head off in front of me. I tried not to look at him. I tried not to feel sorry for him. It was beyond me to understand how it was possible to feel sorry for a person who had done what he'd done to me, what he would do to me again once he found out what a barefaced liar I was. My feelings confused and disturbed me. I tried my hardest to focus on dinner, concentrated hard on not glancing his way at all.

He sniffed. Over and over. Like a child. Worse than any child. And picked at the food with such reluctance that a person coming in might have thought *I'd* called *him* down to dinner and told him he had to sit there till he'd finished it. My nerves were stretched to their limit. My mind raced, trying to find a way to work with his distress to my benefit. Surely, if I supported him through this difficult time, it would be harder for him to rip me up afterwards, even when the truth did come out? But what to say? I didn't want to mention the tears. To be honest, he looked as though he was the tiniest fraction away from breaking down completely. Mentioning my mother might not take the conversation in the kind of direction I needed it to go either. I couldn't think of anything other than what I said in the end.

'I'm sorry.'

He was silent for a moment, then he put down his cutlery and picked up the glass beside his plate. It looked like Coke and ice, but I could smell the rum as he gulped, whether from the glass or him I couldn't say. When he put the drink down he was blinking fast in an attempt to hold back the tears, but it was useless. When the dam broke, he began wiping them quickly away, but it was like shovelling before the snow stopped falling and shortly, he gave up and just left them to run down his face.

'Why has she done this to me?' he asked. 'What is it I don't give this woman and she still treat me so, like a fool, like a bups, like I'm some kind of idiot, fucking bitch.'

It was his tone that chilled me. I could not have vocalized it then, pinned down precisely what freaked me out about it, but it was the monotone he spoke in, the lack of passion, love *or* hate, as though he was beyond feeling, beyond hurt, the fact that he spoke like that while crying. It was the incongruity that got me.

'What kinda woman could just up and leave so? Not even care a shit 'bout nothing she left behind, even her kid.'

Stunned, I realized he was talking about me, about my mother and me, about her not caring, not loving me. My greatest fear confirmed by the man who knew. His nose was running now, his face a sodden, slimy mess. Eyes wild. He stood up and began clearing the table, though technically dinner wasn't finished. I leaned back as he took up my plate and began scraping food on to his.

'I'm gonna bus' her arse for her tonight, you watch! I'm gonna teach her a lesson she won't forget. I'm gonna make sure she never does this to anyone again. Ever. And that's not a threat, it's a promise.'

He took the dishes over to the sink, placed them on the side, then turned and left the room.

For the first time, it struck me that bad as my position was, my mother's was even worse. This crazy, violent man would hurt her even more than he would hurt me. And it would be my fault. Not only had I done wrong but, to top it off, I'd lied. I felt guilty and ashamed and afraid. Guilty that my mother would be made to pay for my wrongdoing. Ashamed that I did not have the courage to go to him then and there and confess. But I was in the house with him, alone. Even if I screamed my head off, no one would help me. Isolated and vulnerable, I was afraid.

For myself.

And then I thought about what he'd said and, actually, it was true. She *had* left me behind without a care or thought. That was all she'd done since he'd come to live here. It wasn't just this party tonight, it was her life, their whole lives that I was excluded from. I was the last thing she thought of now.

And my skin still bore the evidence. Too vividly I remembered what he had done, what she had *allowed* him to do to me. When she got in he'd give her the roasting to beat all roastings, a beating so bad that to say sorry, the coat he'd have to buy her would need to be mink, lined with purest silk, and buttons made from rubies and precious gems, and I would watch from the shadows to see whether this time her beaten body would pirouette and curtsy, modelling it before him, all the while smiling.

It came down then like a guillotine, the coldness in my heart, and deliberately I turned my back on any possibility of owning up. Maybe he would beat me, but he would beat me with what little energy he had left after he'd finished with her. Something like glee began to swell inside me then.

Good! Now she'll know how I felt.

On my way out of the kitchen I turned off the lights Berris had left on, then went to my room. I changed into my pyjamas, turned the light off there too, and lay down in the darkness on top of my bed. I felt too awake to fall asleep. So I sat up, hugged my knees and pressed my back against the headboard, listening out for the first sound of my mother arriving home.

'She never stopped him from beating me. Never said a word to me after. Never kissed me or said, "Try and be good, Jinxy", or "My God! He did *that*?" He could've killed me! If he'd had the energy he could've beat me to death and she wouldn't have stopped him. She heard me screaming, she *heard* me and she did nothing. She would have let me die.'

'That's not true!'

'For years after I wondered, what if he'd been trying to kill me? What if it was me he was stabbing? Would she have tried to stop him then?'

'Yes.'

'But she didn't stop him,' I said. 'I loved her and she let him hurt me.'

'Maybe he told her.'

'What?'

'The things I said. About you being...womanish. Maybe she thought you needed it.'

'Needed *that*?'

'A little hard discipline early, stop you turning out loose. Maybe she thought she was protecting you.'

He was trying to make good of an impossible wrong. And if it had been that alone, maybe I could have gone for it like a grateful sucker, accepted his words with a smile, wiped my eyes and moved on with the rest of my life. But it was more. Always more.

'She didn't even try to stop him killing *her*. She didn't struggle or fight, she didn't raise a finger to defend her own life. Even for me. Even if she didn't care that she'd be dead, didn't she care about leaving me alone for ever?'

'She musta been scared outta her mind.'

'She promised me she would always be there for me. She *promised*.'

'She wanted that. You mother loved you.'

'How can you say that?'

'Mothers love their kids. All of them. Even the bad ones.'

'It's my fault she's dead.'

'It's Berris kill her, not you.'

'But if I'd given him the address, he would've gone to the party late. He would've been vex, but she would've been alive. I didn't. That's why he killed her and I think I wanted him to. What kind of a person am I? What kind of person wishes their own mother dead?'

'Even if you had given him the address, it wouldna made no difference. He would still have done it.'

'That's not true!'

'Berris wasn't making it to no party that night. We came and left and he wasn't coming, whether you gave him the address or not.'

'But if I'd given him the note he would've gotten dressed and gone looking for her.'

'Maybe, but he wouldna found her. Not that night. It was always going to come back to him here waiting for her to come in, and when she did, he would have done what he did. Note or not.'

'How do you know that? How can you say that? How can you be so sure?'

'That was my night, our night, me and her. I never meant from the start for him to come. I told him the wrong time. I got here before he did and took her and left. And when he came in, I knew he would be out to track her down, to link up with us and take her from me. So just to be on the safe side, I did the last thing I knew would ensure he never made it, unless he was gonna search the whole of south London that night; I writ down the wrong address.'

'Oh my God.'

'So you see, whatever you did, that night woulda ended the same way. It was her time, and when it's your time, it's your time.'

14

When I awoke, it was dark outside, the day. The early-morning sounds from the street were familiar; closing front and car doors, engines starting, the neighbours setting out as if this Monday was just another ordinary day.

I felt nothing. Lemon had told me what he had told me and I wasn't hurt or angry or relieved or disgusted or amazed or released; I felt nothing. Nonetheless, last night I had vomited, hunched over the toilet bowl. Violently. Alone. Hoping he'd be gone by the time I came out, and when he wasn't, hoping maybe he'd leave during the night. Even though the house was silent, he was still here. I knew it.

As quietly as I could, I left my room and went into the bathroom. Ignoring the dirty bathtub, I brushed my teeth, rinsed my mouth, then splashed my face with icy water. I dried and studied it, my face, in the bathroom mirror, looking for signs, searching my eyes for change, a subtle shift or clue, some physical evidence of what had happened to me; finding none.

Dressed, I went running. In the biting cold. Pausing first to stretch muscles that still ached from Friday, shaking them out before I began, knowing I had taken them to the extreme so recently, wanting to limit further damage if I could. This time I took it slowly. A single circuit of the park, pacing myself like I'd seen other joggers do, but not from any design or plan; it felt natural. It had gone, the drive, the push, the need to flee. I was going through the motions only, feeling nothing. On the second lap of the park, I realized I no longer even felt the cold.

It had been her time.

Had Lemon meant when he said it that it had been my mother's destiny to die at Berris's hands? That it had nothing to do with me or him, that from the moment she'd met Berris and moved him in, she'd purchased a non-transferable ticket to being a murder victim? It went against the little I believed in to accept that. Every person made their own fate. Hadn't I made mine? Lemon his? If my mum had thrown Berris out the first time he'd hit her, she would still have been alive today.

Or would she?

Suddenly I wasn't sure. If she had insisted he went, would he have quietly accepted, packed his bags, wished her a good life and left?

It was on the third lap of the park that something shifted, something inside me.

I felt it.

My feet were no longer pounding the ground, my arms no longer jerking back and forth at my sides, nothing jarred. It was as if my whole body had become an efficient machine, my limbs pistons, and my head cleared so sharply the world and every detail came into focus. I smelled the cold, heard the sounds of schoolchildren's voices and yapping dogs and traffic. Before my eyes the brittle clay landscape fragmented into one thousand different shades of grey and brown. I tasted the salt of my perspiration against my tongue, felt its heat. It seemed at once as if everything was possible and without limits. Like I might gallop or fly. I felt it. And I ran.

My new body showered and dressed, I made my way back down the stairs to where he sat, fully clothed, on the sofa, like a visitor, a neighbour stopping by for a quick cuppa, family passing through. The room was dark and he had turned on no lights. I opened the blinds at the windows. The greenness of the foliage in the garden was intense, wet-vivid.

'Can I get you anything? Coffee?' I asked, and he nodded.

I made it for us both. Four sugars in his, none in mine; poured them into cappuccino cups like bowls, placed them on saucers, and carried them back in. He glanced up at me as I handed him his. His hands shook and the cup rattled against the saucer as he raised it to his mouth and began to sip, even though it was too hot, sucking in air alongside the scalding droplets, making a sound like a percolator.

I waited.

'You decide what you gonna do about the boy?' he asked.

'I don't know,' I answered, honestly. I hadn't a clue. Somehow I had hemmed myself into a tight corner and whittled my choices down to two: Citizen's Advice or letting Ben go.

Become a real mum or forget it. Two options, each with its own unique set of fears. 'I really don't know.'

He looked at me, his yellowed whites red. He had been talking non-stop for three days, taken me with him, up and down and around it all.

That stuff.

Trying to clear things up while there was still time. Working to build up the merits. Did he believe that fate had brought him to where he sat now? That this was meant to be? What about his son, his grandchildren, *his* family? 'And you?' I asked.

'Ain't got no hard plans.'

He started to raise the cup to his mouth again. This time the rattling was even worse. He changed his mind, and put it down on the floor beside the settee.

'What about John?' I asked, and he shrugged. I watched him as he rummaged through his pockets, found the cigarette box, his lighter.

'Did you ask Berris why he said the things he'd said about Mavis?'

'Didn't have to ask. That was one of the reasons he came to see me. He had things to clear up too.'

'And?'

He inhaled deeply. Blew the smoke out slowly. Answered when he was good and ready. 'You know, after what he done, I thought for a long time he was the hardest-hearted man alive, the coldest, the evilest. But after I spoke to him last time, watching him, *listening*, not how I done most of my life but kind of fair-like, not squeezing him into the way

I wanted to think of him, but looking hard to see who he really was, *what* he was, after all that I come to the conclusion he was just sensitive. Oversensitive. Even small things that wasn't meant to be no slight hurt him. I tried to imagine how it felt to be in his shoes, and they was small and tight and uncomfortable...'

'I can't think of him like that. I don't want to,' I said.

'I'm not telling you what to think. Just saying how it was for me. That it was the first time I saw him proper.'

'So what did he say?'

'You know Berris, for a long time nothing, just bawling. Made a hard drink and gave it to him. Made one for meself and the old legs, to keep them straight and strong under me. Watched him cry and thought hard on the way my life had shaped, about Mavis, the things we coulda done, how our lives coulda been. What Berris told me all them years back set us in a direction that was some kinda one-way street; straight ahead only, no u-turns, no reversing; how could it a been anything else?'

'But what did he say?'

'Berris say he couldn't remember a single bad thing I ever done him, how in prison he pass time counting up every good thing, every favour, every *kindness* from me. He said I was the best friend he ever had, the truest, even more than a brother. To be fair was mostly things I'd heard him say before, but always before was kinda said in jest-like, whereas this time, Berris' voice was so solemn, you woulda think is the Lord's Prayer him ah recite. Listening to them thanks made me feel low.'

The coffee had cooled a bit. Carefully, I sipped it and waited.

'All that stuff about Mavis, the things he'd said, none of them was true. "Man, she loved you." That's what he told me. "She loved you. Only you." Maybe *I* need to go prison, to learn to speak the truth. He confessed all to me and I couldn't, couldn't, couldn't do the same. How could I, with me mouth dry like cassava bread? Didn't know where to begin, or end. Couldn't say a word to him about the things I done to him all those years back, not a peep.'

'So he lied? Trashed your marriage on a whim?'

'Seems so.'

'And about ruining decades of your life, what did he say about that? Please tell me he didn't say *sorry*.'

'He asked me to forgive him.'

'Did you?'

'Yes. Can you?'

It was as if the world's axis shifted for an instant, and I felt something like the panic and confusion of missing a step. Berris had taken so much from me. Altered the shape, the potential of my life from everything that had been possible, left me to survive making do with what little was left over afterwards. Forgive him? I could not.

'It's too much. Too soon. Maybe one day I'll be able to forgive him, Lemon, but not today. Not now.'

'I wasn't asking about him. I'm asking you to forgive me.'

And again the tilt.

I wanted to say *yes* to him but I couldn't, because suddenly it felt like forgiving him and forgiving Berris were one and the same. They were both responsible. They had both done it; killed my mum. Only one of the four hands between them had held the knife, but they were both guilty. Either I forgave the two of them, or neither.

'I don't know,' I said and he nodded. He expected no more. 'I want to,' I said, 'but I can't.'

He nodded again.

I took my cup into the kitchen and put it down on the side. There were dirty glasses there and a couple of empty bottles of wine. I ignored them. Three days it had taken, but it was clear now, the reason he had come. I had a strange feeling, a tightness in my chest that was getting harder to contain. I needed to do something, go somewhere, get out. I went upstairs and pulled on some old boots, found my handbag and took out the keys to the car. I couldn't face Lemon again. Not just now.

'I'll be back in a bit!' I shouted as I left.

Inside the car I studied the *A–Z*, plotting out a route before setting off. On the tail-end of rush hour, it took just over half an hour to get there. Not days or weeks or months. Half an hour to get to a place I had been to the one time and never gone back.

Nothing looked familiar. But then I could hardly remember anything about the funeral. It had been for me as if all memory was concentrated in the fine detail leading up to her death and beyond that there were just snatches here and there for years. I must have been in shock. The thought made me smile. Why should that surprise me? Hadn't I been in shock ever since?

I entered the small building on the right, just inside the gates. Waited till the old guy working there was free and asked him, 'Can you tell me how I'd find a particular grave?'

He pointed to a building opposite. 'Try the office. If you've got the details you can have a look through the register yourself. Or you can pay and they'll do it for you.' He looked at me. 'When'd they die?' he asked.

'Nineteen eighty-three.'

He pointed straight ahead down the road towards a chapel. 'If you wanna take a look yourself just keep going that way. Straight ahead.'

How many people had died in nineteen eighty-three? How many graves would I have to search before I found hers? It seemed easier to return to the office and pay them to tell me where she was, my mother, buried here for fourteen years and I had not visited, even once. But I couldn't do it. I couldn't ask anyone for help. This was a private disgrace.

'Thanks,' I said and, headed in the direction he had pointed, started walking.

There were hardly any people about. The only sounds I heard were birds and the occasional plane. I passed tombs that were ancient. Some said the occupant just 'fell asleep' and I found myself unbearably moved. It sounded such a gentle way to die, having lived first, fully, to simply get into bed one night and not wake up the following day. The way death ought to be. I wondered what had been written on my mum's to explain how she had gone. She hadn't fallen asleep or passed away. She had been wrenched into death. Murdered in hot blood. Did people put things like that on stones?

Beloved mother. Dragged screaming from life.

Past the Chapel of Rest to the end of the road I walked. At the top, I studied the gravestones in front of me. People who died in 1977. Masses of them. To the right there were more flowers in front of the stones than in any other area I had yet passed, the graves being more recent. My mum was buried in 1983. I headed off to the left where the flowers were fewer and the rows of gravestones stretched like incisors into the distance.

I found the graves for the right year but not hers, though I walked the length of the rows slowly, checking every stone. Hers was black. I remembered that. I could tell the plots of those who were truly 'never forgotten' from the ones who had been; the graves visited regularly by the loved ones left behind, flowers brought, notes left. I was searching for the one with the black headstone that looked the most neglected, and that stung.

I turned around when the dates of death went down to 1982. Walked back even slower to the path, then along it. At a junction, there was a triangle of grass with the largest oak tree in it I had ever seen, five or six metres circumference, with a bench beneath it, which I sat on.

It was so quiet.

And peaceful.

That the branches were stripped of leaves made no difference. The tree was majestic. In the summer, was it possible that anywhere in the world there was a more beautiful place to sit and contemplate? Why had it taken so long for me to find it when it had been in that spot for hundreds of years, only thirty minutes away from where I lived? I was bitterly disappointed that I hadn't found her, that I would have to go back to the office and plough through the register like a researcher, felt the disgrace of that weighing on me heavily, that I should need to do something like that in order to find the grave of my family.

My family.

Excited, I stood up.

Directly in front of me were graves from 1967. I walked through a few rows watching the years roll on to 1969. Then I began to walk the rows again. Masses of stones and only the occasional flower here. The too-long dead. Searching and searching and searching. As soon as I stepped into the third row I saw it.

A black heart chiselled from marble. Dulled gold stencilling: *In loving memory of a devoted husband and father, Linville Jackson*; the dates, and below, in brighter golden letters, my mother's name:

who died 1st May 1983
To know her was to love her.

The adjacent grave had a slab of concrete on the ground in front of it. One end had sunk and the earth had risen over it, the grass grown back to cover the earth, and it was as though, in time, even the grave itself would end up buried along with its occupant. But the grave of my dad and my mum was like a garden. The black heart was wrapped in a large red bow. There was a wicker basket in front of it filled with four different plants, the kind of basket you might give someone as a gift. In front of the basket, a band of earth had been cleared and was freshly planted tight with flowering pansies. A sunken vase contained five lily stalks, the buds at different stages of flowering. Two gaped wide in exotic exhibition. The grass before the grave was indented, as if someone had visited regularly and kneeled on that spot. Not Berris. This was the work of years not weeks.

Lemon?

Near the bottom of the stone were two roses beautifully etched into the marble, frosty grey. If they had been coloured they would undoubtedly have been red. She had bought this stone for my father when he died. Had he bought her a space in his plot? It was the perfect place for her. Mr Jackson had always looked after her in life. Loved but not hurt her, cared without breaking her. It was right that he should be the person at her side for the rest of all eternity.

She had promised me she would always be there for me and she hadn't lied or broken that promise. The reason I had not found her before was because I hadn't looked.

I went over it all in my mind, trying to understand the building pressure inside my heart that felt so much like the sadness I had expected to feel when she had died, the absence of which had left an empty space marked out by a perimeter of rage. Inside me I felt a tidal wave building, a tsunami of feeling, as powerful as it was unstoppable.

Fourteen years she had been gone and it had taken me that long to experience grief. My tears when they came were breaking waves crashing downwards, for them, my mum and my dad. For Berris. For Lemon. For Ben. For all that had been done and lost and damaged.

For me.

Then afterwards, kneeling there, I felt like I had ascended into a state of peace, which sat humbled alongside the heartache that had defined every aspect of my life to date. I had wasted so much time, borne so many grudges for so long, and they had made the relationships with the handful of people I had loved in my lifetime impossible. I looked around me at the vast space filled with graves and finished lives and memories. What was the use of grudges when you were sitting here? What was the point?

I would come back. In the week. And bring my own flowers. For them. Walking back to the path I passed another grave like that of my parents', with *Husband* in faded stencilling, and *Wife* added later in newer, sharper letters, and below it, even brighter yet:

And the ashes of their son

And his details.

I was unable to identify the feeling inside me when I read those words, it was too new, a feeling to which I was unaccustomed, but it was so strong I was compelled to stop walking.

I had done everything I could to shun it, employed every measure to help me forget, to pretend it had never existed. Yet in that instant there was no more room for denial. Perfectly still, I let the feeling flood through me, finally recognizing it for what it was.

My mother's name.

Joy.

By the time I arrived back home, there was little left of the short spring day and the house was already in darkness. As soon as I saw it I panicked. I called him even before the front door was properly open but there was no answer. Still I turned on the passage light and the one in the living room. I checked the kitchen then took the stairs two by two. I knocked at the door to my mother's room and at the same time pushed it open and stepped inside.

The bed was made. His things gone. The room as tidy as if he had never slept in it at all. The only sign that he had been here was the window, opened wide, to let the fresh air in.

The ghosts out.

The net curtain rose and shimmied on the slightest of breezes.

I still checked the bathroom, even though, deep down in my heart, I knew.

And I was devastated.

I had no idea where his home was, no number I could call him on, no way of finding or contacting him. When I had the chance and it mattered most, I had not said *I forgive you*, and now that I was ready to, Lemon had gone.

I rang the doorbell once, then waited. The melody went on at length. When he opened the door and saw me standing there he was surprised.

'Hi,' he said.

'Hello, Red.'

He waited a moment for me to say something else and I was unable to decide which of the three million words in my head to say first, so I said nothing. Then he opened the front door wide and let me in.

It was warm, his home. It smelled of burgers and chips.

'I'm sorry, I should have rung…'

'S'no problem,' he said.

The hallway was packed with shoes in two sizes, as if the occupants consisted of a giant and an elf. They were lined up against the wall in ramshackle pairs. There were coats and jackets and scarves strewn over the banister in a heap, and two bicycles were leaned up against the passage wall. I took my coat off and Red took it from my hands, making eye contact, asking questions, seeking answers. I met his gaze.

'Do you want a cup of tea?' he asked.

'Yeah. Sure. Why not?'

'He's in the front room.'

'Okay.'

'I'll get the tea.'

'All right.'

'You want me to come inside with you?'

'Don't be silly.'

'Ben, your mum's here!' he called, then went off and I entered the living room on my own.

He was sitting on the carpet in front of the telly. The room was strewn with his toys. They covered every surface, the settee, the table, the floor. Pictures he had painted and drawn were Blu-Tacked on to the walls. A shelf above the TV housed videos and DVDs; children's ones and family films. There were photos of Ben at every focal point, on top of the TV, above the mantelpiece, and larger ones in heavy frames dominated the window ledge. I thought about his custard-coloured bedroom and felt ashamed.

'Hello, Ben,' I said.

He looked up from the colouring book he was scribbling in, then he looked back down.

'Hello.'

I picked up a muscular male doll in a karate pose from the settee, then sat down in the cleared space, close enough to touch him, though I did not try.

'I'm sorry. I shouldn't have hit you. It was wrong of me. It won't happen again.'

He didn't look up or answer. I was unable to detect even the slightest variation in the rhythm of his colouring-in. I felt the old frustration seeping back and I took a deep breath, trying to check it. I looked around the room wondering how they both managed to live among such chaos and disorder, how they were able to find the space inside it to think. Red came into the room. He looked both pleased and bemused at the same time. Like a person who had come upon the right sign in the right place, unexpectedly. He stared at me as he held out the mug.

'I didn't put in any sugar...'

'That's fine.' It was hot in my hands.

'I wasn't sure if you still took it the same...'

'Yep. Exactly the same.'

'What have you done? You look different.'

'Do I?'

'It suits you.'

'I haven't done anything.'

'Maybe it's love.'

I laughed. Ben looked up. 'Lemon's just a family friend, that's all,' I said.

'Whatever,' Red answered. 'Hey, Ben, you gonna stop that and come and say hello properly?'

'It's okay…' I said quickly.

'Come on,' Red said as if he hadn't heard me.

Ben stopped. He put the crayon in his hand down on top of the page and looked up at me.

Those eyes.

He had her eyes. *My* eyes. I do not know how I had a problem before working out whether he was handsome or not but I had no problem then. The feeling I had inside me was so powerful, I felt weak. I wanted to grab him to my breast and crush him there, kiss every inch of his face, or maybe cry. He was probably the most handsome boy I had ever seen in my life.

So alive.

How had I not seen it before?

He stood up slowly.

'Give your mum a kiss, son.'

As I was putting the mug on the floor beside the settee, politely he leaned over and kissed my cheek, and before he could move back out of reach, I touched him gently, his small head, skiffled low. The short hairs against my skin were springy and soft. The warmth from his head and the heat of my palm became one. I ran my hand over him slowly and the feeling inside me intensified. It was as if he were the first thing of beauty I had ever touched.

Without prompt he moved to sit on my lap and slowly, afraid he would change his mind and get back off, I put my arms around his waist. He smelled of biscuits and ketchup and citrus, and below that something faintly manky, like earth. I wrestled a desire to squeeze.

'How was school today?'

'Okay.'

'You do anything nice?'

'I played with my friends.'

'What did you play?'

'Kites and Globby Heads,' he said.

I scoured my memory banks for some recollection of a game by that name, but came up with nothing.

'How do you play it?' I asked.

'We take off our coats and run around the playground and pretend they're kites. Then we put our coats on top our heads and call each other "Globby Head".'

It was, without doubt, the most pointless pursuit anyone had ever explained to me. My son had spent the best part of his day playing the world's most ridiculous game. I looked into his face to see if he was going to wink at me, or if the corner of his mouth was about to crack a smile, whether his lips were parted in preparation to say the word *Gotcha!*

But his expression was solemn. I could see no humour twitching there. Not only had he just said what he'd said, but he was completely sincere. He really meant it. The welling inside me became impossible to suppress and helplessly, unable to resist a moment longer, I squeezed him tight, then kissed his perplexed face.

And laughed.

Acknowledgements

For their contribution to shaping *A cupboard full of coats*, for every suggestion and criticism, I would like to thank my first readers to whom I am indebted; Elizabeth Galloway, Danielle Acquah, Hilary Facey, Shawn Beckles, Jaclyn Griffiths, and most especially, Olcay Aniker.

I would like to thank Nicky Marcus, who discovered me, and Eve White, my agent, for her belief in my novel and her determination.

I would like to thank Juliet Mabey for her enthusiasm and application and the team at Oneworld Publications who could not have been more constructive and supportive throughout. Additionally, I wish to thank Sarah Coward, most thorough of copy-editors, for every astute observation and her help with the fine-tuning.

I consider myself incredibly fortunate to have a need to say to the friends and family who have given me the understanding, support, encouragement, and space to finish this novel – yes, you know who you are! – from the bottom of my heart, I am grateful and I thank you.

And finally, my love and thanks to Colin Edwards, whose stability both liberates and empowers me to write.

Yvvette Edwards has lived in London all her life. She grew up in Hackney and is of Montserratian-British origin. Yvvette continues to live in the East End, and is married with three children. *A Cupboard Full of Coats* is her first novel.